Lucky

When three single and sexy gorgeous men become dads overnight, they each need a woman – fast!

For their babies' sakes it's…

Mothers Wanted

But will these women ever be wives?

Three brand-new, emotional stories from three fabulous bestselling writers

MILLS & BOON
100 YEARS
of pure reading pleasure

100 Reasons to Celebrate

We invite you to join us in celebrating Mills & Boon's centenary. Gerald Mills and Charles Boon founded Mills & Boon Limited in 1908 and opened offices in London's Covent Garden. Since then, Mills & Boon has become a hallmark for romantic fiction, recognised around the world.

We're proud of our 100 years of publishing excellence, which wouldn't have been achieved without the loyalty and enthusiasm of our authors and readers.

Thank you!

Each month throughout the year there will be something new and exciting to mark the centenary, so watch for your favourite authors, captivating new stories, special limited edition collections…and more!

Mothers Wanted

SANDRA MARTON

MARION LENNOX

JESSICA HART

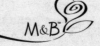

M&B™ and M&B™ with the Rose Device
are trademarks of the publisher.
Harlequin Mills & Boon Limited, Eton House,
18-24 Paradise Road, Richmond, Surrey TW9 1SR

MOTHERS WANTED © by Harlequin Books S.A. 2008

Hot Summer Bride © Sandra Myles 2008
Brand-New Father, Brand-New Family © Marion Lennox 2008
For His Baby's Sake © Jessica Hart 2008

ISBN: 978 0 263 86591 2

24-0208

Harlequin Mills & Boon policy is to use papers that are
natural, renewable and recyclable products and made from
wood grown in sustainable forests. The logging and
manufacturing processes conform to the legal environmental
regulations of the country of origin

Printed and bound in Spain
by Litografia Rosés S.A., Barcelona

Hot Summer Bride

SANDRA MARTON

Sandra Marton, a bestselling, award-winning author for Mills & Boon® Modern™, wrote her first novel while still in primary school. Her doting parents told her she'd be a writer someday and Sandra believed them. In secondary school and college, she wrote dark poetry nobody but her boyfriend understood. As a wife and mother, she devoted the little free time she had to writing murky short stories. Not even her boyfriend-turned-husband understood those. At last, Sandra decided she wanted to write about real people. That didn't actually happen because the heroes she created – and still creates – are larger than life, but both she and her readers around the world love them exactly that way. Sandra has written more than fifty novels for Mills & Boon Modern. She's won the Holt Medallion and has twice been a finalist for the RITA®, the award given by Romance Writers of America. She's won three Reviewers Choice Awards from *Romantic Times* magazine, and this year received a Career Achievement Award from *Romantic Times* as Series Storyteller of the Year. When she isn't at her computer, Sandra loves to bird-watch, walk in the woods and the desert, and travel. She can be as happy people-watching from a pavement café in Paris as she can be animal-watching in the forest behind her home in northeastern Connecticut. Her love for both worlds, the urban and the natural, is often reflected in her books.

Look for Sandra Marton's new book,
***The Sheikh's Defiant Bride*,**
coming from Mills & Boon® Modern™
in August 2008

Dear Reader,

Do you love birthday parties? I know I do. Being surrounded by friends and family, blowing out the candles on a beautifully decorated cake, everyone singing "Happy Birthday"… All of that is wonderful.

Well, Mills & Boon is having a birthday party this year. No cake, no candles, no song – but we, your friends and family, are happy to ask you to celebrate our centenary with us, and to enjoy the gifts we're bringing to you, our wonderful readers.

My gift is the story of Lincoln Aldridge and Ana Maria Mendes. Lincoln is sure he has everything he could possibly want. Ana's sure the only thing she wants is her freedom. They have absolutely nothing in common except a blazing flash of desire…and an orphaned baby, in desperate need of love.

Won't you join me at the party? Open your gift, sit back, and enjoy.

With love,

Sandra

CHAPTER ONE

Rio de Janeiro, April

CARNAVAL had ended almost two months ago, but Rio didn't seem to know it.

Lincoln Aldridge wasn't surprised. He'd been to Rio before. The city could be an endless party, especially for a man with money, rugged good looks and connections.

Linc had all three but he wasn't in a partying mood. He'd been on the go for almost two weeks, first flying to Argentina, then Colombia, then Brazil. His business meetings had gone well but he had a more important matter on his mind.

Too much time had gone by since he'd heard from his sister. Kathryn and her husband, married five months, were on what she'd called a belated honeymoon, seeing the world.

New York City was part of the world, Linc had said wryly, and he damned well expected that Kath and the husband he'd never met intended to make it part of their trip.

"Absolutely," she'd answered, sounding almost like

the kid he still thought of her as being. "We're going to stop there last so we can spend some time with you. And, Linc? Get ready for a wonderful surprise!"

The best surprise would be seeing her again. Kath was twenty-two and he'd all but raised her. Now she lived in L.A., where she'd met Mark and eloped to Vegas. Linc, ten years her senior, would have felt better if he'd laid eyes on the guy before the wedding but at least he would meet him soon.

It was why he was eager to get home.

First, though, he had to finalize the deal he'd made with entrepreneur Hernando Marques. They'd shaken hands on it but Marques wanted to sign the contract at his home. An odd request, maybe, but when a man was about to spend twenty-five million bucks a year giving Aldridge Inc. full responsibility for the security of all his residential and commercial properties, an odd request was okay.

"This is my poker night, Lincoln," Marques had said. "I spend it with a few old friends whose company I am sure you would enjoy. Please. Join us."

So Linc had smiled and said he looked forward to it.

A little before eight, his taxi glided through the massive iron gates that guarded the Marques estate.

Force of habit made Linc check the perimeter. One of his teams had installed the latest security systems a couple of weeks ago. Electric eyes. Hidden cameras. Sensors. He couldn't spot them all, which was as it should be, but what he saw looked perfect.

The taxi stopped at the foot of wide stone steps. His host flung the door open before Linc could ring the bell.

"Lincoln!" Marques grinned and extended his hand.

"I was afraid you might have forgotten my invitation, *meo amigo*."

"Traffic," Linc said with a quick smile, even as he wondered at his host's reaction. Brazilians were a friendly people but Marques seemed to be taking things to a new level.

Marques led him to a leather-walled game room where a dozen or so men stood chatting in small groups near an expansive buffet laid out on a mile-long table.

"Come and meet my friends, Lincoln."

Linc shook hands, smiled, said hello and how are you to men he'd met before and others he knew by reputation. This was a gathering of some of the wealthiest men in South America. Eight years ago, when he'd started Aldridge Inc. with nothing but guts and his Special Forces experience, he'd have given anything to have been invited to an evening like this.

Now, it was Marques's guests who expressed pleasure at meeting him.

He moved from group to group, eating a little, drinking hardly at all, wondering when he could get away. No one seemed in a hurry to play cards.

At last, Marques sought him out again. He was smiling but tiny drops of sweat stood out on his forehead. Something was wrong. Had the man decided against the deal despite the binding handshake?

"Hernando," he said pleasantly. "I was just going to look for you. This is great but—"

"But you have had a long day and you wish for an early night."

"I'm glad you understand."

"I do. So perhaps—perhaps, now, we might adjourn to the library to—to—"

"To sign the contract," Linc said, his eyes on the other man's.

"Certainly. To sign the contract." Marques hesitated. "And to talk."

The library was big and leather-paneled like the game room. A pair of French doors graced the far end; a fire blazed on the hearth of a stone fireplace to ward off the faint chill of the night.

Marques offered brandy. A cigar. Coffee. Linc said no to all three.

"Something's on your mind, Hernando." Linc's tone was polite but cool. "I'd appreciate it if you'd just get to it."

His host nodded. Licked his lips. Fussed at the logs on the hearth with a poker before finally looking at Linc.

"This is difficult for me, Lincoln."

"But?"

"But there is something I must ask." A quick laugh. "I am not good at asking for favors. Not that this is a favor, exactly. I mean, it is something that will surely benefit you, as well as me."

Here it comes, Linc thought, folding his arms over his chest. A request to change the terms of their agreement? To renegotiate the price? What else could it be?

"And what is it you must ask?"

Marques cleared his throat. "You are unmarried Lincoln. That is correct, yes?"

"Excuse me?"

"I said, you are single. Am I right?"

Linc frowned. What did his marital status have to do with anything? "Uh, yes. Yes, I'm single."

"No children, then?"

"Marques. What is this about?"

"Because, you see, it is possible only a man with a child—with a daughter—would understand my feelings on this matter."

"What matter?"

Marques looked at him, then away. "I have a daughter. She is young—but," he added quickly, "mature for her age."

"I'm afraid I don't see what—"

"She is also bright and well-educated. Obedient and well-mannered. And—"

And, Linc thought in horror, as the truth began to sink in, Marques wanted to marry her off. To him?

"I am a modern man, Lincoln. Still, when it comes to my daughter, I have some old-fashioned ways."

Hell. Absolutely to him. He'd heard about this kind of thing, of course, arranged marriages, especially in wealthy families in Europe and South America...

"...would never hand her off to a man I didn't trust and respect..."

They did this back home, too. Not quite this openly but he'd been the target of a couple of attempts at marriage-brokering. He was in his thirties, he was single, he was well-off...

Why think in polite euphemisms? He was rich and that was fine because he'd gotten that way strictly on his own. Nobody had given him anything in this life, which made what he'd acquired, the homes, the cars, the private plane, all the more enjoyable.

And his looks were acceptable.

Okay. Most women made it clear his looks were more than acceptable. He'd always had his pick of women, even back in the days he'd never had more than ten bucks in his pocket. So, yeah, he'd been here before. Approached, you could call it, by some of New York's best-known *grands dames*. They had daughters and he was, by their reckoning, eligible, and so what if his blood wasn't as blue as theirs?

You'd love my Emma, they said. Or, *Why don't you come out to our place in Easthampton this weekend? Glenna will be there. You do remember Glenna, don't you?*

Yes, but nobody had ever come straight out and said, *Here's my daughter. I'd like you to marry her.*

"...a charming young woman, Lincoln, polite and very willing to accommodate. If you'd simply agree to meet her—"

"Hernando." Linc took a deep breath. "I—I want you to know I appreciate how—how direct you're being. This can't be easy for you."

Marques gave a little laugh. "It's one of the most difficult things I've ever done."

"I'm sure it is but the thing is—the thing is—"

A polite knock sounded at the door. A servant popped his head in, smiled apologetically and said something in rapid Portuguese.

Marques sighed. "My wife is on the phone, Lincoln. I'll take the call in my office. She is visiting her sister but you know how it is with women."

Linc didn't. Not with wives, at any rate, and he had every intention of keeping it that way.

"I'll only be a minute. Help yourself to some brandy while you consider my proposition."

Linc waited until the door closed. Then he muttered an oath and decided brandy was a fine idea.

How did a man turn down what Marques called a

proposition? Grimly, he poured an inch of amber liquid into a snifter. He didn't want to insult him. He didn't want to lose this account, either, but if that was what it took to get out of here...

What was that?

Had something stirred outside the French doors? Clouds had moved in to obscure the moon; the light was poor but... Yes. There it was again. He had a better look now, enough to be sure what was out in the darkness wasn't a something.

It was a someone.

Linc put down the brandy glass. He moved slowly, instinctively falling back into survival tactics honed to a fine edge years ago. Adrenaline pulsing through him, breathing steady, he felt himself come alive as he always had in moments like this.

The handles to the French doors were almost within reach. One more step...

He exploded into action, yanked the doors open, threw himself into the night and wrapped his arms around the intruder.

Wrapped his arms around a woman.

Definitely a woman. Her long hair swept across his face. Her breasts filled his hands. Her rounded bottom pressed against his groin. She fought him with all her strength, which was considerable, but it was no match for his.

A cry rose in her throat. Linc sensed it coming and clapped his hand over her mouth. For all he knew, she had an accomplice.

The feel of his hand increased her frenzy. She twisted like a wild thing caught in a trap. Linc lifted her off the ground and drew her, hard, against his body. She grunted. Her elbows slammed into his belly. Her heels rapped his shins.

He put his mouth to her ear.

"Stop it," he hissed.

She fought harder. Deliberately, he spread his hand over not just her mouth but her nose.

"I said, stop!"

Another jab. Another kick. His hand pressed more insistently. After a few seconds she sagged against him but he wasn't fooled. The fight had gone out of her too fast. She was faking it.

He put his mouth to her ear again. She smelled of roses or maybe lily-of-the-valley. He wasn't much on flowers or scents. All he knew was that she fought like a man but she sure as hell smelled like a woman.

"Behave, or it's lights out. You hear me?"

A second passed. Then she nodded. Slowly, carefully, he eased his hand from her face and swung her toward him.

"Who are you?" he demanded. "What are you doing here?"

"Let go of me!"

It was too dark to see her features but he could hear the fury in her voice, sharp with command and condescension. It was almost enough to make him laugh but laughing when your best security system had been breached didn't quite cut it.

"I asked you a question, lady. What's your name? How'd you get past the gate?"

"You asked two questions. And I gave you an order. Let go of me. Now!"

He did laugh then; how could he help it? The woman, who had been speaking in lightly accented English, spat out a phrase in Portuguese he was pretty sure women didn't generally use.

Right then, the moon decided to put in an appearance. It was only a quarter moon but it gave enough light for him to see her.

His breath caught.

She was, in a word, spectacular. Long blond hair. Big blue eyes. Razor-sharp cheekbones, an elegant nose, lush mouth and a body made for sin, poured into a black one-piece thing that lovingly molded every feminine curve.

"How dare you look at me that way?"

He'd seen a lot of thieves in his life but never one who looked like this.

"Damn you," she said, "are you deaf? I said—"

"I heard what you said."

Was that really his voice? So low? So hoarse? Better still, was this really happening? Was he holding an intruder in his arms who looked like every man's dream?

She began to struggle. He drew her closer. Her breasts, her belly, pressed against his. Was it the sense of danger? Was it the feel of her? Whatever the cause, his body responded in a heartbeat.

He froze. So did she.

"Let go," she said, her voice suddenly trembling. "If you don't, I swear, you'll pay for this."

She was right, he would. Once he dragged her into the house, told Marques, the contract they'd yet to sign would go down the drain…

In which case, wasn't he entitled to some compensation?

The thought was cold; the swift rise of heat in his blood was not. He wasn't a man to take what had not been offered but suddenly that didn't matter. Nothing did, except the feel of the woman in his arms.

Deliberately, he cupped her face with one hand. Tilted it up to his. She read what was coming and gasped, beat her fists against his shoulders.

He didn't give a damn. Slowly, he bent his head to hers and kissed her.

She made a sound of protest. Tried to twist her head away. He wouldn't let it happen. He thrust his fingers into her hair, felt it slide like silk through his hand and went on kissing her.

Kissing her. Kissing her…

She ignited like dry tinder under the flame of a match. Her hands slid up his chest. Her mouth softened. She gave a sexy little moan…

A light came on just outside the house.

The woman stiffened. Linc, lost in the moment, started to draw her into the shadows.

"No!" she gasped, and sank her teeth into his bottom lip.

Startled, he loosened his grip. One lithe twist and she disappeared into the darkness.

"Lincoln?"

It was Marques. Linc shuddered. He drew his handkerchief from his pocket and dabbed it to his bloody lip. He was a man who lived by rigid rules of self-control; there was no way to explain what he'd just done. He could only tell his host that an intruder was on the grounds and he had lost her.

No need to supply the humiliating details.

Marques smiled when he saw him. "There you are. I thought perhaps you'd…" His smile faded. "What happened to your lip?"

"It's nothing. An insect bite."

"One of the maids will get you some antiseptic."

"No. No, thanks. I…" Linc cleared his throat. "I'm fine."

"Nonsense. Small wounds can become a problem in this climate. Come inside, Lincoln. I'll ring for—"

"Hernando, listen to me. That security system my people installed?"

"It is excellent," Marques said, smiling broadly. "The best, just as you promised."

"It isn't. I mean, it is but—"

"Papa?"

A girl—obviously Marques's daughter—stood silhouetted in the hallway just outside the room. Marques held out his hand.

"Ana. Come in, child."

Linc smothered a groan. Damn, what a mess! Bad enough he had to tell Marques his high-tech security system had been compromised and he'd let the intruder slip away. Now he had to top that off by saying no, he wasn't interested in marrying a sweet, well-bred innocent young woman while she stood by, listening.

Oh, yeah, this was definitely turning into a fun night, Linc thought glumly…and felt his jaw slide to his shoe tops as Marques's daughter entered the well-lit room.

The sweet, well-bred innocent was the woman he'd just kissed.

The sexy black outfit had been subtly altered by the addition of a pale pink jacket, long and loose enough to hide all those feminine curves. The silky tousle of golden hair was drawn back in a severe knot. But it was she, and one look at her face told him she was as stunned as he was.

"Ana," Marques said, "this is the man I've been telling you about. Lincoln, this is my beloved daughter, Ana Maria."

For the first time in his life, Linc found himself struggling for words. What did you say to a man whose "beloved daughter" had been in your arms moments ago? Whose innocence was obviously a ruse only her father was foolish enough to believe?

His cell phone rang. Ordinarily, he'd have ignored it. Now, he yanked it from his pocket like a lifeline.

"Aldridge," he barked.

"Lincoln," he heard his lawyer say solemnly, "I'm afraid I've had word about your sister."

Somehow, in that instant, he knew what was coming. He turned his back to the room, to Marques, to Marques's daughter. The lawyer was hemming and hawing, stalling for time. Linc interrupted with a sharp command.

"Spit it out, man. What's happened?"

A chartered plane had gone down in a mountain pass. The pilot, the passengers…all of them, gone.

Linc felt the blood drain from his head. Dimly, he heard Marques say something but he ignored him and stepped blindly into the night.

"No," he said sharply. "Not Kath."

"I'm sorry, Lincoln. Your sister and her husband both. But, miraculously, there was a survivor."

One survivor. A baby. A two-month-old little girl.

A little girl who was Lincoln Aldridge's niece.

CHAPTER TWO

New York City, two months later

IT TURNED out that some clichés were true.

Tragedy fell on a man without warning, but life went on. It changed, but it went on.

Somehow, you kept going. Somehow, you adapted.

You adapted, Linc thought groggily, as the piercing wail of the gorgeous, brilliant, impossible four-month-old hellion who now ruled his life shot him from sleep.

He threw out a hand, searched on the bedside table for his watch and peered blearily at the luminescent dial.

Oh, God!

It was five-oh-five. Five-oh-five in the a.m. He had a meeting at eight-thirty with his own people, another at eleven with the European clients he'd taken to dinner last night. He had to be sharp and focused and how could a man be either when he hadn't had a solid night's sleep?

He never had a solid night's sleep anymore. And he rarely had a full day to devote to his work.

First there'd been the awful, sad details of Kath's death to handle. When that was over, the baby—Kath's secret—had taken center stage.

At first, he'd wondered why his sister had kept the child a secret but simple math had explained it. Kath had reversed the usual order of things. She'd gotten pregnant first, then married. Maybe she'd worried he'd have thought less of her for that reversal, which damned near broke his heart. Or maybe she just hadn't known how to break the news to him long-distance.

Whatever the reason, all that mattered now was the baby's welfare.

He had met with his attorney and, of course, immediately agreed to provide the baby a proper home. He didn't know a damned thing about babies—how could he? But he hadn't known a thing about running a business, either, when he'd started out.

No problem.

You didn't know how to do something, you learned. Or, if it was more expedient, you hired people who did. That was what he'd done, what he'd assured the social worker whose job it was to make sure the baby was properly cared for he would do.

And he had.

He'd sent his PA shopping for baby clothes, a crib, a highchair, bottles, formula, diapers and the thousand other things an infant required. He'd had the interior designer who'd done his Fifth Avenue triplex turn the guest suite into a nursery. He'd contacted a nanny agency and interviewed more women eager to clean baby bottoms than he'd have imagined existed in the world, let alone New York.

And, last week, Kath's mother-in-law had suddenly come on the scene. Nobody had even known she existed until then.

Would she ask for custody? If she did, should he

fight her for it? Or would his niece be better off in her care?

Linc couldn't come to a decision. On the one hand, women knew more about kids than he ever could. Wasn't it in their DNA? On the other, the child was his blood. She was his only remaining connection to Kathryn.

What would Kath have wanted? She'd loved him the way he'd loved her. The circumstances of their lives—no father, a mother who drank and forgot they existed most of the time—had made them unusually close. Still, there was no way to know if she'd have wanted her baby raised by him or her mother-in-law. His attorney was checking things out.

The bottom line was that Kath was gone and a small, squalling stranger had dropped into his life. He'd had to leave increasing responsibility for running Aldridge Inc. in the hands of his people. They were all excellent managers, hand-selected by him, but Aldridge had grown into a multimillion-dollar company and he was integral to that growth.

He knew it was time to put the turmoil of the past months behind him and get back to the work he loved and maybe to some kind of social life, but you had to sleep nights to do that.

Right now, the baby's screams were reaching a crescendo, carrying all the way from the guest-suite-turned-nursery on the second floor of the penthouse to his bedroom on the third.

Where in hell was the nanny?

Linc threw back the duvet and started to the door. Halfway there, he remembered he was wearing boxers, his usual sleeping apparel but not what you'd choose for an appearance before Nanny Crispin.

She was the fifth woman he'd hired and the first that seemed to be working out.

The first hadn't lasted a week. Linc had come home an hour early one night and found her rolling on the Aubusson rug in the great room with a guy with studs in his ears, nose and lip and other places he'd glimpsed and tried to forget.

He'd thrown them both out.

Nanny Two had lasted ten days. Day eleven, she'd reeked of pot.

Nanny Three had simply vanished. Her replacement, Nanny Four, had seemed okay until the evening she'd greeted him at the door wearing one of his Thomas Pink handmade shirts, spiked heels and a smile.

Then the agency sent him Nanny Crispin.

She was sixtyish, tall and skinny. Her hair was steel-gray, her small, wire-framed eyeglasses sat squarely on the bridge of a high, narrow nose. Linc doubted if she knew how to smile but she'd come highly recommended and, he supposed, whether or not she ever smiled was immaterial.

It couldn't possibly matter to a four-month-old infant. A baby's needs were purely physical. Food. Warmth. Cleanliness. This baby was getting all that. He'd made sure of it by hiring Nanny Crispin.

Sighing, Linc grabbed the trousers he'd worn last night. The baby's howls had reached earsplitting proportions. Nanny Crispin would have to endure the sight of his bare chest—and what the hell was she doing, anyway, letting the kid scream?

He marched down the hall and went down the steel and oiled teak spiral staircase.

The door to the nursery stood open. All the lights

were on, illuminating the crib where the baby was screeching like a wind-up toy gone berserk. Nanny Crispin, wrapped like a mummy in a flannel robe the same color as her hair, sat in a straight-backed chair beside the crib, arms folded over her flat chest.

Linc cleared his throat. Pointless. Nobody could have heard the roar of a jet engine over the wails of the baby.

"Nanny Crispin?"

As always, he felt like an idiot addressing a woman twice his age that way but she'd made it clear that she expected his housekeeper, his driver and him to call her by her title.

He walked to the crib and waited for her to notice him. When she didn't, he tapped her on the shoulder. She reacted as if she'd been scalded, leaping to her feet, spinning to face him, her mouth forming a perfect O.

"I didn't meant to startle you."

Nanny Crispin stared at his chest.

"I said, I didn't mean to—" Hell. He took a breath, fought back the urge to grab something to cover his naked chest and decided to get to the point. "What's wrong with the baby?"

"Do you not own a robe, Mr. Aldridge?"

"Do I not…?" Linc flushed. Suddenly, he was six years old. "Well, sure, but I heard the baby and—"

"Your attire is inappropriate. I am a single woman and you are a man."

"Yes, but—"

But one of them was crazy. He was indeed a man. She was about as sexually appealing as a stick, never mind the age difference or the fact that she was his employee. If she'd looked like the reincarnation of Marilyn

Monroe, that last fact would have been enough to keep him at arm's length.

Linc jerked his chin toward the crib. "I'm not worried about decorum right now, Nanny Crispin. I want to know why the baby is screaming."

"She is screaming because she is undisciplined."

"Undisciplined. Well, then, of course she…"

His voice faded away. Undisciplined? He frowned. True, he knew nothing about babies, but did four-month-old infants cry because they were undisciplined?

"Are you sure?"

"I have been taking care of babies for forty years, Mr. Aldridge. I know an undisciplined child when I see one."

Linc looked at the baby. Her face was purple. Her arms and legs were pumping. His frown deepened.

"Maybe she's hungry."

"I gave her eight ounces of formula four hours ago. Eight ounces is the proper amount."

"What about her diaper? Does it need changing?"

"No."

"Well, is she too warm? Too cold? Could something be hurting her?"

Nanny Crispin's thin mouth narrowed until it all but disappeared. "She is simply in need of discipline, as I said."

"And that means?"

"It means I shall outlast her temper tantrum. Goodnight, sir."

Linc nodded. "Okay. Sure. Goodnight."

He turned, walked away, got halfway up the stairs and paused. The baby was still crying but her screams had become sobs. Somehow, that was even worse.

Would Kath have let her daughter weep? Would she have called this a temper tantrum?

He swung around, went back to the nursery, ignored the scowl of disapproval and the pursed lips.

"How about picking her up?" Nanny Crispin looked at him as if he'd spoken in Urdu. "You know, take her out of the crib. Hold her, walk around with her."

"One does not reward poor behavior."

"No. Of course not. I mean…"

What in hell did he mean? Suddenly, Linc plunged back in time. He remembered coming home from football practice, finding Kath sobbing her heart out in the corner of the kitchen that had been her bedroom. He'd been maybe seventeen, so she'd have been seven. She'd been crying because some kid had made fun of her, the way she'd looked in the too-big winter coat he'd gotten her at the Salvation Army, and she hadn't stopped weeping until he'd scooped her up, rocked her, told her everything would be all right.

Linc walked slowly to the crib. Looked in. Hesitated. Then he reached down and picked up the baby. It was the first time he'd held her since the day a social worker had placed her in his arms.

This is your sister's daughter, she'd said.

Those simple words, the unfamiliar feel of the kid in his arms, and he'd finally had to accept that Kath was gone.

Now, he stared at the red, unhappy face of Kath's child. His niece. Funny how he never thought of her that way. Awkwardly, he cupped her head with one hand, her bottom with the other, and rocked her back and forth.

A little bubble of spit appeared in the corner of her mouth.

The kid was cute, he thought grudgingly. He hadn't really noticed before, but she was.

"Mr. Aldridge, I must protest. You are undermining my authority in front of the child."

He looked at the baby, then at Nanny Crispin. The look on her face said he was committing a capitol offense.

"She has a name," he heard himself say.

"What has that to do with anything?"

"She has a name. Jennifer. I've never heard you use it."

"Her name is irrelevant."

It wasn't irrelevant, nor was the fact that he never used the baby's name, either. He knew that, deep where it counted.

"Mr. Aldridge. The child needs to be taught a lesson. Either you put her back in her crib or I'm afraid I will have to tender my resignation."

Linc looked down at his niece. Her sobs had stopped. She was staring up at him, her expression solemn.

"Did you hear me, sir? I said—"

"I heard you. Consider your resignation accepted."

Nanny Crispin gasped. Linc almost did, too. What in hell had he done?

"Wait a minute," he started to say, but his cell phone, still in his trouser pocket, beeped. He shifted the baby to the crook of one arm and dug out the phone.

It was his attorney. At—what was it now?—at six in the damned a.m.?

"I couldn't reach you last night, Lincoln."

"Well, you've reached me now, Charles. This better be good."

Kath's mother-in-law had filed for custody. Linc wondered whether he felt relief or maybe something else.

"Yeah, well, we kind of figured—"

"What we didn't figure," his lawyer said briskly, "was that the lady basically abandoned her own son—Kathryn's husband—when he was three. Now she's claiming to have been a devoted mother who had problems."

"Do you buy her story?"

"What I buy is that she just found out about the trust fund you set up for your sister, and that the money in it now transfers to the baby."

Linc's mouth thinned. "Great."

"Indeed."

They made an appointment to meet later in the day. Oh, the lawyer added, the social worker wanted a meeting, too. This afternoon, with him and Linc and the baby.

"She wants to see how the child is doing."

"Sir?"

Linc turned and saw Nanny Crispin, dressed and with her suitcase in her hand.

"I'll see you later, Charles," he said, and ended the call.

"I phoned for a taxi, Mr. Aldridge. Unless, of course, you've changed your mind?"

Two meetings this morning. Two meetings this afternoon. Linc had always been a logical man. There was still time for a logical man to say he'd changed his mind.

"I will reconsider my departure if you are prepared to acknowledge my authority."

Linc's jaw tightened. "Send me the bill for the cab."

He waited as Nanny Crispin stalked from the room. Then he looked down at his niece.

"Well, kid, it looks like it's just you and me."

Jennifer gave a huge yawn. Her eyelids drooped. A second later, she was asleep.

An excellent idea, Linc thought, but there wasn't much point in going back to bed, not anymore.

Okay, then. Time for a plan. When his housekeeper showed up, he'd ask her to do him a favor and watch the baby for the day. He'd go to his office, hold his meetings, contact the nanny agency—again. This time tomorrow he'd have nanny number six and life could return to whatever level of normalcy was possible.

Carefully, he lowered the sleeping baby into the crib.

"Waaaah!"

Linc hoisted her up. She screamed. He rocked her. She roared. Finally, gingerly, he brought her against his chest. Hot drool fell against his naked flesh. The baby gave a shuddering sigh and promptly fell asleep.

Linc waited. Then, very slowly, he sank into the straight-backed chair Nanny Crispin had vacated.

The baby slept on.

Half an hour later, he heard his housekeeper in the kitchen. He rose stiffly from a chair that had surely been designed by a sadist, lowered the baby inch by slow inch into her crib, hobbled to the shower and stepped gratefully under a blast of hot water.

Mrs. Hollowell couldn't babysit.

Her daughter was in the city for the day and she was taking the afternoon off to spend with her. Had Mr. Aldridge forgotten?

Mr. Aldridge had. He'd come close to forgetting his own name. Three hours of sleep could do that to a man.

He told her not to worry.

At eight, he strode into his office. His PA's eyes widened at the sight of Jennifer in his arms.

"I fired the nanny," he said brusquely. "Phone the agency, please. And take care of the kid for the next hour."

Another nod, but when he tried to hand the baby over

those tiny lungs contracted and the baby began to scream. Linc rolled his eyes and reached for her. His PA started to grin but one glance put an end to that.

Frowning, Linc plunked Jennifer against his shoulder again and vanished into his office.

He took his eight-thirty meeting with Jennifer still plastered against him. His people pretended not to notice.

By nine-thirty, she'd drifted off to sleep. After a quick survey of the Italian leather, smoked glass and cherrywood furnishings of his office, Linc sent his PA on another shopping expedition. In short order a thing that looked kind of like a tilted basket stood on the conference table along with diapers, baby bottles and formula.

The basket thing was pink and padded. Linc put the baby into it and breathed a sigh of relief when she didn't object.

His PA had phoned his European clients at the Waldorf. They were not in their rooms but, at Linc's direction, she'd left a message changing the location of their meeting to Peacock Alley, the hotel's posh dining venue.

The trouble with messages was they didn't always get where they were meant to go.

Midmorning, just as Linc was getting ready to leave for the Waldorf, his clients walked in. So sorry, they said, they knew they were early, but...

The baby chose that moment to wake up.

Her face turned pink. Her rosebud mouth pursed. Linc snatched her from her sleeping place before she could shriek.

She smiled, drooled, and—there was a God after all—his clients melted. The meeting went on, the baby gurgled and smiled. Finally, mercifully, his clients left.

Linc started to put the baby in the crib. She began to whimper.

"She's hungry," his PA said helpfully.

Linc looked at her. Looked at the baby. Then he handed the kid over.

"Feed her," he commanded.

His PA started to say something, thought better of it, turned away, opened the door...

Someone brushed by her and walked in. Strode in, was more like it.

A blonde. Tall. Slender. Wearing a black suit, black spiked heels and with a sleek black leather attaché case hanging from a strap across her shoulder. The look on her face meant trouble as she marched toward him, stopped a foot from his desk and slapped her hands on her hips.

Linc's green eyes narrowed. His temper was hot, his patience shredded, his exhaustion a black cloud waiting to burst loose with thunder and lightning...

Holy hell!

The blonde was Ana Maria Marques.

Linc scraped back his chair and jumped to his feet. "What are you doing here?"

"You made my father a promise, Senhor Aldridge. I do not think he will be pleased when he hears that you intend to renege on it."

The baby let out a cry. Linc let out a groan. And assumed, as any intelligent man would, that he had somehow fallen through a wormhole in space and emerged in a nightmare.

CHAPTER THREE

As a boy, Lincoln had taught himself Tai Chi.

Well, maybe not Tai Chi, precisely. The classes had been held after school; they'd cost money and no way would his mother have been able to afford them. Hell, there was no way she'd have paid for something he'd wanted even if she'd been able to afford it.

But he'd spied on the class by cracking open the locker-room door, and he'd learned. Not the finer points, perhaps, but enough to find Tai Chi useful.

The ancient Chinese martial art was as much about self-control as it was about physical strength.

Eventually, he'd figured out that was something you could apply to life in general. He'd used that realization over the years and he thought of it now as he fought the growing tension inside him.

Too bad you didn't think about Tai Chi when you first met this babe, a smug voice inside him said.

Linc ignored it. He'd made a fool of himself with her once. It wouldn't happen again. Besides, Ana Maria Marques looked as furious as he felt.

She also looked spectacular, every man's dream of a dressed-for-success female, the black suit elegant and proper, yet somehow hinting at the rounded contours of her body, the black pumps discreet until you took a look at the height of those heels and what they did for her long, lean legs.

His PA had stepped back into the room, the baby pressed to her shoulder, a bewildered look on her face.

"Sir? My apologies. I don't know why Reception let this woman—"

"It's all right, Sarah."

"If the lady has an appointment, I don't have anything in my calendar about it."

"If you think you are going to throw me out because I don't have an appointment," Ana said hotly, "I assure you, Senhor Aldridge, you are not!"

A muscle flexed in Linc's jaw but his tone was calm.

"Thank you, Sarah. Shut the door, please. I'll ring if I need you."

The door swung shut. Ana didn't blink. She simply glared at him.

Linc folded his arms. "Explain yourself."

"You have it wrong, *senhor*. You are the one who must do the explaining. To me. Or, if you prefer, to my father."

What in hell was she talking about? Better still, what was she doing here? The last he'd seen, she'd been pretending to be a dutiful daughter while her old man worked up the courage to offer her as a bride. In fact, Marques had been so caught up in the offer that he'd gone on talking even as Linc ran out the door that night.

His gut knotted. Had he missed something? Agreed to something? Was that night about to bite him in the tail?

"Because if you think I will not tell him how you have treated me—"

"Sit down, Miss Marques."

He spoke sharply, his words slicing across hers. It worked. Not that she sat down. He hadn't really expected that. But at least she shut up.

Linc took the chair behind his desk, folded his hands on its glass surface and looked at her. How many Ana Marias were there? Three, so far. The sexy night-stalker. The demure innocent. And now this gorgeous sophisticate.

Which was the real woman?

"When you're done mentally undressing me," she said coldly, "perhaps we can get down to business."

Linc raised one dark eyebrow.

"Trust me, Miss Marques. If I wanted to undress you, I wouldn't be satisfied with doing it mentally." He paused. "And neither would you."

A flush rose in her cheeks. "Would you force yourself on me again, *senhor*? As you did the night we met?"

"Is that why you returned my kiss? Because I 'forced' myself on you?"

"I did not return it. And I am not about to be drawn away from the topic at hand."

"What were you doing in that garden?"

"I just said—"

"Among other things, you blew past my best security system."

She smiled the way a cat might when confronted with a delectable mouse. "Indeed, I did."

Time to change direction. "Do you make it a habit to sneak around at night?"

"Do you make it a habit to force yourself on women?"

Back to the beginning. Linc sighed. "Let's move on, Miss Marques. What are you doing here?"

"I am here because of the promise you made my father.

Have you conveniently forgotten? Or did you hope I would not wish to follow through on it? Is that the game?"

Calmer now, Linc decided this couldn't concern a marriage proposal. Her father would be with her if it were. Still, he had no idea what she was talking about but only a fool would have admitted it. Instead, he sat back and flashed a cool smile.

"Why don't you tell me, Miss Marques? You seem to have all the answers."

He was afraid it sounded like a desperate ploy but it worked. A moment's hesitation and then she marched to one of the chairs in front of his desk, sat down, crossed her legs and propped the attaché case in her lap. The pencil-slim skirt of her black suit rode up her golden thighs.

"My father asked a favor of you."

Linc dragged his gaze to her face.

"Funny. I don't remember him asking anything—but then," he said, his tone hardening, "*you* seem to have forgotten that I left your home in a rush that night."

Another splash of color swept across her high cheek-bones. "About that." She cleared her throat. "I should have offered you my sympathy on the loss of your sister."

"Thank you."

Ana narrowed her eyes. The words were polite but she knew what this arrogant *bastardo* really meant was, *Go away.* Anyone viewing the scene would have thought she'd materialized out of the air instead of taking the elevator from Human Resources, two floors below.

Was he playing dumb? Could he really not know why she was so angry? He knew. He had to. He also knew damned well that he'd lied. That he'd said yes to her father only to placate him and had never, not in a million years, expected her to show up in New York.

If only Papa had never asked him.

She'd considered telling him not to, once she'd realized the man who'd forced his kisses on her that night was the man he was going to entrust her to, but how could she?

She'd worked a minor miracle, convinced Papa to let her take a stab at a career in New York, the city where all things were possible. She could have gone off without his approval, yes, but she knew her desire for independence pained him. She wanted to do it without hurting him, and she had.

After months of talk, Papa had finally agreed to let her go, but only if he hand-picked her employer.

"A good man," he had said. "An honorable one with a successful business."

Papa knew lots of good, honorable men who were successful. They were also middle-aged, overweight and balding. That was the kind of man she'd expected.

Instead, Papa's selection had turned out to be Lincoln Aldridge. Tall. Dark. Not middle-aged, not overweight, not balding.

Lincoln Aldridge was a magnificent male specimen.

He was also a sexist pig who'd overpowered her, forced her into his arms, forced his kisses on her, forced her to melt against him and yearn, plead, burn for him to do more, more, more...

Nonsense.

It hadn't been like that. She had been offended by his behavior and she would have told Papa the ugly truth about the good, honorable Senhor Aldridge, but Aldridge had gotten that terrible phone call about his sister.

After that, Ana had assumed Papa's plan was done

with. Then, last week, he'd showed her the letter he'd written and Aldridge's response…

"Miss Marques?"

He was watching her through amazingly green eyes, looking at her as if she were little more than an annoyance. The hell with that, she thought coldly, and lifted her chin.

"Yes, *senhor*."

"I am a busy man, Miss Marques. I don't have time for nonsense."

"A promise is not nonsense."

"I promised your father nothing," he said briskly.

"Not then, no. But he sent you a letter."

A scowl crossed Aldridge's too-handsome-for-his-own-good face.

"A letter?"

"A proposal, to which you replied."

He turned pale. Proof, as if she'd needed any, that he had been lying.

"Your father made no proposal," he said. "And if he had, I surely would not have said——"

"You said yes."

"Impossible."

"You said that you would give me a try."

"I beg your pardon?"

"You said you could promise nothing but that if I showed any talent, you would personally help cultivate it."

He turned even paler. Good. This was what happened when you trapped a liar with his own lies.

"Miss Marques. I could never have said any such thing about——about your talent. And I cannot imagine your father would have agreed to——to such an arrangement."

"He didn't want to, but I explained that a——what

do you call it?—a period of trial is not North American, it is universal. Should my performance not prove adequate—"

"For God's sake, Miss Marques—"

"Should it not, I would not expect you to keep me on. But I can assure you, *señhor*, I am a quick student. I have a degree in business."

He was looking at her as if one of them had gone crazy. Ana frowned. Was it possible Lincoln Aldridge wasn't lying? Could he really know nothing of the employment offer he'd made in response to Papa's request?

No. It was not possible. He had sent that letter. Of course. The letter! Ana opened her attaché case and plucked two sheets of paper from its depths.

"What's that?"

"Something to refresh your memory."

She leaned forward and sent both pages sailing across the expanse of glass that separated them. He stopped their progress with his hand and stared at her for what seemed forever. She was almost out of patience when he finally began to read.

And laugh.

Laugh! This horrible man was laughing at her.

Ana wanted to fling herself across the desk and claw at his eyes. She had come almost five thousand miles. Her plane had landed late so that she'd barely had time to drop her luggage at the hotel and change her clothes before coming here. She'd gone straight to Human Resources, pinned on her best smile, tried to ignore the way her knees kept threatening to knock together…

And found nobody expecting her.

Not the receptionist. Not the manager she'd demanded to see. Not anyone, including this—this oaf sitting across from her, laughing as if he were at the funniest show in the world.

To hell with wanting to claw his eyes. Ana sprang to her feet with every intention of doing it.

"You—you—"

He looked up, not just laughing but guffawing.

"*Tu es um porco*," she snarled as she flew around the desk. He shot from his chair, caught her wrists as she went for him...

His laughter died. What he wanted now burned flame-bright in his eyes.

"No," she said. "Damn you, no!"

He pulled her hard against him and kissed her.

The kiss scalded her; his heart thudded against hers. He swept his hand down her spine, cupped her bottom, brought her body tightly to his. His tongue penetrated her mouth.

It was a macho display of power, of arrogance, of all the things Ana despised...and none of that mattered. She heard herself making little cries. Soft, desperate sounds of desire. Her arms wound around his neck; her hair tumbled free as he tore the pins from it.

His hands molded her hips.

He lifted her. Something crashed to the floor as he sat her on the edge of the desk. Her thighs parted in welcome as he stepped between them. She was hot. Burning hot. And she wanted—she wanted...

"Mr. Aldridge?"

He spun around, blocking her from view, but it was too late. His PA had already seen them.

"Oh. Oh, good grief, Mr. Aldridge!"

The PA's shocked face vanished. The door closed. And Ana wanted to die.

She slipped down from the desk, pushed her hair away from her face with trembling hands. Smoothed down her jacket. Her skirt. Somehow, she'd lost one shoe. Oh, God, she'd lost a shoe…

"Here."

She looked up at the gruff sound of Aldridge's voice. Her shoe was in his hand. She grabbed it, thrust it on her foot.

She was a shaken mess. And he—he looked as if nothing had happened. Every strand of his dark, close-cropped hair was in place. His tie was neatly aligned. His suit jacket was uncreased. Only a glitter in his eyes suggested anything out of the ordinary had happened, though she doubted if this was out of the ordinary.

Lincoln Aldridge was a man who surely had many women in his life and took pleasure when and where he pleased.

She knew all about men like him. You couldn't grow up in Brazil, no matter how sheltered your existence, and not know. It was a man's world. Now she knew it was like that in the States, too.

Just as well Aldridge had decided to pretend ignorance of why she was here. Even if he'd offered her a job, she wouldn't take it.

Ana stepped back. Carefully, she picked up her attaché case. The letters—one from her father, thanking Aldridge for his generosity in offering her a position with his firm, the other Aldridge's response, requesting she show up for an interview today—were still on his desk.

Let them stay there. She never wanted to see them again.

She would give up the foolish idea of the career for which she had been trained, go home, let her father do what he'd wanted all along and find her a suitable husband—

"Miss Marques."

The hell she would. Ana straightened her shoulders and strode to the door. She would not let this one man defeat her. She'd stay in New York, take any job she could get and prove, once and for all, that a woman could succeed without becoming a man's property.

"Miss Marques! Ana. Wait."

She had her hand on the knob but she paused. She would not let this—this idiot write her off as a coward. She would make her exit with dignity.

His hand fell lightly on her shoulder.

She jerked away and spun toward him. At least he had stopped laughing.

"I am happy to have provided you with so much amusement."

Her English had lost the fluidity she'd worked so hard to achieve but so what? There was no reason to impress Lincoln Aldridge with anything except the fact that he could not rattle her.

"Ana."

He ran a hand through his hair. He looked—what was the word? *Contrite*. She didn't believe it, not for a moment.

"Ana." He drew a deep breath, slowly expelled it. "There's been a mistake."

"There most certainly has."

Her voice could have turned water to ice. Linc couldn't blame her. She'd been right about why she was here and he'd been wrong. As for the kiss…a moment of hubris, that was all. He'd never kissed a woman in anger before but there was a first time for everything. Anyway, the kiss didn't require an explanation.

The rest of it did.

"That letter your father sent—" He paused. "I never saw it. It's true," he added quickly, when her eyes narrowed. "Because of what happened to my sister, I had to turn some things over to others the last couple of months. Somehow, that letter ended up on the wrong desk."

"You replied to it."

Linc shook his head. "One of my people did. Obviously he recognized your father's name and assumed we'd grant his request as a courtesy."

"Whatever," she said, as if it didn't matter when it surely did. "My father should not have requested a favor from you. I do not need favors."

A lie, big-time. Linc knew it. "Really?"

"Really."

"Then why did you come here?"

"I came for a job. I certainly did not come here to be laughed at."

"I wasn't laughing at you, *senhora*. I was laughing because I misunderstood what your father…" No, Linc decided. Better not to go there. What he needed was a way out of this mess, one that wouldn't insult her or her father. "You say you have a degree in business?"

"That is correct."

"Can you, uh, can you type?"

She drilled him with a look.

"Okay. I know that sounds sexist but entry-level jobs…" He paused. "We don't have anything here but let me call around. Maybe I can find something."

"I told you, I want no favors from you. I will find a position elsewhere."

"This is New York. Good jobs are tight. If I can come up with something—"

"Goodbye, Senhor Aldridge."

Linc's mouth thinned. Fine. Let the lady take her expensive outfit, her attaché case and her attitude and hit the streets with the thousands of other well-dressed, well-educated hopefuls dreaming of careers.

With luck, she'd end up waiting on tables—which might do wonders for her overblown ego.

He folded his arms as she yanked the door open… and raised his eyebrows as his PA almost fell through it, holding a squalling Jennifer in her arms.

"I'm sorry, sir," she said desperately, "but the baby—"

She held the baby toward him. Linc looked around, as if he hoped Mary Poppins might suddenly materialize. Then he took the baby and held her as if she were an alien life form.

The baby's screams increased.

"Did you phone the nanny agency?" he said, raising his voice over the din.

"They said maybe tomorrow."

Shock sent his eyebrows climbing again. "Tomorrow?"

"Or Monday. They weren't hopeful. They said nobody ever seems to suit you and—"

Ana Maria Marques clucked her tongue and held out her arms. "Give the poor *bébe* to me!"

It was a command, not a request. Linc didn't argue. He handed his niece over.

"Whose child is this?"

"She's my niece. My sister's child."

Ana looked down at the squalling bundle. Her expression softened. "Ah, *pobre bébe*! Where is her papa?"

"He died with my sister."

"How sad," Ana said gently. She cooed at the baby. Whispered something in Portuguese. The child's screams became sobs; the sobs became whimpers. And, to everyone's amazement, the tiny rosebud mouth curved in a smile.

"She likes you," Linc said.

Ana threw him a sharp look. "What a shock."

"I only meant—"

"I have a dozen little cousins. They all like me. What is her name?"

"Jennifer."

"Jenny," Ana crooned, touching the tip of her finger to the baby's chin. "Such a lovely name for a lovely little girl."

Jennifer—Jenny—smiled giddily and blew a bubble.

Linc watched in fascination and upped the count. There weren't three Anas, there were four. Sexy siren. Demure innocent. Tailored cosmopolitan and now earth mother.

He thought of what it would be like to find out which of the Anas was real. To kiss that soft mouth until she melted against him and revealed herself. To him. To his hands, his mouth, his body. Revealed all the rich layers that waited for discovery…

Hell, he thought, and cleared his throat. "Sarah?" he said briskly to his PA "Take the baby, please."

His PA looked him straight in the eye. "I have work to do, sir," she said, and walked out of the room.

Linc wanted to call her back but she was right. What was he supposed to do now? No nanny until tomorrow. Or Monday. Or maybe never, the way things were going. He had an afternoon full of meetings. His lawyer.

The social worker, who'd probably just love to watch as his niece screamed her displeasure to the world.

The baby grabbed Ana's hand and smiled. Ana gave a soft laugh. And an idea so ridiculous any sane man would have dismissed it sprang to life in Linc's brain.

"So, Ana," he said, trying to sound casual, "what will you do now that the job thing hasn't panned out?"

Her shoulders straightened. "That is not your problem."

"Yes, you made that clear. But, ah, but I feel some-what responsible. That letter did go out on my letter-head." He paused. "Actually, I've thought of something that might suit you."

"Thank you," she said, though her tone made a mockery of the words, "but I do not want charity. I have already said that it was wrong to let my father ask you for a favor." She looked quickly at the baby, then held her toward Linc. "You may take her now, *senhor*."

Linc dug his hands into his pockets.

"No charity. This is a real job, but I warn you it doesn't require that degree in business."

"It doesn't?"

"You wouldn't be working for my company, you'd be working for me."

Color flooded her face. "If you think I would take money to—to—"

"I need a nanny for my niece."

Her jaw dropped. Obviously she couldn't believe what he'd just said. Well, damnit, neither could he, but he was desperate.

"Are you up to some honest work?" His tone hard-ened. "Or would you rather hurry home to Papa and admit that your first foray into the world turned out to be too much reality to handle?"

CHAPTER FOUR

WASN'T there a North American expression? Something about being caught between a boulder and a hard surface?

There was, Ana was sure, though maybe she had the syntax wrong. She'd studied English since childhood and she spoke it well, but when she was under pressure her command of the language sometimes faltered.

Besides, language was fluid. And if you lived a medieval existence, if you were sheltered, all but smothered by a well-meaning father and a doting mother, you couldn't possibly keep up with its ebb and flow.

There was, however, no way to misunderstand what Lincoln Aldridge had just said. This was the real world. He lived in it. She did not.

Never mind the college degree. She had one, yes, but the truth was that most of what she'd learned about business she'd learned through her own reading. The college she'd attended was a nice place but it demanded little of the wealthy young women who were its students.

Papa had sent her there to placate her, just as he'd done by sending her north. To Lincoln. First he'd given her a safe education at a school he could trust. Then he'd sent her to New York for a safe job with a man he could trust.

What irony!

Why would anyone trust Lincoln Aldridge? Obviously he lived by his own rules. He'd kissed her because it had pleased him to do so. Now he was offering her a job for similar reasons.

"Well?"

Aldridge's eyes were locked on hers. He looked impatient and arrogant. And beautiful.

A sweet fire engulfed her.

She'd never seen a man you'd describe that way but it suited him. That hard masculine face. The long body. The musculature of it that not even an expensive suit could disguise.

Ana dragged her gaze from his. There was a baby seat in the middle of an enormous conference table. She carried the contented baby to it and took her time securing the safety harness, grateful for the chance to regain her composure.

Of course she would not accept his offer. Why would she even contemplate saying yes? She wasn't a nanny. She adored children but she had not come to New York to burp babies.

"Never mind." A patronizing little smile lifted one corner of his mouth. "That look on your face says it all. You expected me to make you second in command at Aldridge. Instead, I'm offering you good wages to do an honest job—"

"What do you call 'good wages'?"

She could see the question surprised him. Well, it surprised her, too, but what harm was there in asking?

He named a figure. Another surprise. It was a lot of money. Ana did some fast mental calculations.

"Plus, of course, room and board."

"Room and board? You mean, I'd be expected to live in your home?"

"Unless you'd rather get calls from me in the middle of the night if my niece needs tending."

His tone was so flat it took her a second to realize he was being sarcastic. But he was right. You couldn't care for a baby at a distance.

Still, she would not do it. She could not do it. Even if it meant returning home and admitting failure…

"I'll take it."

His dark eyebrows rose. What a pleasure, she thought coldly, to have taken him by surprise again.

"With one caveat."

He sighed. "Health insurance? Paid holidays? Mondays and alternate Saturdays off?"

"Insurance, naturally. As for the rest, when I want time off, I will ask for it."

"Then what's the caveat?"

"You will keep looking within your organization for something for me."

"I just told you—"

"I know how large corporations work," Ana said, lying with aplomb. "People come, people go. When you find a position for which I am suited, you will offer it to me."

Linc's body tightened. He had a damned good idea of what position would suit Ana Maria Marques.

He thought back to how she'd just responded to his kiss. It had been the same way that very first night.

"That night," he said, "in the garden…Were you going to meet a man?"

Her face colored. For an instant she was tempted to tell him the truth, that she'd been doing what she always did when the constraints of her life became unbearable.

For years, she'd slipped out of the beautiful house that was her prison, slipped away from the grounds and wandered the hilly streets in blissful solitude.

A faceless entity named Aldridge Inc. had changed all that.

She'd memorized the master code that bypassed the alarm system, come up with a way to dress that would ensure she'd blend into the darkness. And the very first time she'd tried it…

"Answer the question, Ana. Were you going to meet someone? Or were you coming from a liaison with your lover?" His tone roughened. "Was I the lucky recipient of leftover lust?"

For the second time today, she wanted to hit him. Ball up her fist and smack it right into his jaw. If only he knew how many times she'd relived what had happened, the hours she'd wasted trying to figure out why she'd kissed a stranger…

"Yes," she said with a careless toss of her head, "that's it, exactly. I had just left my lover and you took advantage of what he'd made me feel."

His face darkened; his big body tensed. She wanted to call back the outrageous lie but it was too late. Aldridge had already pulled her into his arms.

His kiss was hard. Merciless. And, oh, God, exciting!

Men had kissed her but not like this, as if the planets and stars were nothing but an illusion and the only thing real was their passion. She told herself not to react, but even as she did she was twisting her hands into Lincoln's jacket, letting herself lean into him—

He let go of her and she stumbled back.

"The truth, *senhora*," he said calmly, "is that your lover left you unsatisfied."

Ana spat a word at him, one she'd heard but never dreamed she'd use. To her fury, it made him laugh.

"What a charming choice of words, Ana. Yes, I know what you called me. I've spent some time in Rio, remember?" His mouth twisted. "Now, do you want the job or don't you?"

"Do you really think I would accept employment in your home after what you just did?"

"What I think," Linc said, "is that you're hardly the trembling innocent your father thinks you are."

"What *I* think," Ana said, "is that you are a—"

"I also think that you're not a fool. You want to stay in New York. That means you need a job. I'm offering you one. Good pay, a roof over your head and food in your belly." His eyes narrowed. "I can assure you, there won't be any other benefits. I've never tolerated personal relationships between management and employees in the office and I'm not about to tolerate them in my home." He shot back his cuff and frowned at his watch. "I have a busy schedule this afternoon. I need an immediate answer. Do you want this job or don't you?"

Was he crazy? Did he really think she would work for him?

He looked up, impatience etched into every hard feature. "Well? Yes or no?"

Ana swallowed dryly. And said yes.

The meeting with the social worker seemed to go well.

Linc met with her alone and then had Ana bring in the baby. Fresh from a bottle, a nap and a diaper change, Jenny glowed with contentment in her new nanny's arms. A few minutes of polite chitchat about babies and then the social worker changed topics.

"That's a great suit, Miss Marques," she said pleasantly. "Armani? Oh, and I love your shoes. Gucci, right?"

The new direction puzzled Linc. Not Ana.

"Yes to both and thank you." Her smile was woman-to-woman. "Of course, I have only just arrived in the city. When you see me again, I am afraid I will be dressed more conventionally. You know, for spit-ups and diapering."

Both women laughed politely. Then Ana leaned forward.

"I hope Senhor Aldridge told you how grateful my father and I are to him for giving me this opportunity."

It was the social worker's turn to look puzzled. "Your father?"

"It is common practice in my country," Ana said demurely, "for young ladies of a certain class to go north, if they wish, and try their hand at genteel employment. Under the close supervision of an old family friend, naturally."

Linc looked at her. Amazing. Nobody would suspect she was lying through her teeth.

"Fortunately for me, Senhor Aldridge is just such an old, trusted friend. When we heard he needed help caring for Jennifer, Papa saw it as the perfect chance for me to do something useful."

The social worker looked as if Ana had just explained the mysteries of the universe.

"Excellent," she said briskly. "Thank you for your time, Mr. Aldridge. I'll see you in another few weeks."

Linc waited until the woman was gone. Then he scratched his head.

"What the hell was that all about?"

"You are a man," Ana said briskly. "I am a woman."

"Really? I'd never have known."

"She was trying to figure me out."

"Tell her to join the club."

"She could tell my clothes are expensive."

"So?"

Ana rolled her eyes. "So, it crossed her mind that you might have bought my things for me. That I am your mistress."

He wanted to say she was crazy, except she wasn't. His lawyer had warned him that his life would come under the closest scrutiny.

"So I told her a story about practices in my country." She smiled sweetly. "You'd be amazed how naive some people are about South America. The taxi driver asked me where I was from. Then he wanted to know all about my encounters with jaguars and head-hunters." Her smile faded. "Satisfied?"

Linc nodded. Who wouldn't be satisfied? His niece was happy. The social worker was happy.

Unfortunately, when his attorney showed up a couple of hours later, he wasn't.

Linc called Ana in and introduced them. She was the perfect nanny: polite, respectful, almost deferential. Charles smiled, said all the right things, but as soon as he and Linc were alone, he shook his head.

"She's a liability, Lincoln."

Linc sat back in his chair. "Since when is a nanny a liability?"

"When she's young, stunning and somebody's spent a million bucks on her clothes."

Linc sighed. "Her old man's loaded."

"The Social Services people won't know that."

"Yeah. They will. They already do."

He told Charles what had happened. The lawyer nodded.

"Young, stunning—and bright. That's one hell of a combo."

"The baby's putty in her hands."

"And you?"

"What, you think I'm gonna make a move on my nanny? Give me a break, Charles. Except for the last one, all Jenny's nannies were young and attractive, too."

"This girl's not attractive, she's spectacular."

Linc sat straight in his chair. "I hadn't noticed."

"Maybe not, but Social Services—"

"I just told you, Ana took care of that."

"For the moment."

"Meaning?"

"Meaning, until they decide you're a fit guardian for your niece—well, just don't underestimate their power, all right? Especially with Kathryn's mother-in-law hovering in the background."

"You have to be kidding. The woman was a failure as a mother to her son. She's only interested in custody of Jenny because of the money I'd put in trust for Kath. No court would—"

"You're male, Kathryn's mother-in-law is female. You're an uncle. She's a grandmother." The attorney held up his hand when Linc would have spoken. "I know it sounds crazy but I've seen judges make decisions that defy logic. We don't want that to happen here."

"No," Linc said grimly, "we don't."

The men rose to their feet and walked slowly to the door.

"All I'm saying is, remember Caesar's wife."

"Meaning?"

"Meaning," the lawyer said, clapping Linc on the back, "remain above suspicion."

"You're serious, aren't you?"

"Dead serious. One wrong move, one blurring of the line between you and Ana, and you'll leave yourself open to losing Jennifer. Unless you've changed your mind about wanting to raise her…?"

Changed his mind?

Forget Kath's greedy mother-in-law. He'd never let someone like her raise Jenny… But there was more to it than that. Early this morning, he'd lifted a tiny stranger from her crib and sat down with her in his arms. Somewhere during the next hour, that tiny stranger had turned into a child he loved.

It defied logic, and Linc was a logical man. But…

"Lincoln? Have you changed your mind?"

Linc held out his hand. Charles took it.

"The only thing that's changed," he said, "is that I'm more convinced than ever I want to raise Jenny. And I'll do whatever it takes to make that happen."

The lawyer smiled. "In that case, just remember to treat Miss Marques like the employee she is and things will…" He hesitated. "…and things should be fine."

Fine wasn't exactly the word Linc would have chosen.

Not for the first couple of weeks. Ana's arrival in his life was like a tornado touching down.

First, there was her luggage.

She'd left it at her hotel. He'd sent his driver for it. The guy was a body builder, long on muscle and stamina, but he'd come back looking stunned.

No wonder.

Six suitcases, each the size of a small truck, were lined up behind him in the marble foyer of Linc's penthouse.

"Oh, hell," Linc said softly.

"Yeah," his driver said, just as softly.

Together, they wrestled the stuff up the spiral staircase and into the nursery. Ana left the baby with the housekeeper and followed them, snapping out directions. When the luggage was placed where she wanted it, Linc cleared his throat.

"I don't suppose you have anything suitable for, uh, for nannying in those bags?"

"Such a typically male attitude," she said with a cluck of her tongue.

Linc brightened. "Good. For a minute there, I was afraid you owned nothing but—"

She opened one suitcase. Then another. And another. He saw suits, silky blouses, more of those pumps that looked so demure until you noticed the sky-high heels.

"I thought you said—"

"What I said was that your attitude was typical."

And right on the mark, Linc thought, but he wasn't foolish enough to say it.

"I will shop tomorrow and buy what is required."

She swung toward him. Strands of golden hair had come loose from the neat chignon at the nape of her neck and lay against her cheek. What if he went to her and tucked those errant strands behind her ear?

"Do you know what would be appropriate?"

He blinked. "Sorry. Appropriate for…?"

"For me to wear."

Lace. Black lace against her creamy skin. Or maybe pale pink. The shade you'd see inside a seashell on a

Caribbean beach. Yes. Definitely. Soft, delicate pink against that soft, lovely body.

Was he losing his mind?

"Of course not," he snapped. "How would I know what you should wear?"

"You have employed a nanny before this, have you not?"

He thought of the long line of useless females who'd filed through his life the last months, flashed on the one who'd worn his shirt and that thong…

"Just buy regular clothes. Casual stuff. Jeans. Cotton tees. Whatever you'd wear to care for a baby, like other nannies."

"I am not like other nannies."

He knew that. Oh, he knew that…

Linc yanked his wallet from his pocket. Tossed a credit card on the bed.

"Leave Jenny with Mrs. Hollowell in the morning," he said gruffly. "Go to the park. Look around. You're bound to see other nannies. See what they're wearing and then go shopping."

"I do not need you to buy my clothes."

He ground his teeth together with enough force to have sent his dentist running from the room.

"And I," he said, "do not need you to argue over everything. Besides, this isn't a gift. I'll take the money out of your pay."

"That will be acceptable."

"Damned right, it will," Linc said, and then, because he wanted to cross the room, haul his impossible, intractable, infuriating new nanny into his arms and kiss her until that look of superiority gave way to one of passion, he turned on his heel and strode away.

* * *

Linc had always worked late, played hard, spent little time at home.

He saw no need to change that.

His days were long. So were his evenings. Longer than usual. With things under control at home, he was giving his little black book one hell of a workout, even though he found himself ending his evenings by giving his dates chaste kisses on their upturned faces and pretending he didn't notice their looks of surprise and disappointment.

Well, hell, that was what happened when a man worked hard. It had nothing to do with the fact that Ana was living under his roof. Why would it? He hardly ever saw her, and when he did they spent a couple of minutes discussing Jenny and then each of them moved on.

He was pleased.

He'd made a wise move, hiring her. Mrs. Hollowell said she was a lovely young woman. Jenny cooed and smiled and squealed with delight. He could hear her in the mornings, could hear Ana laughing with her.

Ana had a terrific laugh. Husky. Sexy.

Not that he cared.

What mattered was that the baby was thriving and nights were peaceful again. No sobs, no screams, no shrieks. Just blessed silence.

What woke him, instead, were his dreams, hot and disturbing and, dammit, ridiculously adolescent. Well, he was human. Having a good-looking woman sleeping one floor down was a little distracting. Once he'd figured that out, he worked his little black book even harder—and left another half-dozen puzzled, unhappy women in his wake.

The first weeks of her employment rushed by. She

hadn't even asked for a day off. She seemed content, spending all her time with Jenny, who loved her. His housekeeper loved her. The doormen and the concierge loved her. Ana was Mary Poppins come to life.

Impossible, a voice inside Linc whispered slyly.

She was, as his lawyer had so succinctly put it, spectacular. And she was filled with passion. That kiss in the garden. The kiss in his office. When would she show her true colors? He kept waiting for the other shoe to fall.

One morning during the third week, Linc picked up the phone to make a quick call before he left for his office. He heard Ana's voice, speaking in Portuguese, and then her low, sexy laugh.

"Oh," he said, "sorry," and hung up the phone.

Who had she been talking to? He frowned, adjusted his tie, grabbed his wallet and went briskly down the stairs and out the door.

That was her business, not his.

By noon, it was driving him crazy.

Who did she know in New York? Better still, who did she know who spoke Portuguese? He knew she hadn't been calling home. She'd bought a cell phone expressly for calls to and from Brazil, and made a point of telling him her father didn't know about her job as Jenny's nanny.

"And you are not to say anything of it, should you speak to him, *senhor,*" she'd added in a tone of voice that made him want to point out that he did not take orders from her…except he wanted to do it by hauling her into his arms and showing her exactly who was boss.

And he wasn't like that.

Certainly he wasn't.

By midafternoon, he was pacing his office. Enough, he thought, reached for the phone and dialed home.

The phone rang a long time. Then Ana answered, sounded rushed. "Hello?"

"It's me," Linc said.

"Yes. What is it, please, Senhor Aldridge? We are in the middle of something. I am very busy."

Not rushed. Breathless. And there was a hint of suppressed laughter in her voice.

Linc tapped a pencil against the edge of his desk. "Very busy with what?"

"I have a visitor."

"A visitor?"

"I am permitted visitors, am I not?"

"Where is Mrs. Hollowell?"

"She left early. She had a dental appointment. *Senhor*, if you are done, I am—"

"Busy. Yeah. So you said." Linc's voice roughened. "Who is this visitor? And where is my niece?"

"The visitor is a friend. And Jenny is, of course, right here with us."

Linc hung up the phone. He thought about who might visit a woman who knew nobody in New York. He thought about that phone call. He thought about Jenny, right there with…

Us.

Twenty minutes later, he stepped out of his private elevator, marched through the foyer and heard his nanny's soft, uninhibited laughter coming from the great room.

"Oh," she said, "*bébe,* you are incredible! When did you learn to do that?"

Linc tossed his briefcase in the general direction of a table and ran.

"What in hell do you think you're—"

Ana, seated cross-legged on the carpet, looked up in surprise. But mostly the surprise was Linc's.

His nanny did, indeed, have a visitor. Another young woman—dark-haired, in jeans and sneakers and cotton shirt. And another baby, sitting in the vee of the girl's legs, just as his niece was seated in the vee of Ana's, grinning and clapping her chubby hands.

"—doing?" Linc finished lamely, and felt his face burn.

Ana's blue eyes narrowed as if the scene he'd expected to find was painted in garish detail across his forehead. The other girl looked from one face to the other, then scrambled to her feet with her charge in her arms.

"Thanks for the coffee, Ana," she said in heavily accented English.

"You are welcome," Ana said, her gaze never leaving Linc's.

"See you tomorrow, at the playground?"

Ana didn't answer for a long minute. Then she shrugged. "Perhaps."

Linc ran his hand through his hair. "Listen," he said, "Ana, your friend doesn't have to leave. I mean, I didn't intend to—"

He was talking to an empty room. Ana's visitor and her charge were gone, and Ana and Jenny were halfway up the stairs.

"Ana. Ana! Dammit, wait!" Linc called as he hurried after her. "Okay. So I was wrong. I'm sorry, all right?"

The nursery door slammed shut in his face. He thought about kicking it open, then decided he'd done enough stupid things for one day.

Ana would get over it.

Besides, what was there to apologize for? She lived under his roof. She took care of his niece. He had the absolute right to hold her responsible for her actions.

She'd taken a lover in Rio.

Why, sooner or later, wouldn't she take one here?

CHAPTER FIVE

ANA avoided him.

She spoke when spoken to, answered questions about Jenny and saw to it their paths hardly crossed.

Why would he want anything more?

Because, he decided after another couple of weeks, because this woman was his employee. He didn't like her attitude. Her behavior was insolent. It was time to put an end to the nonsense.

Friday afternoon, he told his PA to cancel a three o'clock meeting, phone his dinner date and tell her he might be a little late.

Then he headed home.

Ana was in the great room with Jenny. They were sitting on the carpet, playing a game that seemed to involve Jenny giggling while Ana gently tugged her to a sitting position.

"Good girl," Ana crooned. "That's my *pequena preciosa*."

Jenny spotted him first. "Baa baa baa," she said, and shot him a huge grin.

Ana looked up and stopped smiling. "You're early, *senhor*," she said coolly, and rose to her feet.

She was wearing one of what he supposed she'd call her nanny outfits, suitable for a midsummer day. Cropped trousers, a loose-fitting T-shirt, sandals. Her hair was pulled back in a ponytail; her face was make-up free.

She looked about as sexy as a stick. Then why this sudden knot in his gut?

"Jenny and I will be out of your way as soon as I've collected her toys."

"Ana." Linc hesitated. He'd come home angry, wanting a confrontation. Now he knew what he wanted was to offer what she deserved. An apology. "Ana," he said, "I'm sorry."

"There is no need to apologize. You are, of course, free to come into your own home whenever you wish. I should not have brought Jenny in here."

"No! I mean, it's fine that you're here with Jenny." Linc took a breath. "What I'm saying is that I'm sorry about what happened that day you—you had your friend here."

"There is no reason to apologize for that, either."

What she meant was, it was too late.

"Yeah, there is." Linc took a step toward her. "See, I had some, ah, some unfortunate experiences with a couple of the nannies who took care of Jenny before you came along."

"I am sorry to hear it."

Her accent was growing heavier. It made him smile. He'd noticed that about her, that her perfect English always became a shade too perfect when she was angry.

"I have said something amusing?"

"No," Linc said quickly, "not at all."

"Whatever your experiences with the others, you had no reason to distrust me."

You had a lover, he almost said. But so what? Her personal life was none of his affair. Besides, she was right. He had no reason to distrust her. He had no reason to keep remembering the way she felt in his arms, either, the warmth of her body, the sweetness of her mouth.

"You're right," he said quietly.

"I would never bring a man here. How could you think I would?"

"That's why I'm apologizing. I know you wouldn't get involved with a man."

Her eyes became as cold as the Arctic. "I did not say that."

"Sure you did. You said—"

"I said I would never bring a man here, but my life is my own, *senhor*. I did not come thousands of miles to let you take over where my father left off."

"Is that why you left Rio? Because your father found out about your lover and wanted you to stop seeing him?"

She looked at him as if he'd lost his sanity. Hell, maybe he had. Hadn't he just told himself her personal life was none of his business?

"Are you dissatisfied with my work?"

"What? No. No, not at all. I just—"

"Then I see no reason for this conversation."

Ana picked up the baby, turned her back to him and started briskly from the room. Dammit, he'd started to tell her he was sorry for how he'd behaved. Instead, he'd insulted her all over again.

"Ana!"

She stood still, though she kept her back to him.

"Yes, *senhor*?"

"I really am sorry. For what happened last time. For now. For screwing up every time I open my mouth."

Would she respond? Or would she walk away. He didn't realize he was holding his breath until she swung toward him.

"I am sorry, too. Perhaps I am— What is the word?—stubbly?"

"Stub…" Linc grinned. "Prickly."

"Prickly," she said, nodding in agreement. "So, I accept your apology."

"Good." He hesitated. "The thing is, we might get along better if we knew more about each other."

"Certainly. I can give you a copy of my résumé."

"I didn't mean…" He hesitated again. "Are you, uh, are you satisfied, being here? I mean, I know you didn't come to New York to become a nanny."

"I'm happy being with Jenny."

And are you happy being with me? The words were on the tip of his tongue. Hell, maybe he really was crazy.

"Good," he said briskly. "She's certainly happy with you. You're wonderful with her."

Ana smiled. "She's a joy. Did you know she can roll over?"

"No," Linc said, following her lead, carefully stepping back from the thin ice that had appeared under his feet moments ago. "Really?"

"If I put her on her tummy in her play yard, she rolls onto her back." She paused. "If you want to come upstairs with us, she'll show you."

Turn aside an olive branch? He might be nuts but he wasn't stupid.

"Great idea," he said. "Lead the way."

He followed her up the stairs. Ana put Jenny in the play yard and the baby rolled right onto her back.

"Baa baa baa," she chortled.

Linc grinned. *"Baa baa baa* to you, too, kid."

"She's a very special little girl," Ana said, smiling.

"Yeah. She's really something. Kathryn would be…" He frowned, swallowed past the lump that had suddenly risen in his throat and turned to the door. "Well. I don't want to keep you guys from your routine, so—"

"It must be terrible," Ana said softly. "Losing someone you loved as you loved your sister."

Linc nodded. "Kath was one in a million."

A light hand fell on his shoulder. "So is her daughter." Ana hesitated. "Lincoln? It's Jenny's bathtime. Would you like to stay and help?"

Lincoln. She'd called him Lincoln for the very first time. Linc cleared his throat.

"You sure I won't be in the way?"

She smiled. "You won't be in the way if I put you to work."

He smiled back. "Just point me in the right direction and step back."

Clearly, he was going to be second in command.

Linc took off his jacket. Rolled back his sleeves. Held Jenny while Ana put on an oversized apron and filled the baby tub.

She did the actual bathing, though he got as wet as if he'd been part of the procedure. Jenny, it seemed, was great at slapping at the water and giggling.

"All done," Ana said, and that was his clue to wrap the baby in a big towel and dry her during an improvised game of peek-a-boo that sent her into fits of laughter.

"She loves to play," Ana said proudly, and it occurred to him that he didn't know as much as he should about his niece.

It was definitely time to change that.

Ana dressed Jenny in a pair of pajamas with little yellow ducks all over them. Then she looked up at Linc.

"Thank you for your help."

"I enjoyed it."

She smiled. "You're soaked, Lincoln. I should have offered you an apron."

"No problem."

"Well—"

"So," he said briskly, "what's next?"

"Next? Oh." Her face pinkened. "With Jenny, you mean? Well, I'm going to take her down to the kitchen and feed her."

"Fine. Give me five minutes to get out of this wet stuff and I'll meet you there."

"Oh, but that isn't—"

"I think it is," Linc said quietly. "It only just hit me that I don't know a lot about my niece, and I should."

Jenny was eating something noxious-looking when he came down.

"Mashed banana and Pablum," Ana said, trying not to laugh at his expression. "And be careful, Lincoln. Babies are very good at reading faces."

"Yum-yum," he said bravely.

Jenny flashed him a gummy smile.

When the banana-and-whatever was all gone, Linc took the baby in his arms and fed her her bottle. Her eyelids were drooping by the time she'd reached the final inch.

Ana held out her arms. "I'll put her to bed," she whispered.

Linc nodded. He followed Ana into the hall, watched as she started up the steps. The evening was at an end. He was grateful it had worked out well. After all, it was easier to get along with an employee than not to get along with her…

"Ana?"

Ana turned. His heart seemed to rise into his throat. How beautiful she was. How right she looked, with the baby asleep against her breast.

"Ana." He cleared his throat. "Mrs. Hollowell's sure to have left something for supper."

"Oh, she did. There's cold chicken and a salad, and—"

"How about having supper with me?"

An eternity seemed to pass. Ana touched the tip of her tongue to her lips. "Don't you have dinner plans?"

"None," he said blithely, and made a mental note to have his PA send his would-be date a couple of dozen long-stemmed roses in the morning.

"Still, Lincoln—"

"I figured you could bring me up to speed on what's new with Jenny."

"Oh. Of course. I'll be right down."

Linc hurried back into the kitchen. Should they eat here or in the dining room? Summer still gripped the city so building a fire on the hearth in the great room's massive stone fireplace would be—

For God's sake, Aldridge!

"Just get out the chicken," he muttered, "and the

salad, set the kitchen counter and remember this is a meal, nothing more."

Still, by the time Ana reappeared he'd set a table on the terrace. Hey, it made sense. It was a warm night; the trees in the park were an intense green. Why have a terrace if you didn't use it?

He opened a chilled bottle of Sauvignon Blanc for the same reason. Why not? Didn't a meal deserve some *vino*?

They chatted easily while they ate. Ana had a dozen Jenny stories and Linc smiled at all of them. Then they fell silent.

He cleared his throat. "So," he said, "what do you think of New York?"

"Well, I haven't seen much of it but what I have seen seems wonderful."

He almost winced. As brilliant conversation-starters went, his had just fizzled. Ana was being polite. She couldn't have had more than glimpses of the city, and whose fault was that?

His.

She'd come to the States for a nine-to-five job and he'd pushed her into a 24/7 arrangement she'd never have considered under normal circumstances.

"Well," he said, "you should take a day off. I'm sure Mrs. Hollowell can watch Jenny."

"That's all right, Lincoln. I don't—"

"The Empire State Building. The Statue of Liberty. The museums." What in hell was the matter with him? He sounded like a travel brochure. "There's a lot to see."

"I know, but—"

"I'd like to show the city to you."

Their eyes met. He could have sworn he felt electricity sizzle across the table.

"Thank you, Lincoln, but—"

"I like that, too," he said. "The way you say my name."

"What?"

He reached for her hand, enfolded it in his. "Lin-cone. As if it were two separate words."

"My English," she said, her voice a little breathless, "isn't always per—"

"Yes, it is. Perfect. Everything about you—"

Ana wrenched her hand from his and shot to her feet. "I—I have to check on Jenny."

Linc pushed back his chair and stood up. "Ana—"

"Don't," she whispered.

All he had to do was reach out and take her in his arms. He knew what would happen. So did she. He could see awareness in her eyes. But he'd done enough to this woman already. He'd crushed her dream of coming north and getting a job with his company. Worse, he'd taken that dream and used it for his own purposes.

Only a true SOB would want more from her. Except, God help him, more was exactly what he wanted.

He took a step toward her. Saw the pupils of her eyes enlarge and darken. One kiss. Just one kiss—

The baby's tentative cry trailed down the stairs.

"Jenny," Ana said in a rush.

Linc nodded. Jenny. And reality. Just in time.

"Sure." He forced a smile. "Go on. I'll clean up here."

Then, before he could weigh the consequences, before she could protest, he cupped Ana's face in his hands, lowered his head and brushed his mouth lightly over hers.

Her eyes closed. She swayed toward him. For a moment, nothing existed but the magic of their kiss.

Linc dropped his hands to his sides. And Ana fled.

So much for quiet, friendly dinners.

At least things were peaceful. No more sniping cold looks and turned backs. But there were also no more smiles from Ana. No more easy conversation, either, not even when he gave Jenny her bottle or went to the nursery to tuck her in. He was doing those things now, coming home earlier, not going out at night, working hard at getting to know his niece.

The baby made it easy. She beamed whenever she saw him.

He just wished Ana would beam. Or at least smile. She was unfailingly polite, doling out *Yes, senhors* and *No, thank you, senhors* as if they were part of the job requirement—which, he supposed, they were.

But he kept remembering that for one evening, at least, she had not behaved as if this were a job. He knew, deep inside, that was wrong. She worked for him; he had rules about that. Okay. So he shouldn't have kissed her. But that didn't mean she had to stop talking to him, did it?

Saturday, he decided to find out.

He waited until he knew she had Jenny in the stroller. Then he ambled into the foyer.

"You going to the park?" he said, as casually as if they chatted like this all the time.

He'd caught her by surprise. He could tell by the way she looked up from adjusting Jenny's harness.

"Yes."

"Great." He smiled. "I've been cooped up in the office all week. A walk in the park sounds great."

Ana didn't miss a beat. "Jenny will love having you with her," she said pleasantly. "And I can have a little time for myself."

"To do what?" he said, before he could stop himself.

"Go shopping. Wash my hair. You know."

What he knew, he thought grimly as he pushed the stroller through Central Park, was that those were things women offered as excuses when they didn't want to see a man. When they didn't like a guy.

Well, that wasn't what was happening here.

Okay, it was. But not because Ana didn't like him. She liked him, all right. That evening they'd spent together, the way she'd slipped into using his first name, her easy laughter...

It made him angry. At her, for not admitting she'd wanted to kiss him as much as he'd wanted to kiss her. At himself, for doing something stupid.

At the entire situation, because he couldn't seem to find a remedy.

So, as time passed, he did his best not to think about it. He had other things on his mind. Meetings. Appointments. Business.

And there was this thing with the social worker.

The woman had paid two home visits. He'd been there for both. They'd seemed to go smoothly, but he'd caught her giving Ana what could only be called suspicious looks.

"Your nanny is such an attractive woman, Mr. Aldridge," she'd said the last time, when Ana took Jenny from the room to change her diaper.

Linc, remembering his lawyer's initial warnings, had felt something cold tap-dance along his spine.

"I guess she is," he'd said with lazy ease, "but what matters to me is that she's wonderful with Jenny."

He knew it was almost decision time. The social worker asked him more and more questions about the future. Had he thought about Jenny's schooling? About her possible need, as she got older, for a female figure in her life?

Was she measuring him against Kathryn's mother-in-law? What he knew, for certain, was that the mother-in-law was turning up the pressure.

She had the right to visit Jenny. She never came when Linc was there, and at first her visits had been cursory. Hello, goodbye. Ana had told him they'd lasted maybe five minutes.

Lately, though, she said, the visits were lengthier and more frequent.

"She doesn't hold Jenny or anything, but she brings a toy each visit, and she makes a point of asking me the time when she arrives and when she leaves."

His lawyer grew solemn at the news.

"She's building her case, Lincoln. Little presents. Longer visits. It's a way of showing she's interested in Jennifer's welfare."

"But Ana says she never goes near Jenny."

The attorney shrugged. "Trust me, she will if she's there at the same time as the social worker. She's a clever woman, working at looking like Mother of the Year even though we know she isn't."

"Then why hasn't Child Protective Services kicked her out on her butt and given me formal custody? This woman is only after Jenny's inheritance, Charles. Surely they can see that?"

"Be patient, Lincoln. We're gathering information."

Linc had been patient. And finally his lawyer called to say it was paying off.

"The detective we hired came by this morning," he

said. "He gave me a folder two inches thick. The woman has a long history of men and addiction. Give me a week and I'll be ready to move ahead."

Linc sighed with relief. "That's great news, Charles."

"This should all be resolved in your favor pretty quickly. Well, assuming the social worker doesn't pop in for a visit and find you and the nanny in, shall we say, a compromising situation."

Both men laughed.

"Speaking of things going well, how is she working out?"

She's so polite she makes my head ache, Linc thought. "She's working out fine," he said.

He hung up the phone and pushed back from his desk. Why think about that now?. Except for Charles's phone call, the day had been rough. A hush-hush security system his people were installing in a Dallas museum was causing problems. A fire had crippled production of a new computer chip.

Add Ana's attitude to that mix and his head might just explode.

He thought about taking a couple of aspirin, glanced at his watch, saw that it was almost five. Ana would be bathing Jenny. Mrs. Hollowell would be getting ready to leave. His home would be quiet. He could shower, get into jeans and a T-shirt, sit on the terrace with a cold beer for company and watch twilight overtake the park.

It was, he decided, an excellent plan.

Definitely excellent.

By the time Linc stepped out of his private elevator, the ache in his head was easing. And he'd figured right. The place was as silent as a tomb. Ana and the baby were undoubtedly in the nursery. Mrs. Hollowell was still here—he could hear her humming softly in the kitchen—but she'd be leaving soon.

He headed for the stairs. He'd take those aspirin now, then a long shower...

"Whoa!"

He saw the tracks and the gaily colored wooden trains, but by then it was too late. He only had time for a couple of frantic dance steps, a pirouette over the tracks that would have delighted Baryshnikov...

Then he went down on his ass.

The resultant crash was impressive. He heard his housekeeper call out. Ana shouted something, too, and then he heard both women running toward him.

"Mr. Aldridge," Mrs. Hollowell gasped, "are you all right?"

"Lincoln, ohmygod," Ana said, and followed that with a lot of other things he couldn't understand.

He told himself it was because she was saying them in Portuguese. It couldn't be because she was kneeling beside him, wearing nothing but a frantic look and a bath towel.

Venus, Linc thought, *rising from the sea.*

Venus making a fool of him the last weeks, treating him as if they hadn't had that quiet meal together, as if she hadn't sighed when he kissed her. Did he have to break his neck before she deigned to notice him?

"Lincoln. Please, do you need a doctor?"

Linc glared and got to his feet. His tailbone hurt, but he'd sooner have said he was Bobo the Clown than admit to that.

"What I need," he said coldly, "is a no-toy zone in this place!"

She turned pale. Who gave a damn? How much crap was a man supposed to take from a woman?

"There's a closet in the nursery. And a big toy box. That's where these trains belong."

"Yes. You are right." Ana rose to her feet, one hand clutching the edges of the towel together. "I apologize, but—"

"But what? If the nursery needs more storage space, tell me and I'll arrange for a carpenter to build some shelves."

He knew his voice was rising but he was done with tolerating disrespect in his own home, and to hell with anyone who didn't see Ana's avoidance of him as that.

"Uh…uh…" Mrs. Hollowell, wise soul that she was, began backing out of the room. "I'll—I'll just—it's late, sir, and—"

Linc nodded and turned his attention back to Ana.

"If you needed shelves," he snapped, "you had only to say so, but how could you do that without talking to me?."

She was trembling. Good. Let her remember her place here. She was his employee. When had she lost sight of that?

"And what is Jenny doing that you thought you could leave her alone?"

"Jenny is asleep. I would never—"

"People take showers in the morning. They take them at night. They don't take them in the middle of the day."

Her eyes narrowed. "It is not the middle of the day, and I do not need your permission to shower."

"Walking around like that. In a towel. Where's your sense of decorum?"

Where was his sanity? was a better question. She

hadn't been walking around, she'd been in her room until he took that stupid fall, but how could a man be logical when a woman as beautiful as this, as impossible as this, stood before him wearing nothing but a towel?

"Stop yelling at me!"

"I am not yelling," he roared. "And never mind crying. Tears will get you nowhere."

"You think I weep because of you?" Ana jerked her chin up. "Hah! I cry for myself. For ever agreeing to work for a—for a—"

She spat out a word. He took a step toward her.

"What did you call me?"

"Trust me, *senhor*. You do not want to know."

Linc grabbed her by the shoulders. "I've had enough of your attitude!"

"And I have had enough of your dictatorialness. I quit."

"There is no such word," Linc snarled. "And you can't quit. You're fired!"

"You are a horrible, arrogant man."

"You are an insolent, ungrateful woman."

"You—you—"

"That's right, baby." Linc jabbed a thumb into the center of his chest. "Me. *I* set the rules. *I* am in charge. And you are—you are—"

He cursed, hauled Ana into his arms and kissed her. Ana gasped.

The pig! The no-good, despicable brute. The insolence of him. The audacity. The impudence…

Oh, God, Ana thought, and she dug her hands into Lincoln's dark, silky hair, dragged his head down to hers and kissed him back.

He groaned and gathered her closer.

She sighed and rose toward him.

Wrong, her fevered brain shouted, this was all wrong. Lincoln was her employer. There were rules. There was propriety.

And there was this.

This, Ana thought, and opened her mouth to his.

Lincoln said her name. Cupped her face. Tilted back her head and took his mouth from hers just long enough to nip at her throat.

Ana shuddered with excitement. "Lincoln," she whispered.

"Yes," he whispered back. "God, yes—"

His hands slid under the towel and cupped her bottom, lifting her into him. His body was all hard, powerful muscle; his erection, pressing against her belly, made her moan with need.

Another minute and surely her heart would burst. Nothing she'd ever imagined had prepared her for this.

His kiss deepened. Ana felt the sweep of his tongue against hers; delicately she sucked on the tip, and he made a sound deep in his throat that sent heat racing from her breasts to her groin.

His hand moved. Moved again. Slid between her thighs, where she was hot and wet. So hot. So wet. So—so—

Ana cried out. She tore at Lincoln's shirt. Buttons popped and then her palms were against his hot, silky, hair-roughened skin. He lifted her; her legs wrapped around her waist as backed her against the wall…

"What in heaven's name do you people think you're doing?"

The voice cracked through the room with the force of a whip. Linc and Ana sprang apart, just as they had that day in his office, only this was worse.

A thousand times worse, Linc thought in horror.

Ana, damned near naked, was twined around him. His shirt was in tatters, his hands were all over her. And the woman who'd barked those words, who stood staring at them with revulsion, was the social worker.

CHAPTER SIX

LINC swept Ana behind him.

Think, he told himself furiously. Disaster loomed but there had to be a way to avoid it. He'd made presentations that turned hostile CEOs into allies; once, in Colombia, he'd even fast-talked his way out of what associates said would have been a kidnapping.

Surely he could talk his way out of this?

"Miss Harper," he said calmly.

Mrs. Hollowell stepped into view, took in the scene and went white. Hey, why not? A man might as well have an audience for a performance like this.

"I'm so sorry, sir," she said, clasping her hands over her bosom. "The doorman rang and he said this lady wanted to come up and he knew she'd been here before and I said to wait until I spoke with you but you—but you were occupied, sir, and—and—"

"I understand, Mrs. Hollowell. Perhaps you'd make some coffee? I'm sure our—guest—would appreciate it."

His housekeeper shot him a look of gratitude and fled, but the social worker's expression grew even more frigid.

"I am not your guest, Mr. Aldridge. I am here on official business. What we call an unannounced visit."

Linc thought of the joke his lawyer had made about being caught in a compromising position. Damn, damn, damn. Behind him, Ana was trying to tug her hand free of his. He tightened his grasp. The last thing he needed was her racing across the room in that towel.

"We find such visits most illuminating." The woman's smile could have curdled cream.

Ana gave a soft moan of despair and buried her face in his shoulder. Despite everything, this disastrous encounter, his unconscionable loss of control, he wished he could draw her into his arms to comfort her.

What he had to do was think. Hadn't Charles said they had almost everything they needed to push Jenny's money-hungry grandmother out of the picture? To lose the baby now…

And in that instant Linc saw the path to salvation.

"Miss Harper," he said carefully, "I know how this appears—"

"*Appears*, Mr. Aldridge?"

"I can explain."

"I don't think you can. What I have just observed… I must say, Jennifer's grandmother warned us that you had, shall we say, quite a reputation as a bachelor, and now—"

"And now," Linc said briskly, turning to Ana, shielding her still as he shrugged off his suit coat, wrapped her in it and then drew her to his side, "and now those days are over." He smiled for the social worker but tightened his arm around Ana in what he hoped she'd recognize as a warning.

"Over?" The contempt in Miss Harper's voice was almost palpable. "Not from what I just observed."

Linc beamed at Ana, who was looking up at him in confusion. *You don't know the half of it, sweetheart,* he thought, and drew a steadying breath. "What you just saw was a celebration. You see, Senhora Marques has done me the honor of agreeing to become my wife."

Silence fell over the room. Linc figured it was the calm that might precede a tornado.

"Ana?" he said softly, but she was already shaking her head.

"No! Miss Harper. What Senhor Aldridge just said—"

"What I said is not for publication," Linc said pleasantly. He smiled at Ana, though his eyes flashed a warning. "I'm sure you can understand our wish for privacy."

"Lincoln—"

"Darling, surely you can see that we have to let Miss Harper in on our secret?. Otherwise she'd reach the wrong conclusion, and that would not be good for Jenny."

Ana blinked. "Not good for—"

"Exactly."

"Oh." He could almost see her figuring it out. Then she flashed him a dazzling smile and sent another to the social worker. "We would not want you to think Lincoln and I— That we were—" She blushed. "We are, of course, engaged. Otherwise this would never have happened."

The social worker looked dazed. Welcome to the club, Linc thought.

"You're getting married?"

He nodded. "Ana's done me the honor of agreeing to become my wife."

The social worker folded her lips in. "Still, what happened here—"

"We thought my housekeeper had left for the evening. We knew Jenny was in her crib, asleep. And—" He chuckled. "And I guess we just got carried away."

"I see."

"Good. I hoped you would, because—"

"When will this marriage take place, Mr. Aldridge? I wouldn't want Jennifer in this sort of, um, this sort of situation any longer than necessary."

"Nor do we—which is why we've decided to get married at the end of the week."

Ana jerked as if she'd touched a live wire.

"Lincoln," she said, "I told you, it takes time to arrange a wedding."

"I know, sweetheart." Linc tightened his hold on her and gazed down into her eyes. "Which is why I told *you* that I don't care about fancy weddings." He smiled, bent his head, gave her a light kiss and considered himself lucky she didn't snarl and bite him. "Being husband and wife, making a home for our Jenny…that's all that matters. Isn't that right?"

He knew Ana wanted to kill him, but Miss Harper was buying the performance. Moments ago she'd looked as if she'd stumbled into an orgy. Now she was beaming.

"Well, that's just wonderful news, because—well, let me be candid. We've run into some difficulties concerning Jennifer's grandmother."

"Really?" Linc said carefully.

"That's one of the reasons we decided to step up our

visits here." Miss Harper dropped her voice. "I have to admit, after what I saw this evening, I'd have been faced with a dilemma. Would it be better to leave Jennifer in a, uh, a morally questionable situation with you, or place her in foster care while we tried to sort things out?"

"No foster care," Ana said sharply. "Not for our little girl."

"Well, no. Not now. Everything else about Mr. Aldridge checked out well. And now that you and he are getting married…I have noted how much Jennifer's bonded with you, Miss Marques. There's no harm in telling you both that I'm going to file a very positive report." She laughed gaily. "That's a secret, of course, but then, you've already shared *your* secret with me!"

They made small talk for another minute or two. Then Linc pressed a tender kiss to Ana's hair.

"Darling, I'll just see Miss Harper out…"

"You do that, *darling*," Ana said, with another of those dazzling smiles.

It was too dazzling. When he came back, she was gone.

Linc sighed, went up the stairs to the nursery and knocked on the door.

"Ana?" No answer. He knocked again. "Ana. We have to talk."

"We have nothing to talk about."

"You know damned well we do. Come on. Open the door." He waited. Then he cursed under his breath and tried to open it but it was locked. "Dammit, Ana—"

The door swung open a couple of inches, just enough to let him see a quadrant of her face.

"You will wake the baby!"

"Get some clothes on and come downstairs so we can discuss this like rational human beings."

"I told you, we have nothing to talk about. Lying to that woman was stupid. Telling her we were getting married in a couple of days was even stupider. How long do you think she'll believe that ridiculous story? And what about me?"

"Look, Ana—"

"This is twice you used me, Lincoln. First when you forced me to take this job, and now you've forced me to lie about getting married."

"I didn't force you. I offered you employment when you needed it. As for tonight, what did you want me to do? What I told that woman was all I could think of to keep my niece! I love the kid. I thought you loved her, too, but I guess I was wrong."

"You really are a horrible man! How can you say such a thing? Of course I love her."

"Then we're on the same page."

"The same…? What does that mean?"

He considered telling her, in detail, but why ruin things so quickly?

"Just get dressed and come downstairs so we can work this thing out."

"We have nothing to work out," she said with frost in her voice. "The lie was yours. So is dealing with it."

"Okay. You're right. Now, please, get dressed and come down."

She stared at him. Then she gave a reluctant nod and closed the door. He heard the lock fall into place. For some crazy reason, that definitive *click* infuriated him. He wanted to kick the door down, sweep Ana into his arms…

"Ana!"

The door opened again, this time barely an inch. "What now?"

"I'm going to ask Mrs. Hollowell to stay for a couple of hours."

"Excellent," Ana said coolly. "She can play referee."

Linc decided to ignore the gibe. "Put on something suitable for going out."

She looked at him as if he'd lost his mind. Well, maybe he had.

"Nothing fancy. Just what you'd wear for dinner at any little restaurant." Hell, he sounded like a maniac. "Look, we can't talk here. We need a place that's private."

"This is a huge apartment, Lincoln. It has, what? Ten, fifteen rooms?"

"I know how many rooms it has, dammit!"

"Then why—?"

"Because I say so. Because I'm your boss. Because that's how it's going to be. Any more questions?"

He felt it again, the almost overwhelming desire to sweep her into his arms... Jenny, he reminded himself. Jenny was in the very next room.

It was the only reason he was able to walk away.

Dinner. Dinner out, with Lincoln.

Ana bit her lip as she stared into the mirror. She had to be crazy even to consider it.

But what choice did she have? He was right, he was her boss. More to the point, that look in his eyes... Heaven only knew what he'd have done if she'd said no. He wanted to talk, he said, but what was the point? He'd told a lie so enormous it still made her breath catch.

Now what?

He would not actually ask her to marry him any more than he would expect her to agree to it. He didn't want a wife. She didn't want a husband. He was a bachelor, in the prime of his life. She was a woman just finding her way in the world. Each of them was committed to the idea of freedom—and even if they hadn't been, they weren't in love. Her father, people like him, might not believe love had to exist before a man and a woman wed, but she did.

If she ever chose to marry, in the distant future, she would marry for love. For passion. For all the reasons her father didn't understand, like—like feeling your heart lift at the simple sight of your beloved, or wanting to throw yourself into his arms when you saw him, or smiling at the sound of his voice…

Ana's throat constricted.

All right. Yes, she felt those things about Lincoln, which only proved she knew nothing about love. All those emotions had to do with infatuation, not any deeper emotion. And, yes, she was a little infatuated with him. What woman wouldn't be? Lincoln was handsome. He was smart. He was funny and easy to talk to, and when he wasn't barking out orders he was charming.

And—*truth time, Ana*—and what had almost happened a little while ago was what she dreamed of every night.

Lincoln's kisses. His caresses. She wanted them. Wanted him. If the Harper woman hadn't walked in, she would have given herself to him right there, against the wall…

Thank God she hadn't.

What mattered was that he had told a monumental lie, and even though she'd said it was his problem, she would do her best to help him get out of it, for Jenny's sake.

Okay.

She took a deep breath. How did she look? Her hair hung loose to her shoulders; she'd put on a simple silk dress that barely grazed her knees and was the color of rich cream. Her shoes were shiny black leather, the heels spiked. She carried a small black leather purse.

She hadn't worn any of these things since she'd come to work for Lincoln. He was accustomed to seeing her in jeans. What would he think when he saw her tonight?

Her heart thundered.

Who cared what he thought? They were going out to discuss strategy. Dress for dinner at a casual restaurant, he'd said. And she had.

Ana shut off the light, went into the baby's room for one last check, then headed down the stairs.

Would she show up?

Or would she stay in the nursery and lock the door?

Linc paced the foyer, hands in the pockets of his tan chinos.

No. She'd be here. She'd said she would, and Ana always kept her word. Yes, but what would she say when he told her there was only one way out of this—?

"Lincoln."

He looked up. Ana was at the top of the stairs, standing very still with her hand on the railing.

His mouth went dry.

She was beautiful. God, she was more than that. He just didn't have a word for it. Nobody would. There was no single word that could possibly describe Ana. The elegant bone structure of her face. The slender body that curved in all the places it should. And those long, lovely legs. The shoes that made him imagine her wearing just them and nothing else...

Put your eyes back in your head, Aldridge.

"Ana." His voice sounded rusty. He cleared his throat, cleared his brain, shot a look at his watch as if he could actually read it, then looked at her. "Excellent timing. I made a reservation for eight."

He waited for her to say something. To start down the stairs. When she didn't, he jerked his head toward the door.

"Let's go," he said briskly. "We don't want to be late."

She nodded and descended toward him. Lincoln watched the flash of leg, the sway of hip, until he knew it wouldn't be wise to watch any more. Instead, he grabbed his jacket and busied himself putting it on.

A casual restaurant, he'd said.

As restaurants went in Manhattan, Ana supposed this one was casual.

It was Italian, intimate and quietly elegant. It was also romantic. The perfect place for a date, had this been a date, which, absolutely, it was not.

The captain obviously knew Lincoln. He greeted them with smiles, then led them to a candlelit table that overlooked a small garden. He and Lincoln had a brief conversation about wines before Lincoln asked her if she preferred white or red.

"Neither," she said, hating herself for sounding so prissy but, really, what did wine and candlelight and gardens have to do with the reason they were here?

A muscle knotted in Lincoln's jaw. "No wine tonight, thank you, Mario. Just the menus, please."

Ana opened hers, glanced at it, then put it down.

"Have you decided on what you're having so quickly?"

"Actually, I am not very hungry."

Lincoln leaned forward. "Actually," he said, "you don't want to be here. Isn't that right?"

"We are here to discuss the lie you told."

"Is it against the law to eat while we do that?"

Their eyes met. What could she say that wouldn't sound ridiculous? Ana frowned, opened her menu again.

"A green salad," she said crisply. "Chicken Marsala. Coffee." She snapped the menu closed and put it aside. "Satisfied?"

He nodded. "For the moment," he said, and discreetly signaled for their waiter.

The food was probably wonderful, but she couldn't taste any of it.

Lincoln, she kept thinking. She was here with Lincoln. Weeks of living under his roof, of being polite strangers except for that one incredible night when they'd shared a meal and laughed and talked and he'd kissed her, and now she was here, in this elegant little restaurant, sitting at a table with him.

The meal had begun stiffly but he hadn't let it continue that way. When their main courses had arrived—the chicken for her, pasta for him—he'd asked if hers was to her liking.

"Fine," she replied politely.

He said he was glad because, for some reason, he'd just flashed back to the first meal he'd ever eaten in a real restaurant.

"I was a senior in college," he said, "and it wasn't fine at all."

"You'd never eaten in a real restaurant?" she said, before she had time to think.

"Not unless you count McD's as fine dining."

She stopped herself from smiling. They weren't supposed to be telling amusing stories, they were supposed to be planning a way out of Lincoln's monumental lie.

"We didn't have the money for it when I was growing up. And what self-respecting university student wastes his hard-earned money on fancy places when there are school cafeterias and Twinkies in the world?"

He'd been poor? It was hard to imagine. He seemed so comfortable in his life… Although, yes, it would go a long way toward explaining the fire and steel she'd seen within him.

Not that she cared.

"Anyway, I was a college senior, interviewing for jobs, and this guy in a three-piece suit invited me to dinner. I scrounged a sports jacket from my roommate and splurged on a new tie. A good thing, considering he took me to this French place where everything was so expensive I could have lived a week on the cost of one item on the menu."

He forked up a swirl of Pasta Putanesca, put it in his mouth and chewed. Ana waited as long as she could.

"And?"

Lincoln looked up. "Oh. I thought maybe I was boring you."

His eyes glinted with mischief. She wanted to tell him that he was, but how many lies could one evening support?

"Just tell me the story, Lincoln, all right?"

"Well, I didn't recognize anything on the menu, so I decided to order whatever the recruiter ordered."

Ana laughed. "You ended up with snails?"

"Worse. It was Ballotine de Veau Cordon Bleu."
Lincoln put down his fork. "Basically, it was—"

"Boiled parts. I don't even want to think about *what*
boiled parts," Ana said, with a little shudder.

"You've had it?"

"One summer in Tours. When did you find out?"

"When I couldn't chew through my first mouthful."
He smiled. "I asked the guy what we were eating, he
told me, and I guess I turned green."

"And he didn't offer you the job?"

Didn't. She'd said didn't *instead of* did not, *which
meant she was calming down.*

God, how beautiful she was. And that smile...

"Lincoln? Am I right? You didn't get the job?"

"Oh, he offered it. I turned it down. I knew right then
I wasn't cut out for that kind of life."

"But—"

"But I eat in places like this now. And I own that
condo." He shrugged his shoulders. "Yeah, but I came
to those things my own way, if that makes sense."

It made absolute sense. He was an independent man,
her Lincoln. A loner. In another age, he would have
been a knight. A warrior.

Her Lincoln? Ana pushed her plate away. "We came
here to talk."

"Well, we are talking. You're getting to know me,
I'm getting to know you."

"We came to talk about what you told the social worker,
and how you can get out from under that monstrous lie."

His smile faded. "Getting out from under it is easy,
Ana. I just call her up and tell her there isn't going to
be a wedding. The hard part is what happens after." He
paused. "Jenny in foster care."

Ana's face whitened.

"Or maybe Grandma will come up with a hotshot lawyer who'll find a way to make her look like Saint Joan. At the very least, there'll be a long court battle. For all I know, they'd take Jenny from me while it goes on."

"From us, Lincoln. I love her. You must know that."

He did. He'd counted on it. Now he leaned forward. The moment of truth had arrived.

"There's one solution," he said softly. "But I'd need your cooperation."

"I would do anything for Jenny. You know that."

He'd counted on that, too.

"In that case…" Linc looked straight into Ana's eyes as he reached for her hand. "Marry me, Ana. And help me guarantee our little girl a happy life."

CHAPTER SEVEN

WAS this his idea of a joke?

What did she know of North American humor? A joke would fit with their conversation. He'd told her an amusing story a couple of minutes ago, so this could very well be—

It wasn't. Nobody told jokes when they stared at you as hard as Lincoln was staring at her. Ana dragged her hand from his and sat back.

"Are you *luoco*?"

"You have a better idea?"

His tone was as flat as his eyes. He was serious. Tension made it hard to breathe.

"She knows what she saw, Ana. And she thinks it was dead wrong."

"It was."

His eyes flashed. "The hell it was!"

"I am Jenny's nanny. You are her uncle."

"You're a woman." His voice roughened. "An incredibly desirable woman. And I'm a man. We've been dancing around that since the night we met."

"We have not!"

"This isn't the time to argue about it. I did what I had

to do. For all I know, the social worker could have taken Jenny on the spot."

She couldn't argue with that. He had done what he had to do to protect his niece, but marriage…

"I know," he said softly, as if she'd spoken the words aloud. "Marriage isn't at all what you want for yourself. Well, it isn't what I want, either. You know those magazine articles? *One Hundred Things To Do Before You Die?* Trust me, Ana. Getting married wouldn't even make it into my top thousand."

Nor into hers. Then why this sudden ache in her heart?

"Don't look at me that way," he said gruffly. "Do you think I'm happy, asking this of you?"

Did he think *she* was happy, hearing him first suggest the impossible and then describe it as one step up from hell?

"Look, if I could come up with another idea, I would. But I can't, and if you don't marry me, I'll lose Jenny."

Ana reached for her purse. Anger was safer than whatever other emotion was trying to push its way through.

"Just listen to yourself, *senhor*. If *I* do not agree to something *I* do not want, *you* will suffer the consequences."

"That's not what I'm saying and you know it. It's Jenny who'll suffer the consequences."

"You will find a way around it. You always do."

"There *is* no way around it! We get married, or Jenny goes into the hands of the state."

Tears burned her eyes. "How can you do this, Lincoln? It is not fair! To make me feel responsible for my baby's future…"

"Did you hear what you just said? You called her your baby."

"A slip of the tongue."

"The hell it was. You say you love her but you'd let her go into foster care, or into the hands of an avaricious woman who sees dollar signs whenever she looks at Jenny?"

He was pushing all the right buttons. She could feel herself weakening. Desperate, she shook her head.

"No. It's insane."

"Because?"

"Because—because of what you said. That neither of us wants to get married."

"I agree. But this wouldn't really be a marriage."

She blinked. "It wouldn't?"

"We'd only have to stay married until my guardianship of Jenny is secure."

Ana stared at him. "You mean, we would have—what do those romance novels call it?—a marriage of convenience?"

"I don't know the term but, yeah, that's what it would be. My attorney would draw up an agreement. We'd both sign it. You can file for divorce as soon as Jenny's custody is settled." His eyebrows rose. "You didn't think I meant we'd do the until death do us part thing, did you?"

That was exactly what she had thought. Now she realized how foolish she'd been. Lincoln was not an until death do us part person. Well, neither was she. Wasn't that what had brought her to New York in the first place?

Then why did his words stab at her heart?

"Ana." He reached for her hands, clasped them lightly in his. "I know I'm asking a lot."

She nodded. It was the understatement of a lifetime.

"If there were another way…"

She nodded again. He was right, there wasn't.

"We both love Jenny."

Ana nodded a third time. All this nodding. Was that the reason for the ache blooming behind her eyes?

"So, we do what we have to do to keep Jenny safe. A civil ceremony. Something quick but legal. And once Jenny's situation is resolved—"

"We end the marriage."

"Right. I'll tell my attorney to find the fastest way to do it."

"A quick marriage, a quick divorce," she said brightly. "Who could ask for anything better?"

"Of course I'll make a generous settlement on you."

Ana's face whitened. She pulled her hands free of Lincoln's. He knew right away he'd made a mistake.

"Do you think I would take your money?"

"Okay. Okay, no settlement."

"If I did this—if I did it—it would not be for payment!"

Her eyes had gone hot with anger. Linc nodded. He'd have to tread carefully.

"A job, then. Don't look at me like that. I was going to tell you anyway. There'll be an opening coming up in my company in a few months." A lie, but meaningless compared to the other lies of the night. "It'll be perfect for you."

"I just said—"

"Look, we can argue over the details later. Right now, just tell me you'll agree to be my wife for a few months."

Her expression went blank. "That long?"

Why did the question annoy him? It wasn't as if he'd gone down on his knees and offered her his heart.

"I don't know," he said bluntly. "However long it takes, okay?"

She swallowed. He could see the movement in her throat and that made him remember the softness of her skin there, just there, at the hollow where he could see the swift beat of her pulse.

She shoved back her chair. "I need time to think."

"There is no time." Urgency crept into his voice. "The Harper woman will be watching us like a hawk. And I told her we'd be getting married right away, remember?"

Ana's eyes darkened. "Why is everything all about you? *You* came up with that ugly lie, and it was all because *you* forced yourself on me!"

"I what? Ana! Damnit, what the hell are you doing?"

A stupid question. What she was doing was bolting from her chair and racing out of the restaurant. Linc cursed, shot to his feet and dropped a handful of bills on the table.

The captain hurried over. "Mr. Aldridge, sir, is everything—?"

Linc didn't bother answering. He ran, oblivious to the stares, the whispers, flung the door open and stepped onto the street.

Clouds had been scudding high over the city's concrete canyons most of the day. Now those clouds had opened up. A warm light rain was falling, drawing a green, woodsy scent from the sycamores that stood like sentinels along the curb.

Where the hell was Ana?

There! Half a block away, running barefoot, her spiked heels clutched in her hand. Linc took off after her, caught her and spun her toward him.

"Forced myself?" He jerked her to her toes. "You wanted what happened as much as I did, lady."

"That is not true!"

The rain was coming down harder. Drops of it glittered like diamonds on the tips of Ana's lashes.

"Stop lying to yourself."

"*You* are the liar, Lincoln Aldridge. Liar, liar, li—"

Linc kissed her. Ana tried to twist free but he thrust his hands into her hair and held her fast, angled his mouth over hers, kissed her and kissed her, without mercy, without pity...

Without stopping, until, at last, she sobbed his name. *Lin-cone*, the way he loved to hear her say it, and slid her arms around his neck.

He groaned, drew her closer. She was so soft. So delicate.

Somebody laughed, somebody else whistled. "Hey, man," a male voice said, "get a room."

Slowly, Linc raised his head. He looked at Ana's rain-bedraggled hair, her gently swollen mouth, her lashes damp with rain or maybe tears. He had hurt her tonight; he knew he would always despise himself for it, just as he knew what he had to do now.

"Ana." He took a deep breath, then slowly expelled it. "What I did tonight—it was inexcusable." He lowered his forehead to hers. "You're right. Asking this of you was wrong. I'll find a way to deal with—"

Ana laid her fingers lightly over his mouth.

She was watching him as if she were trying to see deep inside his soul. If she could, what she'd see wouldn't make him proud. What he'd just told her was the truth. All of this was his fault.

He'd built his life around discipline. Not just clawing

his way into college or putting his life's blood into building Aldridge Security, but everything he'd done to survive his childhood, to ensure that Kath had a chance at a better life.

Now Kath was gone and he'd screwed up so badly that he was on the verge of losing all that remained of her. But to try and make Ana help him clean up the mess he'd made was dead wrong.

He took her hand in his and kissed it.

"I'll find a way, and it won't involve you. I should never have—"

"I'll do it, Lincoln." She took a deep breath. "I'll marry you and stay married for as long as you want me to."

They agreed to tell no one the marriage would be a sham, and not to tell Ana's father about it at all.

Mrs. Hollowell's excitement made Ana feel guilty.

"Oh, that's wonderful," she said. She kissed Ana, hesitated, then blushed and kissed Lincoln, too. "I wish you all the happiness in the world! Jenny's a lucky little girl."

Only Linc's attorney knew the truth. He met with them the following morning, spoke pleasantly, explained the details of the agreement he'd drawn up and then said he'd like to see Linc alone for a couple of minutes.

"Do you know what you're doing?" he demanded, once the door shut after Ana.

"I know precisely what I'm doing, Charles. I'm gaining permanent custody of my niece."

"Lincoln. This woman—"

"Ana, you mean?"

"This woman, Lincoln… You know nothing about her."

"I know all I need to know."

"This innocent appearance of hers—"

"Charles. I know you mean well but I haven't come here for your advice. I've already decided to marry Ana."

"And then what? Suppose, when the time comes, she refuses to file for divorce?"

"Suppose the sky falls? It's not going to happen, Charles. She's no more interested in making this thing permanent than I am."

"Indulge me, okay? What would happen, do you think, if this woman—"

"Ana," Linc said coldly. "She has a name."

"What if Ana changed her mind? Never mind. Let *me* tell *you*. You'd be up a creek without a paddle."

"Why would she do that? I just told you, she's not interested in staying married."

"She might be interested in money. Lots and lots of money." The lawyer folded his arms. "Who knows what she might demand to go ahead with the divorce?"

"She isn't interested in money."

"I'll let that bit of naïveté go by. What about sex?"

Linc narrowed his eyes. "You're my lawyer," he said coldly, "not my shrink."

"There are no rules about marriages like this, Lincoln. You can have sex or not. It won't change anything legally but it could muddy the emotional waters."

"Just draw up the contract, Charles."

"Answer the question first."

Linc felt a muscle flex in his jaw. "There won't be any sex."

"Well, that's something."

"I'm happy you're happy," Linc said, his tone still icy.

"One last question. What if the time to dissolve the marriage comes and she refuses to grant you a divorce? Would you file instead?"

"Of course."

"On what grounds?"

"You're the lawyer. You tell me. Hell, this is twenty-first-century America. Divorce is easy to come by."

"But no less messy than fifty years ago. You are, in case you've forgotten, a very, very wealthy man."

"Charles—"

"And you're well-known. Your name is in the news about as often as my great-aunt Tillie pets her cat."

"You have a great-aunt Tillie?"

"This isn't funny, Lincoln. I want you to understand that when push comes to shove this contract, any contract, isn't worth the paper it's written on if one party or the other decides to ignore it."

Linc raised an eyebrow. "Are you telling me you're not the *wunderkind* you claim to be?" he said dryly.

"She'd be in position to take a bushel of your money and, in the process, drag your name through the mud."

Linc's expression sobered. "If the truth about the marriage became public after I gained custody of Jenny, could the courts take her from me?"

"After you gain custody? No. You wouldn't lose her."

"In that case, draw up the contract. Let me know when you want us to come in and sign it."

Ana was in the waiting room. When she saw Linc, she rose to her feet. He took her arm and they walked to the elevator.

"He wanted to warn you," she said softly.

Linc thought of saying she was wrong, but how many lies could a man tell?

"He's a good lawyer," he said, just as softly. "I pay him for legal advice and he felt obligated to offer it."

"What did he say? That I was after your money? That I would not divorce you when the time came?"

Linc pushed the call button. "Pretty much."

"And what did you say, Lincoln?"

He swung toward her. "You still say my name that way. 'Lin-cone.'" His voice roughened. "As if there's only you and me left in the world."

"You know that isn't—"

He didn't let her finish the sentence. Instead, he lowered his head, touched his mouth to hers, lightly, gently, then with growing hunger. She leaned into him, let herself fall into the kiss before she gasped and pulled back. "It will be a marriage of convenience," she said breathlessly. "That means—"

The elevator doors swished open. It was crowded.

"—no sex."

Someone giggled. Ana felt her face heat. She stepped into the car, Lincoln by her side, and refused to make eye contact with him until long after they were home.

CHAPTER EIGHT

MRS. HOLLOWELL left early the next evening, which gave Linc the chance to tell Ana what he'd planned.

"There's this guy I play racquetball with. He's a judge. I've dropped by his chambers a couple of times. I thought I'd ask him to marry us. His chambers are handsome, plus he's a nice— Why are you shaking your head?"

"I don't want to be married by your friend, Lincoln."

Linc raised his eyebrows. "Because?"

"Because he will think he has to say something personal."

"And?"

"And I would rather not make this more of a lie than it already is."

"Really?" He could hear his tone hardening. This was no blissful occasion, but it wasn't exactly a funeral, either.

"Yes. Really."

"So, you want to do what? Act as if we're planning a visit to a dentist who doesn't believe in Novocain?"

To his surprise, she laughed. She had, he thought, a lovely laugh.

"I know it seems silly but I feel guilty. We're lying to everyone."

He felt guilty, too. Not so much about lying to the world but about…He wasn't sure, exactly. Maybe it had to do with what this day should be like for Ana, because no matter what she said, he was sure she would marry someday.

She was meant for the comfort and love of a man's arms, just not for his. No woman was meant for that. He was too removed. Too dedicated to his work. Relationships weren't his thing. A dozen women had told him that. So had Kath, only she'd been more blunt.

"You don't want to open up, Linc," she'd said. *"It makes you feel too vulnerable. I understand it's because of how we grew up, but you're going to regret it someday."*

Not true. It was the worst kind of dollar-store pop psychology—and, dammit, what did all this looking into his navel have to do with anything?

"Okay," he said briskly. "We'll get the license tomorrow, get married at City Hall as soon as the law says we can."

"Fine." Ana got to her feet. "What time shall I be ready?"

Linc rose, too. Oh, yeah. Definitely she looked as if she were getting ready for a trip to the dentist.

"It's only eight in the evening. Why are you going up?"

"I get up early."

"Me, too, but I go to bed later than this."

"So?"

"So," he said, watching her face, "we'll have to coordinate our hours. I'd lay odds newlyweds don't go to their bedroom a couple of hours apart."

Color swept into her cheeks; she looked as if he'd

just told her he had a predilection for wearing animal skins and dancing around campfires.

"What do you mean, *their* bedroom? Surely you do not think—?"

"Surely I do think," he said, walking around the table to her. "Mrs. Hollowell thinks we're getting married because we're crazy about each other." He smiled thinly. "Sleeping in separate rooms might put a dent in that."

"Lincoln." She took a step back. "No sex, remember? This is a marriage of—"

"I know what it is." Slowly, he hooked his hand behind her neck and drew her forward. "I also know we're going to have to make it look real." He put a finger under her chin, raised her face to his. Her mouth was trembling. The sight put a knot in his gut. "No sex doesn't mean we won't share a room. Or an occasional kiss." He lowered his mouth to hers. Kissed her gently. Waited for what he knew her response would be, that little sigh, the sweet moan…

What in hell was he doing? he asked himself, and stepped back.

"Goodnight," he said, as calmly if he hadn't just kissed her, as if he weren't aching to lift her in his arms and carry her to his bed.

Ana fled. He couldn't blame her. He'd run, too—except it was too late.

He'd asked Mrs. Hollowell to take care of Jenny for the day.

Ana waited until the housekeeper left for the park. Then she handed Lincoln a piece of paper. At first, he thought it was a shopping list.

Then he looked more closely.

1. No sex

2. Do you have a chaise longue in your dressing room? If not, please order one. It is where I will sleep.

3. Signs of affection should be brief and occur only if someone is observing us.

4. No sex.

He looked up. She was standing with arms folded and lips compressed. He told himself not to laugh.

"You have one item listed twice."

"I thought it a very important item."

He nodded. His soon-to-be-wife was definitely an interesting woman.

"Well?"

Linc handed the paper to her. "No problem."

"Including the chaise longue?"

"Including the whatever-it's-called."

"Thank you. I thought you might be opposed to some of my requests. I am happy to see that you are not."

"They're fine."

Kissing her last night had been a momentary lapse in judgment. A man shared his home with a gorgeous female, he was bound to react. It wouldn't happen again. As for the *chaise* thing—he'd call Macy's and order one right after they went to City Hall to apply for a license. Or after they went to Charles's office and signed the pre-nup.

Somewhere in there he'd take care of it.

The pre-nup was as thick as a dictionary. Linc, who'd been dealing with his lawyer long enough to trust him, signed it after a cursory look.

Not Ana. "I would prefer to read it through," she said.

It took her an hour.

Charles tapped a pencil against a pad of yellow legal paper, watched the clock, watched a couple of pigeons on the ledge outside the window, watched the people in the office across the street.

Linc watched Ana.

She frowned, chewed on her lip, made notes. She was wearing one of her dress-for-success suits and she'd pulled her hair into a knot at the nape of her neck, but strands had escaped and fallen against her cheek.

She pushed them back impatiently.

Linc thought about doing it slowly. Very slowly, so he could bend down and breathe into her ear, touch the tip of his tongue to it.

He shot from his chair. Ana and Charles both looked up. "Just stretching my legs," he said brightly. "I'll be back in a minute."

He went out of the office, paced the corridor, counted to a hundred, then headed back.

Ana saw him and scowled.

"What?"

"This clause about payment…I told you, I want nothing for my part in this."

"Yeah, and I told *you* that you deserved something."

"This money is out of the question. I do not need it. I will not take it."

"Independence is expensive, Ana. You want to be on your own when this is over, you'll want that check."

"I will not accept money, Lincoln!"

"Fine. Scratch out the clause and initial it. That's the way. Here, I'll initial it, too. Okay. Now, just sign the damned contract."

She glared at him. Then she scrawled her name on the document and stood up. "I will wait outside," she said, and marched out without a backward glance at Lincoln or Charles.

Linc waited until she'd closed the door. Then he took an envelope from his pocket and put it on the desk.

"What's this?" Charles said.

"A check, made out to Ana."

"But she said—"

"I know what she said, but I'm not going to let her do all this for me without compensation. Put it away until this thing is over. I'll give it to her then."

His lawyer nodded. "An excellent idea."

"Yeah," Linc said—except the truth was, nothing about this idea felt the least bit excellent.

They made a quick stop at Tiffany's for a plain gold band, then hurried to City Hall, where Linc produced his birth certificate and Ana produced her passport.

Linc took out his wallet. Ana took out hers.

"I will pay half the fee," she said.

He decided not to argue. Her accent had grown so thick that soon he'd need an interpreter to understand her.

The clerk issued their license. In twenty-four hours, he said, they could marry.

Back home, Jenny grinned and held out her arms. They played with her for a while. Ana said she would take over, but the housekeeper tut-tutted.

"Don't be silly, dear! Tomorrow's your wedding day. You go and relax with Mr. Aldridge and leave the baby to me."

But once they were alone Ana said she was exhausted. "It has been a very long day, Lincoln. I think—I think I will go to my room."

Linc tried to see past his fiancée's wooden smile. Was she angry at what he'd forced her into, or was she terrified?

Suddenly, he had to know.

"Ana. Listen to me. I promise, you'll be fine—"

Her eyes flashed. "What do you know of how I will be?"

He thought about pulling her into his arms. Showing her that he knew, that he would never hurt her...

His mouth thinned. Did she think this was any easier for him? Because it wasn't. Why would he want to get married, even if the marriage was a lie? Why would he want to marry a woman who didn't want to marry him?

"What I know," he said coldly, "is that you've agreed to perform a role in a charade and I expect you to do it well."

"Do not worry, Lincoln. I will be the best actress the world has ever seen."

"Just remember that," he said, and even though he hated the way her mouth trembled, he stood his ground in silence as she ran up the stairs.

Late the next afternoon, they stood before a clerk at Centre Street. Two minutes later they were husband and wife.

"You may kiss the bride," the clerk said, smothering a yawn.

Linc knew there was no need for what Ana had labeled a "sign of affection." Nobody was, to use her word, *observing* them, except the clerk and a stranger pressed into duty as a witness. Still, they were in a public place. The pretense might as well begin now.

He turned Ana to him.

Brides were supposed to glow but her face was the color of milk. And when he tilted it to his, he saw the glitter of tears in her eyes.

His heart constricted.

"Ana," he said softly, "I'm sorry. For what I said last night, for today…"

She shook her head. "Never mind. We're doing this for Jenny. It's all right."

It wasn't all right at all, and he knew it. He kissed her. Kissed her tenderly. Until she melted against him and he tasted the salt of her tears on her soft mouth.

My wife, he thought. *My wife*.

And then the clerk said, politely, that there were others waiting and it was going on closing time. Linc put his hand in the small of Ana's back as they left the building and felt her trembling. He slid his arm around her waist. She stiffened, but then she leaned into him the way she would have done if the ceremony binding them together had been real.

He had arranged for Mrs. Hollowell to stay overnight to care for Jenny.

Ana had objected, until he'd pointed out that his housekeeper would be the one person who'd be in a position to comment on their marriage, if that became necessary.

Mrs. Hollowell had said of course she'd stay, but wouldn't it be better if she took the baby home for the night? She had grandchildren so she had all the things Jenny might need. He'd thanked her and said that wouldn't be necessary.

Now, watching Ana, he knew he'd made a big mistake.

Mrs. Hollowell had set out champagne and caviar. Ana didn't notice. She'd filled the sitting room with vases of white roses and freesia, which was more than he'd thought to do, but Ana didn't notice that, either.

The housekeeper was giving her worried looks. Ana was supposed to be a happy bride. Instead, she looked like a woman who'd lost her best friend. Who knew what she might say or do? What if she blurted out the truth about their marriage?

He had to do something, he thought, and gently gathered Ana into his arms.

"You must be exhausted, sweetheart," he said, smiling, hoping she'd get the message and smile in return. "Why don't you go upstairs? Take a long bath, even a nap. I'll be up after a while."

She not only got the message, she all but sighed with relief. "I will do that, Lincoln. Thank you for thinking of it."

He waited until she'd left the room, then he turned to Mrs. Hollowell.

"My wife's been under a lot of stress," he said. "She's worn out."

"Yessir," his housekeeper said evenly. "You haven't given her time to breathe."

A day of firsts. He'd never been married before and his polite housekeeper had never before commented on his personal life.

"That offer you made," he said, "to take Jenny for the night… Is it still good? Ana and I need some quiet time together."

That won him a smile. "Two minutes to get the baby ready, Mr. Aldridge, and we'll be on our way."

"I'll phone for my car. And Mrs. Hollowell?" Linc smiled. "Thank you."

He gave Ana an hour.

Then he knocked on his bedroom door. *Their* door, he reminded himself, and felt the tension in his gut.

Ana opened it. She'd worn one of those dress-for-success suits for the wedding and she was still wearing it now. She was also wearing an expression that could best be described as halfway between disbelief and anger.

"Someone moved all my things!"

"Well, yeah. Mrs. Hollowell. She suggested it and—"

"You should have asked me."

"We went through all this, remember? You're my wife. You sleep with me."

"I have no intention of sleeping with you."

"A figure of speech," he said, holding up his hand.

"And what," she hissed, "is this?"

Bewildered, he started to look around. Ana muttered something, grabbed his lapel, hauled him into the room and shut the door.

"Do you want Mrs. Hollowell to hear us, Lincoln?"

Maybe this wasn't the time to tell her Mrs. Hollowell was gone.

"What's the problem?"

Ana swept her hand around the room. "What do you see?"

"Uh—"

"Dresser. Chest. Tables. Chairs. Bench. Lamps," she said, answering her own question. "Now come into the dressing room. What do you see?"

Linc cleared his throat. "Clothes?"

Ana folded her arms and glared at him. "Do you see anything even resembling a chaise longue?"

"A chaise…?" *Damn!* "I forgot. In the rush, I just… I'll order it tomorrow."

"And where, pray tell, am I to sleep tonight?"

He looked at her, at the beautiful eyes flashing with anger, at the defiance, the courage, the spirit his Ana radiated…

"Here. It's a big bed. You take one side, I'll take the other."

She glared at him for what seemed a very long time. Then she narrowed her eyes.

"Touch me," she said through her teeth, "and you are a dead man."

He believed it.

CHAPTER NINE

ANA lay wrapped in her robe, all but clinging to the edge of the bed, as far from Lincoln as she could manage.

The clock read 2:22 a.m. She had not slept at all.

Lincoln, on the other hand, had gone into the bathroom, come out in a pair of sweats, climbed into the bed, put his head on the pillow and drifted off to happy dreamland.

This sham wedding was upsetting only to her. He'd gone through it without hesitation, saying "I do" and "Yes" and kissing her at the end of the ceremony as if their reasons for marrying were the same as everyone else's.

He wasn't supposed to have kissed her.

That was part of the deal. No touching. No kissing. A separate bed for her. He'd agreed to it all and now she knew just how much that meant. He'd touched. He'd kissed. Now they were sharing a bed.

Ana swallowed hard.

Maybe the real question was why she'd melted into that kiss? Leaned into his embrace? Why she'd wanted to weep when she saw the champagne, the caviar, the flowers that it had taken Lincoln's housekeeper to arrange?

She wasn't a bride. Not a real one. She was a woman

playing a role opposite a man who thought marriage was an unnatural act. But so what? She thought the same thing.

There it was again, that ridiculous sting of unwanted tears. Ana blinked them back and looked across the endless expanse of bed. Lincoln still hadn't stirred. For all she knew, in a little while he might even start to snore.

Such a romantic wedding night.

She sat up, eased from the bed and the room. She thought about stopping at the nursery to check on Jenny, but Mrs. Hollowell was sleeping there and the last thing she wanted to do was rouse the housekeeper. Instead, she made her way downstairs and onto the terrace.

The late summer night was warm. Below, a lone taxi prowled south along Fifth Avenue. Across the street, the trees stood like silent sentinels in the darkness.

This time, when Ana's eyes filled with tears, she let them come.

What a fool she'd been to marry Lincoln. Hadn't she realized this would not work? That to live this kind of lie would be—?

"Ana?"

She spun around. Lincoln was standing in the doorway. Her heart did a stutter-step. He was so beautiful. So masculine. He was her husband—and she could still remember the taste of his mouth, the scent of his skin...

"Lincoln. I didn't mean to wake you."

"You didn't." He stepped outside and leaned his elbows on the railing beside her. "I wasn't sleeping. I just figured it was simpler to let you think I was." He sighed. "And I know exactly what you were thinking just now."

She felt the rush of color in her cheeks. "You do?"

"You were thinking, what in hell did we do?"

"Oh." The breath whooshed from her lungs.

"Me, too. I thought it would be so simple. Get married, pretend everything's great. But it's turning out to be complicated." He turned around and leaned back against the railing. "Well, we'll just have to uncomplicate it."

"How?"

"I don't know," he said gruffly. "And, frankly, I'm not up to figuring it out at this hour. The only thing I'm sure of right now is that we never had supper."

She looked at him. "Didn't we?"

He grinned. "No. Not even that caviar. You were too busy chewing me out for forgetting to order the bed."

"About that…" Ana hesitated. "I shouldn't have been so angry. With everything you had on your mind—"

"I should have remembered. I'll take care of it tomorrow, I promise." He touched the tip of his index finger to her nose. "Right now, it's the middle of the night."

"I know. I'm just not very sleepy, that's all."

"What you are is hungry."

She would have said he was wrong but her belly gave an unladylike growl of affirmation.

"See?" he said, laughing. "So, let's have something to eat, okay?"

He held out his hand. Slowly, she took it.

"I suppose I could find something in the refrigerator and make sandwiches."

"Forget that. We'll do take-out."

"At three in the morning?"

"This is New York, sweetheart. The city that never sleeps." He turned on the kitchen lights, drew a stool from the counter and watched as she scooted onto it.

"And bachelors know all about take-out. Mrs. Hollowell only started cooking for me after Jenny came along." He opened drawers, cupboards, poked through shelves and finally fanned a dozen menus on the counter in front of her. "Pick one."

"You decide. I'll be happy with whatever you choose, Lincoln."

Lin-cone. There it was again, that softness in her voice, that way she made something as simple as his name seem to shimmer. There was that smile, too. He'd wondered if he'd ever see it again after the fiasco about the unordered bed, the fiasco of the entire day. He'd moved too fast, hadn't taken the time to ease her fears or maybe even make her see how good this could be, being together for whatever time they had.

Hell.

Linc grabbed for a menu, then for the phone.

"Chang's Kitchen," a voice sang in his ear. "What would you like?"

Ana, Linc thought, and the realization stunned him.

He built a fire and they ate seated on oversized silk pillows before the hearth. He set out heavy white napery and Baccarat flutes that he filled with the chilled champagne.

Ana laughed when she saw how much food he'd ordered. Moo shu pork, orange chicken, shrimp in black bean sauce and half a dozen other things sent their fragrance wafting into the air as he opened the white take-out boxes and arranged them in a circle.

"No plates?"

"No plates. No forks. Just chopsticks. Trust me," he said solemnly. "It tastes better this way."

She smiled and dug in. He waited a while, watching

as she transferred small bits of food to her mouth. Once or twice she licked the chopsticks. Damn if it didn't make his belly clench.

"What?" she said, laughing. "Are you going to criticize my chopstick technique? I'll have you know my very first nanny was born in China. Well, Taiwan. She had me using sticks before I was five."

"A nanny, huh?"

Ana lifted a shrimp to her mouth. "A long succession of them. Nice, mostly, but I think it must be nicer to be raised by your mother."

"Probably."

"Probably? Didn't your mother—?"

"She took care of herself," he said, shrugging as if it hadn't mattered when it damned well had. "I took care of me."

"And your sister," Ana said softly. "Kathryn was lucky to have you in her life."

"She was my sister," he said simply. "My responsibility."

"And you are a man who takes responsibility to heart."

How had this conversation grown so serious? This wasn't a night for that. It was a night for being alone with Ana. For realizing how important she had become to him. For wanting—for wanting—

"Ana."

What he was thinking must have been right there, in the way he spoke her name, the way he looked at her. Color rushed into her face. Carefully, she put down her chopsticks.

"It is late," she said, rushing the words together. "Mrs. Hollowell will probably be coming down in a little—"

"She's not here. She took Jenny home with her."

Ana stared at him. "Why?"

"Because this is our wedding night."

"No." Her voice was a whisper. "It isn't."

"It is, Ana. No matter the circumstances. I thought it would be easier this way, not having someone else here in the morning."

He was right. Lincoln, the ever-responsible man. She forced a smile.

"Thank you."

"What are you thanking me for, Ana?" His voice roughened. "That you won't have to pass an early-morning inspection? Or that you won't have to make love with me?"

Ana felt her heartbeat quicken. *Get up right now*, a voice inside her ordered. *Get up and walk out of this room!*

"Because what I want, more than anything in the world," he said, "is to make love with you."

"No. You should not say—"

"I should. I've told enough lies lately. Tonight, at least, I'm going to speak the truth."

She sat very still, feeling his gaze on her skin like a silken caress. She knew he wanted her. She knew it the way every woman knows when a man wants her.

And she wanted him.

"Ana? There's a drop of sweet-and-sour sauce on your mouth."

All she had to do was pick up her napkin and touch it to her lips. But she was an adult. Independent. Capable of making her own decisions.

"Where?" she whispered, and saw the heat flare in his eyes.

"I'll show you."

He leaned forward and covered her mouth with his.

It was a long, sweet kiss; his lips were cool, the abrasion of his end-of-day beard against her skin sent a tingle of electricity down her spine.

"Did you get it all?" she said against his mouth.

"Not yet. There's more…"

So much more, Ana thought, and then, somehow, her lips were clinging to his. Parting beneath his. His tongue was in her mouth and she…

She was on fire.

"Lincoln. Please. Kiss me. Kiss me. Kiss—"

The bedroom was too far away. He knew he'd never make it that far. He, the man who prided himself on his self-control, could never seem to manage it when it came to this woman.

Instead, he drew her down against the soft pillows. Kissed her, drank in her sweet moans and whispers as he undid the sash of her robe. It fell open around her, an ivory chrysalis exposing his Ana to his eyes.

She was exquisite.

Small, rounded breasts tipped with deep rose. A slender waist that blossomed into a woman's hips. Long, elegant legs. And at the junction of her thighs a cluster of pale gold curls that seemed to beg for his caress.

Her skin was flushed with color; she was trembling, as if she'd never been with a man. Selfishly, even though he knew better, he wished it were true.

"You're beautiful," he whispered.

Gently, he cupped her breasts, watched her face as he swept his thumbs over her nipples. She moaned and he bent to her and kissed her throat, the slope of her breasts, the delicious crests. She made a little sound in her throat and he felt a wave of hot, raw need sweep through him. He wanted her now, wanted to bury himself inside her, but she deserved more from this night and he was determined to give it to her.

He kissed her breasts again. Drew the sweetness of her nipples into his mouth. Kissed her navel, her belly. Kissed the delicate whorl of gold. Parted the petals of that most beautiful of flowers...

And touched her.

Ana screamed and came apart in his arms.

He drew her close, held her, rocked her until she calmed. A fierce sense of fulfillment swept through him, knowing he had done this for her. For his wife.

"Lincoln?"

Her voice shook. He kissed her, pulled off his sweats and came back to her again, covering her with his body as she sighed his name. Slow down, he warned himself, but her cries were the aphrodisiac men had sought through all eternity.

"Ana," he said, "look at me."

Her lashes lifted. Her eyes met his.

"Yes," she said, and he let his swollen sex brush against hers. God, he thought, surely he was going to die from such pleasure...

Sweet heaven! He didn't have a condom.

He jerked back. Felt his erection starting to fade with the shock. But Ana reached between their bodies and closed her hand around him.

"Ana," he said, trying to hold on to sanity. "Ana, sweetheart..."

She tilted her hips. "Please, Lincoln," she whispered, and the world blurred as he surged forward and thrust deep into his bride's feminine heart...

And tore through the fragile barrier of her virginity.

* * *

They lay entwined, his arm around her, her head on his shoulder, her leg over his.

Linc's heartbeat slowed. The room came back into focus and so did his brain. God, what had he done? He had shredded his no-sex promise to Ana. He had taken her virginity. And as if that weren't enough, he had committed the ultimate sin.

He'd made love to her without a condom.

The room was cool, the air chill against his sweat-slick skin. Ana had to feel it, too. Carefully, never letting her go, he reached for her discarded robe and drew it over them.

"Sweetheart." He rose on his elbow, just enough so he could see her profile, half hidden by strands of golden hair. Where to start? he thought, gently thumbing it aside.

She sighed. "You want to know why I didn't tell you I was a virgin."

"No. Yes. That, too. Damnit, why didn't you?"

"I don't know." She looked up at him and smiled. "Maybe because it was none of your business."

"Of course it was my business," he said, even though he knew she was right. They'd never intended to become lovers; why should she have told him anything so personal?

"Besides, even if I'd wanted to, when was the right time? Would you have had me say, 'Lincoln, this moo shoo pork is delicious and, oh, by the way, I am a virgin'?"

A deep laugh rumbled in his chest. "Okay. Maybe not like that, exactly, but…" Gently, he brushed his mouth over hers. "How come you didn't slug me when I said maybe you'd come from your lover that night we met in Rio?"

"Mmm. I should have." She smiled. "But I took pity

on you. I knew you were furious because I'd violated your security system."

"Mostly I was furious at myself for losing control and kissing you." His tone grew husky. "If you knew how many times I thought about that kiss after I got back to New York…"

"I'll bet you thought about your security system, too. 'How could that woman have defeated it?'" she said, in almost perfect imitation of his low growl.

Lincoln grinned and nipped lightly at her throat. "Are you going to tell me?"

"It's very complicated, Lincoln. I sat down at a computer, worked up some algorithms…" She grinned at the look on his face. "I memorized the code when Papa set it. You think I'd let a hotshot Norte Americano keep me from getting outside for a nightly run without bodyguards?"

"A run?" His voice rose. "Alone, in those hills? For God's sake, Ana! Anything could have happened to you."

"But nothing did." Her voice softened. "In fact, Lincoln, I don't think anything at all ever happened to me in my entire life until now. This was—it was wonderful."

"Yes," he said gruffly. "It was. But—" He tried to say it lightly. "But I broke rules one and four."

"No sex," she said softly.

He nodded. "Can you forgive me, sweetheart? I swear, I didn't plan—"

"It was my choice, too. That's why I came to New York, remember? To live my own life, not anyone else's."

But she was part of his life now, Linc thought. Except she wasn't. When this marriage ended, she would go her own way. It was what she wanted. What he wanted, too.

Wasn't it?

"Lincoln? What's the matter?"

"Nothing. I just—just—" He took a deep breath. "Ana. I didn't use a condom."

She nodded. "I know."

"I'm healthy, sweetheart, but I could have made you—"

"This is my safe time of the month, Lincoln."

"Yeah, but just so you know, should anything happen—"

"I'm an adult. I take responsibility for myself."

There it was again, another arrogant little statement about independence. He admired her for it, but would it be wrong if she leaned on him, just a little? If she needed him, just a little? If she—if she felt something for him besides desire?

"Ana." He drew her tightly against him. "Ana—"

She silenced him with a kiss, not wanting to hear how grateful he was that she'd married him for Jenny's sake, because, if he did, she knew she would not be able to let the lie pass. She would have to tell him the truth. That she loved Jenny, yes, but that what she'd done was for him.

She had fallen in love with her temporary husband, even though loving him would surely break her heart.

CHAPTER TEN

LIFE was wonderful.

Jenny was a delight. Surely a baby like no other. Bright. Sweet. Absolutely adorable.

And Lincoln…Lincoln was everything a woman could want. Generous. Attentive. Tender. Intelligent. Charming and gorgeous and sexy and passionate.

Sometimes, lying in his arms at night, Ana would imagine what life would be like if their marriage were real. She didn't want to think that way; it hurt too much to know it would not happen. But her thoughts drifted to how it would feel to be with her husband forever, and her throat would constrict.

Maybe she made some little sound, maybe Lincoln could sense something, because, inevitably, he'd turn her toward him.

"Sweetheart?" he would whisper. "What are you thinking?"

"Nothing," she would say, and thank God for the darkness of the bedroom that kept him from seeing how close she was to tears.

Sooner or later all this would end. Lincoln would

come home and tell her that their deception had worked, that Jenny was his, that their marriage had run its course.

That was how she'd thought it would go. In the end, it was not like that at all. He didn't come right out and tell her. Instead, he just began to change.

He came home late. Meetings, he said. Last minute stuff.

He left early. Breakfast appointments, he told her. Unavoidable.

But the surest indication of what was happening came at night. He began letting her go to bed alone. The press of work. Reports to read, plans to make...

"You understand, don't you, Ana?"

Yes, she said, yes, of course.

When he finally came to bed, she pretended to be asleep. Sometimes, he'd climb in beside her so carefully she knew he was determined not to wake her, and she'd want to sit up and tell him not to worry, that she would not let him make love to her even if he tried.

A lie, because every once in a while he'd suddenly roll toward her, wake her with his kisses, take her in his arms and love her with a passion that bordered on frenzy. She'd seen a movie once about a soldier leaving for war. He'd made love to his wife that way. It was how he'd said goodbye.

Life was not a movie, but it wasn't a fairy tale, either. There would be no happy ending here.

Then came the morning—this morning—when she knew it was time to admit the marriage was over. She'd awakened to find Lincoln at the window, fully dressed, staring out at the park.

"Lincoln?" she'd said, sitting up, drawing the duvet

to her chin because, for the very first time, she hadn't wanted to face him naked.

Slowly, he'd turned toward her. What she'd seen in his face had made her breath catch. "We have to talk."

Not yet, she'd thought. Oh, please, not yet…

"Now, if you like. Or this evening, Ana. Whichever you prefer."

She'd known she needed to compose herself. Weeping in front of him would be too humiliating. So she'd lied. She'd said she'd gotten her period during the night. Her back ached. She had cramps. Talking tonight would be best.

Lincoln had breathed what could only have been a sigh of relief. Why wouldn't he? It was almost four weeks since they'd made love without a condom. Her responsible husband would have stood by her if she were pregnant…

But that wasn't what he wanted.

It wasn't what she'd wanted, either. Amazing how what you wanted could change.

He'd nodded. Asked if he could get her some tea. Responsible to the end, she'd thought, and stretched her lips into a smile.

"Don't worry about me," she'd said brightly, and she'd held the smile until he left the room without kissing her, without a backward glance, without anything to show that, for a little bit of time, they'd been lovers.

It was only then that she'd let herself weep.

Now, sitting on a bench in Central Park, sitting near the statue of Alice in Wonderland, by the model boat pond with Jenny asleep in her stroller, a bright autumn sun beating down from a cerulean blue sky, Ana wondered how she would get through tonight's conversation.

She would, though. Lincoln had married her for Jenny;

she had married him for love. That wasn't his fault, it was hers, and she would never let him know that she—

"Miss Marques?"

Startled, she looked up and saw Lincoln's attorney standing beside the stroller.

"May I join you?" he said, even as he sat down beside her.

She knew, instinctively, this was no accidental meeting.

"What are you doing here, Mr. Hamilton?"

"I stopped by Lincoln's place. Lincoln's housekeeper said I might find you here."

Lincoln's place. Lincoln's housekeeper. And he'd addressed her as Miss Marques. Nothing like reminding the hired help who and what they were.

"I wanted to speak with you privately, Miss Marques. I hope you don't—"

"You've come to tell me Jenny's custody has been settled."

She spoke the words through wooden lips, knowing, as she'd known for days, they had to be true.

Hamilton raised his eyebrows. "Well, that's a relief. I thought there might be a problem."

Ana's throat tightened. "What do you mean?"

"The ruling came through more than a week ago. I suggested to Lincoln that the three of us meet right away, but—well, I gather he thought he'd have some difficulty sharing the news with you."

A week? Lincoln had known for all that time but he had not told her. Had he been silent out of pity? Or had Lincoln, the ever-responsible man, been waiting to find out if she were pregnant?

"So, on his behalf, as his attorney and his friend…"

"Please. You do not have to say anything more." Ana

rose to her feet. "Lincoln and I had an agreement and now there is no longer a need for it."

"I'm glad you're taking this so well, Miss Marques." Hamilton stood up, too. "We can set an appointment for our meeting. Or..." He held out an envelope. "Or we can deal with the remaining legality right now."

She took the envelope and stared at it. "What is this?"

"Your check."

"My what?"

"I know you insisted on crossing out that clause in the contract but Lincoln feels you've earned yourself a generous— Miss Marques?"

Ana stood, released the brake on Jenny's stroller and began pushing it toward the park exit, her pace quickening as she heard the traffic on Fifth Avenue.

"Miss Marques," Hamilton called, but she saw no reason to answer. She saw no reason to do anything but take Jenny home, kiss her goodbye and get out of Lincoln's life as swiftly as possible.

To think he'd imagined he had to buy his freedom from her...

Tears blurred her eyes. She blinked them back and kept going.

"What do you mean, she's gone?"

Mrs. Hollowell stared at her employer. His voice was low and dangerous, his face white, his eyes bright and hard as emeralds.

"Just that, sir. Ana is—"

"You did nothing to stop her?"

"Me? How could I have stopped her, Mr. Aldridge?"

"How in hell do I know? You were here, not—" Linc stopped and drew a deep breath. He had to get control of himself, fast.

"I'm sorry," he said. "Let's start over. Ana's gone. She packed her things and left?"

"Yes."

"No note?"

"No, sir."

"No forwarding address?"

"No, sir. I told you. She told me to take care of Jenny. Then she called a taxi and—"

"Nobody just calls a taxi and disappears." So much for control. Linc ran his hand through his hair, then started over. "What brought it on? Did she say?"

"Only that she should have left a long time ago." Mrs. Hollowell bit her lip. "She was crying, sir. And when she kissed Jenny goodbye... Oh, it was awful."

Awful, and his fault. If he hadn't been afraid she'd turn him down, if he'd taken his wife in his arms anytime during the whole miserable week and said, *Ana, the court has given Jenny to me, but I don't give a damn how badly you want your independence, I love you and I'm not going to let you leave me,* at least he'd have had a chance.

His last hope had been that maybe she'd conceived his child and he could use that to make her stay married to him. Then, this morning, she'd launched into that little speech about getting her period.

And she'd been smiling, as if she was glad he understood there'd be nothing binding her to him once the terms of the contract were met.

So he'd walked away rather than say something he'd regret, spent the day trying to figure out a way to approach her that would change her mind.

In midafternoon he'd thought, Screw this. Forget about work. Forget about a plan. He'd just go home, take Ana in his arms, tell her he adored her and that she had to feel the same way about him, she had to…

Except she was gone.

"Mrs. Hollowell. Exactly what happened here today?"

"Nothing out of the ordinary. Well, except maybe Ana seemed a little, I don't know, sad. So when Mr. Hamilton stopped by after lunch, looking for her—"

"My lawyer was here?"

"Yes. Looking for your wife. And since she'd seemed a bit down, I thought perhaps a little visit with someone would cheer her up. I told him she'd gone to the park and that I knew she almost always sat near the Alice statue."

"Charles Hamilton went to see Ana?" Linc said in a low voice.

"As far as I know, he did. And, oh, I almost forgot. There was one other thing. When your wife returned home…" The housekeeper dug in her apron pocket. "She left this on the kitchen counter, Mr. Aldridge. I didn't know whether to throw it out or—"

Linc stared at the bits of paper in Mrs. Hollowell's outstretched palm. He took them, spread them on the counter, shuffled the pieces…

And groaned.

He was looking at the check he'd made out to Ana and given to his lawyer for safekeeping, right after they'd signed that goddamned contract.

At the time it had seemed the responsible thing to do.

"Charles," he said through his teeth, crushing the pieces of paper in his fist, but he knew better than to give in to his fury. There'd be time to deal with it later.

Now, finding Ana was all that mattered.

* * *

Where would she have gone? Home to Brazil? He didn't think so but anything was possible.

He took his Porsche. It was a fast car and every minute counted. When he'd started doing business in Brazil, he'd stored the phone numbers of all the airlines that flew to Rio from Kennedy in his cell phone.

Now he punched them up. Only one had a flight leaving, and it was leaving soon. Was an Ana Maria Marques on the passenger list? Nobody would tell him. Security was his business so he understood why they wouldn't, but if his Ana was on that flight…

He drove like a madman, ignored blaring horns and raised middle fingers, but by the time he reached the airport the plane was gone. Five hundred bucks slipped to a counter agent got him the information he needed.

Ana had not been on the plane.

Where next? There were eight million people in the city. How was he going to find one woman, one incredible woman whom he loved with all his heart?

Think, he told himself furiously, *think.*

The hotel where she'd originally been registered? Where she'd stashed all those suitcases filled with her dress-for-success suits? It was as good a guess as any.

He got there fast, skidded the Porsche into the no-parking zone in front of the door and ran into the lobby.

"Ana Maria Marques," he said to the desk clerk. "Is she registered here?"

She was, but the guy wouldn't tell him her room number. More security, and Linc, the security expert, wanted to reach across the desk and grab the man who was only doing his job and shake the information out of him.

Yeah, but that would only get him arrested. So would

banging on the doors on every floor, yelling Ana's name.

He took another look at the front desk. The hotel was old. The clerk had a computer, but a wall of numbered mail slots stretched behind him. Did they use those or were they for show?

Only one way to find out.

Linc got the hotel's number from a stack of brochures on the desk and punched it into his cell phone. The clerk answered; Linc said he wanted to leave a message for Ana Maria Marques. He made something up, held his breath, watched as the clerk wrote it down—and stuffed it into slot 916.

He ran to the elevator. Halfway to the ninth floor it hit him that maybe Ana had been crying because she was angry he hadn't told her they didn't have to stay married anymore. She'd torn up the check but that didn't prove anything. She was hot-tempered and impossibly independent.

And she'd left him.

What kind of woman did that to a man who loved her? Okay, so he'd never said the words, but she should have known. A woman loved a man, she knew what he felt for her. Women were supposed to sense those things, damnit.

The elevator doors opened. Linc stepped onto the ninth floor and started walking.

Ana had to love him—or what was he going to do with the rest of his life?

Ana peered at the thermostat in her room and edged it up another notch. It was set on high, she had not yet taken off her jacket and still, she was shaking. Maybe she was coming down with something? Or maybe it was what she'd seen on that little stick in the bathroom a few minutes ago?

No. She would not think about that now. Though why she hadn't thought to check until after she'd lied about her period this morning…

Tea. Hot tea. That was what she needed. She phoned Room Service, placed the order, then sat down on the edge of the bed.

What now? She had to make plans. Go home to her father? Not an option, especially now. She would remain in New York. Find a job. A place to live. One step at a time, and not one of those steps would involve weeping over Lincoln.

He had needed her to care for Jenny and warm his bed. Then he hadn't had the courage to tell her that was all finished, so he'd let his lawyer do it for him, with money.

Tears welled in her eyes. She was a fool to cry over such a man.

The knock on the door surprised her. Room Service. She'd almost forgotten. She wiped her eyes with the back of her hand, went to the door, released the security chain…

And gasped.

"Ana—"

She slammed the door in Lincoln's face.

He knocked again. Pounded the door until it shook. Ana reset the chain and cracked the door an inch.

"Go away!"

"Open this door, Ana."

"Are you deaf? I said—"

"This is an old hotel. That chain might as well be made of paper clips. Open the door or, so help me, I'll kick it down."

She stared at him. The grim look on his face said he

would do exactly that. Her mouth narrowed; she shut the door, undid the chain and turned the knob. Lincoln stepped inside and began to shut the door.

She stopped him. "Leave it open."

"You should know better than to open a hotel door without looking through the peephole."

Ana folded her arms. "Thank you for your professional advice. I will remember it for next time."

"Well, the odds are you won't need it next time."

Her eyebrows rose. "And why is that?"

"Because the next time you're in a hotel room, you'll be with me."

"I do not work for you anymore, Mr. Aldridge. I quit my job."

"You can't quit your job."

"I most assuredly can."

"Actually, *job* is the wrong word."

"It is the correct word to describe a nanny's duties."

"But not the duties of a wife."

She looked so cold, sounded it, too. And that rigid posture, the voice saying "Mr. Aldridge" in tones that would have given a penguin the chilblains... He'd known his Ana was upset, but the truth was he didn't know if it was because she didn't want to see him or she was surprised to see him. Now, as color flowed into her cheeks, he felt the first stirrings of hope.

"I am not your wife. At least, I will not be for very long. I phoned your attorney's office and left him a message. I told him to start divorce proceedings as per our contract."

"My attorney is an ass."

"Because he did what you were too much the coward to do?"

"Because," Linc said, starting slowly toward her, "he

knows all about the law and not a damned thing about the human heart."

"For that you would need a physician." Ana took a half-step back. "Stay where you are, please, Mr. Aldridge, or—"

"Or what, Mrs. Aldridge? Are you going to call Security and ask them to throw your husband out of your room?"

"You are not my husband. You are—you are—"

"I love you, Ana."

Ana's heart seemed to bump against her ribs. "You are an excellent liar."

"I adore you."

"Is that the reason you told your lawyer to give me that check?"

"I wrote that the day we signed that damned contract. I wasn't going to let you put your life on hold without giving you something for it. How in hell was I to know Charles would take it into his head to deliver it? Ana. Listen to me. I love you!"

She wanted to believe him. Oh, she wanted to! But there was just so much pain her heart could take before it shattered.

"Why are you doing this?" she said, hating the way her voice broke. "Lincoln, I'm not going to play these games anymore. What are you doing?" she said, which was a foolish question, because what he was doing was reaching for her and gathering her to him. "I just told you—"

"No games," he said softly. "Not anymore. Come back to me, Ana."

Tears rose in her eyes. "None of this is necessary. I know that Jenny is legally yours now."

"Jenny is ours, sweetheart. If you're willing, I'd like us to start adoption proceedings."

"Lincoln." Ana began to weep. "Do you really love me?"

Linc drew her into his arms and kissed her. His kiss said everything she'd ever longed to hear, and as she wound her arms around his neck she realized he had been kissing her that same way since the first time they'd made love.

"Last night," she whispered against his mouth, "you were so removed…"

"I'd been trying to find a way to tell you about Jenny, but I was afraid you'd say you were happy for me and now it was time you went on to live your own life."

"For shame, Lincoln," Ana said, laughing and crying at the same time. "Didn't you know how much I loved you?"

"I let myself hope, but when you said you'd gotten your period…" He leaned his forehead against hers. "It wasn't the news I'd hoped for, Ana. You're probably going to hate me for this but, see, I figured you couldn't possibly leave me if you were carrying my child."

"Our child," she said, smiling.

"That's what I meant. Our child. And—"

"I lied to you, Lincoln. I didn't get my period during the night."

He lifted his head and looked into her eyes. "No?"

"I didn't get it today, either." She moistened her lips. "A little while ago I took one of those home tests."

Could a man really survive without breathing? "Ana. Are you? Are we—?"

She nodded. "Jenny's going to have a little brother or sister for company."

He didn't move. Didn't speak. Just as her heart started to plummet, Lincoln lifted her off her feet and whirled her in a circle.

"Sweetheart. Ana. I love you so much…"

He kissed her. She kissed him back. And gradually they heard the sound of applause.

The Room Service waiter stood, smiling, in the open doorway. Half a dozen people were clustered behind him. They, too, were smiling. And clapping. Someone even whistled.

Ana laughed and buried her face against her husband's throat. Linc grinned at the little crowd.

"I," he said proudly, "am the world's luckiest man."

He gave his wife another long, tender kiss. When he finally lifted his mouth from hers, Ana sighed and looked deep into his eyes.

"Lincoln, my love," she said softly, "let's go home."

Brand-New Father, Brand-New Family

MARION LENNOX

Marion Lennox is a country girl, born on an Australian dairy farm. She moved on – mostly because the cows just weren't interested in her stories! Married to a 'very special doctor', Marion writes Medical™ romances as well as Mills & Boon® Romance (she used a different name for each category for a while – if you're looking for her past Mills & Boon Romances, search for author Trisha David as well). She now has over seventy published romance novels to her credit.

In her non-writing life Marion cares for kids, cats, dogs, chooks and goldfish. She travels, she fights her rampant garden (she's losing) and her house dust (she's lost).

Having spun in circles for the first part of her life, she's now stepped back from her 'other' career, which was teaching statistics at her local university. Finally she's reprioritised her life, figured out what's important and discovered the joys of deep baths, romance and chocolate.

Preferably all at the same time!

Look for Marion Lennox's new books,
***A Royal Marriage of Convenience* and**
***His Island Bride*, coming from Mills & Boon®**
Romance in March 2008 and Mills & Boon®
Medical™ in April 2008.

Dear Reader,

Mills & Boon is a hundred years old. Or a hundred years young. How cool is that?

Romance crosses generational boundaries. It crosses international boundaries. Women the world over, generation after generation, have shown their devotion to the company by immersing themselves over and over again in the pages of our wonderful love stories.

Invited to participate in this Mother's Day anthology as part of our centennial celebrations, I bore this theme in mind. I wanted to create a romance that brought together international players – a hero and a heroine who try to solve the troubles of the world, and in doing so find each other. Mike and Harriet build a family from disparate pieces. They prove to each other – and to all of us – that love can conquer all.

Mills & Boon has blessed us with that message now for a hundred years. I hope in another hundred years the message will be even stronger.

Love to you all,

Marion Lennox

CHAPTER ONE

'KYLE has a father?'

Harriet McDonald, house mother of Number 4 Bay Beach Children's Home, stood in the midst of a battle-ground of kids and felt sick and tired and grief-stricken.

She should be intervening in what was threatening to become World War III. Robbie and Kyle had built a fort at one end of the hall. Erin and Katy had built a fairy palace, at the other. Now, however, the boys were in the fairy palace threatening Barbie with death by dismemberment if the girls didn't leave their fort. But the girls had found the boys' war paint and Barbie was on her own.

Five-year-old Kyle was deeply incensed—more by the girls' callous abandonment of Barbie than by their use of his war paint. Kyle. Harriet loved him with all her heart.

'Tell me what's happened,' she whispered, and on the other end of the line she heard her supervisor give a sigh of sympathy. The huge risk of this job was attachment to the children in care. Kyle had been with Hattie inter-mittently since birth. Everyone knew Hattie was in love.

'His father's a Major Michael Standford,' Veronica told her. 'He's American. Hattie, I'm so sorry.'

'It's...it's great he has a dad,' Hattie managed, struggling mightily to sound professional.

The boys had found plasticine and were sticking Barbie's head onto the floor so she stood upside down and naked. The girls should crack, but there was something wrong with the boys' thinking.

The boys cared deeply about their fort. The girls were more pragmatic. Barbie's rescue could wait until all options were explored.

'You know Leslie never said who the father was?' Veronica asked.

'I know that.'

Kyle's mother had been a brittle diabetic, a lovely, erratic loner who'd lurched from crisis to crisis. At three months old Kyle had been put into Hattie's care— 'Just for a few days, until I sort myself out.' Those few days had turned into six months. Kyle had then gone back to Leslie. Three weeks later Hattie had been called on again. Over and over.

Kyle might be her one true thing, but Hattie was also Kyle's. More and more Kyle regarded her as his mother, and more and more she thought of Kyle as her son. When Leslie had died last month everyone in Social Services had assumed that she would finally adopt him. Leslie would never countenance it, but Kyle's grandparents didn't care, and there'd been no hint who the father was.

But now...

'It seems Leslie's mother went through her belongings after she died,' Veronica told her. 'She found a diary, and it had the name of Kyle's father. He's a lawyer with the US armed forces. According to the diary, Leslie had a fling with him for a weekend and got pregnant.

She never told him. However, her mother's made of sterner stuff. She tracked him down and told him he needs to face his responsibilities. He's done DNA testing and paternity's proven. He's coming this weekend.'

This weekend.

Hattie wanted very badly to cry—to sink to the floor and sob. But she had four kids surrounding her, and her boss was on the phone. She was a professional. Reuniting kids with parents was what she did.

'That's fantastic,' she managed.

'It's not fantastic for you,' Veronica said bluntly. 'You know we all hoped…'

'For a stable, loving home for Kyle,' Hattie finished for her. 'That's all I care about.'

'You care about Kyle.'

'That's what I mean.'

'This is a beast of a job sometimes,' Veronica said gently. 'I know what this is doing to you. Hattie, I'm so sorry.'

'Don't…'

'I won't,' Veronica said. 'I know you don't want sympathy. We've both got a job to do and we'll do it. I told Major Standford you'll be expecting him on Saturday. You have the parents' suite empty? I thought you did; great. There are formalities to complete—taking Kyle back to the States is going to take more paperwork than you can imagine—so it'd be good if he could use that time getting to know him.'

'But he will take him?'

'On the phone he sounded appalled that he had a son,' Veronica said. 'But he also sounded responsible. There's a lot of legal stuff to see to, but he'll sort it.' She hesitated. 'Actually, Hattie, I looked him up on the Web.

It seems he's some hotshot lawyer employed by the army to investigate human-rights violations in war zones. He sounds amazing. He certainly doesn't sound like the sort of guy who'd leave his kid in a foster home for the rest of his childhood.'

'No,' Hattie said miserably. 'I mean…that's great.'

'So, expect him on Saturday,' Veronica said, back to being professional again. 'At least this means you'll have a space free again soon. So many kids…'

She disconnected and left Hattie to face her own demons.

He'd expected some sort of institution. The woman he'd spoken to had said Kyle was being cared for in the Bay Beach Children's Home. He'd seen orphanages in his war postings, and the thought of what he'd seen there made him cringe. This wouldn't be as bad—he knew that—but he'd envisaged at least a stereotypical building, like a hospital or a school. Instead, when he'd stopped at the post office just over from the beach to ask for directions, the lady he'd asked had said, 'Which one?'

'Number 4,' he'd said, checking the instructions Veronica had given him.

'That's Hattie's place,' the postmistress told him. 'The Rabbit Hutch. Second on the right and third house along. You can't miss it—it has a ruddy great rabbit painted on the sign in the front yard.'

There was indeed a rabbit. There was also a large, unkempt garden, shaded by a vast gum tree with a wobbly-looking treehouse in the lower branches. Kids' bikes and skateboards littered the yard and a huge sandpit took up most of one side. Two little girls were in the sandpit, intent on digging.

'Hi,' he said as he opened the gate. 'Is Hattie home?'

'She's in the kitchen,' the smaller of the girls said, digging a bit harder now she thought someone was watching. 'But I wouldn't go in if I were you. She's crabby.'

'Why is she crabby?' he asked, intrigued.

'Robbie and Kyle had a competition to see whose wee went furthest,' the littlest girl—the digger—said. 'They're scrubbing the bathroom and she's cross. We thought we'd stay out here.'

'Very wise,' he said.

'Why are you using a walking stick?' The oldest child—a girl of maybe about eight, too thin, a little bit haunted—was watching him intently.

'I hurt my leg.'

'That's an army uniform.'

'That's right.'

'Did you hurt your leg in a war?'

'Just an accident,' he said. 'I need to…'

But they were no longer listening. 'Robbie!' The little girl stood up and yelled as hard as she could. 'Robbie, there's a guy from the army here. He's got a uniform. He hurt his leg in a war.'

A head stuck out from the nearest window. A little boy, seven or eight, looked out. And stilled. A look of total awe crossed his face.

'You're a soldier,' he breathed.

'Yes.'

Another head appeared fleetingly beside the first head—a mop of dark curls, half hidden—and he heard the sound of a woman's voice calling from inside.

'You need to come with me, Kyle.'

The front door opened. A young woman stood in the

doorway. She was wearing jeans and an oversized windcheater, frayed at the cuffs. She looked as if she'd been painting—red, yellow and iridescent blue paint liberally adorned the windcheater and her nose and forehead. She had rich chestnut hair bunched into two masses of shiny curls. There was a hint of freckles under the paint.

She was holding a small, curly-headed boy by the hand.

'You must be Major Standford,' she said, and she smiled. 'I'm Harriet McDonald—Hattie—and this is Kyle.'

It was a gorgeous smile, warmly welcoming, but Mike wasn't looking at her. He was looking at the little boy by her side. He was… He was…

Him.

There was a picture of Mike aged five, taken over thirty years ago, when Mike had figured out how to manage without training wheels on his bike. His nanny had brought out the camera. When she'd left soon after—his nannies had been as changeable as his mother's moods—she'd presented him with a photo album. He'd held on to that picture of him and the bike.

Here were those same deep black curls, always rioting. Huge brown eyes. Freckles.

Enough. He found himself blinking, trying to focus, trying to figure that it couldn't be. But this little echo of his childhood was looking up at him, doubtful, almost scared.

'This is Kyle,' Hattie repeated, and bent down and scooped the little boy into her arms. She didn't look big enough to lift him, Mike thought. She was only five feet four or so, slim, a diminutive woman, but she held the child with the ease of practice.

'It's okay, Kyle,' she said gently. 'This is the Major I was talking to you about. Major Standford.' She looked a question at Mike, and he knew at once what she was asking.

He wasn't prepared for this—but would he ever be?

He'd come this far. There was no way he could back out now. And paternity had never been an issue. Sure, when he'd first got the phone call he'd thought it was some sort of con. But when Leslie's parents had outlined just what had happened, when they'd sent him a photograph of their daughter, he'd remembered Leslie.

Six years ago... Could he ever forget? The fighting had lurched into the civilian zone. What had happened had been unimaginable horror, and Mike had been called on to collate evidence for future war crimes tribunals.

On his return to headquarters his immediate boss had looked at his face and told him to take some leave. 'Go to Paris for the weekend. Find a girl, take in a movie, look at normal people enjoying themselves. Remember that this is an aberration.'

He'd met Leslie in a bar that first night. She'd seemed as brittle as he'd felt—as needful.

And this was the result, looking fearfully at him from the safety of Hattie's arms. This small boy who looked at him with his own eyes.

He had this one moment to walk away, and he couldn't do it.

'I guess I'm your dad,' he said softly, so softly that he thought no one but him could have heard.

But Hattie nodded. A look of something that he thought for a moment was pain washed across her face, but then she smiled and hugged Kyle tighter.

'Kyle might take some time to get used to the idea,' she said. 'You talked to my boss? She's suggested you stay for a while in our parents' suite if you can. Would you like to do that?' Her eyes were pleading a little. 'Kyle would find it hard if you took him straight away—and in fact, you can't. There's lots of paperwork to be done before then. And you do need time to get to know him.'

He nodded. 'You've been taking care of Kyle for a while?'

'Intermittently since he was a baby,' she said. 'Haven't I, Kyle? Kyle's mum had diabetes—really badly. She was often sick, so whenever she wasn't able to take care of him I took over.'

'Hattie's my real mum,' Kyle said suddenly, and hugged her hard, burying his face in her shoulder.

She smiled sadly and lifted him back a little.

'You know that's not true, Kyle,' she said. 'I'm your house mum. I look after kids when their real mum and dad can't care for them. You know the boys and girls who come here don't stay very long.'

'I've been here for ever and ever.' He seemed close to tears.

'Not that long,' she said, then gave up trying to pry him loose and turned to the other kids. To the little boy hanging out the window. 'Robbie, this is Major Standford. Robbie wants to join the army more than anything in the whole world. You'll be staying with us, Major Standford?'

'Mike.'

'Mike,' she said, and smiled again. This time he was able to take in the smile in its entirety. It was a smile to give a man pause.

It was a smile to make a man think that maybe he'd be best staying in a motel down the road.

But things were being taken out of his hands. 'Can Robbie help take your gear inside?' she asked. 'He's longing to. As you're wearing uniform, I suspect you don't have anything so normal as a suitcase.'

'I have an army duffel,' he admitted, and Robbie was tumbling out of the open window, flying down the path to the car before anyone could say another word.

'Small boy heaven,' Hattie said wryly. 'Carting an army duffel. Kyle, do you want to help?'

There was a frantic shake of Kyle's small head.

'What about you girls?' Hattie said. 'Mike, these are Erin and Katy. Erin's the oldest. Katy's the one with six Band-Aids on her leg. She had an accident with roller-blades and came off worst.'

'I could put the duffel bag on my rollerblades,' Katy offered. 'That way we wouldn't have to carry it.'

'That's a very good idea,' Hattie said warmly. 'But I think the whole three of you might need to hold it on. Robbie, you're in charge—the rest of you do what Robbie tells you. Off you go and show Major Mike to his quarters. Then you can all wash up in Kyle and Robbie's newly scrubbed bathroom and come for lunch. There's hot dogs and apples and cordial. Major Mike, welcome to our home.'

Mike unpacked his kit in relative peace. The rooms he'd been shown into by the three kids were comfortable and warmly furnished, a bedroom with an *en suite* bathroom, and a small sitting room looking out over the bay. There was everything he needed for a reason-able stay.

How long was he intending to be here?

Who knew? He was officially on leave, starting today. When Leslie's parents had contacted him he'd been thinking of coming to Canberra for a conference anyway. He'd asked for leave afterwards.

'Take as much time as you need,' his boss had told him. 'You're well overdue for a break. See something of Australia while you're there. Do some surfing. Have some fun. See if you can remember what fun is.'

This was a pretty good part of Australia to have fun in, he conceded. Bay Beach seemed to be an unimaginative name for a small town which seemed breathtakingly lovely. Mountains rose steeply behind the coastal fringe. The beach looked fabulous.

He could use a swim.

Hot dogs and apples and cordial were waiting.

What had he let himself in for? And where did he start? Kyle was his biological son, but the knowledge of his existence had blown him sideways.

There was a knock on the door. Hattie's head poked round, looking anxious.

'Hi,' she said. 'Can we talk?'

'Sure.' He motioned her inside. She came in, closed the door behind her and leaned on it. Looking worried. She still had a yellow splodge on the side of her nose.

'I need to know where we stand before we take this any further,' she said. 'Kyle's really unsettled.'

'It's the last thing I want,' he said. 'To frighten him.'

'We need to work through it with care. Veronica said you didn't know of his existence?'

'Not until four weeks ago.'

'It must have been a shock.'

'You can say that again.'

They seemed to be circling, he thought. Figuring each other out. Hattie was Kyle's house mother. The social worker, Veronica, had spelled the relationship out for him.

'Leslie was an erratic mother. She'd never consent to give Kyle up for adoption, or even for permanent foster care. She was always coming to get him tomorrow, or tomorrow or tomorrow—which is why he's had to be placed in one of our community houses. Hattie's a house mum, trained to look after itinerant kids—kids with short-term problems. But she took Kyle in as a baby, and to give him some sort of continuity we've always reserved a place there for him. Hattie's been his constant.'

'So I'll be taking him away…'

'Hattie's a house mother. Her job is to look after traumatised kids and if possible reunite them with their parents. Yes, you might have trouble forming a relationship with Kyle, but it won't be because of Hattie.'

But now Hattie was watching him, wary as a she-bear with a litter of cubs, scenting wolf. *He* was the wolf?

'Are you planning to take him back to the US?' she asked.

'I'm not sure.'

'Or stay in Australia?'

'I'm in the US armed forces.'

'I can see that. Do you have a permanent base?'

'No.'

'Will that fit in with having a child?

'Other men have kids…'

'Other men have partners to take up the slack when they're away. Do you have someone?

'No.'

'Or other kids?'

'No! Look, what is this?'

'I just need to get the facts,' she said gently. 'Kyle needs the truth. He's an intelligent little boy. He knows his mother's dead. His grandmother came to see him yesterday—the woman's never lifted a finger to help before, but she arrived and told Kyle straight off that you were his father and you'd be taking him overseas. I've been trying to pick up the pieces since then—explain it in a way that's not threatening. But you yourself don't know what's happening?'

'This has happened too fast.'

'You need to work it out pretty soon,' she said, still gentle. 'I know it's hard for you, but it's harder for Kyle. He's lost his mother and he needs to be settled. I'm not sure what your situation is. If you intend to stay in the army then maybe you should think about adoption. There are many couples out there who could give Kyle a lovely home.'

'I couldn't…'

'No, it's way too soon,' she said. 'And I don't want you to be overwhelmingly pressured. You're looking as terrified as Kyle. But adoption laws aren't what they were. You can set it up so you have a say in who adopts him. Maybe find a couple in the US so access isn't a problem, and organise it so that you can have as much access as you want. We can start things rolling from here. Anyway, all I'm saying is that there are lots of options. Come out and have some lunch, and then we'll take the kids over to the beach. Did you bring your togs?'

'Togs?'

'Swimmers,' she said, and grinned. 'Boardies or budgie smugglers.'

'Pardon?'

'Aussie,' she said. 'Board shorts or the alternative.

Think about how you might go about smuggling a budgerigar into the country and you have our version of a skimpy men's swimsuit. Welcome to Australia. So you do have togs?'

'I… Yes.' He thought about it and gave a faint grin. 'I don't hold with budgie smugglers. I'm more a board shorts man.'

'Excellent,' she said, and smiled. But the worry didn't completely fade. She was trying very hard to sound light-hearted, he thought, but it didn't quite come off. 'Men think budgie smugglers look sexy, but they so don't,' she added. 'Board shorts are much more manly.'

She coloured a little and her smile became more genuine. 'In my opinion, that is. Whatever. Come and wrap yourself round a hot dog or six, and then we'll hit the beach. The best way you can get to know Kyle is to get to know us all. Relax and have fun. Starting now. That's an order.'

'Yes, ma'am,' he said, startled, and she grinned.

'Excellent. Finally a little obedience. If you knew how hard that is to come by here…'

CHAPTER TWO

THEY had lunch. As promised, it was hot dogs, as many apples as anyone could eat and jugs of homemade cordial.

Mike sat at the big wooden table in the kitchen and felt absurdly out of place.

'Why did you take your uniform off?' Robbie asked in tones of deep disappointment.

'I'm not on duty now,' he said. 'I'm on leave, and on leave I wear jeans and T-shirt like anyone else.' Then, on impulse, 'Would you like to try on my army cap and boots tonight?'

There was an awed hush.

'I could take your photo in them,' Hattie offered. 'We could e-mail the photos to your mum in hospital.'

'Cool,' Robbie breathed.

'Me, too?' Erin asked diffidently. Erin was the skinny, haunted one. 'Aunty June's going to see Mum at the weekend.

'She'll be able to take the photos, then,' Hattie said, agreeing.

'But Mum doesn't like uniforms,' Erin ventured, thinking it through a bit further.

'That's just cops,' Robbie said scornfully. 'Your

mum doesn't like cops 'cos they put her in jail. Major Mike's not cops. He fights in wars.'

'How did you hurt your leg?' Erin asked, for the second time.

A fall. He almost said it—and then he didn't.

That was the line he gave casual enquirers. He'd said it so often that it was almost out before he caught himself.

But now he stopped himself before he gave the easy lie, and he didn't know why. All he knew was that they were watching him: Erin, Katy, Robbie, Kyle—and Hattie.

This wasn't a house for wimps. He could see that at a glance.

Or maybe not a glance. On the surface these were normal kids with a single mum. But Erin was way too thin, and a couple of savage burn marks marred her skinny forearms. They looked like burn marks he'd seen before, on adults. Burn marks he didn't want to think about.

Robbie looked better—better fed, more outgoing. But he seemed almost aggressive. Mike had seen young recruits act like this when they were scared. His mother was in hospital? He wondered why.

Katy was almost as quiet as Kyle. She was drinking her cordial and her eyes over the rim of her mug were huge.

This was a state home for desperately needy kids. His son was one of them.

His son.

The thought was gut-wrenching on so many levels he didn't know where to start. Firstly he had a son... How was it that his precautions hadn't worked? He'd steered clear of commitment all his life, moving from country to country, never wanting roots. The memories of his parents' relationship chaos meant that he'd never been tempted to go down that path. He knew the hurt relationships did to kids.

Yet here was another kid—his own son—scarred already by the relationship that had formed him. A desperate coupling between two flawed individuals.

Something of what he was feeling must have been showing in his face, for Hattie leaned over and put another hot dog on his plate. She smiled at him, her expression warm and sympathetic.

'There's no need to tell us if you don't want to,' she said. 'There's no need to say anything you don't want to in this house.'

'It's the rule,' Robbie said grudgingly. 'But if it was in a war…'

'A bomb went off near my car,' he said, and there was a stunned hush.

'Oh, Mike,' Hattie murmured.

'Was people killed?' Robbie asked.

'Yes,' he said, and met Robbie's awed look head on. 'It was a terrible situation. That was why we were there—to try and keep people safe. Mostly that's what our soldiers do now. They go to places where there's fighting and they try and keep people safe.'

'You don't do any fighting?' Robbie asked, prepared to be disappointed.

'What's more important?' he asked. 'To learn to fire a gun and shoot people? Or to learn how to persuade people to put their guns away.'

'That's what you do?' Robbie asked.

'That's what I try to do,' he said. 'I think it's the most important job in the army.'

'But you still see guns?'

'Robbie…' Hattie said warningly, but Mike shook his head.

'No. It's okay. Yes, I see guns. But I'm doing my very best to see less and less of them. If you want to grow up to be a soldier and help keep peace in the world it's a truly heroic thing to do.'

'Wow,' Robbie breathed.

'I'll show you my medals after lunch,' he said, and Robbie's face said there could be no greater pleasure.

'Me, too,' Kyle said, and Mike smiled at him fleetingly and nodded. He had this figured. He talked to the other kids and Kyle would listen.

Hattie was smiling, and he glanced at her and realised she knew exactly what was going on. She approved, he thought. But still, there was that flash of pain.

She'd let herself get attached to Kyle. He could see that. She was trying her best to hide it. She was great to all the kids. But there was that tiny, deeper softening when she looked at Kyle.

He couldn't ask her about it now. It'd have to wait until the kids weren't present.

He did need to stay here, he thought. When the kids were asleep he could talk to her. The thought was suddenly appealing on more than just a needs basis.

'Okay, let's get this show on the road,' Hattie was saying, starting to clear away and jerking him back to common sense. 'This is a very busy Saturday afternoon. Agnes has rung saying she's opening the clothes store for us at four o'clock, so we can get our school uniforms. That means we need to hit the beach now, and be home and washed and changed by three-thirty. Anyone not in their togs in ten minutes gets to carry the picnic basket down the cliff!'

Fate worse than death. There was a gasp of horror and four small bodies catapulted out of their chairs and headed for their bedrooms.

It was only three blocks to the beach. Hattie and the kids walked. Mike came after in his car.

'There's no need for you to come,' Hattie told him. 'If you want to stay and rest…'

'I've just come from Canberra this morning,' he told her. 'Not the US. Jet lag's not a problem.'

'And the leg?'

'Yeah, well, walking three blocks is still a pain,' he admitted. 'So I'll drive. But I'll take the picnic basket.'

So he did. But he took his time, and by the time he pulled into the little car park overlooking the beach they were all in the water.

Hattie and her kids.

They looked fabulous, he thought. Hattie was wearing a multi-coloured swimsuit, a one-piece that showed every curve to perfection. The two little girls were wearing crimson bikinis and the boys were in board shorts.

They were splashing up a storm in the shallows, but they saw him arrive. Hattie waved at a guy in a yellow windcheater that said 'Bay Beach Life Guard' and walked up the beach to meet him.

He watched her come. She was totally natural, he thought. She used no artifice to attract. She just…was.

Hell, what was he doing, sitting in the car? He climbed out stiffly as she reached him. Her curls were dripping wet, she was sand coated, and she was laughing over her shoulder at something the life guard had called to her.

She was gorgeous.

'Sorry,' he said, feeling dazed. 'I didn't mean you to leave the kids.'

'Simon's watching them,' she said. 'The life guard. He's my nephew. Family has to be useful for something.'

'You're a local, then?'

'Born and bred in Bay Beach. I went away for a bit to do my training, but this is home.'

'So you're just waiting for Mr Right to give you your own babies rather than take care of everyone else's?'

Whoa! It was the wrong thing to say. It was appalling. It was intrusive on all sorts of levels. It was only because he was feeling dazed and shocked and right out of his comfort zone that his senses had slipped enough for him to say it.

And as well as intrusive it was hurtful. The look of pain that flashed across her face was unmistakable. He'd sensed her unhappiness this morning. Now...

'I'm so sorry,' he said, fast. 'That was a boorish, dumb question, and I had no right to think it, much less ask it.'

She blinked. And then she regrouped and managed a smile. And then a bigger one.

'Wow,' she said.

'Wow?'

'For my brothers to give me an apology like that I'd have had to have threatened to tell Mum at the very least. You do a lovely line in sorries.'

'I guess I've had practice.'

'And you being a lawyer? Who'da guessed?' She hauled open the back door of the car and tugged out the picnic basket before he could stop her. 'We asked about your leg, and we had no right there, either.'

'My leg's fine,' he said, reaching for the basket, but she refused to relinquish it.

'I'm very sure it's not. You don't have to play the macho bit with me.'

'How many brothers do you have?' he demanded.

'*Two*,' she said. 'And *three* sisters. Don't mess with me in this town.'

'No, ma'am,' he said, but he still didn't let go of the basket.

'Mike?'

'Yes?'

'Let go.'

'Over my dead body. You go back and play with the kids.'

'You're coming in swimming, too?'

'I'm thinking about it.'

'Think about it while I carry the basket.'

'Hattie?'

'Yes?'

'Let go, or I'll carry you and the basket down the beach.'

'You wouldn't dare.'

'Watch me.'

'You're using a walking stick.'

'I've carried a woman before, with my leg worse than this,' he said, and then he realised what he'd said and stopped dead.

He'd never talked about it. The day of the bomb. The awfulness. The sheer tragedy…

'Okay, Mike, you can carry the picnic basket,' Hattie said gently into a silence that was suddenly loaded, and she knew—he could tell that she knew—that he'd reached the point where it scared him to go on. 'I only fight for things that matter. But, Mike…' She hesitated. 'I have a feeling that there's all sorts of things happening in your life that matter,' she said gently. 'And Kyle's only one of them. But that's what this place is for. Respite and regrouping, gathering resources to face the world again. Leave the picnic basket this side of the high tide mark and come in and join us. And remember we're all the same,' she whispered. 'Some of us have scars on the inside and some of us have them on the outside. Just because they're hidden it doesn't mean they don't hurt. And admitting you're hurting… Well, that's what these kids are doing. Welcome to the club.'

She watched him swimming.

He kept himself far away from them. The kids were playing in a pack—they often did, knowing there was safety in their own little group. So they splashed and whooped around Hattie, while out past the breakers Mike swam slowly, strongly, from one end of the bay and back, over and over again.

Leaning on his stick, he'd looked vulnerable, and she'd seen the savage scars on his thigh as he'd entered the water. But now the water was taking the weight from his injured leg and he was revelling in his freedom, revelling in the strength of his upper body.

He was seriously good.

He was seriously sexy.

Yeah, and that was a dumb way to react, Hattie decided as the allotted hour for swimming wore on. Don't even think about sexy, she told herself crossly. He's a parent and he's a high-flying international lawyer. He probably has a string of high-flying women all over the world.

Right.

Robbie barrelled into her under the water and she fell

backwards, ended up sputtering, laughing, and emerged cuddling the normally non-tactile child. She was working. She was helping Robbie have fun.

But she was just ever so slightly watching Major Mike Standford out of the corner of her eye.

And, at the other end of the bay, Major Mike Standford was watching her.

CHAPTER THREE

HATTIE'S house was run like clockwork. At three they were out of the water, and by a quarter to four she had them washed and dressed and lined up, ready to go to town.

'Tuesday's the first day of school term,' she told him. She was doing a visual check as each kid appeared at the door—clothes neat, shoes on, hair combed. Robbie got sent back twice.

'Isn't it a bit late to be buying uniforms?' he asked cautiously. Not that it was any of his business. He was way out of his comfort zone. But he remembered his own childhood, carefully controlled. His school uniforms would have been ordered and fitted months ahead.

'These kids are itinerant,' she said. 'Did I know last week that they'd be here this week? No. There's no guarantee they'll be with me on Tuesday, but this is the latest I can leave it.'

'Don't any of them have school uniforms?'

'They might have six or seven,' she admitted. 'Our rule is to fit 'em out in the uniform here, regardless of where they've been in the past. There's only one thing worse than starting a strange school, and that's starting off looking different to anyone else. So uniforms it is.'

'Could Kyle stay home with me?' he asked diffidently.

'No,' she said bluntly, doing up Katy's top button.

'No?'

'Don't force it,' she said. 'Kyle doesn't know you properly yet, and neither do I. Even if I wanted to say yes, I couldn't. Your paperwork hasn't come through, so leaving Kyle with you would leave me criminally liable.'

'But I…'

'I know. You're a trustworthy citizen.' She caught Robbie as he hared past and sighed. 'Robbie, you call that combed?'

'I combed the front.'

'You comb all over. Do it,' she growled, and then smiled at Robbie's retreating back. 'He tests me all the time,' she said, and Mike found himself smiling back before he thought about it.

If he was a kid in trouble he wouldn't mind ending up in Hattie's care, he thought. She seemed to have just the right mix of discipline, humour and love.

Love? Yeah, love, he thought, as Robbie raced out again. She caught him, swung him round, and then rumpled his newly combed hair.

'There,' she declared. 'Perfect.' And she kissed him and propelled him forward to the minibus.

'Aw—yurk,' Robbie said, and wiped away the offending kiss with vigour. But he didn't mind at all, Mike thought. Well, why would he?

But he still didn't have a handle on what was going on. 'So Kyle will get a uniform even though he'll only be here for the next couple of weeks?' he asked.

'Tell me where he's going then?' she demanded, suddenly stern.

'I haven't worked that out.'

'No. So my job is to give these kids security until the adults around them *do* work it out.'

'That sounds accusing.'

'I'm simply stating facts. Kyle is your son, but you haven't worked out his care, so it's up to me until you do. But you're welcome to come with us.'

Did he want to go and buy school uniforms with a bunch of foster kids? He could stay home and read a book, take the weight off his leg for a bit.

'Your leg's hurting,' she said suddenly.

How the hell did she know?

'No.'

'Something is. Go take a nap and we'll see you in an hour.'

'I'm coming with you.'

'Okay,' she said, neither pleased nor displeased.

He had an irrational need to know which she was. In one sense he felt judged—she was so carefully non-judgmental, but she must be thinking of him as yet another of the world's messy parents who let their kids fend for themselves.

But in another sense…

'Fine,' she added, and she smiled, and when she smiled the sun came out and all was right with the world. She had *some* smile. 'You want to come in the minibus with us?'

'I…'

'Squash over, kids,' she called. 'Major Standford's coming with us. But he doesn't need a uniform—he already has one.'

So he went. He sat with Kyle. He didn't know how it happened—it just sort of did. It was the natural way the seating fell, but he sensed that it hadn't happened by chance.

He was on the long back seat of the bus, and Kyle was sitting beside him.

'This is the best place on the bus to sit,' Kyle confided.

'Yes,' he agreed. 'I used to like the back of the bus when I was your age.'

'Do you still?'

'I guess I do.'

'You won't take me away from Hattie, will you?' he asked suddenly, and Mike was left floundering.

He glanced forward and caught Hattie's eyes. She was watching him in the rearview mirror as she drove.

This was a hugely important question.

Hell, he felt so hemmed in that he wanted to get off the bus right now. Four weeks ago he'd been a totally self-contained soldier, with no commitments, no responsibilities, apart from his career. Now he was being watched by a woman and by a small boy. One expected nothing of him and the other wanted nothing of him.

Could he just walk away? Leave Kyle to Hattie?

Leave him in a home for troubled kids for ever?

No. A decision had to be made soon, and no matter what it was it would involve taking Kyle from Hattie.

'Kyle, I honestly don't know what's going to happen,' he told Kyle, speaking softly, knowing that Hattie couldn't hear him but knowing that she was still watching him, still sensing what was going on. 'I've just learned that I'm your dad,' he said. 'I've never had a son before, and I don't know where to start. All I know so far is that you love Hattie. I think that's great. Hattie is obviously a really good house mum, and I can see why you love her. So no matter what happens we'll figure out a way that you and Hattie can still see each other.'

'Can I still live with Hattie?'

'I don't think so,' he said, knowing he had to be honest, no matter how much he hated that his words made his little son flinch. 'But let's not worry about that yet. I have a long time here—weeks—to get to know you, and then Hattie and you and I will sit down and figure out how we can make you happy.'

'I want to stay with Hattie,' Kyle said, but he said it in a tiny, faltering whisper that said he already knew it was impossible.

He'd be used to Leslie carting him away at short notice, Mike thought. And Veronica had told him enough of Kyle's life for him to know that those periods had been unmitigated chaos.

'Let's just wait and see,' Mike said. 'And let's keep talking to Hattie about it. We'll think of some way we can keep you happy.'

'Hattie's clever,' Kyle whispered.

'Yes,' Mike agreed. 'I can see that.'

The uniform-buying was not the sort of uniform-buying Mike was used to.

For a start, everything smelled funny.

They'd stopped at a church hall, and when they'd filed out and Hattie had opened the door the smell had hit before they walked inside. The fusty smell of used clothes, stored badly.

A middle-aged woman was there, in a bad tweed suit and the sort of blue hair rinse Mike hadn't seen for twenty years.

'Hi, Hattie,' the lady said. 'How many poor wee things do we need to fit out today?'

The 'poor wee things' paused as one, and their expressions changed. Mike saw it. From a tribe of kids on an excursion they were suddenly kids from a home.

He saw Hattie brace herself, and he saw that the smile she returned was forced.

'Not a single poor wee thing,' she said brightly. 'Just a bunch of kids who've come up from the beach and need school uniforms. Agnes, this is Robbie and Erin and Katy and Kyle, and Kyle's father, Major Standford.'

'You've got a *father* staying with you?' Agnes said, giving him the sort of stare he guessed was the one she used for any degenerate, drug-dealing, violent criminal. Or similar.

'Isn't that great?' Hattie said, refusing to be distracted. 'Okay, Agnes, sweaters first. We need a size ten, an eight and two sixes.'

Mike watched on. Fascinated. Five minutes later the four kids were wearing grey sweaters with the faded emblem of the local school.

They were all faded. They were all…old.

The smell was getting stronger as the clothes were disturbed.

'Shoes next,' Hattie said brightly, and Mike could stand it no longer.

'Hattie, we don't need to do this,' he said.

'Sorry?'

He was looking at Kyle. The elbow of the sweater Kyle was trying on was patched. The fact that Kyle was looking in the mirror admiring himself was a help, but not so much of a help that Mike could get over the patch. And the smell.

And this was his son.

'Is there somewhere in town where we can buy new gear?'

'No,' Hattie said shortly, and sat Kyle down and tugged his shoes off.

'Surely there is,' he said.

'There is,' Agnes offered.

'No,' Hattie said.

'But I'm willing to buy—'

'Agnes, can you help Kyle with his laces? The rest of you can do your own. Mike, can I talk to you outside?' She didn't wait for a response, but whirled away and walked out, expecting him to follow.

He followed. When he'd closed the door behind him she turned to face him and her expression was strained.

'Mike, if you buy new clothes for Kyle, the rest of the kids are going to hate it,' she said. 'They're all pretty pleased about their school uniforms now, and a good wash will get rid of the smell. I guess it's your prerogative to buy new for Kyle, but it'll cause problems for me. Please don't.'

'I'll buy new gear for all of them,' he said tightly. 'My son's not going to wear musty hand-me-downs. Hell, look at him.'

'I did look at him. I saw a kid who looked like he was really pleased.'

'Agnes called them: "poor wee things."'

'Agnes is a well-meaning fruitcake.'

'My kid's not going to wear hand-me-downs.'

'Do you think he cares?'

'I care.'

'Then care for the right reasons,' she snapped. 'You care that there's a patch on Kyle's elbow. Big deal. You think he notices? So you'll solve the problem by buying them all sparky new uniforms. Which means they'll know what sparky new uniforms feel like, and next time they need a uniform—which might be as early as next week, when a parent comes to claim them—they'll know that there's an alternative to shabby. This little town is a working fishing town—not wealthy—and a lot of local kids will be in hand-me-downs. These kids will turn up to school on Tuesday and they'll fit right in—which is what I want them to do. So I'm asking that you don't get in the way of that.

'But I do have rules,' she admitted. 'You are the parent. You can take Kyle and buy him new gear and I can't object. I'm just asking you not to. Please. For all our sakes.'

She met his look square-on. Directly. Challenging. And all of a sudden…

All of a sudden he was hit by a crazy, irrational, overwhelming urge to kiss her. The urge was so great that it took an almost superhuman effort not to. He had to physically root himself to the spot and not move. It was as if a tsunami had hit him—a force so powerful that he was almost swept away. She was so…so…

'I'm going back to tie some shoelaces,' she told him, casting him a doubtful look. 'If you'd like to join us you're welcome. I'll leave you to think about it.'

He had so much to think about that his head spun, but any thought of kissing was clearly ridiculous.

He returned to the Rabbit Hutch, helped unpack the kids' parcels, ate toasted sandwiches and fruit salad in front of a silly movie, read the boys a bedtime story while Hattie read to the girls, and then discovered he was expected to retire to his suite.

'I'm sorry, but I need time to myself when the kids are in bed,' she told him. 'There's a television in your room.'

There was. But he felt rebuffed. He felt…weird.

Why was he reacting so strongly to her?

It was this situation, he thought, a little bit desperately. He couldn't get his thoughts in order. His normally cool, calculating brain had been addled almost as badly as if a bomb had gone off.

That was how he felt. Shell shocked—almost as severely as he'd been six months ago.

She was just through the wall, he thought. She was doing a pile of sewing, taking up hems on school uniforms, reinforcing patches, listening to Abba on her sound system.

He could turn his television on, but then he wouldn't hear her Abba, and he sort of wanted…

He didn't know what he wanted.

His leg ached.

He lay on his bed and picked up a crime thriller he'd been enjoying.

He couldn't enjoy it now. He was too…too…

Involved.

He didn't do involved.

His brain did a fast switch—as unwelcome as it was unexpected. One minute he was lying on the bed, listening to the sounds of Hattie patching pants, the next he was in hospital on the other side of the world.

It was the first day he'd been allowed out of bed. He was being flown out later that day, and he couldn't wait to get out of there.

One of the guys in his ward had wanted something, and he'd offered to go and find a nurse. He'd rolled down the corridor in his wheelchair and seen the nurse he wanted through the glass windows into another ward. So he'd pushed through.

The child had been sitting in a cot by the door. Just sitting.

She'd been about three years old, maybe even younger. She had a mop of tousled blonde curls that needed a wash. Her shadowed brown eyes had been a little crusted and her face ancient for its years.

Her left leg ended in a massive dressing just below the knee.

He'd come so close to losing his own leg that such a sight had carried even more horror than it otherwise would have—if such a thing were possible.

He'd tried to wheel past, but it had been as if the wheels on his chair were glued. He'd stopped by the cot rails and looked in.

She'd looked at him. And such a look...

It hadn't been despairing. It had simply been lost. Expecting nothing. Hoping for nothing.

'Hi,' he'd said weakly, and she hadn't responded.

The nurse had come up to him then. He oughtn't to be here, she'd said. This was the civilian part of the hospital, not the side the army had taken over for their casualties.

'How can I help you?' she'd asked.

He'd explained his friend's needs. But before they'd left he'd turned to the cot. She'd still been watching him.

'What's her story?'

'She's waiting to go to the orphanage,' the nurse said. 'She's been here for too long already. There's nothing more we can do for her.'

'Her parents?'

'They died in a bomb blast. Much like your incident, sir,' she said diffidently. 'But with more civilian casualties.'

'So she has no one?'

'There's lots more like her. Our orphanages will provide for her.'

'She'll be adopted?

'There's plenty of cute babies with four limbs to adopt. Why take this one? But, sir, you're not meant to be in this ward. I'll take you back now, and then we need to get your medication organised for your evacuation.'

And that had been that. A momentary glimpse of a tragedy that was played out all over the world. Why should it have affected him as it had?

'I'm doing cocoa,' Hattie's voice called from the other side of the wall. From the other side of the world. 'You want me to make you some?'

'I'll come out.'

'I'll bring it in,' she said, and she did. But she wouldn't stay. She presented him with his cocoa, smiled warmly—her best care-worker-taking-care-of-families smile—and left him with his thoughts.

Which were a tangled muddle of Kyle, and a little girl in a cot in his war-torn past.

And Harriet McDonald.

CHAPTER FOUR

SUNDAY was pretty much a repeat of Saturday, without the uniform-buying. Hattie kept them busy pretty much all the time. She had little time to herself, he realised.

'Don't you ever say, Go outside and play?' he asked her, and she smiled a bit sadly and shook her head.

'Well, I do. But only when it's to give one of them one-on-one attention. These kids are high-energy. High-risk, too,' she admitted. 'You let them get bored and the troubles come flooding back. It's more trouble than it's worth.'

'So you're on duty all the time?'

'I take time off.'

'And what happens to the kids then?'

'Another house mother comes in. Not perfect,' she admitted, 'but it's the best I can do.'

'So does Kyle…?'

'Kyle comes with me when I'm off duty.'

'So he really is special?'

'He really is. You want to take him down looking for shells?'

'You'd trust me alone with him?'

'I would,' she said. 'Twenty-four hours is enough to give me a measure of a person. You're okay.'

What was there in that to make him feel like blushing? *'You're okay.'* Some praise.

'So you're starting to hand Kyle over?'

'Yes,' she said bluntly. 'Are you ready?'

'Maybe I have to be.'

'There is the adoption road.'

'I don't know whether I want that.'

'What about your own parents?' she asked. 'Will they be interested to know you have a son?'

'They weren't particularly interested in the fact that *they* had a son,' he said, before he thought about it, and then he thought what the hell was he doing, displaying all for this woman to see?

'You really are a loner,' she said softly.

He didn't answer. He didn't know where to start to respond.

'Kyle, would you like to take your dad over to Shelley Beach and look for cowries?' Hattie called, before he could get his face together.

Kyle thought about it gravely from the sandpit. 'Does he want a cowrie?'

'I don't know what a cowrie is,' he admitted.

'I found five last week,' Kyle said shyly. 'You want me to show you?'

'Yes, please.'

'Can Katy come, too?' Kyle asked, but Katy shook her head.

'I'm bored of cowries.'

'Just you and your dad,' Hattie said, and the world held its breath.

'Okay,' Kyle said, obviously not figuring it for the big deal it was to Mike. 'Just wait until I get my bucket.'

Mike smiled. And then he turned to Hattie. And there it was again. Pure, unmitigated pain.

'Hattie, I'm so sorry,' he said, not exactly understanding what he was sorry for.

'Don't be,' she said, and put her hand to her side. Suddenly he wasn't sure if it was physical pain or emotional. 'There's no need to be sorry,' she whispered. 'We all need to get on.'

Sunday night. More solitary television-watching. More cocoa. More figuring out the boundaries.

The boundaries were Hattie's, and he wasn't permitted to cross them. He was one of her parents and he wasn't permitted to get closer.

Monday came and went, and with it went the remains of the school holidays.

On Tuesday morning they all walked the four blocks to school. Even three days of swimming had helped Mike's leg. He made it the four blocks without flinching.

The pain belonged to the children. The kids were dead quiet on the way there, and as they stopped by the gate Erin started to cry.

'They won't like me,' she sobbed.

'I'll hit them if they don't like you,' Robbie said, but he sounded as nervous as Erin.

'There'll be no hitting. There'll be lots of learning and lots of fun, and you all have your favourite things in your lunch boxes,' Hattie said, sounding bossy. 'And at three-thirty I'll be here to walk you home again.'

'I'll be here, too,' Mike said, and got a surprised look from Hattie.

'Promise?' she said urgently, and suddenly he realised what she was doing. She was giving these kids certainty. It was no light statement—*I'll be here to pick you up.*

'I'll be here,' he repeated, and she smiled.

Which pleased him.

And it also pleased the kids. They relaxed. Just a little, but enough so that when they met the teachers, and when the melee of kids in the playground became ordered pairs, when the kids were ushered into school, Erin's tears had dried and Robbie's belligerence had faded.

And then they were gone, and Hattie and Mike were left looking at each other in the sun.

This was the hardest time, Hattie thought. Having parents staying was hard enough when the kids were on holiday. To have Mike staying longer…

It hardly ever happened. Most parents didn't like their parenting skills under scrutiny. They came if it was absolutely necessary, before they were trusted with a child again, and they left as soon as they could.

Mike could leave, she thought. Maybe come back at weekends until he had things sorted out.

She said as much, tentatively, and he thought about it.

'Yeah, I could.'

'You have somewhere to go?'

'I can find a hotel. Maybe that'd be best. But then I have to be here at three-thirty…'

'You have nowhere else?'

'I'm American.'

'How much leave do you have?'

'Indefinite.' He stared down at his leg as if it was somehow not connected to him. 'The shrink's saying I have post-traumatic stress. They're telling me I can take off a year if I want.'

'Do you want?'

'I don't want even this much,' he snapped, and then shrugged. 'Sorry. That's no problem of yours. I'll take myself off.'

'There's no need.'

'What do you do when they're at school?'

'Housework,' she said glumly. 'Have you seen the state of the house after the holidays?'

'I'll help.'

'You have to be kidding.'

'I can wield a mop.'

'It's my job.'

'Because you're the mum? Hey, I'm the dad, aren't I?'

'You don't want to wield a mop.'

'Neither do you,' he retorted.

'Yeah, but it's in my job description.'

'I'm just figuring out *my* job description,' he said, and grinned. 'Let's see if we can fit a bit of housework in before I work out that it's not my role.'

'But your leg…'

'The doctors say to exercise. I'm sure mopping fits with the rest of the physiotherapy I've been doing.'

So they scrubbed the house. It was weird, Hattie thought as they worked through the morning. She usually hated this job. In truth she often called on one of her sisters to help her. Physically, she just wasn't up to it.

But today she was feeling no pain. Mike had checked her music collection, winced, but then decided it was Music to Mop By, and they'd attacked the house together.

It was almost…fun.

It *was* fun.

They started at the top and worked down. By lunch-time they had a vast load of washing flapping on the line, and the house was as sparky clean as a kids' house was ever likely to be.

'Lunch,' Mike said, deeply satisfied as he surveyed the shine on the kitchen linoleum. 'Champagne, I think.'

'Sandwiches at the kitchen table,' Hattie said, but he was having none of it.

'No one makes sandwiches in this kitchen,' he said. 'At least not until *News of the World* and *Vogue Interiors* get here with their photographic equipment. I'm taking you out to lunch.'

'I have things to…'

'I'm very sure you don't,' Mike said. 'I just did half your things for you.'

More, Hattie conceded. Post-school-holiday cleaning would have taken her at least two days to get through. But to go out to lunch with him…

It seemed personal. And this guy was too big and too male and just too…too Mike for her to want to go out with him.

Wrong. She'd like very much to go out with him. But there were complications every way she looked down that path.

'Your leg must be aching,' she told him. 'Why don't I walk down to the corner store and bring us back—'

'A sandwich? No. Champagne or nothing.'

He really was a bit…well, irresistible. The way he smiled at her…

'And you're hurting, too,' he said gently. 'Hattie, why do you keep putting your hand to your side? Don't tell me that's an old war wound?'

She pulled her hand from her side as if she'd scalded it. 'No.'

'Problem?'

'It's none of your business.' She bit her lip. 'Sorry. That sounded rude.'

'It did,' he agreed mildly. 'Especially since I told you about my leg.'

'You didn't tell me very much about your leg.'

'I was in a car when a roadside bomb went off,' he told her. 'Four onlookers were killed, but all I got was a fragment of flying metal in my leg. I ended up with a fractured knee and the lacerations that have left the scars you can see. That was six months ago. I'm only just off crutches, which explains the limp. Give me another six months and I'll be ready to run marathons.'

'Really?'

'Maybe not,' he conceded, and smiled. 'I never was one for marathons in the first place.'

'There's residual damage?'

'I may be a bit stiff-legged. But, considering what happened to the civilians nearer to the bomb, I'm not complaining. Okay, that's me. What about you?'

'I'm fine.'

'Hattie…'

'Okay, I get pains in my side sometimes,' she said, driven against the ropes. 'But I'm not telling you why.'

'Women's troubles?' he said cautiously, and she smiled despite herself. He'd said it in just the way he might have said: *detonating bomb.*

'That's right.'

'So you'll be better tomorrow?'

'Most likely.' As if. But to stop it… The next step seemed so final. So appalling.

'Hattie, what is it?' he asked gently, and she stared at him and read the concern in his gentle probing eyes and she felt like weeping.

Yeah, like *that* was going to happen. This man was the parent of one of her charges, and that was all. She needed professional distance.

'Sorry,' she said, snapping out of it and brushing a cobweb off her windcheater with care. 'I was away with the fairies. I need to talk to a couple of the other house mothers about some planning issues. I'll meet you back here at three, and we'll walk to the school together. That is, if you'd like…?'

'*After* we've had some lunch,' he said, firmly but gently. 'I'm not going to probe into your women's issues. I'm not going to probe anywhere I'm not wanted. But I *will* take you down to the pub, which I had the forethought to check out yesterday. They have rump steak on the menu, and I'd kill for a cold beer. And champagne for you.'

'A sandwich is fine—'

'For a snack. But you're a grown woman with a sore side, and I'm a grown man with an injured leg, and both those things need iron. I read that somewhere. Women's troubles equals lack of iron equals red meat.'

'You watch too much television. Mike…?'

'Yes?'

'I don't want to have a steak.'

'Now, that's a porkie,' he said, still in that gentle voice that had the power to unnerve her completely. 'The moment I said steak something lit up in the back of your eyes and it's stayed sparking. I bet you hardly ever make steak for the kids.'

'No, but…'

'Then it's me. You don't want to have steak with me. Because you're worried about me? That I might over-step the bounds of professional?'

'Yes, there's—'

'Hattie, Kyle needs continuity. We both know that. Wherever he ends up, I hope he can stay in contact with you.'

'Yes, but—'

'Then we need to get to know each other,' he said. 'As friends. Agreed?'

'Yes, but it doesn't feel like friends,' she said, sounding a bit desperate.

He nodded. Thoughtful. 'You're right,' he conceded. 'It doesn't. So we need to work on it. Starting with steak. And then you can go see your fellow house moms and I'll put my leg up for a bit—but you won't knock me back because of dumb scruples. Will you?'

'I…'

'Dumb scruples, Hattie.'

'Fine,' she said, and threw her hands in the air. 'Fine, fine, fine. You just don't know Bay Beach. Two minutes after I enter the pub with you it'll be all over town.'

'You take notice of gossip?'

'No,' she said, giving up altogether. 'I'm above gossip. In my dreams.'

But in the end it was great. Having made the decision to eat with him, it was as if she'd also decided to let her guard down.

They went to the big old seafront pub. The place was almost deserted. They slid into a wainscoted booth full of saggy cushions, and the bartender greeted Hattie with easy camaraderie. He brought them champagne and beer, followed by the biggest steaks Mike had ever seen, and then he left them to it.

Hattie was tense as hell, so Mike patiently asked the

dumb getting-to-know-you questions he'd learned from
being a guy in strange places all his life.

'Tell me about the town. How many people live here?
What's your favourite place? What's the best food round
here? Tell me about your family.'

The questions were impersonal enough to make
nervous civilians relax a little, but he'd used the
same questions on dates. Most women gave carefully
thought-out answers, designed to show they thought *he*
was interesting—not the town, not their family.

Hattie did no such thing. She relaxed quickly, answering with passion, humour and high energy.

'This town drives me crazy,' she told him. 'I left here
when I was eighteen to do my nursing training and I
swore I'd never be back. But it's like a great sticky
magnet, luring me back, holding me in its clutches.'

'That sounds scary,' he said faintly.

'Scary is right,' she said darkly. 'See the barman?
He's currently dating my great-aunt. He's on the phone
now, and I'm betting it'll be to Aunty Gertie. Gertie will
ring my mother, and my mother will ring Mary and
Shanni, and Nick and Rob, and...'

'Your brothers and sisters?'

'I have three sisters, two brothers and their associated
partners. They're the local mayor, magistrate, police
sergeant, newsagent, kindergarten teacher, CWA
president—anything you name, they're it. It's a huge
support-cum-spy network that sometimes threatens to
overwhelm me. If you're still here next week you can
meet them. We're having one of our regular beach bar-
becues and it's family only—which means at least half
of Bay Beach is there. What about you?' she asked. 'Tell
me about your family.'

It wasn't supposed to work like that. He'd asked a question, she'd been enthusiastically honest, and now he was confronted with little choice.

'It's not exactly a big family.'

'Siblings?'

'No.'

Her face creased in sympathy. 'Your parents?' she asked, dropping her voice a notch, expecting bad news. 'Are they still around?'

'I have no idea.'

'You have no idea?'

'It sounds bad, doesn't it?' he said. 'But my father disappeared before I knew him, and my mother dumped me with my grandparents when I was six, and I pretty much haven't seen her since. There's always been money—my grandparents were wealthy—but my mother was a petted, indulged brat. Last time I heard she was in Thailand with someone I don't want to even think about meeting. Which suits her, as she's never been interested in keeping in contact with me.'

'Oh, Mike…'

'It's cool,' he said coolly. 'My grandmother looked after me very well.'

'She didn't cuddle you,' Hattie said hotly, and then blushed, all the way up. He gazed at her, fascinated, as she fought desperately to get her composure back. It was almost worth telling his family secrets, he thought, to get a gorgeous reaction like that.

'Sorry,' she said, and gulped a mouthful of her champagne too fast and choked. Badly. He grinned and got up, and thumped her between her shoulderblades.

Her reaction was interesting, to say the least. She held up her hands in surrender, then subsided, sliding down the chair until she was on the floor under the table, completing her cough in relative privacy. When he bent to check she wasn't dying, she glared and choked some more.

'Men,' she managed at last. 'My brothers just love that, too. One mouthful of champagne goes down the wrong way and it's into the Heimlich manoeuvre.'

'You're gorgeous.'

She choked some more, and backed further under the table.

'Hey, is he bothering you?' the barman called, and wandered over to see what was happening. He stood above the table with Mike, the two of them a picture of solidarity in male concern. 'Come on out and I'll thump your back,' he offered.

'She doesn't like having her back thumped,' Mike said.

'She's a very definite lady, our Hattie,' the barman said. 'All the McDonald girls are. You should meet her aunt. You thinking of dating her? You'll have your hands full.'

'I'm one of her kids' parents,' Mike said. 'I can hardly date her.'

'Yeah, well, I'm not even going to think about interfering in that relationship,' the barman said. 'The families she sorts are legion. You want a glass of water, Hat?'

'No. Go away.'

Mike strode over to the bar, filled a glass of water and carried it solicitously over to her. He stooped down and handed it over.

'I'm fine,' she spluttered.

'And not even pink,' he agreed. 'Or not as pink as you were a minute ago.'

'Mike? Just back off.'

'I have,' he said, and stood up again. And watched her drink her water. And thought…

He thought: things are changing here, very fast. And he wasn't in the least sure which way was up any more.

Because looking down at her made him feel odd. Protective and…well, just odd. She was gorgeous, but she used no arts to attract. She was treating him as she must treat her brothers. She didn't seem the least bit…well, interested.

But she'd blushed, and now she was refusing to look him in the eye. She had him entranced, and it was a long time since Mike Standford had been entranced.

He watched her sip her water and thought he was enjoying the sensation more than he'd enjoyed anything for a long time.

'I have to go,' she said at last, hauling herself out from under the table, refusing his proffered hand and thumping her glass on the table. She turned to the barman. 'And you destroy that security footage. I only had one glass of champagne and "House Mother on Pub Floor" is not a good look. Thank you for lunch,' she said politely to Mike. 'I'll see you at school time.'

'You don't want coffee?'

'I don't want anything,' she said, too forcefully, and then fought back mounting colour again. 'Nothing,' she reiterated. 'Nothing, nothing, nothing. Except to get my composure back. I'll see you when the kids are out of school and not before.'

She stomped out of the pub, leaving Mike and the barman looking after her.

'Tetchy,' Mike said cautiously, and the barman grinned.

'A woman with spirit. Don't mess with her.'

'I won't,' Mike promised, but then thought, maybe, just maybe, messing with Harriet McDonald might be a whole lot of fun.

CHAPTER FIVE

HAVING fun with Hattie wasn't on the agenda. What followed were three quiet days—days when Hattie treated Mike with extreme caution. It was as if her outburst about cuddles and her own overreaction had sent alarm bells ringing and she wasn't about to ignore them.

She treated him with warmth and friendliness, but when he came into a room she found a reason why she needed to go out. After meals she'd apologise and say she had work to do, then wait politely for him to return to his allocated space.

He was here for a reason, and she wasn't about to let him change that reason.

So she was purely professional. She encouraged him to spend as much time as he wanted with Kyle, actively approving Mike's tentative ventures into forming a friendship with his small son.

At least that was working. Kyle was relaxing, little by little. The excitement of being at school helped break the ice—every afternoon he came home full of things to tell, and if Hattie was listening to the other kids then he'd turn naturally to Mike.

Which Mike thought was great. To have this small

person entrusting him with confidences was nothing short of amazing. In truth, it filled something inside him that he'd never realised had been empty. It was… humbling.

And this was what he was here for, he told himself. This was why he'd come. It might even be okay. It was good that he was focusing on his relationship with Kyle to the exclusion of everything else.

But there was always Hattie. She had him fascinated. He wanted to know more of her.

For Kyle's sake, he told himself. But he knew in his heart it was no such thing.

What the hell was he getting into? It was crazy to even think about getting to know Hattie better, but as he saw her taking care of this odd assortment of waifs and strays he found himself in increasingly unfamiliar emotional territory.

But she wasn't the least bit encouraging. In fact, she was downright discouraging. After that one day of housework—that one pub meal—she was back to being professional.

And then, on Friday night, Katy's mother came.

It was Katy Mike knew least about.

He had the kids almost worked out. Hattie wasn't supposed to discuss her charges' backgrounds, but he'd been in the house for almost a week now, and he knew most of it. Robbie's mother was in rehab, and was hoping to be out in a week or two. Hattie thought he'd be okay. His mother was really trying.

Erin's mother was in jail for drug-trafficking. Erin had been mistreated by an abusive stepfather, but he was now out of the picture. Her mother had twelve months of her term to go, so by rights Erin should be in long-term foster care, but there was an aunt who was tentatively trying to reorganise her life to include a niece she was clearly fond of. The aunt was getting more and more involved, and Hattie was encouraging the relationship all she could. Any contact with the family was to be valued, so that was why she was in this short-term facility.

But Katy…

'Her parents are dysfunctional,' was all Hattie would say. The little girl was a cheerful imp, almost too social, ready to be friends with anyone. In the short time he'd known her Mike had found himself charmed. And also…strangely he'd almost recognised her. Katy had developed a sort of armour, he thought, an armour not dissimilar to his own. She got on with her life and didn't let anything upset her.

On Friday night they'd just finished dinner when they heard a car pulling up outside. It had a hole in its muffler, Mike thought, and when Hattie opened the front door and he saw past her to the car he thought there was more than just a hole in the muffler. The car looked a complete rust bucket.

There was a couple on the doorstep. Aging hippies, he thought. Forty or so years old? Both had dreadlocks. The woman's dress was tatty, hanging down to her ankles. She was wearing a filthy old shawl. The guy was in tattered jeans and a windcheater that was far too small for him, and both had bare feet.

'We've come for Katy,' the woman said. Katy looked along the entrance hall from where she was sitting at the kitchen table and didn't say a thing.

'Hi, Katy,' the woman called, and Katy put her mug down with care.

'Hi, Mum.'

'Get your stuff, love,' the woman called. 'This is Gerry. He's taking us up to Nimbin. He really likes kids.'

'May, you need to come in and talk to me first,' Hattie said. 'You know the drill.'

'Yeah, I've got answers to all the questions,' May said, proudly. 'Me and Gerry did them this afternoon.'

'I need the proof, though,' Hattie said. She ushered them into the kitchen, where all four kids were watching. The expression on Katy's face was exactly the same as all of them.

'Mike, can you take the kids into the living room?' Hattie said. 'Put on a video. I won't be long.'

'Sure,' he said, and rose. The kids rose with him. They obviously knew the drill, too.

'Get your stuff, Katy,' May said.

'Hattie will fix my suitcase like she always does,' Katy said with quiet dignity. 'I'll watch videos while I wait.'

Half an hour later they went.

They drove off into the sunset, and Hattie watched them go with a face that showed no expression. Mike watched her from the window of his bedroom. He listened as she came inside and gathered the other kids and sent them to bed. She did the bedtime stories for all of them. He'd been reading to Kyle each night, but some sixth sense told him to stay back now.

Usually after the kids were in bed Hattie went straight into clean-up mode. Mike would hear her clattering in the kitchen. Usually she'd put music on, and often she'd hum along or even sing.

But tonight there was deathly silence. Nothing and nothing and nothing.

It wasn't his place to enquire. He was just a parent, he told himself. He was one of her responsibilities—like the little family that had just left.

He couldn't bear it. He walked out to the kitchen.

She was sitting at the table, her head down on her arms. Her bright curls were sprawled out over the table. Her shoulders were slumped in an attitude of total defeat.

'Hattie?' he said cautiously. She lifted her head and her face was streaked with tears.

'Hattie,' he said again, and before he knew what he'd intended himself, he'd hauled up a chair beside her, tugged her to him and was holding her.

She held herself rigid for all of ten seconds—and then she let herself slump into his arms. She sobbed, but he couldn't hear her sob. To sob aloud in this place would be to disturb and frighten the children. She was a professional. Her sobs were rigidly contained, not at any level permitted to be heard. He had the feeling that if a child appeared at the door she'd be in control in seconds, wiping her eyes, blaming hayfever, desperate to allow their world to be undisturbed.

But *her* world was disturbed. Dreadfully.

'Katy?' he said cautiously. He wanted, quite desperately, to put her back from him, push the curls from her face and kiss her. It was an illogical, irrational longing that he had to subdue, for he knew that to do such a thing right now would drive her right back into her solitary grief.

'I shouldn't tell you…'

'Then don't,' he told her, and he held her some more, forcing himself to give her all the time she needed. It was a reward in itself—to be allowed to hold her.

Five minutes. Ten. He didn't know. He didn't care. He simply held her and let her take her own time to recover.

And finally she did, pulling away, swiping a fist angrily across her eyes, standing up and crossing to the stove.

'Sorry. Thanks. I don't know what…'

'If you want to tell me it won't go further,' he said mildly, and waited.

'Tea,' she said fiercely. 'I need a cup of tea.'

'Not a whisky?'

'Don't tempt me. I'm on duty.'

'Okay, let's both be on duty and have tea,' he agreed.

'You can have whisky.'

'I don't need it.'

'You don't love Katy.'

'I've only known her for a week.'

'I've known her for three years,' she said. 'We all have. Her mother is an irresponsible fruitcake. She goes from man to man, and every time she finds someone new she fancies playing happy families. So back she comes and collects Katy. And every time it's a disaster. The dumb thing is that every time we get her back she's a bit more self-contained. She's bright as a button, and she's learning how to defend herself. She's six going on eighteen. Here she lets her guard down, just a little, but she's doing that less and less.'

'So she won't be looked after?'

'For a while,' she said soberly. 'May always has the right answers for the conditions she has to fulfil to take her away. So she'll have a little money and a place of residence, and she's promised that Katy will go to school. But it'll fall apart in weeks. I've packed Katy's gear, and I've packed the bottom of her duffel tight with a few supplies. She'll use them if May gets too stoned to remember to feed her. She also knows that there's a prepaid mobile phone under the lining. I bought that with my own money last time she went, and she can use it in an emergency to ring us. We'll collect her and bring her back. Maybe here. Or maybe to somewhere in Queensland or Western Australia or wherever May's latest whim takes her. But she's not safe.'

The last words were said on a note of desperation, and Mike rose and took her into his arms again, just because he couldn't bear not to.

'How do you do this?' he asked wonderingly, running his fingers through the silkiness of her curls. He wanted so badly to kiss her that it was a physical pain not to. 'Put yourself through this over and over again. Why?'

'Because I have to believe I make a difference,' she whispered.

'You're a trained nurse. You don't think nursing would be easier?'

'Of course it would be easier. But these kids…'

'Are tearing you apart,' he said, still holding her close. 'You can't keep doing this for ever.'

'I don't have a choice.'

'Maybe you do,' he said cautiously, the idea that had been floating nebulously at the edges of his thoughts crystallising into a solid form. 'Maybe I can offer you an alternative.'

'Like what?' He heard the catch in her voice as she realised that she'd gone well past the boundaries of where she was supposed to be. She tugged back from him, and he released her with real regret.

'Have you ever been to the States?' he asked, and he watched as she grew even more confused.

'Pardon?'

'This is the wrong time to be asking,' he said ruefully. But then he looked at her ravaged face and thought, no, maybe it was the right time. This job was tearing her apart. A break might be just what she needed.

'Kyle is my son,' he said softly. 'But I'm based in the States. My job takes me away often, and I can't predict my absences. I've been trying to figure how I can fit Kyle into my life.'

'You want to fit him round the edges?' she asked, in a strange little whisper, and he knew that he didn't have this right. But then he wasn't sure what right *was* in this equation. He was flying in the dark, hoping like hell he could land safely.

'If I had an extended family it would be easy,' he said, trying to sound logical. 'But there's no one. And Kyle needs permanence. Even I can see that.'

'That's good,' she said, still in that strange little voice.

'I was wondering if I could employ you.'

'As?'

'As his nanny.'

'His nanny?'

'Nannies brought me up,' he said. 'I know it's not great, but it's the best I have to offer. And I will be around.'

'When you're not out saving the world.'

'My job's important,' he said.

'As is mine.'

'Yes, but you love Kyle,' he reasoned. 'I've been watching you with him. You try so hard to treat him as you treat the others, but when you look at him… Hattie, what would have happened to Kyle if I hadn't appeared?'

'He might have been adopted,' she admitted. Softly, as if the words hurt. He could still hear the ache of tears in her voice and it was enough to make him falter.

'Veronica said you've been caring for him off and on almost since birth. She says he loves you.'

'Veronica talks too much.'

'Would you have been permitted to adopt him?'

'Maybe—yes,' she whispered. 'Because of that relationship.'

And because of a lot of things, she thought. Adoption by single parents was generally frowned on, but there were extenuating circumstances here. Many, many circumstances.

'I do want him to come back to the States,' he said, frowning, thinking it through as he spoke. 'I need him to be where I can see him whenever I'm off duty.'

'Of course you do,' she agreed. She had herself under control again now. Outwardly at least. 'There's never been a question of me adopting Kyle since we knew he had a father. You have absolute rights.'

'Like May?'

'Like May,' she said, trying hard to keep her voice steady. 'But I hope you'll use them more wisely. And if you're offering me a job—'

'I want you to listen,' he said, before she could continue. She was all set to refuse and he couldn't bear that she would—for her sake, as well as for Kyle's. And maybe even for his. 'Hattie, my family is old money. My grandparents left everything they had to me. I own a big place on the east coast that hasn't been used for years. It's right on the beach, in one of the loveliest little towns in the country. You and Kyle would be happy there,' he said. 'Gloriously happy. It's the most fabulous house…'

'Better than this?' she demanded, astounded.

He looked round at the battered kitchen, at the

stained bench-tops, the ripped linoleum, the signs of constant occupancy by kids whose behaviour patterns didn't fit with *Vogue Interiors*.

'Much better than this,' he said. And it was the wrong thing to say. He saw the wash of anger and thought, *uh-oh*.

'How better?' she snapped. 'Better than comfy beds and a mother figure only just down the hall? Better than a little village school and knowing every kid in town? Better than having my parents and my siblings here as back-up family, as they're back-up family—to these kids, as well as to me? Better than…what? What would my role be there? Live in a great mausoleum of a place, fall deeper and deeper in love with Kyle, fill my time while he's at school polishing your possessions, being polite to you and standing back when you deign to visit Kyle a couple of times a year. And then one day you'll meet and marry the woman of your dreams and there I'll be as part of the furniture—the nanny—or maybe you won't want me at all, and the heartbreak will be there, just the same, hanging over me day after day.'

'I won't get married,' he said, and that was the wrong thing to say, too.

'Yeah, it's exactly the same,' she said, scornful. 'Of course you won't. You've been hit by the same tragedy that every one of my kids is facing right now. So your answer to that is to be fiercely independent for ever more. And you'll teach Kyle to be the same. You'll stick him in your wonderful house with a *nanny*.'

She said *nanny* with such scorn that he flinched.

'Hattie, it's what you are,' he said, trying to figure it out. And she nodded.

'Yes, it is. Why do you think I waved goodbye to

Katy just now? Because parents are better. Even bad parents. Even dippy parents. As long as there's love there…You know, there's just a chance May will work this out. That she'll wake up one morning and figure she's stuffed up with her daughter too much and she'd better do something about it. Over and over the re-search says that parents are best. It's worth taking risk after risk to get it right. That's why as soon as we knew Kyle had a dad who'd take responsibility there was no way I could ever adopt him. Kyle's yours, Mike. And, no, you're not employing me to absolve you from care.'

'I never meant…'

'You don't know what you mean,' she said wearily. 'Neither does May. But you have your son lying in bed down the hall and you're his father, and, no, I'm not the answer for you. Yeah, I'm tired of this job—bone-weary from all the goodbyes, from all the trust I have to give, warranted or not. But sticking me in a beach house in America while you go off and save the world isn't an answer for me and it isn't an answer for Kyle. Keep thinking. Meanwhile, I'm sorry I wept on you. You were in the wrong place at the wrong time. Now, if you'll excuse me, I'm going to bed.'

'You haven't had your tea,' he said helplessly.

She told him what he should do with his tea.

Yeah, well, he'd stuffed that up. Mike lay in bed and stared at the ceiling. There was no way sleep would come. He felt…pierced.

There had been scorn in her eyes as she'd responded to his invitation. As if he didn't have a clue and he was being criminally negligent in his proposals for Kyle.

Hell, it was better than what May was proposing for Katy.

Katy.

He'd only known the little girl for six days, but even so… The thought of her sitting in the back of a clapped-out sedan heading for heaven knew where, with her bag full of cookies and an emergency phone secreted in the lining, made him feel sick. He felt like he'd felt when he'd looked at that little girl in the hospital six months ago.

This is what happens when you get involved, he told himself. He knew that. Hell, of course he knew that.

He coped with the big picture. His work was to try with all his might to prevent the worst of war's atrocities—to give the big guns of this world pause when they were considering the little people, to let them know that consequences would ensue even ten, twenty years after.

It was desperately important work. He couldn't afford to be deflected by the little people themselves.

He didn't even know her name, he thought savagely. The little girl in the cot…

Hattie would love her. Hattie would know how to make that blank look go away.

Hell. He got up and walked to the window.

Hattie was out there, on the kids' swing under the big tree. Not swinging. Just sitting, staring out at the night.

She was so alone. She was breaking her heart.

He could…

No.

The night closed in on him. He couldn't, and he knew he couldn't. Go out and take her in his arms as he so desperately wanted? Hold her close and comfort her?

She wouldn't be comforted. He was one of her parents, one of the many to be reunited with their kids and then sent on their way.

She was staring down the road as if she could still see the tail-lights of Katy's car.

How could he say his work was more important than hers?

Maybe he could just…?

No.

The barriers were too strong. Too carefully built up over too many years.

Katy would do the same thing as he, if she survived, he thought, and he wondered whether he should go out and tell Hattie that. *Katy will be fine. She's a smart little girl. She'll figure out the armour thing.*

He'd watched Katy's face as she walked out through the door and he'd recognised his own. As he'd said goodbye to yet another nanny. As he'd…

No matter. That was in the past. He was fine, as Katy would be fine.

But Hattie wouldn't be comforted if he told her. He knew that.

She'd scorn what he'd achieved.

Independence.

He closed his eyes. Enough. *Enough.*

But he couldn't go to bed yet. On impulse he walked into Kyle's bedroom and stood looking down at him in the moonlight. This child who was dependent on him. His son.

He felt a light touch on his shoulder and it was Hattie.

'He needs you,' she whispered. 'Only you. His dad. Goodnight, Mike. But while you sleep…see if you can let yourself fall in love.'

CHAPTER SIX

Two days later Fiona arrived with her suitcase. Fiona was nine years old, smart, street-savvy and cheerful. She knew the ropes—as Mike was starting to realise most of these kids knew the ropes. But Fiona was what Hattie described as *stable*. Her mother had coeliac disease. Every now and then she needed to be hospitalised for a few days, and there was no one to take Fiona.

'Fiona could probably look after herself,' Hattie told Mike as they washed up after dinner. It was almost routine now—she'd admitted him into her life this far, but no farther. Still, he was content enough. It was time out from his high-stress life, and, strangely, it seemed more and more something he'd desperately needed. Washing dishes…a normal life.

'She's too young at nine,' Mike said, thinking of Fiona's cheerful bossiness at dinner. As the oldest, she'd gone straight into organisational mode, and Hattie had simply watched her with bemusement and a certain amount of enjoyment.

'Her mother is pretty much incapacitated,' Hattie said. 'Fiona was born bossy, and I reckon she started organising her mum when she was about two. You should see them together. They're great.'

'Like Kyle and Leslie?' Mike asked cautiously, and Hattie shook her head.

'Chalk and cheese. Oh, Leslie loved Kyle in her own distracted way, but she'd never put Kyle's needs above her own. Leslie had the choice to look after her diabetes and she refused, even though it meant Kyle ended up not having a mother. May…I'm not sure she's even capable of caring. But even though Fiona's mum is too ill to look after Fiona properly she loves her to bits, and Fiona knows that. That's why she's happy tonight. She knows why she's here, and she knows her place in the world. Even Robbie and Erin…they both have hopeless mothers in the eyes of some, but they're loved. In the end that's all that matters. Money…nannies…physical care…yeah, okay, they're important but they don't count for anything if there's not love behind them.'

'Can I ask you something personal?' he said cautiously, concentrating on wiping a fry-pan.

'I reserve the right not to answer. But go ahead.'

'Why aren't you married?' he asked. 'You're what? Thirty? You live in a little town where marriage is the norm. You love kids. Why—?'

'I was engaged once,' she said shortly, before he could take it any further. 'It didn't work out.'

'And there's no one else to marry?'

'Why would I marry?' She handed him a washed jug, frowned at the soapsuds she'd left on the lip and took it back again. 'Do you think I should?'

'No, but…'

'You do.' She let out the water and started washing down the sink. It was weird domestic stuff to be doing while such a conversation was being played out, but it worked, distancing them enough so they could continue. 'So why aren't *you* married?

'I never wanted to be married.'

'Because of your background?'

'I guess.'

'But you have girlfriends, right?'

'I move around a lot,' he said uneasily. 'But, yeah…'

'I was just checking you weren't gay,' she said, and he grinned and some of the tension eased.

'Not gay.'

'That's good for Kyle.'

'Would it have made a difference?'

'To how we'd react to you? No. A father is a father is a father.'

She said it with a snap of finality and tossed down her dishcloth.

'Wouldn't you like your own kids?' he asked.

There was no disguising the pain on her face at that. It was as if he'd physically hit her. She put her hands behind her on the bench, holding on, gripping, gathering herself.

'Hattie, I didn't—'

'Leave it,' she whispered. 'Leave it, Mike. I'd love my own kids more than anything in the world, but it's not going to happen. Now, if you don't mind, I have school lunches to make. Can I ask that you return to your own quarters?'

He thought about it. He thought about it over and over again as the days wore on. As Kyle grew accustomed to him, started liking him, started relaxing with him, started talking to him with the ease of friends.

He was here to do this—to establish a relationship with his son before he left—but there was more in his head now than the prospect of taking his son back to the States.

Hattie had knocked back his job offer. Yeah, but she couldn't keep doing this for ever. He watched her face when she didn't think he was watching. He watched her interact with the kids. On the surface she was laughing and bubbly and bossy—a loving house mum. Inside… Maybe it was because he recognised the same strain he'd been under himself. He could attribute the strain to war-time horror, but what Hattie was doing… throwing her heart into the ring over and over and letting it come out bruised and battered, collecting it together and then tossing it into the ring again… It had to end.

How…? How…?

On the Friday night of the second week he went to the beach barbecue with the McDonalds. As Hattie had told him it was a weekly event, cancelled the first Friday because it had dared to rain. But this Friday was fine, so off they went to the beach. Hattie, Robbie, Erin, Fiona, Kyle and Mike.

He'd been reluctant to impose on what was obviously a family party, but the kids would have none of it.

'Everyone comes,' Kyle said. 'Everyone and everyone and everyone. And Grandma McDonald says a friend of yours is a friend of mine, and she laughs and puts more sausages on the barbecue.'

'Grandma McDonald?'

'My mum,' Hattie said, colouring. 'Yes, you'll be welcome.'

'Do you want me to come?' he asked.

'Kyle wants you to come,' she said. 'He's invited you, and that's what matters. Of course you'll be welcome.'

So he went, feeling like an intruder, knowing Hattie would be much more comfortable if he wasn't there. He'd messed it up by offering the job. They'd been starting an embryonic friendship and he missed it.

Or if he had to be honest it wasn't exactly an embryonic friendship. On his part it was a fierce, mind-blowing attraction, and maybe she sensed that. Maybe she scorned the fact that he was taking this thing he was feeling and calmly offering her a nanny job.

She wasn't saying, but the way she looked at him… It was with caution now. She was wary and she was hurt.

He'd added to the strain behind her eyes.

Still, there was little he could do about that this night. He helped load the van with the kids' beach paraphernalia, and then helped unpack at the other end, and then he was suddenly in the middle of McDonald chaos.

'Mike.' His hand was gripped at least a dozen times. 'You're Kyle's dad. Welcome to Bay Beach. Have a beer.'

Hattie's father and her brothers were big men, cheerful, open-faced—the kind of men he'd want in a tight situation, he thought, and he wasn't surprised when he found one brother was a cop and her dad and the second brother were farmers.

'Hey, Kyle's dad.' Women were pressing food on him, smiling at him with smiles that matched Hattie's, drawing him into their circle with unmitigated friendliness.

The kids melted into the bunch of McDonald kids, eating, whooping, heading into the sea, while the adults watched with obvious tolerant affection. One adult was the designated life guard—a yellow and red hat was passed around, and whoever was wearing it at the time was responsible for not taking his eyes off the kids in the surf.

But there were so many adults that their job was never onerous—it was passed on after ten minutes or so to the next adult who happened to look sandwich- or beer-free.

Hattie was in her element. She had kids around her from the time she arrived, and she took her family's kids under her wing as easily as she took the foster kids. She had them making sandcastles, competing for the tallest, the neatest, the prettiest, helping the littlies, cheating when cheating helped. She had them swimming races, swimming with them, diving underneath the water, surfacing under the tummies of those in the lead, making them squeal with delight. She and a gangly adolescent with a slight limp—a kid named Harry—seemed to be in cahoots, between them making sure everyone was in fits of laughter.

Harry surfaced under Hattie when she least expected it and the entire family dissolved as she spluttered and coughed and giggled.

'She's a kid,' Mike said softly, wonderingly, and it was Janet, Hattie's mother, who was standing beside him and heard the comment.

'Do you really think that?' she asked, curious.

'I guess I don't.' No, he didn't. Not when Hattie was wearing her fabulous swimsuit and looked a million dollars. Not when her eyes were dancing with wicked laughter, when her curls were dripping wetly around her face, when she was lifting Kyle and whirling him round and round before launching him towards the shore on a shallow wave.

A kid? Maybe, yes. But all woman, as well.

'She's been like this ever since she was tiny,' Janet said, handing him a lamington. 'Bossy, happy, funny, loving. Our Hattie.'

It was said with a tinge of sadness, and he glanced down and saw that sadness compounded on Janet's face.

'So why the sadness?' he asked.

She winced. 'Sorry. That's… I didn't mean…'

'To sound sad? Okay—but you did. I know it's none of my business, but I'd like to know. Why are you looking at your daughter feeling sad?'

'She's breaking her heart over Kyle,' Janet said honestly. 'He came to her…well, at a bad time. She's had it rough, my Hattie, for all she puts a brave face on it.'

'She said she'd had a broken engagement.'

'Did she tell you that?' Janet said wonderingly. 'Usually she doesn't say that much. She bottles up her problems, my baby daughter.' She sighed, but then shrugged. 'Sorry. She'd hate it if she knew I was talking about her. And there's no way she'll ever let what she feels for Kyle influence what she's doing now. Which is passing over responsibility to where it really lies. It's a wonder she's not pulling you in to be with Kyle now.'

As if on cue, there was a yell from the water.

'Mike! Surely you should be finished your dinner by now? Kyle wants to show you how he can do a handstand under water.'

'You see,' Janet said, almost to herself. 'She'll stand back and let other people do the loving. Over and over. She breaks my heart.'

'Why doesn't she have her own family?' Mike said, frowning, ignoring Hattie's call for the moment.

Janet shook her head. 'I doubt…'

'Mike.' Two women approached from the sidelines. Two McDonald women. He'd been introduced to Hattie's sisters—these two were Mary and Shanni.

Shanni was carrying a toddler, and Mary was tossing orders over her shoulder to adolescent twins.

'Yeah?'

The women looked at each other. 'You ask him,' Shanni said. 'It was your idea.'

'Nope,' Mary said. 'You're the bossy one.'

'Right,' Shanni said, and sighed. 'I'm always the patsy in this family. Mike, we've been talking. You're over from the States for a month while you get to know Kyle. Right?'

'Right,' he said, cautious.

'But you're hardly seeing anything stuck in town. So we had an idea.'

'Blakes,' Shanni said, sounding breathless, and beside him Janet gasped. 'We're paying for the two of you to go to Blakes.'

'Blakes? Are you out of your minds?' Janet demanded.

'No,' Shanni told her. 'We've just done a whip-round, and Mary rang Blake in person, and there's one table available tomorrow night. Blake's going to see that they get the best one there, and Mary and I are babysitting.'

'Whoa,' Mike said, confused. 'What the hell is Blakes?'

'It's the classiest restaurant in Australia,' Janet said, sounding bemused. 'It costs a mint. It's half an hour's drive north of here. They have their own heliport, so the wealthy can pop in for pre-dinner drinks.'

'And it's just what Hattie needs to cheer her up.'

'Nothing's going to cheer Hattie up,' Janet said, and they all four turned to look at Hattie, who was engaged in a splashing war in the shallows.

She looked joyous. But these women said she needed cheering up. Mike himself was starting to figure there was a whole lot going on under the surface he didn't have a clue about.

'Do you think she'll go with me?' he asked dubiously, and then thought, hell, did he *want* to take her out to dinner? But suddenly the thought of taking her out, taking her away from the kids, sitting at a restaurant and being able to talk to her—really talk—was irresistibly appealing.

'It's already paid for,' Mary said. 'Nick gave Blake his credit card number.'

'No,' Mike said, revolted. 'If we go, I'm paying.'

'She won't go, then,' Shanni said bluntly. 'But if she thinks we've spent our hard-earned cash…'

'Why won't she go with me?'

Shanni and Mary exchanged sisterly glances.

'No,' Janet said, suddenly forceful. 'You're not to betray your sister's confidences.'

'Okay, we won't,' Mary said regretfully. 'But the boys tell us you're okay—our boys can suss character at a hundred yards. You look hunky. We bet you dress up a treat. And the last time Hattie got to sit in a classy restaurant with a hunky guy was about a hundred years ago. So I'm going to tell her. Hattie, love! Guess who's taking you to dinner tomorrow night?'

What the McDonalds wanted as a family, the McDonalds got. If the powers for good had this family available to them in the Middle East they might well achieve world peace, Mike thought, stunned, as he watched them destroy systematically every single one of Hattie's objections.

'It's already paid for. Aunty Eva put in ten dollars. Ten dollars, Hattie! You're not going to look a gift horse like that in the mouth. And Harry wants to read Kyle his bedtime story. You can't deny him that when Kyle's leaving.'

He had it figured now—sort of. Harry was another Bay Beach waif and stray, but he'd been adopted by one of Hattie's sisters and her husband when he was little more than a toddler. Waifs and strays were a family speciality, it seemed.

And so was bulldozing.

'I don't want to go out with Mike,' Hattie wailed, and she was met with hoots of derision from the entire family.

'A free meal at Blakes? An excuse to frock up? Does the man have a beer gut and bad breath? Hattie, we've promised Mike. We've told the kids what's happening. Say thank you very much, and go.'

She had no choice. But as they all drove home that night she looked tense. And she was really, really quiet.

'We could always tell them we went and go find a picture theatre,' he said, but didn't elicit a smile.

'They'll ask Blake. We have to go.'

'Will it be so bad?'

'They don't know what they're playing at,' she snapped. She shook her head. 'No. They do. But, oh, I wish they wouldn't.'

He almost had the perfect excuse. When they arrived home from the beach there was a message on his cell phone.

'Gray's flying in for a meeting of the combined heads in Canberra. He needs a couple of hours' briefing. Can you do it?' his boss asked when Mike rang him back.

'Sure.'

'So the break's doing you good? Things are getting back to normal? Great news, Mike. You're missed. I'll send the chopper at nine.'

He went to find Hattie. She was sorting washing. What the hell was sexy about a woman sorting washing?

.Everything was sexy about Hattie. He just had to look at her and…

And, hell. *'Things are getting back to normal?'* he'd just been asked. What was normal about this situation? His son?

This woman?

'I need to go to Canberra tomorrow,' he said, and watched the flicker of hope quickly disguised.

'I… That's fine.'

'It means…'

'Don't worry about tomorrow night,' she told him. 'I'll tell Shanni and Mary to cancel.'

'I'll be back in time,' he said gently. 'They're sending a chopper for me. They'll fly me there and back.'

'A chopper?' She set down the pile of clothes and turned to face him. Awed. 'You must be important.'

'Some of what I know is important.'

'Have you been off work since you hurt your leg?' she asked cautiously.

'I went back three months ago.'

'But it didn't work out?'

'I guess I wasn't as recovered as I thought.'

'Head-wise? she said, and nodded. She'd composed herself now and was sorting socks. 'It's a hell of a world out there. But you'll be tired when you get back tomorrow. The last thing you'll want is to come out with me.'

'The first thing I'll want is to come out with you,' he said, before he could stop himself, and her hands stilled on her socks.

'Mike, don't,' she whispered.

'Don't what?'

'Don't push. Don't make me…' She faltered, and then she glared. 'No. I'm not going down that road.'

'Hattie, let's try it and see,' he said urgently, before she could go further. 'Like you, I don't think I want… what seems to be happening between us. I've surely never wanted it in the past. But suddenly…'

'You feel it, too?' She met his gaze wonderingly, and he wanted to gather her to him and hug her, socks and all.

'I'd be inhuman if I didn't feel it.'

'It can't go anywhere.'

'We might—'

'We mightn't.'

'Let's just see,' he told her. 'Let's just say thanks very much to your family for tomorrow night and go out for dinner like normal men and women do all the time. We might discover that I pick my teeth and belch and you tell rude jokes.'

'We might,' she said. Not sounding hopeful. 'But…'

'It's only for one night,' he said. 'We don't want to hurt your family.'

'That's blackmail.' She stared at him, perturbed, obviously torn.

'I'll be gone in a couple of weeks,' he said. 'You can get on with your life again.'

'There is that.'

'So tomorrow…?'

'Okay, I'll come,' she said, throwing her hands up in the air, and the socks with them. They dropped all round her and she let them fall. 'Just once. Just because my family is insistent and interfering and you'll only be here for two more weeks. But don't you dare talk about any…thing…between us, Mike Standford, or I'll be home again so fast you won't see me for dust. I don't want any…thing.'

'Neither do I,' he said, as she stomped off with her arms full of clean clothes. And then he added under his breath as he picked up the socks and followed her, 'But I think I've got it all the same.'

They sent a Black Hawk helicopter. It was the stuff of every small boy's dreams, and the girls weren't averse to being blown away by it, either. The chopper landed on the sports oval a block from the house. The kids insisted on escorting Mike—once more in full military uniform—to the chopper. Once there, Mike faced a small delay as there was a real and urgent need to give four kids a quick tour of Bay Beach by air.

He left soon after, disappearing into the northern sky, and Hattie was left with four awed, almost speechless kids. Robbie especially was too overwhelmed to speak. His small face shone.

'Mike says I can learn to fly when I grow up,' he breathed. 'If I get good at school work.'

'Then we'd better help you at your school work,' Hattie said, blessing Mike.

'He's my dad,' Kyle said, softly but proudly. And then louder. 'He's my dad.'

They walked slowly home. Mary was sitting on the front fence, waiting for her sister.

The kids took off with Mary's twins. The women were left in the front yard together.

'So he's just flown out of your life?' Mary commented. 'It was some exit.'

'He's coming back tonight.'

'I hoped you might say that.'

'He's not… I'm not…'

'You're falling in love,' Mary said softly. 'Well, why not? I always did fancy a man in uniform.'

'Mary, I can't.'

'Tell me why you can't.'

'He asked me to be his nanny.'

'That's clearly ridiculous. But you've moved on from there. I watched him watching you on the beach. He's not thinking of you as nanny material.'

'He doesn't want a wife.'

'Why not?'

'He comes from a hell of a family background.'

'Which is your speciality,' Mary said softly. 'Healing the soul.'

'I don't think he knows he's wounded.'

'Does he know *you're* wounded?' Mary said.

Silence. The kids were whooping inside. There was a bunch of pink galah birds in the big gumtree overhead, and their screeching was almost ear splitting. But it felt like silence to Hattie.

'I'm not going to tell him that,' she said at last.

'You might have to,' Mary said bluntly. 'You're going into hospital next month.'

'Yeah, but it's nobody's business except mine. And he'll be well away.'

'Hattie, it should be all of our business,' Mary said, and moved to give her a hug. 'We all love you so much. And Mike…he's gorgeous, Hattie. Let him close.'

'I can't help him…'

'Until you have yourself sorted. I understand that, but maybe by then it'll be too late.'

'It's too late anyway,' Hattie whispered.

'That doesn't sound very assertive,' Mary chided her. 'It's not a McDonald woman thing to say at all.'

'Sometimes I don't feel so tough,' Hattie confessed, and got another hug for her pains.

'Oh, love… So tonight…?'

'Nothing's going to happen. Thank you all for organising it. It will be lovely. We'll go out for dinner, and I'll enjoy myself a lot because I'm still girl enough to soak up dinner in a place like that with a man as gorgeous as Mike Standford. But it goes no further. He doesn't want it.'

'And you?'

'I don't want what I can't have,' she whispered. 'I'm getting good at it.'

CHAPTER SEVEN

MIKE was late.

By eight the kids were in bed. Shanni and Mary were ensconced in the living room with three rented movies, a vast box of chocolates and two bottles of wine.

Hattie was dressed. Not as she'd have liked to be dressed, in her nice, sensible black skirt and neat white blouse, made classier with her mother's pearls in honour of the restaurant's reputation. Shanni and Mary had taken one look at her, hooted in derision and gone through her wardrobe as if she had no rights at all.

She was now dressed in a jade-green silk dress—or almost a dress, Hattie thought, staring in the mirror in dismay. It was a tiny, curvy, clinging number, with shoe-string straps, a plunging neckline, and a slit up the side to allow her to move. Her sisters had had to fight to get the zip done up, as it clung to her body like a second skin.

'I've put on weight since I bought this,' she'd gasped. 'It's far too small.'

'I bet Mike doesn't think it's too small,' Mary had said, grinning. 'Just don't let him mess with that zip in the dark, 'cos once you've eaten dinner there's no way he'll ever get it done up again.'

'I can't wear it.'

'I'm not undoing the zip,' Mary had said smugly. 'What about you, Shanni? Are you undoing the zip? And there's no way you can reach, Hattie.'

'I hate my sisters.'

'No, you don't,' Shanni had said. 'You love us to bits. Just like Mike is going to when he sees you in this dress.'

Except he was late. It felt like first-date stuff, pacing the living room with her sisters watching, trying not to care, trying to tell herself this was a fine, social thing to be doing to keep her family happy.

And then he arrived, and it was worse than first-date stuff, for he opened the front door and she'd forgotten how drop-dead gorgeous he was.

He'd been wearing his uniform when he'd left this morning, but then he'd been surrounded by kids and excitement. Now, standing in the doorway, coming home to collect her and take her out to dinner, he simply took her breath away.

He was a big man, wide-shouldered, strong, weathered—how could a civil-rights lawyer be weathered? No matter. He might just as well be a combatant out in the field; he had that been-there-seen-things-he'd-probably-never-discuss sort of containment about him. Containment? Tension. Yeah, he was tense, she thought. And maybe she was, too. Okay, she definitely was tense. This was weird dating territory, and her sisters were appraising him with frank appreciation.

'Woohoo—he's a babe,' Shanni said. 'You reckon we ought to let our little sister go out with this guy?'

'A man in uniform,' Mary said dreamily. 'No. Hattie, you stay home. I'll take him out myself.'

'Down, girl,' Shanni said, laughing, and prodded

Hattie forward. 'Were you planning on getting changed, Mike? I only ask because Blakes doesn't take arrivals after nine.'

'I'm ready if you're ready,' Mike said, and smiled at Hattie. And everything melted, right there, right then.

It was the uniform, she thought desperately as she let him usher her out of the door. It was because he looked so big and so masculine, and he was so…so…

So Mike.

She'd blown his mind.

He'd opened the door and she'd been standing in the living room in her little green dress and he'd thought he'd never seen anything more beautiful in his life.

He'd intended to change. He'd intended to take a few minutes and say goodnight to Kyle.

But they were ushering him out through the door. Kyle was waving goodbye from the window; the other kids were hooting with excitement.

'Make them go to bed,' Hattie yelled to her sisters, but Shanni and Mary were standing on the front porch and weren't about to move until they left.

'Are you going to kiss her?' Robbie yelled, and the kids whooped with laughter as if Robbie had said something incredibly witty.

Mike thought it sounded pretty clever, too. It seemed a really good idea.

But not here. Not now. Not when she'd sunk into the passenger seat of his hire car and was staring straight ahead in disgust.

It behoved a man to tread warily.

But kissing…

Maybe. Maybe.

CHAPTER EIGHT

THEY drove to the restaurant in near silence. Hattie gave terse directions. Mike tried to think of light conversation and failed. They stared ahead at the highway and things were left unsaid all over the place.

Finally, almost as they arrived, Hattie broke the impasse.

'How was your day?' she tried.

'Dear?' he said, and regretted it almost immediately.

'Pardon?'

'You're supposed to say, How was your day, dear?'

'Over my dead body,' she said, and he grinned.

'So, have the children been well behaved?'

'No,' she said. 'And I'm not going to get your slippers for asking.'

'No?'

'No.'

'Good,' he said. 'I don't feel like slippers. I'm starving.'

'They didn't feed you?'

'A sandwich at midday.'

'You mustn't be very important after all.'

'I'm not.'

'But they sent a helicopter to get you.'

'Good training,' he said, and there was a spot of that silence again.

'You are on leave, though?' she said cautiously.

'This was urgent.'

'You want to talk about it?'

'I can't.'

'There's lots of your work you can't talk about.'

'Just lucky I'm not a great talker.'

'Right,' she said. 'That's put me in my place. Let's both shut up.'

They did. It was weird, he thought. It was a date and not a date. He should be relaxed—he was going to an excellent restaurant with a beautiful woman—and yet he felt stiff and worried and so intensely aware of her that he felt as if he was behaving like a gauche school-boy.

The meal would make it better, he thought. Please.

The restaurant certainly looked the deal. They were ushered into a vast room overlooking a moonlit sea. The place was at the edge of a biggish coastal town to the north of Bay Beach. There were yachts moored in the harbour, their swing lights illuminating the sea. The moonlight shimmered over the whole scene, brilliant in its beauty.

They were sat down by an officious waiter and offered champagne.

The chairs were stiffly upright. The linen was stiff and white, and the cutlery magnificently ornate silver.

There were couples all around them, magnificently dressed, deep in intimate conversations.

'Proposal city,' Hattie said, sounding a bit disparaging. 'How many velvet boxes can we spot?'

'So much for my plans for the night,' Mike said, and Hattie smiled.

'You'd have more sense. What is this, do you think?'

'French,' Mike said, looking at the menu.

'I'd like things to be a bit more specific,' Hattie said. 'French goat? French tofu?'

'I'll translate,' he said and did. And fifteen minutes later they were served an entrée which Hattie thought was small and Mike thought was minuscule.

'Just lucky I ordered steak for main course,' he said as the plates were cleared. This wasn't going well. Hattie was looking more and more tense as the night progressed.

The couple at the next table had a tiny velvet box as a centrepiece. They were holding hands over the table. They weren't seeing their food.

'I'll walk over and take their food from them if they don't eat it soon,' Mike growled. 'Hell, I'm starving. Your family doesn't own shares in this place, I hope?'

'I don't think any of them have been here,' Hattie said. 'They heard about it as *the* place to come and thought it'd be fun to send us here.'

'I'm grateful,' Mike said, but he still looked hungry, and when his main course was put in front of him his expression was almost ludicrous.

He was trying very hard to be polite. This meal was a gift. But...

He'd asked for prime beef steak. Waiguaru— supposedly one of the most magnificent steaks available anywhere in the world.

So it might be. But this... It was a piece of eye fillet, about three inches square, and not so thick as you'd notice. The salad surrounding it was gorgeous—if you were into flower arranging. There was a perfectly sculptured offering of what looked like butter on the centre of the steak, but it wasn't melting. It sat looking like…

'Like something you might see in an expensive art gallery,' Hattie said, giggling.

Her own offering was even more sparse. She'd ordered salmon. There weren't a lot of salmon laying down their lives in order to feed this restaurant tonight.

'I think it's nouvelle cuisine,' she said doubtfully, and Mike snorted.

'That crap went out with the eighties. This place is playing on its reputation. Look at these guys… They've all come for the night of a lifetime. They're paying a fortune.' He ate his steak in four mouthfuls, and then glowered and watched as Hattie finished her dinner— which took only about a minute longer.

'Okay,' he said. 'We're done. We can go back to your family and say thank you very much for the gift—it was magnificent. But what came after was better.'

'What came after?'

'Fish and chips on the beach,' he said, rising and holding out an imperious hand. 'I saw a place as we came into town and their sign said open until ten. We'll make it. Don't tell me you want to sit here any longer?'

'N-no.' Of course she didn't, but eating on the beach…

'I'm not about to ravish you,' he said, seeing her doubt. 'I'm too damned hungry.' He raised his voice. 'Excuse me, can someone bring the bill, please?' he asked, in a voice which was commanding and assured and carried right across the restaurant. 'My partner and I need to find somewhere to eat before we die of hunger.'

* * *

So they bought fish and chips—a lot of fish and chips—and drove down to the foreshore. There were tables and chairs right where grass met sand. The night was balmy and moonlit.

The restaurant had been lovely, but this was lovelier, Hattie thought, and the fish and chips tasted great.

'I can't believe you said that,' she said, as she finished her first piece of crunchy battered fish and eyed a scallop with intent. 'Criticising Blakes is like thumbing your nose at the Queen.'

'I'd never do that to Her Majesty,' Mike said, seriously. 'Her Majesty has served her country with distinction for eighty years. There's not a lot of distinguished service about that place. Have another scallop. I've had three already.'

'Yum,' she said, and did.

The silence was changing. The tension had somehow evaporated with the change in venue and with the truly excellent food they were now devouring. It felt good. Hattie felt good. More, she felt…right. He really was a gorgeous guy, she thought. He was a man of principle who acted as he saw fit. How many men would have had the courage to do what he'd done?

What else had he done? She watched his face in the moonlight and she knew that he'd been in some of the worst places in the world and they'd left their mark.

He was an unknown soldier. He was still in his uniform—it seemed almost part of the man. Part of the protective barrier?

Maybe.

They finished their meal in contented silence and fed the remainder of their chips—even Mike couldn't finish as many as he'd ordered—to a bunch of sleepy gulls who deigned to wake for the occasion. Then Mike stood and smiled and held out his hand.

'Walk on the beach before home?' he asked.

'I shouldn't.' Of course she shouldn't. The night was too beautiful. This man was too gorgeous. The situation was all too precarious.

But he was holding out his hand and smiling, and it would have taken a stronger woman than Hattie to resist. Dangerous or not, she put her hand in his and let him lead her down to the sand.

They paused to take off their shoes. That took Hattie a whole two seconds, while she slipped off her sandals, but Mike had to remove his army boots and she stood patiently, smiling.

'Just as well the enemy aren't over the nearest hill,' she retorted. 'I can just hear you… Oooh—wait, guys. No attacking yet, until we've got our shoes and socks off and we can escape by water.'

'Today's armies have dress rules for these kind of situations,' he said. 'Any army causing another army to get its feet wet violates at least three conventions and two international war codes. That's what makes my job as a lawyer with them most satisfying.'

'And lucrative?'

'As you say.'

She smiled, and he grinned, and then he held her hand again and they wandered into the shallows.

Once again they walked in silence, but it was getting better. Deeper. Warmer.

'Hattie, I need to go home,' Mike said, and the warmth stopped—just like that.

'You mean, America?' she said, knowing by the flatness of his voice that it could be nothing else.

'That was what today was about,' he said. 'There's a big case coming up. If I want to be involved I need to be in on the beginning.'

'And what about Kyle?'

'I've said not before two weeks. They've agreed. I'll report for duty at the end of the month. I talked to Veronica by phone today—she thinks all the paperwork can be done by then.'

'I don't believe this.' They'd been strolling in the shallows. She stopped dead and the waves lapped in and out around her. She felt sick. So soon… So soon…

'So you'll take Kyle home the minute the paperwork gets done? And then what?' For a moment there she'd been desolate, letting the personal hold sway, but suddenly desolation was overtaken by fury. Deep, burning anger that threatened to overwhelm her. 'You'll arrive, what? On the Saturday? Show Kyle to whatever childcare facility you can organise and then head off and save the world on Monday?'

'My work's important,' he said.

'Sure,' she said savagely. 'Important enough to sacrifice one small boy? If you—'

'Hattie, I'm hoping I don't have to.'

It caught her. The note of desperate urgency. The need. She paused mid-tirade and stared at him in the moonlight. He looked troubled and unsure. Almost afraid.

'Hattie, I've already asked if you'd come with us,' he said. 'As Kyle's nanny. I was dumb. I didn't think it through—that's a course of action that could only lead to misery all round. But I'm putting another offer on the table now. It's one you'll probably reject out of hand when you hear it first—it does seem crazy. But I've been thinking and thinking… Maybe we could make a go of it. If you want a family…We could come back here a couple of times a year to visit. We could have your family over. If you'll—'

'What on earth are you talking about?' she demanded, confused, and he shook his head.

'I'm making a mull of it. I know this isn't the right way, but neither is handing over velvet boxes in fancy restaurants. Hattie…Harriet…I'm asking if you'll marry me.'

It took her breath away.

One minute she was feeling bereft and furious and lost. The next she was so confounded she could hardly speak.

She took a deep breath and backed a little into the shallows. A wave, bigger than most, broke over her calves and splashed up to the hem of her little dress.

She didn't notice.

'I have to think you're joking,' she whispered.

'I'm not joking,' he said, and there was such depth in his words that she knew them for the truth.

'Then what…?'

'I've fallen in love with you,' he said. And there went her ability to breathe. This big, gentle man, standing in the moonlight, looking down at her with such tenderness…

Quite suddenly she wanted to weep.

'How can you?' she whispered, and he spread his hands, looking lost.

'I don't know,' he said honestly. 'This is uncharted territory for me. I've spent my life steering clear of any sort of emotional commitment. But in little more than two weeks I've met my son, and what I feel for him… I can't tell you. It's tearing me in two, keeping my distance, giving him space to get to know me. But, hell, I'll do whatever it takes. And at the same time there's you. I watch what you do with the kids—'

'I know what this is,' she said, not knowing at all. 'It's shock. You've just met your son for the first time. I don't come into it. You're just seeing us as an all-inclusive package.'

'I'm not,' he said, and reached for her hands, but she stepped back further. 'Hattie, you're quite simply the most beautiful woman I've ever met,' he said.

Yeah, well, that took her breath away all over again. This was not to be taken lightly. He was sounding deadly serious. That he could think he loved her…

But to go straight from this to marriage…

'You know, we seem to be missing a bit in between, here,' she said cautiously. 'Girl meets boy. Girl gets asked out on first date. Girl marries boy. Have I been reading the wrong romance novels? There's no middle bit.'

'I know,' he said ruefully. 'It's not fair.'

'I don't think fair comes into it. Sanity might.'

'You think my proposal is insane?'

'Tell me why it's not.'

'Because I can make a great life for you,' he said, and the urgency was back. 'I can, Hattie. Hell, you can't go on the way you're going. Giving and giving and giving. Look, I don't know how you feel about me—' He stopped, appearing suddenly to think this might be an important omission on his part. 'Do you think I'm okay?'

She took a deep breath, totally bewildered, but he was waiting for an answer. 'I might,' she admitted at last, and he grinned.

'Like I might think you're okay?'

'You're not wanting to jump me,' she said, and his grin faltered. Then returned.

'It's not for want of wanting.'

'I'm not seeing any evidence of it.'

'I'm a cautious man,' he said. 'I need to get my bases covered first.'

'So you'll ask me to marry you and then think about the jumping?'

'I don't want to frighten you.'

'Golly,' she said. And then, more definitely. 'Golly. Um…are you proposing to a sixteen-year-old, here?'

'You think I might have messed with the order?'

She was so confused she felt as if she was about to fall over. Dizziness didn't describe it. The night was out of kilter, so crazy it was like a dream. Any minute she'd wake up and smile at what she'd dreamed.

But meanwhile Mike was looking at her with an expression that was part anxious, part tender—and part something else.

He *did* want to jump her, she thought. There was blatant desire in his eyes, and it was far too long since anyone had looked at her like that. Mostly because she'd driven them off if they'd so much as looked at her. After one broken heart…

But this was Mike. Mike who sat at her breakfast table every morning and made the kids laugh. Mike who'd fallen for Kyle in a way she hadn't thought possible. Mike who even looked like Kyle. Mike who cared enough about Robbie to bring him a whole sheaf of helicopter flight manuals—yeah, she'd seen him surreptitiously put them on the hall table before they left.

This was Mike who made her toes curl just to look at him.

He was proposing marriage.

Yeah, marriage was crazy. But right now wasn't crazy. Right now she was standing in the shallows, without a kid in sight, in her gorgeous dress, her feet in the water, and she felt unbelievably desirable. And Mike was in his very sexy uniform, and she looked at him, and things twisted so hard and so fast that there was no way she could stop herself saying the obvious.

'You can't propose before you kiss me,' she said. 'It isn't proper. I'm not even sure it's legal.'

'You want me to kiss you?' he asked, sounding confused.

'You need me to ask twice?'

He smiled at that. His eyes creased with the lovely laughter that she adored. He reached for her hands and she put her hands in his, willing herself to be drawn forward.

She tilted her face to meet his and he kissed her.

Her life changed. Just like that.

It was supposed to be a kiss. Just a kiss.

She'd kissed men before—of course she had. She'd even enjoyed it. But not like this.

From the moment his mouth met hers she felt herself change, melt, merge. As though this first contact was enough to join them for ever. It was a crazy thought, coming from nowhere, but suddenly it seemed an immutable truth.

And that was all she was able to think before logic shut down. There was no room here for thought. There was room for nothing. Not for laughter. Not for wonder. Not even for how damned sexy he looked, or how male, or strong or how wonderful. His mouth was lowering on hers—and her thoughts shut down.

Mike.

His lips were on hers, claiming her as his own. His big, gentle hands were holding her waist, tugging her into him.

Major Mike Standford.

Mike.

Her home?

He'd wanted to kiss her since the first time he'd seen her. Even when it had seemed totally inappropriate—dumb, even.

Maybe it was dumb even now, but he wasn't thinking that. He was thinking he was where he most wanted to be in the world. That nothing else, no one else, mattered—except Hattie and here and now. And she was kissing him as fiercely as he was kissing her.

There was no way he wanted to fall in love. He wasn't absolutely sure it had happened now. But he'd surely fallen in lust.

That must be it. He wasn't falling in love, he told himself dazed. He wasn't.

So he shouldn't kiss her?

That was a no-brainer. Not kiss her when he had the opportunity? A man would have to be crazy.

She was pressing into him as he deepened the kiss, and his hands came up to cup her face. Her hair was a mass of lovely curls, tendrils escaping every which way. He could feel her curls against his face. The sensation was indescribable.

Lust?

Love. He knew it must be. He felt for this woman as he'd felt for no other. If he needed to lay down his life for her right now he surely would.

Harriet McDonald. Hattie.

His wife?

The thought almost overwhelmed him. He'd proposed to this woman and she'd asked to be kissed. He'd proposed, thinking she'd probably knock him back, but for her to kiss him…

For her not to reject his proposal out of hand…

It could work, he thought, dazed. It could.

His arms were around her, holding her close, closer… Her breasts were tight pressed against his chest, fitting into place as if she belonged. She *did* belong, he thought exultantly. There'd been a hollow there—an emptiness—but suddenly the emptiness was gone. The other half of his whole…

The sensation was wonderful. Magic.

They were deepening the kiss together, mutually needful, mutually wanting to be as close as man and woman could be. This was not the time or the place to take things to what might be their inevitable conclusion—they were knee-high in surf, for a start— but it hardly mattered as this joining was as meaningful as any deeper joining could possibly be.

He was entranced. Enchanted. Bewitched. He was slowly, wondrously exploring this sensation that was as unexpected as it was amazing.

Hattie. It was a crazy name for a beautiful woman. There was no sophistication about his Hattie. What you saw was what you got. She was pressed tight against him, tighter, tighter, and he heard a tiny sigh of pleasure as her fingers raked his hair, pulling him closer, closer, closer.

A wave slapped against their thighs, higher than the rest. Hard enough to have them break apart for a moment. Long enough to check there wasn't a tsunami on the way.

There wasn't, and he reached for her again. But the shock of the wave had given her pause, allowing a semblance of sanity to return.

'No,' she said.

'No?'

'Um…I need to get this sorted in my head. Not…not that I didn't want to kiss you.'

'I seem to remember you asked me.'

'That was only because you had the order wrong.' He had her hands back in his now, but she was resisting being tugged closer. 'Mike—whoa. We need to think this out. I don't know where this is going.'

'I'm not sure, either,' he said gently. 'But that kiss… I knew it'd be like that. I just knew.'

'You did no such thing,' she whispered, fighting for a semblance of control. 'I never knew kissing like that.'

'No,' he said. Meekly.

She cast him a look that was half suspicion, half fear. 'So that's why you asked me to marry you? Because you thought it might be different?'

'Because I knew it'd be different. It *is* different.'

'Different enough to justify marriage?' She sounded lost, which was pretty much how he was feeling. But he had to get things under control. Hell, he could keep a courtroom in order. He just had to get this conversation between the two of them to proceed in the right direction.

'Your mother says you'd love to get married,' he tried, and she stilled.

'What's this got to do with my mother?'

'Nothing. I just thought—'

'You talked about me to my mother?'

'Yes. I thought—'

'You asked her for my hand in marriage?' She was sliding fast into anger, he thought in dismay, and he had to do something to retrieve the situation. Fast.

'Hattie, nannying's crazy,' he told her urgently. 'I was dumb to even think it could happen. You love Kyle as much as any mother could. And me... Kyle's knocked me sideways. I never thought I could care for a kid, but here I am thinking I'd do anything in the world for him.'

'Like marry me?' she said carefully. 'The supreme sacrifice?'

He really did have this wrong.

'It's no sacrifice at all,' he said, trying hard to retrieve the situation. 'I know you well enough by now to realise you'd throw that in my face. But, Hattie, I've been watching you caring for those kids, loving them to bits, breaking your heart over and over again. And I've seen what I want for my son. A wonderful, vibrant, loving mother.'

'So we're back to square one?' she said, almost cordially. 'Only the terminology's changed. Will you be Kyle's mother instead of will you be Kyle's nanny?'

'I want you to be my wife.'

'See—that's the bit I don't understand,' she complained.

They'd stopped noticing their surroundings now— they were wet to the core but it didn't matter. What was being said was too important for anything else to intrude.

'It's impossible to understand,' he told her, choosing his words with care. Aware that this was his only chance to state his case. To get this right. 'What I want is to take you away for a fabulous weekend somewhere, where we can concentrate on you for a change. But this is the best I can get. Four hours of freedom and then back to living with four kids. I can't figure out how to sweep you off your feet.'

'You want to sweep me off my feet?' she whispered.

'More than anything in the world.'

'But you can't because witching hour is midnight?'

'It's a bit short for a hot seduction scene,' he said ruefully. 'And I know you think I'm crazy, but I don't think it's crazy at all. Hattie, I've been collecting evidence for war crimes which come to trial at the Hague in four weeks. I have to be there. There's little alternative—it was spelled out for me today. You do wonderful things here. I do what I can on a different scale. But, Hattie, I need your help. I can't take care of Kyle by myself. He needs you. And I'm starting to think I need you, too. So come to the States with me. No, I'm not asking for you to be Kyle's nanny. I'm saying be Kyle's mother. Marry me and assume every right true parenthood entails.'

'While you go off and save the world?' The sheer, unadulterated bliss she'd felt as he'd kissed her had completely gone. She didn't understand what was in his head—his sense of marriage was obviously light years from hers.

The joy was being replaced with desolation.

'So how much time would you be spending with us?' she asked carefully, as if treading on eggshells.

'I get long spells of leave. I work a big case—it might take three or four months—and then I take three or four weeks off. I'm normally based in Washington, but I can commute.'

'To the beach? To where you'll park me and Kyle?'

'That's a bit unfair.'

'What about your leg, Mike?' she asked suddenly, changing tack a little. 'What are you doing about that?'

'What do you mean?'

'I mean, I'm a nurse, and I've been watching you. It hurts like hell. If I were your doctor I'd be saying take more serious time off, get some decent rehabilitation, or you'll be stuck with the consequences for ever.'

'I don't have any more time.'

'Because the world can't be saved without you?'

'My work's vital.'

'No one else can do it? That's arrogance.'

'It's what I am,' he said. 'It's the reason I get up in the morning. I need to make a difference.'

'So do I,' she whispered. 'And I do. You're saying what you're doing is more important than my job.'

'No, I'm saying you can still make a difference,' he said, starting to sound exasperated. 'You can love Kyle to bits. In doing so you can free me to do what I need to do. In my breaks we could have a fantastic time—these couple of weeks have been the best healing my head could ever have. I think you're the smartest, sassiest, most gorgeous woman I've ever met, and making you my wife would be the most amazing thing I'd ever do. And, Hattie…'

'Yes,' she said, in a dull little voice that he was concentrating too hard on his words to pick up on.

'Hattie, I wouldn't mind a family,' he said. 'I mean… not just Kyle. I know your family is everything to you. I'd hate for you to be separate from them, but I'm wealthy enough for you to come back here for at least two long holidays a year. You could make it while I'm away, to fill the time a bit more. If any of them want to come over I'd be more than happy to pay expenses. And if you wanted to go back to part-time nursing…'

'To fill more time…?'

'If you want,' he said diffidently. 'But, Hattie…' He paused, knowing what he was saying was almost too big to contemplate. But he'd been thinking of almost nothing else since watching her on the beach with her charges and her nieces and nephews. 'Hattie, I'd like to have our own,' he said. 'I never thought I'd say it. I thought I was an absolute loner, but it seems I'm not. Kyle's the best little kid, and he loves the other kids, weird and troubled as they are. If you wanted…maybe we could give him brothers and sisters.'

He had it all wrong. He had it totally, totally wrong. While he'd been speaking she'd been watching him with bemusement, as if he was speaking some sort of language she didn't understand. But at the back of her eyes there was something that he thought—hoped— was longing.

He knew how she'd reacted to the kiss. He'd caught her watching him, and he'd thought the attraction was definitely not one-sided.

But now…

Her face had lost all its colour. She took a step back from him, and as he instinctively reached for her she lashed out.

Her hand met his face in a stinging, fiery slap that had him stop dead in the water and stare down at her in amazement.

She gazed at him in horror. Then she gazed down at her hand as if it somehow belonged to someone else— as if it had no part of her.

'Hattie…'

'I hit you,' she whispered, shattered. 'I've never hit… I'd never hit…'

'I don't understand.'

'Neither do I. Mike, take me home.'

'Is it because—?'

'It's because of all sorts of things,' she said, anger fading, leaving bleakness, but also some semblance of returning control. She stepped back far enough from him so that even if her errant hand wanted to slap she couldn't reach. 'Mike, you don't know me. You've seen me only as Kyle's foster mother, and it's like seeing me only through professional eyes. I'm a good house mum. It's what I do. But to ask me to marry you for such a reason…'

'It's not just that. Of course it's not.'

'No,' she said brokenly. 'And if I was stupid enough, then I'm probably attracted enough to you to say yes, and we'll work things out, and of course I'll support you in your very important work. But maybe I'm selfish, too, Mike. Maybe I have needs you don't even want to know about. So let's leave this. Let's haul up the professional barriers again and restart. As soon as the paperwork's through then you get to take Kyle home. You set up whatever you need for him over there. I have a feeling you love him more than you think you do. I suspect the Hague is going to feel pretty lonely without him. But that's your problem and Kyle's. Not mine. Leave me out of the equation. And now…just take me home.'

He took her home. There was no argument she'd listen to. And he knew he'd hurt her. She sat as far away from him as she could, and she shivered, even though he'd turned the car's heater up so high that he was sweating.

She was right. He didn't know her at all. And he'd hurt her…

He couldn't bear it, but he couldn't put it right.

Back home, she disappeared into her bedroom the moment they arrived, leaving him to face her sisters.

'Uh-oh,' Mary said, looking at his face. 'Bad oysters?'

'A bit of a bad call,' he said ruefully.

'You didn't try and jump her?' Shanni asked.

Mary gave a shocked gasp. 'That's none of our business,' she said primly, but then grinned. 'But she looks upset. I can't see our Hattie upset by a man as gorgeous as you taking the odd liberty. Unless you did something ghastly, like ignored the No Means No rule.'

'Ooh, who's out of line here?' Shanni demanded, and Mike smiled despite himself. These two were incorrigible. They'd be great sisters, he thought. Great sisters-in-law?

'I asked her to marry me,' he admitted, and their humour disappeared just like that.

'You didn't,' Shanni breathed.

'Oh, my dear,' Mary said.

'She slapped me,' he said.

'Oh.'

There was a long drawn-out silence. Then Mary said, 'Did she tell you—'

'No,' Shanni said strongly, before Mary could go one word further. 'Sorry, Mary, but we can't interfere. You know, as well as I do that when relationships get as serious as this then there's no place for us. And telling Mike stuff Hattie would never allow us to tell is going to help nothing. Besides,' she added bluntly, 'we'd be crossed off her Christmas list for ever.'

'She's had a tough relationship in the past?' Mike said cautiously, but both women had decided they'd gone far enough.

'We need to go,' Mary said, gathering her coat. 'Come on, Shanni.'

'You don't think we should talk to her?' Shanni asked.

'We're going,' Mary said, and pushed her sister out through the door. 'Good luck,' she called over her shoulder. 'You'll need it.'

She wasn't coming out.

She heard Mike talking to her sisters, and she thought if they started talking about her she was going to have to kill them.

Maybe she should have been honest about the reason for her violent reaction. Her palm still hurt. She sank onto her bed and cradled her hand as if it hurt far more than it did.

As if in echo, the pain in her gut stirred and shifted and clamped. Worse than the last. Worse than ever.

Two more weeks until the operation was scheduled. Two more weeks until she could never have babies for ever.

She'd held it in. Even her sisters couldn't know how much it hurt, how much she ached. And now here was Mike, calmly taking away her beloved Kyle and saying, *It's okay, come with us and have a few more babies.*

She shouldn't have hit him. He wasn't to know.

She'd hurt him. She'd seen the flash of matching pain in his eyes and she'd thought that asking her to marry him had been a really big deal for him—a huge concession. The fact that he couldn't go any further than he'd done—promising part-time parenthood, part-time marriage—wasn't his fault. It had been instilled in him since birth.

And she'd hit him.

She should go out and apologise. She heard her sisters leave. She heard him walk to her bedroom door and hesitate. If he knocked…

'Hattie, are you okay?' he asked, and she wanted more than anything in the world to open the door, fling herself into his arms and sob. *No, I'm not okay. No, I'm bereft and frightened and I hurt and you're taking Kyle away and I love you, you big oaf, and more than anything else in the entire world I want what you're suggesting—marriage, kids, happy ever after.*

But that wasn't what he was offering. He was asking her to be a part-time wife. No commitment necessary. No.

'I'm fine,' she whispered, trying desperately to make her voice loud enough for him to hear. 'I'm sorry I slapped you. I overreacted and I had no right. And thank you for the marriage offer—it was really sweet. But you and Kyle…you have to work it out on your own. I'm sorry, Mike. Thank you for a very nice evening—apart from the slap. Goodnight.'

'You don't want to talk about it?

'I have talked about it,' she whispered. 'I've talked all I'm going to talk. Goodnight.'

They had two more weeks together, and Hattie used the time to withdraw.

She was good, Mike had to acknowledge as the weeks wore on—seriously good at the job she did. Without ever appearing to, she shifted Kyle's care to him. At the school pick-up the other three kids would be diverted to visit someone and he'd be left with Kyle, listening to the events of the day, taking him home, watching him have his milk and cookies. She'd sort the washing at night and toss Kyle's unsorted stuff to him. Domesticity—the sort of things he'd never imagined himself doing—was starting to envelop him.

He might even have enjoyed it. But at the same time as Hattie distanced herself from Kyle she was also distancing herself from him.

Three nights before he was due to leave she said to Kyle, 'Right, it's time you and your dad started being a family. From now on you get to sleep in the family suite with your dad. Off you guys go after dinner. You can watch television together, and read each other bedtime stories and be a real family.'

Which meant Mike wouldn't see Hattie after dinner. But he couldn't object, for Kyle was looking really, really anxious. This was a very big test—to separate himself from the other kids and be Mike's son. He was torn.

'Maybe we could go down to the video store and choose a movie?' Mike suggested, and the awful decision was made.

So hand in hand they walked to the store and chose a video, and when they got home there was a note on the kitchen table saying Hattie and the rest of he kids had gone to see friends. He and Kyle looked at each other and they knew they were thinking exactly the same thing.

They wanted to be where Hattie was.

'But we're family,' Mike said, watching his little son's face begin to crumple. 'It's okay, mate.' He stooped and gathered Kyle into his arms and hugged him. And it felt okay. It felt right. A shared grief.

'We'll never let her go completely,' he promised his son. 'Twice a year we'll visit. I promise. And you can phone every night if you want.'

'It won't be the same,' Kyle said brokenly, but he was hugging Mike as hard as Mike was hugging him, and Mike thought Hattie had succeeded. She'd given him his son.

'It won't,' he agreed, stroking Kyle's hair. 'Hattie's one in a million. But we'll be all right together. You'll see.'

And three, four days later the last of the red tape was cut. Mike loaded Kyle's possessions into his hire car. He hugged each of the kids and he tried to hug Hattie, but she wasn't having any of it.

She shook his hand formally. Her face was so blank that he knew inside she was tearing apart. Inside the car Kyle was weeping inconsolably, and Mike felt like doing the same himself.

'Just go,' Hattie whispered, gathering the rest of the kids around her like a shield. 'Don't make it harder on all of us by stretching it out. Just go.'

'So you never told him?'

'Why would I tell him?'

'Because you love the guy.' Mary was seriously exasperated. 'And he loves you. You just had to look at him…'

'Yeah, he'd have loved me. Twice a year and on Bank Holidays.'

'What do you mean?'

'I mean, he's out saving the world and he has a tiny son, and he would have used me to justify not getting any closer. You know that was never going to work.'

'But where does that leave you?'

'Right where I've always been,' Hattie said. 'Here in Bay Beach, where I belong.'

'And Sydney next month for surgery. Oh, Hat, how can you bear it?'

'Leave it,' Hattie said shortly, and got up from the front porch and walked inside. 'Everything's fine. Everything's always been fine. Sydney's just formalising something we've known for ever. It's no big deal.'

'But losing Kyle…and Mike.'

'Leave it,' she snapped, and slammed the door.

CHAPTER NINE

Saving the world with a five-year-old in tow was really difficult. Impossible, really.

For a start, finding Kyle a nanny in the States and leaving him was never going to happen. By the time they arrived back in the States, Kyle was overawed, overwhelmed and totally dependent on his dad. Whenever Mike made a move as minor as going to the bathroom Kyle got anxious.

So when Mike left the States, Kyle went with him. Also along for the ride was Heidi, a sweet young thing straight out of nanny school, who thought an all-expenses-paid holiday overseas was cool. Heidi and Kyle had bonded enough in the weeks before the case started to make Mike think things might be okay, but every night Kyle was watching for him, checking the clock against Mike's promised home-time. How the hell was that going to work when things started getting serious?

And every night they rang Hattie.

'I'm going to school here. Heidi's taught me to play Ping-Pong. Dad's too, too busy.' Kyle would chatter away happily for about half an hour to Hattie, who, half a world away, was getting up early so she would have time to talk to Kyle as much as he needed.

It didn't include time to chat with Mike. 'I'm sorry, Mike, I'm afraid I don't have time,' she said softly when Kyle handed the phone over to him. 'Robbie's hurt his knee and I need—'

'Robbie's hurt his knee? How badly?'

'Nothing a sticking plaster won't fix, but it's my business,' she said, gently enough. 'And, Mike…can you tell Kyle I won't be able to talk with him for a few days from Friday? I'm taking time off.'

'A holiday?'

'Sort of.'

'Are you sure you're—?'

'I need to go.'

So the next night they didn't ring. Or the next. Then, on the supposition that she might just have meant the weekend, they rang again and got Veronica.

'I'm house mum while Hattie's away,' she told them. 'But Hattie's fine.'

'Why shouldn't she be fine?' Mike demanded, hearing nuances where maybe none were intended.

'I just meant she's on holiday.'

'When will she be back?'

'We're not sure.'

'Why not?'

'I'll let you know,' Veronica said brusquely. 'I have to go.'

'Veronica said she's fine,' Mike said, replacing the receiver and looking down at Kyle's worried face. 'Why do you think she said that?'

'I don't know.'

'Neither do I,' Mike said, worrying. And then he said, 'Let's call Janet.'

He rang Janet. 'I need to know about your daughter,' he said bluntly.

'Why?' she said, and he told her. He told her everything. And Janet listened in silence, and then made a decision and told him everything back.

And when the call was over Kyle was looking really worried. He knew his dad well enough now to hear worry.

'Okay, Kyle,' Mike said, lifting his small son into his arms and hugging him, because he, Mike, badly needed a hug. 'I think we need to do some reorganising.'

Three days post op was probably the time a girl looked her worst. For the first couple of days she'd looked wan and interesting, hooked up to tubes and monitors and generally looking like a sick person. By day three she was unhooked, sitting up, feeling exceedingly sorry for herself, and thinking her abundance of floral arrangements smelled funny. But she wasn't about to stretch her stitches by getting out of bed to shift them.

Her hair needed a wash—but what the hell? Her mum had just brought in a bunch of glossies—but who cared which celebrity was bonking who?

She was desperately lonely. Janet was staying in Sydney until she was out of hospital, but her hospital-visiting was limited, to say the least.

'Hospitals make me nervous,' she told her daughter honestly. 'It's the smell.'

'Help me get rid of the flowers.'

'You can't get rid of them,' Janet said, shocked.

'They're floral arrangements from all your friends. They cost a fortune. No, you just lie back and get better, and I'll see you tonight. Though you might want to put on a bit of lippie before I come again. You look like a ghost.'

Right. She left, and Hattie managed a trip to the bathroom, and thought who the hell cared if she had lippie on or not? She slunk back down under the covers, decided she wasn't going to cry, even if she really, really wanted to, and then the door opened.

Two heads appeared around the door. One high. One low.

Mike. And Kyle.

For a moment she thought she was dreaming. She blinked and blinked again.

'Can we come in?' Mike said, and hauled off his cap. He was in his army uniform. She loved his army uniform.

She loved him. She loved him so fiercely the emotion was almost overwhelming. But here was her first love, Kyle, edging past his dad, heading for her like an arrow straight for her heart.

'Don't forget she'll have a sore tummy,' Mike said urgently, and Kyle checked his arrow rush to a more sedate launch. But he was still fast, up on the bed, into her arms, hugging her close before she'd accepted she wasn't dreaming.

'We've surprised you,' he said, burying his face in her neck. And that was the end of whatever self-control she might have liked to retain. She stared blindly up at Mike. She closed her eyes in sheer disbelief and hugged Kyle's little body to her as if she'd never let him go.

She wept, and things had changed. This wasn't the controlled sobbing of the house, where she feared frightening the children. This was a weeping for *her*. A release of self-control that had held for far, far too long.

And when Mike sat gingerly on the bed beside them, carefully lifting Kyle far enough away to prevent pressure on her dressings, carefully gathering both woman and child into his arms, carefully hugging her close, she kept on weeping—weeping as if she would never stop.

They didn't try and stop her. Neither of her boys. They didn't pull back or try and mop her up or say anything. They simply held her and let her sob, these wonderful men who shared the intuitive knowledge that something inside her was crumbling and that all they could do was wait until the pieces reassembled in whatever fashion they cared to re-emerge.

A nurse came in—probably to take obs or something similarly non-vital—and Mike gave her a look that would have quailed an army of Huns. She retreated without a word.

And Hattie cried on.

But finally, finally she cried herself out. She hiccupped into Mike's by now sodden shirt, and sniffed, and Mike gathered a handful of tissues from the box on her bedside table and handed them over.

She blew her nose—hard—and he laughed and grabbed more tissues and mopped her sodden face.

'We love you,' he said simply, and it was all she could do not to start again.

'Why…? Why…?' She couldn't make her voice work.

'We came to marry you,' Kyle said solemnly, handing his father more tissues. They had an assembly line going here. 'Dad's got a ring.'

'But I—'

'Hey,' Mike said, half-laughing. 'This is for me to say, young Kyle.'

'But you already said,' Kyle said indignantly. 'And we chose the ring at the jewellers at the airport. It's a really big diamond,' Kyle told Hattie, and she was so bamboozled that Mike took pity on her and took her into his arms again.

'I guess I already asked Hattie to marry me,' he said to Kyle, his voice thick with raw emotion. 'So maybe it's better if this time it comes from you. But Hattie said no last time. I think we ought to explain that the parameters have changed.'

'What's *parameters*?' Kyle said, confused.

'The reasons why we should be a family,' Mike said and he drew back a little, smiled anxiously into his love's eyes. 'Sweetheart, are you well enough to listen? Janet said it'd be okay.'

'Janet…?'

'We got worried and phoned her,' he said. 'She told us what exactly you've had wrong with you. Endometriosis. Constant pain for years. And now a hysterectomy. She said at least this final step should make you pain-free, no matter how gut-wrenching it is for you now.'

'Janet had no right…'

'No,' Mike said. 'She doesn't. I had to tell her that Kyle and I love you more than anything else in the world before she'd tell us. She said you can't have babies. She said you've known that for years, and that was the reason that shallow bas— That low-life of a fiancé threw you over. And she also said that was the reason you threw my proposal back in my face. Offering to let you have children…'

'You weren't to know.'

'No, but it was a hugely arrogant thing to even think, much less propose,' he said. 'Hattie, Kyle and I think you're the most wonderful woman in the world. But we always knew that. What's changed over the last few weeks is that I've figured I'm not prepared to be an absentee father, much less an absentee husband.'

'You're not?'

'No,' he said soberly. 'It tears me up, leaving Kyle to go to the office. Okay, he has school now, and I need to get realistic. Kyle and I both know we have to face a bit of time apart. But separation nine to five is enough. Twice a year access is not on the agenda. I was nuts to think it ever could be. And I've been away from you for three weeks, and that's nuts, too. Kyle will tell you I'm going out of my mind.'

'Dad used to listen in on the other telephone while I talked to you,' Kyle said seriously, trying very hard to keep up in this adult-to-adult conversation. 'He said it made him feel better. When you said you didn't have time to talk to him it made him sad.'

'So…?' A flare of hope had lit, way down deep. It was tiny to start with, but it was building. Building, building and building.

'I think we should both stop saving the world,' Mike said, and she blinked.

'But…your work…' she whispered, confused.

'Yeah, and your work, too,' he growled. Kyle had wriggled between them. 'Kyle, let me get an edge in here.'

But Kyle was hugging Hattie, and Hattie wasn't letting him go. She was holding him like a shield. In case…in case she didn't know what.

'Hattie, what we've both been doing is incredibly important,' Mike told her, abandoning hugging but holding

her with his eyes. He was caressing her from a distance
of inches. Loving her. 'But we've been doing it for a
long time, and I've been thinking. Saving the big world
can only happen if individual worlds are safe. Yes,
you've been looking after individual kids, but now it's
our turn to find love for each other, for us, for our tiny
family.'

'Oh, Mike…'

'When I was in Canberra I was head-hunted,' he told
her, scarcely pausing for breath, knowing what he had
to say was desperately important and determined that
she hear everything before he be interrupted. 'The
Australian government would like to take me on as an
advisor. I'd be a liaison person, a policy person—someone who maybe still makes a difference but in a quieter
way. I'd be a backroom boy, Hattie. A nine to fiver. I
might need to make the odd trip overseas, but I'd be permanently based in Canberra.'

'But Canberra is only…'

'A couple of hours from Bay Beach by road,' he said,
still talking too fast. 'When they first approached me—
before I met Kyle—I dismissed the offer out of hand. I
thought what I was doing was too damned important to
entrust to anyone else. Maybe part of that was my injured
leg. When I got out of hospital everyone was saying it
was time to get out of the war zones, let others take a turn.
And it felt wrong. Like I was being sidelined. But now…
All of a sudden it feels right. All of a sudden…sitting
with Kyle in some damned impersonal five-star hotel
room on the other side of the world…it felt like the guys
were right. I've done my bit. As you have.'

'Mike…'

'We could still have a house somewhere in the Bay

Beach area here,' he said, desperate to state his case in full, not giving her a chance to interrupt. 'That is…that is if you'd consider moving. I can organise myself work where I can be home a lot, and we can move between one and the other, but I will be based in Canberra. For the foreseeable future I can't base myself solely around here.'

'I wouldn't want you to,' Hattie whispered, awed, trying really hard not to burst into tears again. 'Families should stay together.'

'So you'd consider moving to Canberra?'

'With me,' Kyle said urgently. 'With me, with me, with me.'

'Yes,' said Hattie.

'You'd be leaving Bay Beach.'

'We could come back most weekends, right? And on vacation?'

'I'll sell my place in the States and buy the best holiday house in the district,' Mike said, slowing down a bit, his face lighting with hope. 'Plus a wonderful big home in Canberra. If you could bear to come with us.'

'But why?' she managed, struggling desperately to think clearly, to force herself to remember that this man had asked her to marry him before, and he'd asked her for the wrong reasons and she couldn't bear it if she had to say no again.

But the reasons had changed. Or maybe they were the same, but he was seeing them clearly for what they were.

'Hattie, I love you,' he said simply, and he lifted Kyle aside and put him at the end of the bed, like it or not. 'Kyle, I'm asking Hattie to marry me,' he said. 'And a man needs to hug the woman he proposes to, so if you don't mind?'

'Well, hurry,' Kyle said, looking pleased.

'I do love you,' Mike said, and he took her hands in his. 'Hattie, I loved you from the moment I first saw you. You had yellow paint on your nose.'

'But how can you…?'

'How can I not? You're someone I never thought I could find. You're my beautiful Harriet. My beloved Hattie. You're beautiful, you're sexy, and I want you as my best friend and my lover for the rest of my life. But most of all, Hattie, I want you to be my wife. I would be the proudest, most fortunate man in the world if you'll agree.'

'But I can't have children,' she whispered. 'How can you want me?'

'How the hell can I *not* want you?' he demanded, in so fierce a voice that she flinched. Then, as he saw that she was serious, he took her in his arms and held her as if she was the most precious thing in the world.

'We already have Kyle,' he said, and Kyle, tired of being shunted to the end of the bed, edged in between them again. 'He's a really good start.'

'But…'

'Then there's Katy,' he said solemnly. 'I'm thinking you might need to stop being a house mother—it's too hard to do for ever. Let's launch Robbie and Erin back to their respective families and then call it quits. But if Katy was to need a home…we could be interim foster parents for her whenever she needs us. More permanently, if it works out. If you'd like.'

'Of course I'd like,' she said, feeling breathless.

'I don't know whether you'd like to go back to nursing…'

'I might,' she said, taking breath. 'Then again…'

'If we filled the house with enough kids, maybe not for a while?' He was holding back from her a little now, searching her face. 'Hattie, I do love you. I left you, and we tried for a whole three weeks to get on without you. We failed miserably. Kyle and I need you in our life. Mostly, *I* need you in my life. I'll do whatever it takes, my lovely Harriet.'

'So you're taking on the kids as a supreme sacrifice?' But she was smiling. She knew him now, this man, and she knew enough to know that his world had changed. The solitary Major Mike Standford was no more. This man was as needful of a quiverful of kids as she was. He was a family man. *Her* family man.

'If we're talking kids…there is one thing,' he said, unable to believe his luck but knowing that this time he had to say what was in his heart.

'Give her the ring,' Kyle said, urgent.

'There's something I have to say. Before I tie her to us completely.'

'You've got a wife and kids somewhere else?' she asked, smiling and smiling.

'A child.'

Her smile faded. She searched his eyes, knowing instinctively that this was no threat to their happiness.

'You have another child somewhere?'

'Hattie, when I was injured in the bomb blast, there were civilian deaths,' he said soberly. 'I hauled a woman out of a burning car and she died in my arms. I know her family is all right—and I've made a financial commitment. That's nothing. But later, in the hospital, I saw a child. A little girl, aged about two or three. I don't even know her name. She's lost a foot, Hattie, and she has no one. She'll need more medical assistance than

she can get where she is. The authorities have said she'll
be impossible to adopt, because why would anyone
choose a child like her?'

'Oh, Mike…'

'It's going to take a huge effort to get her here,' he
said urgently. 'And more effort to give her back some
semblance of a childhood. Hattie, to ask you to take her
on with me…it seems dreadful, but I can't get her out
of my dreams.'

'And why would you?' she demanded, and the
smile was back.

'Hattie, it's a huge ask.'

'It's a gift,' she whispered. 'Mike, what you're
giving me—'

'I'm giving you nothing,' he said fiercely. 'You love
and you love and you love…'

'Yeah, and you haven't even given her the ring,' Kyle
said disgustedly. 'Dad…'

Mike regrouped. He searched Hattie's face, and what
he saw there made him smile. He sat back and fished
in his pocket and produced a velvet box.

'I need three square inches of salmon to go with
this,' he said. 'And white table napkins.'

As if on cue the nurse popped her head around the
door, determined this time not to be repelled by a glare.

'I've given you all the time you can have,' she said
briskly. 'I'm sorry, but I need to change Ms McDonald's
dressings and give her her medication.'

'New dressings,' Mike said. 'And medication. Better
than table napkins and nouvelle cuisine any day.'

'But will you marry him?' Kyle said urgently as the
nurse got closer. 'You haven't said yes.'

'I don't have to,' Hattie said, and she opened the

box, lifted out the truly awesome diamond, and slipped it onto her finger before the nurse or anyone else could get near. 'Your father's committed himself before witnesses and he's announced his intentions in front of my mother. If I know Janet she's out shopping for wedding dresses right now.'

'Really?' Mike said faintly.

'Welcome to the family, my love,' she managed, but only just.

And then she couldn't say anything else for a very long time.

For Major Mike Standford could bear the suspense no longer. He calmly turned his back on the waiting nurse, and took his affianced wife into his arms.

And while the nurse and Kyle looked on—with absolute approval—he kissed her for just as long as he wanted to.

Which meant the two o'clock medication for the patient in Ward Nine had to be charted as administered very late indeed.

The paperwork took months. Months of going back and back, getting to know the tiny girl, growing to love the tiny, waif-thin sprite with mischief in her eyes and a courage that would be up to any challenge the world threw at her—as long as she had a family loving her every step of the way.

And when the adoption papers finally came through it was no longer Mike Standford and Hattie McDonald, but Mr and Mrs Standford with their son, Kyle, who walked into the orphanage dormitory on that day, to gather one confused but courageous little girl into their arms and take her home.

Their daughter.

Hattie held her. She held her and held her while Kyle and Mike stood back, hand in hand, and let the women bond.

'I've just had a thought,' Mike said at last, in a voice thick with emotion. 'I hadn't realised. But my Palm Pilot just beeped to remind me.'

'Remind you of what?' Hattie asked, hardly able to drag her attention away from the little girl in her arms.

'It's Mother's Day,' Mike said softly, wonderingly. He lifted Kyle up and the four of them managed some sort of sandwich squeeze which enveloped all of them.

'Happy Mother's Day,' he whispered to Hattie, and he kissed the top of her hair. 'Happy Mother's Day to us all.'

For His Baby's Sake

JESSICA HART

Jessica Hart was born in West Africa, and has suffered from itchy feet ever since, travelling and working around the world in a wide variety of interesting but very lowly jobs, all of which have provided inspiration on which to draw when it comes to the settings and plots of her stories. Now she lives a rather more settled existence in York, where she has been able to pursue her interest in history, although she still yearns sometimes for wider horizons. If you'd like to know more about Jessica, visit her website www.jessicahart.co.uk.

**Look for Jessica Hart's new book,
Promoted: to Wife and Mother, coming from
Mills & Boon® Romance in March 2008**

Dear Reader,

I don't know about you, but I waste a lot of time wondering, 'What if…' I know it's pointless, but it's impossible not to speculate about how differently things would have turned out if I had said 'yes' instead of 'no', if I'd stood firm instead of compromising, if I'd made that phone call, or not sent that e-mail. Perhaps it's just me, but whenever I make a decision, however trivial, there's always that niggling feeling that I might have made the wrong choice.

Rose, the heroine of this special story for Mother's Day, has to make a difficult choice of her own: stay with the man she loves or make a new life for herself with the chance of having a baby. Either way, she loses something very special.

Luckily for Rose, she gets a second chance and this time, if she and Drew can make the right decision, they can have everything…

Best wishes,

Jessica

CHAPTER ONE

SHE couldn't afford it. Rose threw down her pen with a sigh. No matter how many different ways she tried it, the figures just didn't add up. Which left her with a problem.

'What,' she asked her small son, 'am I going to do with you?'

There was no reply from Jack, but Rose hadn't really expected one. At twenty months, his vocabulary was too limited to suggest the practical solution she needed, but he looked up at the sound of her voice and offered her instead a smile of such sweetness that Rose felt her heart contract. Jack might not be able to deal with her current childcare crisis, but his smile was all she needed to reassure her that somehow, some way, she would manage.

Leaving the depressing bank statements on the kitchen table, she went to sit on the floor beside him while he returned his attention to the brightly coloured bricks that were scattered around him. Absently, Rose piled three on top of each other, showing him how to make a tower.

'I need that contract, but I can't take you with me to the studio,' she said, as Jack instantly reached out to knock the precarious tower over. 'Peter and Peter are lovely, but their place is much too perfect for toddlers. There are too many sharp edges and antiques, and any-way, I wouldn't be able to concentrate on work if you were there.'

She quite often talked to Jack, knowing that he couldn't understand. He was happy to listen to her voice, and it made her feel less alone to be able to talk things through, even if the conversations were inevitably rather one-sided.

Jack was looking aggrieved at the disappearance of the tower, and Rose quickly built another one, higher this time, and his face lit up as he realised that he could demolish that, too.

'Perhaps I should have married your father when he asked me,' she went on guiltily.

Thinking about how sensible it would be to marry Seb always made her a little uncomfortable. It wasn't that she had any problem with being sensible normally, but it was a big step to marry someone you didn't really love, no matter how practical an option it seemed, and Rose still hadn't been able to commit herself further than saying that she would think about it.

'But that wouldn't have solved the problem of what to do with you now,' she reminded Jack quickly, setting a blue brick precariously on top of the pile. 'He'd still have had to go to Bristol for that job, and I would still be here wondering how I can afford someone to look after you. I can't do that unless I start work on this contract, but I can't work unless I can find someone to look after you.'

Sitting back on her heels, she smiled as Jack de-stroyed the second tower with a shout of triumph. 'It's a problem, isn't it?'

'Ya!' yelled Jack delightedly.

'That sounds like a yes to me.' Rose sighed as she looked at her watch and levered herself upwards. She had better start making Jack's supper. Perhaps some magic solution would occur to her when he was in bed and she had some quiet time to think.

Leaving Jack trying to build his own towers, she went over to the kitchen. She loved this room. Apart from the narrow hallway leading up to the stairs, the whole ground floor of the Victorian terraced house had been knocked through to make a bright, open-plan living room, with comfortable sofas towards the front, and a kitchen with a big table and French windows opening onto her little garden at the back.

Although, strictly speaking, it wasn't her garden at all. It was Drew's. Not that he had ever lived here, or would have done anything to the garden if he had. Whenever Rose thought of the absurdly low rent she paid, she felt quite dizzy with relief and gratitude. Without Drew she really wouldn't have been able to manage since Jack had been born. He had always been generous.

Irresponsible, restless and ridiculously scared of commitment, but undeniably generous.

Her gaze fell on an old photo clamped to the front of the fridge with a Snoopy magnet. It showed her squinting slightly into the sun, and Drew with his arm around her. They were both smiling, both radiating happiness and confidence in the future. Both looking very young.

It seemed right to keep a picture of him up since this was his house, although Rose always felt a pang when she looked at it. Drew, with his crooked smile and his dancing eyes and that odd, distinctive pale star-shaped splodge in his dark hair. She had always known that she loved him. She just hadn't realised how much until he had left.

Drew. Where was he now? 'I'm off to Africa,' he had said cheerfully the last time she'd seen him at some awful party she'd gone to with Seb. 'I've been seconded to an aid project, putting in water supplies to remote villages.' Rose always forgot exactly where he had gone—one of those sub-Saharan countries whose capitals she couldn't pronounce. All she had really taken in at the time was the fact that he was leaving.

That he would rather go and work in the heat and the dust and the danger than stay at home and have a family with her.

Her eyes rested on his face in the photo. She could imagine him so clearly, standing under the African sun, sleeves rolled up, eyes screwed up against the light. He would be loving the tough conditions. There had always been a reckless, restless side to Drew, and he had a wonderful capacity to turn even the direst situations into good fun.

How long was it since *she* had had fun? Rose tried to remember wistfully.

Not since she had handed Drew that ultimatum. Settle down with me and start a family, or let me find someone else who does want children, she had told him.

And Drew had chosen to let her find someone else.

'But we'll still be friends,' he had said, and he had meant it. When Rose had asked if she could rent the house he had bought as an investment while he was away, he hadn't hesitated. 'You'll be doing me a favour,' he had said. 'I couldn't ask for a better tenant than you, Rose.'

Rose stopped the sigh that threatened just in time. Drew had moved on, and so had she. Firmly, she opened the fridge so that the photo was out of sight, and put Drew out of her mind as she made herself think about feeding her small son instead.

Pulling out a piece of chicken and a bowl of fresh tomato purée that she had made earlier, she decided to cook some pasta, as well, and see if she could sneak in some peas. It was amazing how early Jack had come to regard certain green vegetables with suspicion.

She was filling a saucepan with water for the pasta when the doorbell went. Jack looked up, and Rose saw his surprised expression mirroring her own.

'Who do you think that is?' she asked him as she turned off the tap. 'We don't usually have visitors at this time.' Jack was so mobile now that she was wary of leaving him on his own even for a moment, and she bent to pick him up. 'Let's go and see who it is.'

Balancing him on her hip with the ease of long practice, Rose squeezed past the pushchair that blocked the narrow hallway. She could see a man's shape through the opaque glass panels in the front door, and she frowned slightly. If this was someone doing a survey it was really inconvenient timing, and so she would tell him.

But the words died on her lips as she opened the door and saw who was standing there.

Drew.

Drew!

With a baby.

Drew shifted the baby awkwardly in his arms. She was heavier than he had thought, but at least she was still asleep, he thought gratefully. What a day this was turning out to be! He had had no idea when he'd set out to see the Clarkes after lunch that he would find his life completely changed by teatime.

'I'll be fine,' he had assured Betty Clarke. 'I've got an old friend called Rose. She'll help me.'

He should have called, Drew realised, but the situation was much too complicated to explain on the phone. He had just known that Rose was the person he needed, and he'd wanted to get to her as soon as possible. He hadn't let himself think about anything but finding her.

It was only when he stood on the doorstep, ringing the bell to his own house, that Drew wondered if he should have checked after all. What if Rose were still at work? What if she had decided to go out for the evening? Would she still have the same mobile number?

Then, to his immense relief, he saw through the glass panels that someone was coming towards the door, and for a moment he even forgot the baby in his arms as a rush of anticipation at the thought of seeing Rose again swept through him. It was nearly a year and a half since they had last met, and then she had been with some colourless guy that Drew hadn't liked at all. With any luck she would be on her own this time, and they could talk properly, the way they had always used to talk.

Drew had hoped that going to Africa would get Rose out of his system at last. That had been the plan, anyway. Rose had moved on, and so would he. Not only would he move on, he would move somewhere so different that he would never even *think* of her.

But it hadn't worked like that. All those crushingly hot nights when he lay on his makeshift bed and listened to the relentless shrilling of a million million insects, the memory of her had been as cool and refreshing as iced water.

Drew suspected that he had romanticised Rose's image in his memory, but when the door opened at last, his first impression was that she was as lovely as ever. She had the same straight silvery blonde hair, the same wide grey eyes, the same sweet curve to her mouth that had haunted his dreams.

But she wasn't on her own. All those long African nights, and he had never once pictured her with a toddler on her hip.

Which was funny, really, when he had known all along that what Rose really wanted was a baby.

And now it seemed that she had one.

Drew's carefully prepared speech evaporated from his mind as he looked at her. *Rose.* He had been planning to cajole her and charm her—to beg her for her help, if necessary. But now all he could think was that he was too late.

Much too late.

'Hello, Rose,' he said simply, unable to think of anything else to say, but his smile felt stiff and he had the oddest sensation of stumbling and falling into a deep, dark pit.

Rose's expression was almost cartoon-like in its astonishment. 'Drew!' she gasped, finding her voice at last, although it sounded quite unlike her own. 'Drew…what…what…?' She was stuttering with surprise, bewildered by so many questions that it was impossible to decide which to ask first. 'What are you doing here?' she managed at last. 'I thought you were in Africa!'

'It's a long story,' said Drew, realising that he had the advantage. At least he had been expecting to see her, even if he hadn't been prepared for the shock of realising that she had a child, or for the way his heart had slammed into his throat at the sight of her. 'Can I come in?'

'Yes…of course…' In a daze, Rose stood back, and Drew edged awkwardly past her in the narrow doorway. For a devastating moment they were very close, and she was overwhelmed by the sudden realisation that this wasn't a dream. This was real, and Drew was right *there*, bare inches away from her. Browner than she remembered him, tougher somehow, but otherwise exactly the same.

Apart from the baby in his arms, of course.

Rose felt very strange. She didn't know what she wanted to say or do or know first.

'Sorry about the pushchair,' she said breathlessly, for want of anything better to say until she could make up her mind. 'There's nowhere else to keep it.'

'That's OK.'

Drew made it past the pushchair and into the living room. He looked around him, recognising the house he had bought as an empty shell, but barely. The furniture was his, but Rose had made the room unmistakably her own. She was a designer, of course, and she had always had the gift of making a house stylish with just a few carefully placed pieces.

The brightly coloured bricks scattered over the floor didn't belong in any style scheme, though, and nor did the plastic highchair at the table or the rest of the unmistakable baby paraphernalia. Rose's life had changed.

Without him.

Drew made himself smile again as she followed him into the room, and he looked properly at the little boy in her arms for the first time. Grey eyes identical to Rose's stared back at him.

'Who's this?' he asked. He was trying to sound jovial, but he was uncomfortably aware that his tone wasn't quite right.

'This is Jack,' said Rose, holding Jack a little more tightly than normal.

'Is he yours?' said Drew, then cursed himself for a fool as she nodded. Of course Jack was hers. He had known that as soon as he looked into the little boy's face.

'Hello, Jack,' he said, but Jack, overcome by shyness suddenly, hid his face in his mother's neck.

Drew could remember just what it felt like to bury his face into the curve of her throat like that. He knew exactly how her skin smelt there. He looked away, ashamed to find himself jealous of a small child.

'He'll come round,' Rose said. 'Just give him a minute or two.'

Drew put his smile back in place. 'Well... congratulations,' he made himself say. 'I know how much you wanted children. You must be very happy.'

'I am. Jack's everything I ever wanted.'

No, not everything, Rose, she corrected herself, remembering how many times she had ached to rewind time and unsay that ultimatum. But then she wouldn't have Jack, and how could she wish that?

'Why didn't you tell me you were having a baby?'

Rose lowered Jack to the floor, where he clung to her legs. 'I didn't think you'd be that interested, Drew. You've always gone out of your way to avoid babies.' She looked at the sleeping baby in his arms, but avoided the obvious question. 'Why should you care if I had one?'

A dull flush spread along Drew's cheekbones. 'I thought we were friends,' he said. 'Of course I'd care about something so important to you. Maybe it wasn't my business, but…' He paused, and then shrugged. 'I wish I'd known, that's all.'

'You've been out of touch,' Rose reminded him, trying for a lighter note. 'You can't expect to keep up with all the news when you take yourself off to the middle of nowhere for years on end!'

'Just under eighteen months,' said Drew, not sure why he was feeling so defensive. 'I've been out of e-mail contact, it's true, but there's a postal service. You could have written.'

'Yes, I could have,' she conceded. Walking awkwardly, with Jack clinging to her leg, she went over to one of the sofas and gestured to Drew to sit down on the other one. 'I'm sorry,' she said honestly. 'It's just that you seemed a long way away.'

She should have told him about Jack. Especially since they were living in his house. She just hadn't been able to find the words.

'I did mean to write, in fact, but…' She lifted her shoulders hopelessly. 'To be honest, I wasn't sure how to tell you.'

'Well, there's no reason why you should have done,' said Drew after a moment. 'It's just strange seeing you with a baby.'

'I could say the same about you.' Rose looked meaningfully at the baby, still sleeping peacefully in his arms. It was obviously a little girl, and someone had dressed her carefully in a dress and little coat, with a cute striped hat, although Rose guessed that someone hadn't been Drew. He was holding her as if she were an unexploded bomb. 'What's her name?'

'Molly.'

'Nice name,' said Rose, puzzled by the expression on his face. 'Whose is she?'

Drew hesitated. 'She's mine,' he said after a moment. 'Molly's my daughter.'

There was a long, long silence. Even Jack seemed to sense the tension, pausing in the middle of scrambling up onto his mother's knee to look up into her face.

'Your *daughter*?' Rose said in a frozen voice. It was the last, the very last thing she had expected.

'I've only just found out myself,' said Drew. He swallowed. This was much more difficult than he had imagined when he had gaily assured Betty Clarke that he would be able to look after Molly. 'Rose,' he confessed, 'I really need your help.'

Rose stared at the baby. At Drew's daughter. After everything he had said about not wanting children, he was a father. Another woman had had his baby. Rose was unprepared for how much that knowledge hurt.

Mechanically, she lifted Jack onto her lap. Swallowed. Dragged her gaze from the baby to look right into Drew's eyes.

'I think you'd better explain,' she said.

CHAPTER TWO

DREW raked a harassed hand through his brown hair, making the distinctive Pemberton streak stand up on end. 'I don't really know where to start…'

'There's usually a pretty obvious point when babies start,' said Rose.

He acknowledged that with a twisted smile. 'Yes, but you usually get a few months' warning that a baby is going to appear in your life, too. I had none at all. Molly is just as much a surprise to me as she is to you.'

She frowned. 'How long have you known about her?'

'About two and a half hours,' he said, with a glance at his watch. 'I had no idea of her existence until then.'

'What? Not even a suspicion?'

'Of course not,' he said indignantly. 'I would never have gone off to Burkina Faso if I'd known. What do you think I am?'

'I think you're a man who never wanted a baby.'

'I didn't. That's what makes this all so…' Drew looked down at the baby. 'I feel like I've been in a car crash,' he admitted a little helplessly to Rose. 'One minute I'm a bachelor, fancy-free, with no responsibilities, and the next I'm a father. I can't really take it in.'

He did look shell-shocked, Rose had to admit. Almost as shocked as she felt. Her heart was still bruised and fluttering with shock from its plummet the moment Drew had looked at her and told her that he was a father. Drew, who had always ruled out the possibility of babies with *her*.

Jack, settling into her lap, stuck his thumb in his mouth and stared at Drew and the baby as if fascinated by them, and she put her arms around him and hugged him close, not sure if she was giving reassurance or taking it.

'How old is Molly?'

'The Clarkes told me she was nearly eight months old.'

'The Clarkes? Who are they? And where's Molly's mother?'

'She's dead.' Drew heard Rose's sharp intake of breath at the bald statement, and he rubbed his hand wearily over his face. 'Look, you're right. I need to start at the beginning.'

'When you slept with Molly's mother?'

'Yes,' he said, flinching slightly at her directness. 'Her name was Hannah and she was a technician at the office. She'd do the technical drawings and… Well, it doesn't matter what she did. I'd known her for a few years, ever since I went to work there, and we'd always got on well. Hannah was attractive, I suppose, but I never really thought about that much. She was just a friend.'

She wasn't you, he wanted to say to Rose, but didn't.

'If you had a baby together you were clearly more than friends,' Rose said crisply.

Typical Rose, thought Drew with rueful affection. She looked so sweet, but there was a refreshing and sometimes uncomfortable astringency to her, as well.

'That really *was* all we were until my leaving party,' he insisted. 'But that night I was… Well, the truth is that

I wasn't sure I was doing the right thing in going to Africa, but I didn't want anyone to know that I was having doubts, so I did my best to cover it by having a good time. Drinking too much, in fact,' he added dryly. 'Hannah was in a strange mood, too—almost wild. I didn't realise at the time, but her parents told me today that she had decided that she really wanted a baby.'

'And she'd picked on you as the father?' Rose raised her brows in disbelief.

'I know what it sounds like…but she definitely didn't want a relationship. She told her parents that she liked me, and thought I'd have some healthy genes to pass on, but that I'd be a disaster as a father.'

'Hah!' snorted Rose, thinking that Hannah had obviously had no illusions about Drew. Sensible woman.

'I'd told her about why we'd split up, so she knew I didn't want children myself, but she didn't care about that. She just wanted to get pregnant.'

Jack was beginning to squirm. He had evidently decided that Drew and Molly weren't going to do anything alarming, and was ready to go back to his toys. 'It takes two to get pregnant,' Rose pointed out, putting out a protective hand just in case Jack fell as he scrambled down from the sofa. 'Didn't you take any precautions?'

Drew shifted in his seat. 'The thing is, I wasn't expecting to sleep with anyone that night. I thought I was just going out for a few drinks, but one thing led to another, and then Hannah was inviting me back to her flat, and…When things started getting a little…you know…'

'I know,' said Rose expressionlessly.

'I think I did say that I didn't have anything with me, but Hannah was insistent that she was on the Pill and…' He glanced at Rose's face. 'Don't look like that! I *know* it was irresponsible, but it wasn't as if she was a total stranger.'

'Hannah lied to you?'

'She wanted a baby. That's what her parents said, anyway. It was just luck, from her point of view, that she managed to get pregnant that night, but apparently she knew that she was ovulating and all the signs were good. It even suited her that I was going away a couple of days later, as I wouldn't be around to put two and two together.'

'She told her *parents* all this?' said Rose in disbelief. Her own parents had died in an accident when she was nineteen. She had loved them dearly, and missed them still, but she certainly couldn't imagine telling them that she was ovulating and hoping to become pregnant by a man she knew didn't want to be a father. It would have been hard enough to tell them about Jack.

'Hannah was a very strong personality. You'd have liked her,' said Drew. 'No, you would,' he insisted, when she looked sceptical. 'Her parents told me that she'd been completely straight with them about wanting to do it on her own. All she would say about me was that I worked at the office and that she liked me, but that I was the last person she wanted to get involved with.'

He didn't add that Hannah had told her parents that he was still in love with Rose, and that she knew that any attempt at getting together for the baby's sake would be doomed to disaster.

'So you went off to Africa none the wiser?'

'Exactly. Hannah was very casual about it when I saw her the next day. She said it was just a fling for both of us, and that as far as she was concerned we were just friends. And that was a bit of a relief, to be honest.'

'I'm sure it was,' said Rose acidly. 'You wouldn't

have wanted to have to take any responsibility for your actions, now, would you?'

A dull flush crept up his cheeks. 'It wasn't like that,' he said. 'And I've taken responsibility now. When I heard that Hannah had died, I wanted to see her parents and say how sorry I was, how much I'd liked her…it seemed like the right thing to do somehow.'

It had been. Rose studied him, a little frown between her brows. She had been so staggered to see him, and so thrown by the news that he was a father, that she hadn't had a chance to look at him properly yet. Now she looked at him more carefully. He was browner, yes, and leaner. There were more lines around the green eyes, but otherwise he looked just as she had remembered him.

But something had changed. He seemed more solid somehow. His face was still humorous, with that long, curling mouth and the glinting amusement in his eyes, but there was a new assurance to him now, a thoughtfulness that hadn't been there before. Africa had changed him. His time there seemed to have made him responsible rather than reckless.

He was different. Rose couldn't quite put her finger on why or how, but she knew that it was true. And it wasn't just to do with the baby sleeping in his lap.

'What happened?' she asked.

'I wasn't looking forward to it,' Drew said. 'I didn't know what on earth I was going to say, but in the event I didn't really have to say anything. As soon as Mrs Clarke opened the door she just stared at me, and then stood back to let me inside. I couldn't understand what was going on, but she showed me into a sitting room and there was a baby in one of those bouncy chair things.'

'This is Molly,' Hannah's mother had said.

'Is she Hannah's?' he had asked, and she had nodded with a wavering smile as Drew approached the baby. His tentative smile had been wiped off his face as he'd looked at her properly and seen the telltale splodge in the baby's soft dark hair. Dumbly, he had raised his eyes, and Betty Clarke had nodded again.

'And yours,' she had said.

Now Drew pulled the cap off Molly's head, and Rose saw for herself. It hadn't taken her long to get so used to Drew's hair that she hadn't even noticed it after a while, but she vividly remembered how startled she had been to meet his father and see exactly the same pattern on his head.

'It's a form of vitiligo,' Drew had explained to her once. 'It's an auto-immune thing. For some reason melanin isn't produced, and in our family it's inherited, a sort of genetic quirk, because if we get it at all, it always shows up in exactly the same pattern.'

Molly was dark-haired, with a distinctive star-shaped streak of pale hair above her right eyebrow. Exactly like Drew.

There was no doubting whose daughter she was.

Rose watched Drew tentatively smooth Molly's hair, and something painful—jealousy? Bitterness?—gripped her heart so hard that she had to look away.

'Didn't Hannah's parents try and find you when she died?' she asked after a moment.

Drew shook his head. 'She'd been very careful not to give any information away, but they'd noticed that she'd smiled when she'd seen that streak when Molly was born. "Just like your dad," she'd told Molly. So at the funeral they hoped that someone with that hair would turn up, but of course, I was overseas. They didn't have much choice but to carry on looking after Molly themselves, but they're struggling. Betty—her mother—is due a hip operation soon, and her husband has a bad heart. They were just wondering whether they would have to call in the social services when I turned up at the door. It seemed like providence. There's no need to do a DNA test with that hair—all the babies in my family have that.'

'I remember,' said Rose slowly.

Drew looked down at Molly and then straight at Rose. 'I couldn't just walk away when they needed help. It takes two to make a baby, as you pointed out, and I had to take some responsibility, so I said I would look after her at least until after her grandmother's operation, and then if that goes well we would try and sort something out.'

'But you don't know anything about babies,' Rose protested. 'I can't believe they just handed her over to you.'

'Betty was a little reluctant at first, but there didn't seem to be any option, and I…I told them you would help me,' he confessed in a rush.

Rose drew a sharp breath of exasperation. That was typical of Drew. He had always taken her for granted, always believed that he could charm her into doing whatever he wanted. 'You hadn't even told me that you were back in the country, Drew!'

'I know,' he said. 'I only got back yesterday. It all happened so suddenly. Everything was going well on the project when we had word that insurgents were making their way towards us. We were ordered to withdraw to Ouagadougou, and then the decision was made to repatriate us until the situation became clearer, and who knows when that will be?'

'So you suddenly found yourself back in London?'

He nodded. 'I'd been seconded to the project in Burkina Faso from my company, so I reported back to head office to see what I should do in the meantime.'

'What did they say?'

'They told me to take a couple of weeks' leave, and if I'd heard nothing by then they'd find me another job. I could probably go back to the team I was working with before I left. I went to see them, and that's when I heard about Hannah...'

Drew sighed. 'You know, there's part of me that wishes I'd never gone to see the Clarkes.' He glanced down at his daughter. 'Molly has changed everything,' he said, sounding almost baffled.

'Babies have a habit of doing that.'

Rose tried to imagine what it had been like for him, arriving back in London from Africa. Working in a dusty rural village one day, checking in at swish City offices the next. Believing himself to be as irresponsible and free as ever, then discovering that he was a father. She wasn't surprised that he still looked faintly shell-shocked. He must be reeling from jet-lag and cultural shock, let alone the terrifying and unexpected responsibility of fatherhood.

But, dammit, she didn't want to feel sorry for him! How could he turn up here with a *baby*, after all he'd had to say about not wanting to be a father, and just assume that she would drop everything to help him?

'So you thought of me?' she said, her voice hard.

'I was going to come and see you anyway,' said Drew. He wanted to tell her that the thought of seeing her again had been the one thing he had held onto in the muddle and chaos of leaving, but this was clearly not the time. He hadn't really thought about how she would feel when he turned up with a baby, but it had clearly been a tactless thing to do.

'I was looking forward to seeing you,' he persevered, 'but I thought you'd be working until the evening, and when I heard about Hannah I felt I should go and see her parents straight away rather than keep putting it off.'

He hesitated. 'When I saw Molly and understood the situation…you were the first person I thought of, Rose.' He couldn't explain how strong his feeling had been that she was one person he needed, and that if he could only find her and show her Molly that everything would be all right. 'You know what my mother's like. She was never exactly hands-on with her own child, so I can't imagine she would be much help, even if she could be persuaded back from Spain. My father might have helped, but he's ill, and my stepmother is taken up with him at the moment. I could only think of you.'

'You didn't think that I might be busy? That I might have my own child to look after?'

'No,' said Drew. 'I never thought of you having a baby. I thought you'd be just the same, and that I could rely on you the way I've always done before.'

His green eyes looked straight into hers. 'There's nowhere else I can go right now. I knew you would know what to do with a baby, and I had to bring Molly somewhere.'

'And this is your house,' Rose added for him in a dull voice, her gaze sliding away from his. 'Don't forget that bit.'

'I hadn't forgotten, but I don't want to use that to threaten you. You live here, and nothing's going to

change that. You can tell me to leave if you want to, and
I'll go, but I'm begging you, for Molly's sake, to help
me. I'm a water engineer, Rose. I don't know the first
thing about babies. I'll get a nanny for Molly tomorrow,
but for tonight I really need your help.'

Rose looked at Molly. She was just a baby. How
could she refuse to help her? Drew had known that she
wouldn't be able to do that. Her grey eyes lifted to meet
his green gaze once more.

'All right,' she said. 'I'll help you tonight, but then
we need to talk about this, Drew.'

'Whatever you say,' said Drew, unable to hide his relief.

As if she had been waiting for some signal, Molly's
face puckered and she began to squirm. Rose saw the
relief in his expression wiped away by panic.

'Oh, God, she's going to wake up,' he said desperately, sitting rigidly still, as if he could will the baby
back to sleep. 'What shall I do?'

The words were barely out of his mouth before
Molly began to wail, startling Jack, who looked up from
the box of toys he was emptying.

'Ga?'

'It's all right, Jack, it's just the baby,' said Rose, getting up to take Molly from Drew, who looked frankly
terrified. 'Let me take her.'

Lifting Molly against her shoulder, she held the
warm little body close and rubbed her back soothingly as she bawled. 'It's all right, sweetheart…Shh,
now…you'll be all right…' she murmured, swaying in
a comforting rocking motion.

Drew watched them both nervously. 'Is she OK?
Why's she crying like that?'

'She's woken up in a strange place with strange people, Drew. Wouldn't you want to cry if you were Molly?'

Out of the corner of her eye, Rose could see that Jack had stopped what he was doing and was regarding her with a scowl, jealous of the attention she was giving the baby. She badly wanted to tell Drew exactly what she thought of him, but that was going to have to wait.

'Jack needs his supper,' she told Drew, 'and Molly will need something to eat, too. Did her grandmother give you food for her?'

'I've got a whole car full of stuff.'

'Why don't you go and bring it in?' she suggested, resigning herself to the inevitable. 'We need to get both these children in bed, and then, Drew, we're going to have to talk.'

CHAPTER THREE

BY THE time Drew had struggled in with the last of Molly's stuff, the front half of the living room was crowded, but Jack's supper was almost ready. Rose had made it largely one-handed, while inviting Jack to patronise Molly for being so small and helpless that she couldn't do half the things that he could, like pick up his bricks. Showing off about that kept him occupied for a while, but she could tell that resentment at the attention Molly was getting wasn't far off, and she was very glad when Drew had finished and she could hand his daughter back to him.

'Here—you take her,' she said.

Before Drew had a chance to protest, she had laid the baby in his arms. Molly stared up at him, and he stared back, suddenly overwhelmed. His daughter. Her eyes were the same colour as his. She had the same streak in her hair. His throat seemed to close with an emotion he couldn't name, a mixture of terror and love.

And then Molly began to wail and the moment had passed.

'Hold her against your shoulder and walk around with her,' Rose told him. 'Talk to her. She doesn't know where she is or who we are or what's going on. Try and comfort her.'

Gingerly, Drew did as he was told while Rose put Jack in his highchair and set his supper in front of him. She offered him a plastic spoon, as well, but without much hope that he would use it. Jack hated being fed but, while he would occasionally have a go with the spoon, generally he preferred to use his hands. He loved his food, but there was no denying that he was a messy eater. By the time he had finished, half his meal seemed to have ended up garnishing his hair or ears. It was never a pretty picture.

Rose was used to Jack's eating habits, but she noticed that Drew averted his eyes. 'Better get used to it,' she told him. 'I don't suppose Molly's table manners are much better! And, talking of which, we'd better find her something to eat…'

He wouldn't have known where to begin, Drew realised, feeling horribly inadequate but profoundly grateful at the same time that Rose seemed to know what she was looking for as she dug through the pile of stuff the Clarkes had sent with Molly, emerging eventually with a bib, a jar of prepared food and a smaller version of Jack's highchair.

'OK, we're in business.' Rose carried the chair over to the table and set it next to Jack's as she pretended to marvel at how much he had eaten. 'Do you think you deserve some pudding now?' she asked him, and Jack shouted an enthusiastic reply and banged his plate on the plastic tray.

Drew liked watching her with her little boy. She was so relaxed and natural with him. Would he ever be like that with Molly? he wondered, glancing down at his daughter. It was hard to imagine. All he had to do was hold her at the moment, and he felt much, much more tense just doing that than he had done when he had heard that rebel troops were closing in on the village. Insurgents he could deal with; an eight-month-old baby was a much more alarming proposition.

'Shall we just get Molly settled first?' Rose was still chatting to Jack, wanting him to feel pleasantly superior rather than resentful. 'She's just a baby. She's not a big boy, like you, and she probably doesn't know about puddings, does she?' She glanced over her shoulder at Drew. 'Do you want to put her in the chair?'

'Um…Rose…' Drew held Molly away from him with a grimace.

'What is it?'

'She…smells.'

Rose couldn't help it. She started laughing at his expression. 'I should have thought of that! Time for your first lesson: changing a nappy!'

Digging out the changing mat, she laid it on the kitchen floor and talked Drew through the whole process as she gave Jack his pudding and encouraged her son to condescend to Molly. She could have changed and fed the baby in half the time it was obviously going to take Drew to do it, but she would have to be careful not to make Jack jealous—and besides, Drew had to learn. She had only promised one night.

One night with Drew.

How different this night would be from all the others they had spent together, from all those long sweet nights when they had tumbled, laughing, into bed, and woken cosily entwined the next morning. Rose could still remember the smell of his skin, the heart-cracking feel of his arm holding her close into the curve of his body. The warmth of his breath on her shoulder, the touch of his lips at the nape of her neck, sending that telltale shiver of response down her spine no matter how hard she tried to pretend that she was asleep…

Hastily, Rose yanked her mind back on track. This night wasn't going to be like that. Drew wasn't here because he had changed his mind. He wasn't here because he wanted her. He was here because he needed her help, that was all.

Because he had had a baby with somebody else.

Think about Jack, Rose told herself with a kind of desperation. Think about Molly. Think about anything other than what it's going to be like lying in bed tonight, knowing that Drew is at the other end of the hall—there, but not with her.

'Whew!' Drew screwed up his nose as he pushed the dirty nappy into a plastic bag. 'Who would think something so small could make such a stink?'

Rose pushed the thought of the night to come aside, and got up from her chair next to Jack's to dispose of the nappy. 'Welcome to my world,' she said.

After the nappy-changing, learning how to feed Molly would be relatively painless—or at least that was what Drew thought, until he discovered that there was a lot more to it than simply popping a spoonful of food into her mouth every now and then. Molly turned out to have a will of her own, and if she didn't feel like having what he offered she would close her little mouth firmly and avert her face, batting the spoon away with an imperious hand. Drew ended up with more food on him than in the baby, but Rose didn't seem to think it mattered.

'She's had something to eat, that's what's important,' she said, wiping Molly's face with the deftness of long practice and lifting her out of the highchair. 'Now, what about a bath?'

'That would be great,' said Drew, looking down at his smeared shirt. 'Are you sure you don't mind?'

'Not you, dummy! Molly and Jack.'

Drew was exhausted by the time Molly was finally ready for bed. 'Do you mean to say you have to do this every day?' he asked, appalled.

'But this is the best bit,' said Rose, unable to resist cuddling the warm, clean baby who snuffled into her neck.

Drew watched Molly's fat little hands clutching at Rose's hair and felt inadequacy wash over him again. 'I'll never be able to do this on my own,' he said despairingly.

'Yes, you will. Have a cuddle,' she said, reluctantly handing Molly over. 'You'll realise it's all worthwhile.'

Drew was terrified that Molly would start crying again, but after a momentary stiffening she relaxed against him. 'She's almost asleep anyway,' said Rose quietly. 'Offer her the bottle,' she said, handing over the milk she had brought up.

So Drew sat in the chair and fed his baby daughter while Rose sat Jack on her lap and read him a story. Jack seemed to have accepted the idea that Molly would be sharing a room with him, and they had set up her cot in the corner.

I can't believe I'm doing this, Drew kept thinking. *I can't believe I'm a father. I can't believe Rose is right there, after all this time.*

With one part of his mind he marvelled at how small and perfect Molly was. Her hands were like tiny dimpled starfish on the bottle, and she was making soft, snuffly noises as she drank her milk. Drew was very conscious of how warm and solid and real she felt, of the surprising weight of her in the crook of his arm.

But with the other part of his mind he was terribly aware of Rose on the other side of the room, of her quiet voice as she read the story, of the curve of her throat and the sweep of her lashes and the tenderness of her expression as she smiled down at her son, cuddled trustfully into her lap, lashes drooping and one thumb stuck in his mouth.

Rose hadn't said anything about Jack's father. Shouldn't he be here, enjoying this quiet time with them? Didn't he want to be there? Drew wondered. Or would he come home any minute now? Would the front door slam, followed by eager footsteps up the stairs to find wife and son? Somehow Drew didn't think that was going to happen. Rose would surely have mentioned him, and in any case there had been no sign of a man in the bathroom or kitchen. Drew didn't really want to analyse how reassuring he had found that.

And yet why wouldn't Jack's father want to be with Rose? She was warm and loving and beautiful—everything a man could want.

So why did you leave her? an inner voice asked acidly. Drew knew the answer to that. He hadn't wanted children, and Rose had. He hadn't wanted the feeding and the crying and the nappy-changing and the quiet evenings sitting in a nursery. He hadn't wanted any of this.

He looked down at Molly. He hadn't asked for any of it, but now that he was here everything felt…different.

Molly's eyes were fluttering, lifting, then falling again, until with a little sigh the teat of the bottle slipped from her mouth.

'She's asleep,' said Rose softly. She had already

tucked Jack into his cot and kissed him goodnight. He had been so tired he had gone down with barely a token protest. 'Let me take her.'

Very gently, she lifted Molly from Drew's arms and laid her in her cot. Drew stood looking down at the baby in the dim light. At his daughter.

His *daughter*, he thought again, suddenly overwhelmed by the enormity of it. Wordlessly, he looked at Rose, who smiled as if she knew what he was thinking.

'It'll be all right,' she said quietly. 'Molly will be fine. You'll be fine.'

Drew hoped she was right. Leaving the two children sleeping, he followed her downstairs.

'God, what a day!' he said, collapsing onto one of the sofas.

'How do you feel?' asked Rose. On automatic pilot, she began to put back all the toys Jack had emptied out of the box.

'I'm not sure,' Drew confessed. 'Terrified… overwhelmed…but incredible, too.'

Rose smiled. 'I know what you mean. I feel like that almost every time I look at Jack.'

She threw the last of the toys back in the box and closed the lid, then got up off her knees and headed for the kitchen. Realising that she wasn't going to sit down until the mess from the babies' supper was cleared away, Drew got up to help her.

'Do you do this every night?' he asked as he wiped down the highchairs.

'Pretty much.'

'On your own?'

Rose wrung out the cloth. 'Usually, yes.'

'Rose…where's Jack's father?'

There was a tiny pause. She gave the cloth an extra twist. 'He doesn't live here,' she said.

'So you're not married?' Drew was appalled at the sudden feeling of lightness as she shook her head.

'No, but Seb is still Jack's father. He plays an important role in his life.'

Drew watched her wipe down the worktops. 'I was sure you wouldn't have a baby until you were married. I thought that was what you wanted.'

'That was what I thought, too.' Rose had found a bottle of wine, and without asking Drew she pulled out the cork and poured two glasses. 'But things don't always work out the way you plan them.'

Handing Drew a glass, which he took with an absent-minded word of thanks, she went over to the sofas, stretched out on one with a weary sigh.

'You've found yourself a father by accident,' she said. 'In lots of ways I'm an accidental mother, too. I met Seb a few months before you left. He's a nice guy—very kind, very responsible.' Very unlike Drew. 'He'd just come out of a relationship, too, and neither of us had any expectations that it would be a long-term thing. We were friends more than anything else.'

'Clearly more than friends if you had a baby together.' Drew quoted her words back at her, and she flushed.

'All right, we were more than friends,' she admitted. 'But it honestly wasn't a big thing for either of us. And then…I was on the Pill, and I got food poisoning one night… I didn't think it would make that much difference, but it did. I was three months pregnant before I even thought about going to the doctor.'

'And what happened then?' Drew wasn't enjoying this story at all.

Rose sighed. 'I bought myself one of those home pregnancy testing kits and at first I was horrified. I wasn't in the right situation to have a baby, and I knew Seb wasn't ready for a full-time commitment any more than I was. I'd always had a romantic dream about getting married and having a family, and I was appalled at the idea of being a single mother, but…it was my baby inside me. I couldn't let anything hurt it. And I knew that I might never have another chance to have a child.'

'What did Seb say when you told him?'

'He was shocked at first, but when we talked about it neither of us wanted to contemplate a termination. We agreed that we would both be responsible for the child, and that it would be better for us to be friends than to feel stuck in an unhappy relationship which neither of us wanted. So Jack has a mother and a father. We just don't live together.'

Rose took a sip of her wine. 'Seb lives not far from here, which is one of the reasons I was so keen to rent from you. I knew I would never be able to afford anything in this area by myself.'

'So you knew you were pregnant when you asked me if you could have this house?'

'Just,' she said. 'Perhaps I should have told you then, but I didn't feel ready to talk about it to anyone. I was overwhelmed by the idea of having a child, and not at all sure how I would cope with everything. It wasn't how I'd imagined having a baby,' she admitted a little sadly.

'But you went ahead and had Jack anyway?'

'Yes,' Rose said. 'And I've never regretted it for a moment. But it hasn't been easy. I certainly couldn't have done it without Seb. We've been sharing the childcare as much as we can, and I can always talk to him if I'm worried about anything to do with Jack. He's a huge part of my life—and of Jack's, obviously.'

Drew was getting a bit sick of hearing about how important Seb was to her. 'So where is he now?' he asked in a hard voice.

'He was made redundant recently,' Rose told him, picking her words carefully. 'It was a shock for both of us, but he's just got a temporary job, and there's a chance that it might become permanent. The trouble is that the new job is based in Bristol, which obviously isn't ideal from a childcare point of view.'

'Bristol isn't that far from London,' Drew pointed out. 'It's—what?—an hour and a half? A couple of hours by car?'

'If you've got a car,' said Rose. 'I haven't. There's no point in making any plans until we know if Seb's job is permanent or not, but in the meantime I've got a problem.' She glanced at Drew, sprawled on the opposite sofa, speculation in her grey eyes. 'I'm wondering if we could come to some arrangement,' she said.

'What sort of arrangement?' asked Drew cautiously.

'A practical one,' said Rose. 'You said you would have to get a nanny for Molly while her grandmother is in hospital. Why don't I be that nanny?'

He stared at her. 'You want me to *employ* you?'

'No, I'm offering to look after Molly and Jack during the day if you'll come back after work and babysit in the evenings so *I* can go to work. It would be a straightforward exchange of childcare, with no money involved.'

Rose kept her voice even, not wanting to betray how desperately she wanted Drew to agree. She had been thinking about it while they bathed and fed the two children, and it made perfect sense. It might not be the magical solution she had been fantasising about just before Drew turned up on her doorstep, but really it was pretty close.

Drew, however, wasn't looking convinced. 'Why would you want to do that?' he asked, puzzled by her offer.

'Well, for a start it would mean that I could stay here,' she pointed out. 'This is your house, and you're going to need it now that you've got a child to look after. It's going to be a push with the four of us, and there certainly isn't any room for nanny. So, if that's what you want for Molly, Jack and I would have to find somewhere else to live, and with everything else so uncertain at the moment I really don't want to have to do that.'

'I wouldn't make you leave your home,' said Drew, offended by the very suggestion.

'You might not have a choice, Drew. You have to put Molly first now, and if she needs a home and someone to care for her while you're at work, you're going to have to make sure that's what she gets. All I'm suggesting is that I be that someone. I may not be a trained nanny, but I'm here and I won't cost you anything. It's the perfect solution for both of us.'

CHAPTER FOUR

DREW looked doubtful. 'For me, perhaps,' he said, frowning slightly. 'I don't see what you get out of it. You're not really proposing to go to work after looking after two children all day, are you? I've only done it for a couple of hours—with help—and I'm exhausted!'

Rose shrugged. 'I'm used to it. I'd be just as tired if you asked me to go and dig a well in Africa, but you probably wouldn't think anything of *that*. The evenings are the only time I can get any work done. It was better when Seb was around, because he used to work at home one day a week, and he would have Jack then, so I could go into the studio and have any meetings then. The rest of the time I've had to work on the kitchen table when Jack's sleeping. I'm lucky Peter and Peter have been so supportive and are prepared to be flexible.'

Drew raised his brows. 'Peter and Peter are still together?'

'Very much so. They've got a much better track record than the rest of us,' Rose said dryly. 'And they've been fantastic to me. Their design business has really taken off in the last couple of years, and I've had a steadyish supply of freelance work from them. Ideally,

I'd spend more time at the studio with them, but that would have meant finding childcare for Jack and that was simply too expensive for me.

'Besides,' she went on, picking up her glass once more, 'I didn't want to miss out on being with Jack. Babies grow up so fast, and they change every day. I'm just lucky I've been able to arrange my work around him. A lot of people don't have that option.'

Drew had got up to find the bottle of wine, and now he leant across the coffee table and refilled Rose's glass. 'It sounds as if you've got things under control,' he said slowly. 'Why not carry on as you are? There's no need for you to put yourself out for Molly and me, after all.'

'There is if I need you to put yourself out for me,' said Rose. 'And I do need that. Peter and Peter have just asked me to work on a big contract. It's really important to them, and for me it would be good money and great on my CV, but there's a catch this time. The deadline is very short, and if I want the work I'd have to commit myself to working there for the next six weeks. Peter and Peter have said they'd be happy if I spent three evenings a week in the studio with them and did the rest at home, but with Seb away I wasn't sure that what I'd get for the work would be enough to cover the childcare I'd need. I was feeling desperate just before you arrived, but now that you're here everything's changed…'

She trailed off as she looked across the coffee table and met Drew's green gaze, and the air evaporated from her lungs all at once as the unreality of the situation suddenly hit her afresh. How could she have guessed when she woke up this morning that Drew would be sitting there sharing a bottle of wine with her before she went to bed again? That he would be there, looking at her, after all this time, after all those months and weeks and days of missing him?

But there he was, as if the last two years, ten months and nineteen days had never happened, as if nothing had changed.

Only Rose knew that everything had changed. Drew was a father. She was a mother. The most important experience of their lives, becoming a parent, and they had done it with other people—not together, the way she had always dreamed. A wave of sadness swamped Rose for a moment, before she managed to shake her mind free of it. What was done was done. There was no point in getting maudlin about it.

Not wanting Drew to guess how much she still felt for him, Rose made an effort to pull herself together.

'The *situation* has changed since you turned up with Molly,' she corrected herself with a show of briskness. 'I was beginning to think I'd have to turn down Peter and Peter's offer, but now that you're here there's a chance I can do the work after all. All you need to do is agree to a bit of babysitting.'

Drew made a face. 'It sounds so easy when you put it like that. But what if something happens when you're out? What if Jack or Molly wakes up and cries? I wouldn't know what to do!'

'You'll have to learn.'

'How?' he said, thinking of the competent way Rose had dealt with Molly earlier. He would never have that kind of confidence.

'The same way every new parent does, by doing it,' said Rose. 'You can spend the next week or so getting used to the routine, and Jack and Molly can spend it getting used to you, then I'll be able to leave you to it.'

Drew couldn't help thinking it wouldn't be as easy as Rose made it sound, but he would sound pathetic if he made too much fuss. After all, she had managed. Why shouldn't he? Could it really be *that* hard to look after a baby? He could install water supplies in hostile terrain. He could negotiate his way around government departments and design workable solutions to improve sometimes desperate conditions. He could work when the temperature hit a hundred and twenty in the shade, usually when there wasn't any.

So he could manage a baby.

Couldn't he?

'There you are, then,' said Rose. 'You can have a crash course in fatherhood starting tomorrow, and then we can sort out a routine which means that we can both work and that both our children are looked after.'

Drew studied her over the rim of his glass. She was leaning back in the corner of the sofa, legs curled up under her, pushing the pale blonde hair tiredly behind her ears. The grey eyes were as beautiful as ever, but shadowed by weariness and starred with lines that Drew suspected might have as much to do with worry as with laughter.

It must have been tough for her, bringing Jack up on her own, and money was obviously tight. She had always been such a warm, loving person, and she deserved better than she seemed to have got from Jack's father.

But who was he to criticise Seb? Drew realised in a moment of insight. What had *he* ever done to make Rose happy? He had insisted that he didn't want children, had refused to even consider the possibility of giving up his precious freedom for her. And he had discovered the hard way that freedom wasn't all that it was cracked up to be. It hadn't meant so much without Rose by his side to be free *with*.

Rose had been sensible. She had found someone else. And he couldn't complain now because he hadn't been the one to give her the baby she wanted. The least he could do, Drew thought, was to help her with Jack as she had asked, so that she could work.

He just wished he didn't feel guilty about the fact that she was going to end up looking after his daughter for him. The truth was that he needed Rose much more than she needed him.

She was right, too. Looking after the two children between them was the obvious solution to their difficulties. Drew could see that. It was just that it didn't *feel* quite right. It felt as if Rose were proposing some kind of business arrangement. The Rose he remembered wasn't brisk and practical. That Rose wouldn't have worried about money and childcare. She would have wrapped her arms around him and told him that everything would work out, that nothing mattered as long as they were together.

But they weren't together any more, remember? Drew reminded himself fiercely. That was the whole point. They might be spending the next few weeks in the same house, but it wasn't about loving each other. It wasn't about being together any more. It was nothing more than a practical solution to a practical problem. Rose had made that very clear, and he had better not forget it.

'OK,' he said. If Rose wanted to keep things practical, that was what he would do. 'Let's do what you suggest. If you tell me what I need to do, I'll look after Jack and Molly in the evenings while you're at work.'

Rose exhaled slowly. She hadn't realised until he agreed how tense she had been waiting for him to decide. 'Thanks,' she said simply.

'I should be thanking *you*,' said Drew as he topped up their glasses once more. 'Let's drink to our deal.' Leaning forward, he chinked glasses with Rose across the table.

'To our deal,' she echoed, faint colour staining her cheeks as she settled back into the cushions. It felt all wrong to be talking about a *deal* with Drew—as if they were strangers coming to a business-like arrangement, as if they had never lived together, never loved together.

There was a pause.

'It'll be funny to be living together again,' Drew said as the pause lengthened into an awkward silence, and Rose wondered if he had been thinking the same thing as her.

Her colour deepened. 'It won't be the same with two children.'

'No, I suppose not.'

Silence threatened again, and Rose shifted uncomfortably on the sofa. It was her turn to think of something to say.

'Are you OK about sleeping in the third bedroom?'

Which was one way of making it clear that he wouldn't be sleeping with her, Drew thought wryly. Not that he had expected that for a moment.

'Of course,' he said.

'There's not much room in there,' Rose persevered. 'It's not much more than a cupboard. I don't mind sleeping in there if you'd rather have my room.'

Once there would have been no question of sleeping in separate rooms.

'I'll be fine,' he said, forcing a hearty note into his

voice. 'That little room will be luxury compared with the places I've been sleeping in recently, and it's not as if it'll be for ever.'

'No,' Rose agreed flatly. 'It's not for ever.'

They drank their wine in a silence that stretched and twanged with the memory of all the times they had slept together, all the times they had made love and believed that they would be happy for ever. All the times when it would have been impossible to imagine that one day they would sit opposite each other like strangers and be unable to say what they were thinking or feeling.

'Did you see where I put my phone?' Drew said at last with a kind of desperation. He looked around the room, at anything other than Rose. 'I should ring the Clarkes and let them know that Molly's OK. They'll be worried.'

'It's over there,' said Rose, pointing. She got to her feet, very grateful to him for breaking that awful silence. The Drew she remembered would never have been as thoughtful, she reflected. Was it Africa that had made him more responsible, or the shock of suddenly becoming a father? Either way, it was a change for the better. 'I'll try and find something to eat while you call them.'

Drew stopped in the middle of opening his phone. 'You're not going to cook now, surely?' he objected. 'It's been a hell of a day, and the last thing you must want to do is start thinking about a meal—and the last thing I want to do is feel guilty because you are! Let's order a take-away.'

'That's not very healthy.'

'We can be healthy tomorrow,' he said firmly. 'Where's the nearest pizza place? I haven't had pizza for eighteen months!'

He bullied Rose into fishing a flyer for a local pizza

delivery service from the recycling box while he quickly called the Clarkes to reassure them that Molly was safe and well. Before Rose quite realised what had happened, he had ordered them a pizza each and was switching off his phone with an air of satisfaction.

'They said they'd be about twenty minutes,' he told her. 'They can't come quick enough for me! I'm starving…' He stopped, realising that Rose was regarding him with an odd expression. 'What?' he said.

'What did you order for me?' she asked, very quiet.

Drew shook his head slightly, not understanding what the problem was, but understanding that there *was* a problem. There was definitely one of those. What had he done?

'Four cheeses with extra pepperoni,' he said.

'Was that what I asked for?'

'No,' he said slowly, feeling his way, and then only just stopped himself from slapping his head as he suddenly realised what he had done. 'I didn't ask you what you wanted. I'm sorry, Rose.' He tried a winning smile. 'It always used to be your favourite. I didn't think. Do you want me to ring and change the order?'

'No,' said Rose. 'I just don't want you to assume that you know me when you don't.'

Drew considered for a moment. 'I can't pretend that we're strangers, Rose,' he said finally.

How could he pretend that he didn't know her? That he didn't know how she tasted, how she felt? He knew everything about her, from the gurgle of laughter in her voice to the funny look she got on her face when she was about to sneeze. He knew how blotchy she got when she cried, how her tongue stuck out between her teeth when she was concentrating hard.

How her smile lit the beautiful grey eyes. How her silky hair brushed his face when she leant over to kiss him.

How could he pretend he didn't know every turn of her head, every dip and curve of her body, every quirk of her personality?

Drew's heart twisted. God, he had been a fool to walk away. But how could he have known how much he would miss her?

'You could try,' Rose said. 'I've changed, Drew, and so have you. We're not the same people we were three years ago.'

Three years ago, when she had told him that she wanted a baby and he had decided that his freedom was more important.

'Surely we haven't changed *that* much?' Although three years ago he certainly hadn't realised what an idiot he was to leave her. He knew now. That was a change, true, but at heart surely they were both still the same? 'We still like the same pizza,' he pointed out, in an attempt to lighten the atmosphere.

But Rose refused to respond to his cajoling smile. 'Pizza isn't important,' she said sharply. 'We need to get to know each other all over again.'

Drew threw himself back down on one of the sofas and linked his hands so that he could stretch his arms above his head. 'All right,' he said, grimacing as he tried to release the tension in his shoulder muscles. 'So, tell me about the new Rose Walters.'

Rose eyed him suspiciously, but she could hardly refuse to talk when she was the one who had insisted that they didn't know each other. Suddenly limp with tiredness, she slumped down opposite him once more. 'What do you want to know?'

What Drew really wanted to know was what Jack's father was like. He wanted to know if Rose had been in love with him, if she loved him still. She wasn't the kind of person who had casual relationships, so Seb must have meant *something* to her. She hadn't changed that much, whatever she claimed.

Once he could have asked her anything, but he couldn't do that now.

'What do you do every evening when Jack's in bed?' he asked instead.

Rose contemplated her life. 'Work, usually,' she said. 'It's the only time I can really concentrate. Sometimes friends will come round, but they've either got babies of their own and are equally tired or they're working and on a completely different routine.' She flushed. 'It doesn't sound very exciting, does it?'

Telling Drew about her life made her realise how small it had become. When they had been together there had always been something happening. They had gone out often—to films, to plays, to gigs and concerts, whatever took their fancy. They'd had friends round to casual suppers where they would sit around the table and laugh. They'd gone for long walks at the weekends. Drew had played for a very amateurish hockey team; Rose had wandered around galleries and dreamed of being an artist. And even when there had been nothing else to do it had been fun just to stay in and cook together, to watch television and argue about what they were watching. To make love knowing they had all the time in the world and no one else to think about but each other.

Drew had given all that up. No. Rose pulled herself up. She had pushed him to make a choice. Family life or a single life.

And he had chosen a single life. She only had her-self to blame.

Sometimes Rose wondered what life would have been like if she hadn't started handing out ultimatums—if she had just let things drift on until Drew was recon-ciled to the idea. But she hadn't felt able to take that risk. He had been adamant that he didn't want children, and she'd been equally certain that she did. Separating had been the only sensible option.

But now here he was, sprawled on the other sofa as if he had never left.

CHAPTER FIVE

DREW thought about what she had told him. It didn't sound as if her life was much fun. 'Don't you ever get lonely?' he asked.

Rose's first impulse was to deny it, but what was the point? Drew was a single parent, too, now. He would learn for himself soon enough.

'Sometimes,' she admitted. 'I love Jack, and when he's up and awake I don't usually have time to feel lonely. But when he's in bed, of course there are times when I'd like to have an adult conversation and talk about anything except babies. Toddlers are the centre of their own worlds, and it would be nice to have someone who cares about *me* occasionally, who's there to help me if I'm tired or sick.'

'You didn't want to make a go of it with Seb?' He was unable to resist probing this time. 'It must be a lot easier if you're part of a couple.'

'I'm sure it is.' Rose sighed a little. 'Seb did ask me to marry him when Jack was born, but I said no.'

'Why?' Drew hoped he didn't sound too glad.

'Because I wasn't sure that I loved Seb enough,' she told him honestly. 'And I wasn't sure that he loved me enough, either. I knew that he wouldn't have asked me if it hadn't been for Jack. I suppose I was still holding on to that dream of marrying someone who would love me for ever.'

Someone who would make her feel the way Drew had done.

'I didn't want us to get married because we felt that we should, and then find that we couldn't live together,' she tried to explain. 'I didn't want us to end up like your parents, arguing and fighting and hating each other. I saw what happened to you.'

Drew was startled into sitting upright. 'What do you mean? Nothing happened to me!'

'Your experience of family life was so different to mine,' Rose told him. 'Of course you didn't want to settle down and have children when all you knew about marriage was bitterness and disappointment. Your parents put you off the whole idea of having a family, didn't they?'

'Well, yes—partly,' he admitted reluctantly. 'But it's not as if I had a miserable childhood. I was away at school most of the time.'

'I wasn't prepared to take the risk that some time in the future Jack would say that the best part of his childhood was being sent away school,' she said flatly.

'You're making it out to be my fault you're not married,' said Drew, only half joking.

'Of course it's not your fault. But knowing you did make me wary of committing myself unless I was absolutely sure that I was doing the right thing.'

'You can never be absolutely sure, Rose. Even I know that. And divorce doesn't have to be the end of the world, you know. Most people manage better than my parents,' he added dryly.

'I know,' said Rose. 'That's why I've been thinking about marriage again recently.'

Drew's heart jolted at her words, which was ridiculous, he knew. Why shouldn't Rose think about marriage? Hadn't he just been telling her how much easier it would make her life? And it wasn't as if *he* had ever wanted to get married.

'Oh?' he said. 'What's brought that on?'

'When Seb left for Bristol he asked me again. If this new job works out he'll be based down there permanently, and it would be difficult for him to see much of Jack.'

'And what did you say?' Drew's voice sounded harsh even to his own ears.

'I said I would consider it seriously,' Rose told him.

'Even though you don't love Seb?'

'I do love him,' she corrected him. 'Just not…' *Just not the way I loved you*, she almost said. 'I love him as a friend,' she went on hastily, before Drew wondered what she had been going to say. 'There are lots of wonderful things about Seb, and the best thing about him is that he adores Jack as much as I do.'

'If he loves him that much, why did he go off to Bristol?' asked Drew, who was fed up with hearing how wonderful Seb was.

Rose gave him a look—she might as well have just rolled her eyes. 'That's where the job is,' she said with exaggerated patience. 'If he'd had the choice, of course Seb would have stayed here. As it is, I need to think about Jack. He needs a father around all the time. Seb and I don't love each other passionately, it's true, but we might love each other enough to give him the family he needs.'

Why had he started this conversation? Drew wondered, feeling as if a cold fist had curled around his entrails. 'What about your dreams?' he said with a note of desperation. 'Are you really going to give those up?'

'If I have to.' Rose's voice was even. 'I'll do whatever I have to for Jack. That's what being a parent is all about. It's true, I used to dream about having everything. I wanted an adoring husband, a big, happy family, a lovely house, a successful career…but I've had to grow up, Drew. I'm a mother now, and I've learnt that I can't have everything. But as long as I've got Jack, and he's happy, I've got enough.'

'This is your early-morning wake-up call!'

Drew surfaced blearily to find a baby plonked down between him and the wall. For a moment he just stared at it blankly. A baby? What was a baby doing in bed with him?

A *baby*? He shot upright at the realisation that it wasn't, in fact, a dream, and then slumped back against the wall with a groan as memory returned.

'Your daughter's in need of some quality time,' said Rose, standing back hastily and averting her eyes from Drew's bare chest. It wasn't that she hadn't seen it before. It was just that she had forgotten what an effect it could have on her, even at this time of the morning.

Drew yawned hugely. 'Didn't we have enough quality time last night?' he asked Molly, who was lying on her back, gurgling and playing with her toes, the picture of innocence.

It was hard to believe that she was the same baby as the one who had screamed and screamed until Drew had made it to her cot. Rose had told him to try and keep her in her bed and calm her by patting her soothingly, but Molly had been so distressed that he hadn't been able to resist picking her up. And after that, of course, he had had to do it every time.

It seemed to Drew that he had spent the entire night walking Molly up and down the tiny landing and making up bottles of milk from which she'd taken a few sucks then batted them away. Amazingly, Jack had slept through it all, and although Rose had appeared once or twice at the beginning, she'd evidently decided to leave him to get on with it as the night wore on. Drew didn't blame her at all. Molly's sobs had subsided to heart-rending little hiccups until eventually she'd grown heavy with sleep and he'd laid her very gently back into her cot, tiptoeing away to crash back into his narrow bed for all of two minutes before she started to wail again.

That was what it felt like, anyway.

Now, as Drew blinked away sleep, he was amazed to see that it was morning. Molly smiled and waved her chubby arms when he spoke to her, and he couldn't help smiling back. Hauling himself back up on his pillows, he tickled her tummy and laughed when she squealed with delight, the misery of last night quite forgotten.

'I've changed her and fed her,' Rose said briskly, to cover the constriction in her throat as she watched them together. 'If you keep an eye on her, I'll bring you some tea.'

Drew glanced up from Molly. 'Tea sounds great! Thanks, Rose,' he said gratefully, and smiled at her.

Rose wished he hadn't done that. Last night she had done really quite well at keeping him at a distance. Drew had helped, of course, asking her about Seb and unwittingly reminding her that she was supposed to be thinking about making a family for Jack, not pursuing useless dreams.

She had told him that she would do anything for Jack, and it was true, but it was hard to think about marrying another man when Drew was there, making her heart turn over every time he smiled, making her remember the warmth of his hands, the pulsing excitement of his touch, the love and the laughter and the way the world had seemed bright with promise when they were together. It must have rained sometimes—this was England, after all—but all she remembered was day after day awash with golden sunshine.

Marrying Seb wouldn't feel like that, but Rose had so nearly made up her mind to do it anyway. Why had Drew had to come back now, just when she had thought that she was over him at last and ready to start a new life? It wasn't even as if he had come back for her. *He* wasn't following a dream or trying to recapture the past. No, he was just looking for someone to look after his daughter. They had come to an arrangement that suited them both, and she had to keep that in mind, Rose told herself sternly. There was absolutely no point in dreaming old dreams. There was no point in wanting him still.

It wasn't even as if he were looking his best. His hair was dishevelled and there were pouches of tiredness under his eyes. He couldn't have got much sleep last night, she thought with some compunction.

She cleared her throat. 'I'll go and get that tea, then.' She bent down to Jack, who was clutching the bottom of her dressing gown but staring at Drew as if fascinated. 'Come along, you.'

But when she picked Jack up, he stretched out his arms to Drew and made it plain that he wanted to stay.

'Can you manage two?' she asked Drew doubtfully.

'I'd better get used to it if I'm going to be babysitting when you go to work,' he said, moving over so that she could put Jack down next to Molly, safe between his body and the wall.

That meant leaning a little too close to Drew for comfort, and Rose's eyes let her down. Instead of fixing on Jack, as she'd intended, they skittered sideways to meet Drew's warm green gaze, and in spite of the stern talking-to she had just given herself she was hit by a gust of longing to pretend that the last three years had never happened, that they were still in love and she could sink down on top of him, press her lips to his chest, to his throat, kiss her way all over him the way she had always used to do, until he loosened the belt of her robe and ran his hands over her body and rolled her beneath him…

Jack pushed Molly, who toppled against Drew with a wail of surprise, and Rose jerked fully upright at the sound. Her face was burning, and unconsciously she tightened her belt, as if Drew really had tugged it apart.

'Jack!' Her mouth was so dry that she had to clear her throat twice before she could speak. 'You mustn't push Molly like that. She's just a baby.' Avoiding Drew's eyes, she bent to retrieve the teddy Jack had discarded on the floor. 'Look, why don't you let her have your teddy?'

Jack's lip stuck out, and he scowled. For a mutinous moment it seemed as if he would refuse, but suddenly he took the teddy and shoved it towards Molly. Fortunately Drew was quick enough to anticipate the gesture, and stopped it hitting the baby just in time. He propped Molly upright against him, and her tears cleared miraculously at the sight of the teddy.

'Oh, look, she likes *you*,' said Rose as Molly smiled, and Jack visibly swelled with self-importance. He waved the teddy some more, Molly laughed some more, and a happy relationship appeared to have been established.

If only it were that easy when you were an adult, thought Rose with an inward sigh.

'He'll be happy showing off now,' she said to Drew, not sorry that the incident had deflected attention from her burning cheeks.

Drew grinned at her. 'Well done! It's an education to see a master at work!'

Oh, dear. There was that smile again. Rose yanked her gaze away.

'Tea,' she said firmly, for the third time.

She could hear Jack and Molly laughing as she made the tea downstairs in the kitchen. They were obviously enjoying themselves. This was her favourite time of day with Jack, when he was rested and happy and very loving.

Smiling, Rose poured boiling water onto the teabags. There was just something about the sound of a baby's laughter. It made all your worries about money, about how you would manage, about the present and the future and the past, seem somehow unimportant. Nothing really mattered as long as Jack was content—as he clearly was now.

Carefully, she carried the two mugs of tea upstairs, and paused in the doorway of the little bedroom. She could barely see Drew for Molly and Jack, who were crawling over him, shrieking and squealing, as he blew raspberries at them and tickled them, and let them pat him and stroke him and tug at his nose.

Lucky Jack. Lucky Molly.

'Those two look happy,' she said. And why wouldn't they be? They could clamber over Drew and touch him however they wanted.

Drew looked up at the sound of her voice. He had been laughing as he played with Jack and Molly, but his smile faded as looked at her. She was wearing a shabby dressing gown, and her hair was all mussed, as if she hadn't bothered to brush it since she'd got out of bed.

She looked warm and incredibly sexy, and he couldn't help remembering how close she had been when she'd leant over him to put Jack safely on the bed. He had been able to smell that fresh, clean, peculiarly Rose scent, and it had taken all he had not to grab her and pull her down onto the bed with him, to find out if she had really changed as much as she said she had.

Drew knew that he was staring, but he didn't seem to be able to do anything about it—until Molly recalled him to the situation by grabbing his nose and twisting it in her tiny fingers.

'Ouch!' exclaimed Drew, his hand going involuntarily to his nose, and Rose laughed, making his heart twist. 'I hope you've come to rescue me,' he said. 'I'm exhausted!'

'You look as if you're doing very well,' she told him. 'They're having a lovely time.'

She sounded faintly wistful, Drew thought, and he patted the bedcover. 'Come and join us,' he said. 'Then we can all have a lovely time together.'

A little bedside table was squeezed into the corner of the room, and Rose set Drew's mug down on it before perching a little nervously on the edge of the bed.

Well, what else could she do? It would look odd if she took her tea and went back to her own room, and she didn't fancy her chances of getting Jack to come with her. He was enjoying himself far too much using Drew as a trampoline. And, given that mere politeness

meant drinking her tea here with Drew, there was nowhere else to sit.

But it felt terribly intimate to be sitting on the edge of
his bed in her dressing gown while he leant bare-chested
back against the pillows and let Jack bounce all over him.

Momentarily excluded from all the horseplay, Molly
let out an aggrieved squawk and tried to roll towards
Jack, but she ended up floundering until Rose saw what
was happening, put down her tea, and scooped her up.
She was perfectly happy to sit comfortably on Rose's
knee, then, from where she could see what Jack and
Drew were doing, but still enjoy some undivided attention of her own.

'Do you ever get to drink your tea?' asked Drew,
amused.

'Eventually. You soon get used to drinking it cold!'
Lifting Molly in one arm, Rose retrieved her mug and
held it well away from the baby so that she could sip
the tea. 'Jack, calm down now, and let Drew have some
tea.'

Drew pulled the mug cautiously towards him, although he was careful to keep it out of Jack's reach.
'Thanks for the this—' he began, and then broke off,
raising his brows in exaggerated surprise. 'It's got milk
in it!'

Rose was taken aback. 'Milk, no sugar. That's
right, isn't it?'

'Did I ask for milk?'

'No, I—' Rose stopped. She could see where this was
going. 'Sorry, you're quite right,' she said ruefully. 'It
wasn't fair of me to object to you assuming you knew
what pizza I wanted and then to make exactly the same
assumption about your tea.'

Drew laughed at her chastened expression. 'But, as it happens, I do still like milk in my tea.'

'The way I still like four cheeses pizza with extra pepperoni, in fact.'

'You see,' he said in a different voice. 'Not everything's changed, Rose.'

Rose smoothed Molly's hair and kissed the top of her head, just where the distinctive Pemberton smudge of fair hair stood out against the dark. It was easier than looking at him.

'No,' she conceded, wishing she wasn't so aware of how *close* he was, of how easy it would be to slide along the side of the bed and lean down to kiss him. It was such a narrow bed that even perching right on the edge she could feel his leg beneath the duvet, pressing against her.

Her physical reaction to him certainly hadn't changed, thought Rose. Only Drew could set her senses trembling just by sitting there. No one else's touch could suck the air out of her lungs. No one else's smile made her heart turn over, no matter how often she steeled herself to resist it.

'No,' she agreed again in a low voice. 'Not everything.'

CHAPTER SIX

ROSE had warned him that he would be on a crash course in parenthood, but even so Drew was unprepared for how much he had to learn. She had to show him how to prepare food for Molly, how to feed her, clean her and change her, and then how to dress her. This last wasn't nearly as easy as he had thought it would be, as Molly wriggled and squirmed and kept rolling away from him as he fumbled with her clothes. His hands felt huge and unwieldy, and he envied Rose her calm competence and the deft way she dealt with the children.

No sooner was Molly up and dressed, it seemed, than she was ready for a nap. But when that was over Rose decided they would all go shopping together. 'This'll be good experience for you,' she told Drew, who was beginning to wish he could have had a nap like Molly. It had been non-stop ever since Rose had woken him that morning, and he was feeling the effects of his sleepless night.

Drew couldn't believe how long it took to get ready to go out. Both children had to have their nappies changed, and then there was a huge palaver about making sure that they had little boots and coats and hats, because there was a cold wind blowing. Only Jack didn't want to wear his hat, and kept pulling it off, threatening a tantrum until he realised that Molly thought it was funny and was trying to pull her hat off, too.

Through it all Rose remained astonishingly calm, ignoring the way Jack was showing off and packing a drink, clean nappies and goodness knew what else into a bag. They were almost ready to leave the house when they realised that Molly's car seat would have to be transferred to Rose's car, and as Drew struggled with the unfamiliar fittings he thought longingly of the simple task of laying water pipes under the fierce African sun, where he only had to deal with flies and broken equipment and an approaching insurgent army. He had rung his office that morning and arranged to take leave for a fortnight at home, starting the following Monday, but he was beginning to wish they hadn't been quite so understanding. He wasn't sure he could take two weeks of this!

'I think we're going to need to invest in a double buggy,' said Rose as she strapped Jack into his seat. 'Otherwise you'll be stuck in the house all day next week when you're on your own.'

Drew was still searching for the last strap on Molly's seat while she arched and wriggled and protested, but he looked up sharply at that. 'On my *own*?' he said in alarm. *'Next week?'*

'I might as well make the most of the fact that you've got two weeks off,' she said, coming round to help him. She pushed him out of the way and sorted out Molly's straps in no time, clipping them all together and telling Molly quite firmly to be quiet and sit still. 'I'll be able to go to Peter and Peter's studio every day, so I can really get going on the project.'

Drew looked deeply uneasy as he got into the passenger seat. 'I'm not sure I'll be ready to look after them on my own by then.'

'Of course you will,' said Rose, getting in beside him and poking the key around until she found the ignition. 'Look how much you've learnt already.'

'That's just it. There's so much to think about. I'll never be able to remember all of it.'

'Don't worry about it. It'll all come naturally after a while. It's just a matter of practice.' Rose put the car into gear. 'By the time you've changed a few nappies, you should be able to do it in your sleep.'

Drew sighed. 'I can't wait.'

The whole process had to be reversed when they got to the supermarket, where Jack and Molly were unstrapped and loaded into a special trolley. Rose could see that Drew was appalled by the tedium and frustration, although he was doing his best not to show it. Part of her wanted to laugh at his determinedly upbeat expression, but there was another part of her that felt sorry for him, too. It must be quite a contrast—to be leading an important project, doing life-changing engineering work in Africa one day, and pushing a baby and a toddler in a trolley round a suburban London supermarket the next. On the whole, Rose thought that he was dealing with it pretty well.

She had written out a shopping list over breakfast, and now she pulled it out of her bag as they headed into the fruits and vegetables section. 'Bananas,' she murmured to herself. 'Apples…'

'What about a pineapple?' Drew held up a magnificent specimen and sniffed its bottom. 'This one's ripe.'

'We don't need a pineapple, Drew.'

'What you mean is, pineapple isn't on your list!'

'No, and it's not on my list for a reason,' said Rose, with a slight edge to her voice. 'Pineapples are too expensive.' She had learnt to be very careful about money since Jack's birth, when her income had dropped dramatically. 'Jack doesn't like it, anyway.'

'I bet Molly likes pineapple.'

'I'm quite sure she doesn't. It'll be far too acidic for her.'

'OK, then—I like it.'

Rose gritted her teeth. 'Fine—you buy yourself a pineapple, then, Drew, but don't put it in this trolley. I said *don't*!' she said, voice rising, as Drew wedged the pineapple in next to the bananas.

'Look, I'll get all this. What harm is my pineapple doing?'

'I don't like people messing with my trolley,' she said, a touch sulkily, and Drew laughed.

'God, how could I have forgotten what a control freak you are when it comes to shopping?'

'How could I have forgotten how deeply annoying *you* are?' she snapped back.

Drew's eyes gleamed. 'Do you remember that huge fight we had in Sainsbury's that time? When you broke that bottle of wine?'

'*You* broke it! I was just trying to put it back on the shelf. It would have been fine if you hadn't turned it into a tug of war and then let go when I wasn't expecting it,' Rose protested. 'It was really embarrassing!'

It *had* been embarrassing, but it had been funny, too.

Everyone had turned to stare at them as they regarded the broken bottle, aghast at the waste of good wine, and then their eyes had met and the argument was forgotten as they both started to laugh. They had paid for the bottle and, still laughing, had gone home and made love.

The memory sent warmth spilling through Rose, and she felt her face burning as she looked away from Drew and busied herself picking out tomatoes.

'I should have remembered how incompatible we were on the shopping front before we came out,' she muttered.

'We weren't always incompatible,' he reminded her softly.

As if she needed reminding! Rose didn't need to look at him to know that he was remembering how they had laughed all the way home on the bus, how they had abandoned their shopping bags as soon as they got in and kissed each other, still laughing. How they had made love all afternoon.

'We were very young,' she said, tying the plastic bag full of tomatoes, not meeting his eyes. 'Nothing really mattered then.'

The only thing that had mattered was being together. She had met Drew at a party thrown by mutual friends soon after she came to London. She had been twenty-two, he twenty-four. They'd both been starting out on their careers, and neither of them had had much money, but they'd had a wonderful time.

They'd been inseparable for seven years, until Rose had seen her thirtieth birthday approaching and had started to think about a family. That had been almost three years ago. There had been an awkward year or so afterwards, when they had tried to be friends if they bumped into each other at occasional parties, but for Rose it had been part pain, part relief when she heard that Drew was going to Africa. Once he had gone she would be able to stop hoping against hope that he would change his mind and come back to her. Only then would she be able to move on and make a life with someone else.

That was what Rose had told herself. It just hadn't quite worked out like that.

Rose was thoughtful as they drove home. Living with Drew was going to be more difficult than she had thought if she was going to be ambushed by memories like the one in the supermarket at every turn. She should have expected it, though. He had always had the ability to turn her inside out, to charm her out of the most ferocious sulk, to make her laugh when she was most determined to be serious.

This time, though, she couldn't afford to succumb. It was all very well remembering the times they had laughed and loved together, but she hadn't forgotten the pain of saying goodbye, the misery of knowing that he didn't love her enough to imagine a future together. Drew might have become steadier and more responsible when he was in Africa, he might be a father now, but he hadn't said or done anything to suggest that Rose was anything more to him than a friend he could count on when he needed her to look after his child.

No, Rose wasn't about to trust Drew with her heart again. She could accept that the physical attraction was still there—it was hard to deny it when it was zinging in the air between them—but she couldn't let herself be hurt the way she had been hurt before. Much better to let him think that this really was just a practical arrangement, and that he meant no more than a convenient solution to her childcare problem.

So when Seb rang that evening, as she was cooking supper for Jack and Molly, she greeted him with much more warmth than usual. Drew was lying on the floor, letting Jack clamber over him, while Molly gurgled and bobbed up and down in her bouncy chair.

'Seb!' she said brightly, and Drew lifted his head, obviously listening. 'How lovely to hear you!'

Seb sounded a little wary, as if uncertain what to make of her encouraging tone, but she chatted determinedly on for a while, knowing that Drew was listening to every word, until she called Jack over. He was the reason Seb had rung, after all, although there was no need for Drew to know that.

'Jack, do you want to talk to Daddy?'

Jack didn't really understand, but when Rose held out the phone he scrambled off Drew and ran over so that she could put it to his ear. His eyes went round at the sound of Seb's voice, and he beamed up at Rose, but a moment later had lost interest and went trotting back to carry on rough-housing with Drew.

Rose laughed and went back to Seb. 'Sorry, it's hard when you can't see his face, but he really does love hearing your voice. He misses you. We both do.'

It was true, in a way. If Seb had been around there would have been no problem about him looking after Jack while she worked. There would have been no deal with Drew. She wouldn't have needed to suggest that he moved in, and he wouldn't be here, unsettling her with his presence, turning her careful world inside out and upside down.

If Seb had been around she and Jack could have moved in with him while Drew had his house back and found himself a nanny. If Seb had been here he would have kept her steady and she could have concentrated on him and the life he'd offered Jack and her.

She wouldn't be racked by temptation and tortured by memories if only Seb were there, Rose decided. Of course she missed him.

In the background, Jack was shrieking with delight as Drew tossed him in the air. Molly was watching from the bouncy chair, her excited squeals adding to the noise. Rose was quite sure that Drew was stirring them up deliberately because she was talking to Seb.

'It sounds like a madhouse there,' said Seb, amused. 'What's going on?'

'Oh, that's just Drew playing with Jack,' Rose said carelessly. 'I haven't had a chance to tell you yet,' she went on, super casual. 'I've solved the problem about care for Jack when I'm at work. Drew and his daughter are staying here for six weeks, and we're going to look after Molly and Jack between us.'

'Drew? Isn't that the guy you used to live with?'

'Yes, we were together for a while, but it was just one of those relationships you have when you're young and then grow out of,' she said dismissively, her words aimed more at Drew than at Seb. 'We stayed friends when we split up. This is his house, actually, and he's just here temporarily until he decides what to do with his little girl.'

'Why did you need to justify yourself to Seb?' Drew demanded, as soon as Rose had said goodbye and switched off the phone. Jack's attention had been diverted by his favourite plastic truck, which meant that

Drew could get up at last and follow Rose to the kitchen area. 'What business is it of his whether I'm here or not?'

'Seb is Jack's father,' said Rose, lifting a lid and poking the potatoes with a knife to see if they were cooked. 'Of course he needs to know who's living here and spending time with Jack.'

'And has Seb given permission for me to stay in my own house?' said Drew sarcastically.

'Don't be silly, Drew.' Infuriatingly calm, Rose turned off the heat under the potatoes and drained them in the sink. 'I explained how you would look after Jack when I'm at work, and he can see that it's a sensible solution.'

'So he doesn't mind?'

'Mind what?'

'That I'm living here with you and Jack.'

'Of course not,' she said. 'What's there to mind? It's not as if there's anything going on between you and me. It's just a practical arrangement, and even if it wasn't, Seb's not the jealous type.'

Unlike *him*, Drew thought. He could still remember how devastated he had been when he'd heard that Rose was going out with someone else only a month or so after they'd split up. He had bumped into them at some party, and he'd wanted to push his hand into the man's smug, smiling face. Had that been Seb?

'Seb knows there's no reason for him to be jealous, anyway,' Rose went on, searching in the drawer for the potato masher. 'I told him that we used to be together, and that our relationship was over a long time ago. He knows that I've moved on,' she said. 'He's very secure.'

Good for Seb, Drew thought vengefully. If he had to hear any more about how marvellous Jack's father was, he would throw up. Seb was clearly the model father—apart from being stuck at the other end of the motorway, of course. All these stories about how secure Seb was, how understanding, how much Jack missed him, made Drew feel inadequate—and that wasn't a feeling he liked at all, although he sensed that he was going to have to get used to it. He couldn't imagine anyone ever saying that he was a perfect father to Molly. He would never be as confident dealing with her the way Rose dealt with Jack.

Still, it was extraordinary how quickly he adapted to the new routine. He learned how to sterilise bottles and make up milk, and while he couldn't say that he enjoyed the nappy-changing experience, at least he got quicker at it. Rose showed him how to bathe Molly, how to feed her and dress her and play with her and calm her.

It didn't take long to establish a nighttime ritual, too. Rose would make up the bottles while Drew sat on Jack's bed, with Molly on his lap and Jack tucked into the circle of his arm, and read them a story. Whenever Rose came back upstairs, she'd see the three of them there, Jack's eyes enormous, while Molly kept lunging for the pages. Drew went to great lengths to vary his voice, doing a deep growly one and then a high, squeaky one to make Jack giggle, even though he probably didn't understand more than one word in five. She would watch them from the doorway, and every time she felt her heart constrict with if onlys…

Drew found Dorothy Grebe's book on caring for babies and toddlers amongst the great pile of stuff the Clarkes had given him to take away with Molly, and he pored over it when Rose wasn't looking. She tended to get cross when he quoted it at her.

'Dorothy isn't here. I am!' she snapped. 'If you think

you can do better with a book, be my guest! I'll go back to work right now!'

'No, no,' he said hastily. 'We'll do it your way.'

But he read the section on safety very carefully, and slipped off one afternoon to the local hardware store. Soon the house was bristling with safety equipment, with guards across every conceivable danger, safety locks on every door, and every socket childproofed.

'What on earth are you doing?' Rose asked as Drew fixed covers to the sockets above the kitchen units.

'Making these sockets safe.'

'But Molly would have to be at least four foot before she could reach them! And when she is that tall, I hope she'll be sensible enough not to stick her fingers in the sockets!'

'Better safe than sorry. That's what Dorothy says,' said Drew with an austere look, and Rose rolled her eyes, muttering darkly about what he could do with Dorothy.

'And Dorothy says you have to be very careful about using bad language in front of children, even if they can't speak properly themselves.' Drew grinned provocatively, and tutted at her response. 'I don't think Jack and Molly should be picking up phrases like *that*, either!'

Rose threw a cushion at him, but she was laughing.

They did a lot of laughing. Drew hadn't realised quite how much fun children could be. Molly loved to be tickled until she squealed with glee, and she and Jack were fascinated by each other. Jack could keep her entertained for ages just by jumping importantly on and off a step, visibly delighted by his ability to keep her happy. He was deeply patronising to Molly, so much so that Rose often had to cringe when Drew caught her eye, but Molly didn't mind at all. She loved Jack.

Both children adored bouncing on the bed and clambering over the adults, and Jack liked to play football—in a very loose sense—with Drew, in the little garden at the back. Drew was surprised at how much he enjoyed those times. He liked the determination and concentration on Jack's face as he tottered after the ball or picked it up with a crow of delight to try and throw it. Sometimes, thought Drew, Jack looked uncannily like his mother. He had the same gleam of fun in his grey eyes, the same trick of pressing his lips together when he was cross.

It wasn't all fun, of course. There were plenty of times when Drew found himself dealing with Jack's tantrums or, worse, with Molly when she was tired. Her fretful crying set his teeth on edge. He wished he was as calm as Rose, who seemed to have limitless reserves of patience.

Drew couldn't help wondering sometimes if he would have felt differently about having children if his own mother had been more like her. He loved his mother, of course. She could be great fun. But she had always been highly strung and very volatile, too, smothering him with affection one minute and shouting furiously at him the next. Rose was different. She was steady and safe and endlessly loving. Jack had no idea how lucky he was.

CHAPTER SEVEN

EVERY night Drew had to get up to Molly, but she had settled into the new routine with remarkable ease. She never cried as often as she had done that first night, but there were still times when Drew had to drag himself out of bed and along to her cot.

The broken nights weren't the only downside. Drew was finding it harder and harder to lie in his narrow bed and know that Rose was sleeping only a few yards away. It was harder and harder not to think about sliding into bed beside her and losing himself in her softness and her warmth.

He wondered if she had any idea what it did to him to see her yawning in her old dressing gown, her hair tousled and her eyes sleepy, or wandering unselfconsciously back from the bathroom wrapped only in a towel. She was usually practically dressed, in jeans and easily washable tops, but one sunny day she wore a short, flippy skirt, and Drew could hardly drag his eyes away from her legs. His desperate awareness of her made him twitchy. It was incredibly difficult to keep his hands to himself. He longed to touch her, to feel her, to taste her, to bury his face in her hair and breathe in the fresh, wonderful smell of her, to hear her whisper in his ear that she loved him and ached for him, too.

But Rose wasn't going to do that, was she? She wanted Jack to be with his father, but it was easy to forget that she was thinking about marrying Seb when the days passed in a reassuring routine, and there were the evenings to look forward to, when Jack and Molly were in bed and they could eat a simple supper together. Sometimes they watched television and had furious disagreements about everything from politics to hairstyles, but at other times they just sat over a glass of wine and talked.

Rose asked him about Africa, and he told her what an amazing experience it had been. He told her how much he had liked the people he had worked with there, but how frustrating he had found it to deal with officialdom. He described the sense of satisfaction when a job was completed and he saw how life in a village could be completely changed. He told her what it was like to sit with a beer and watch the sun set behind the acacia trees, suffusing the huge sky with dramatic reds and golds, to listen to the throaty croaking and whirring and shrilling of the African night.

Drew asked Rose about her work, too, and she talked about Peter and Peter, and how excited she was about the new project which could change things for all of them. They talked about mutual friends. Sometimes they remembered things they had done together.

But they never talked about how much they had loved each other or why they had split up.

Drew couldn't help noticing that Rose never once gave any indication that she wanted to go back to the way they had been. Seb rang almost every night, and she was always delighted to hear from him. She was always ready to talk about *him* and what a good father he was.

How could he tell her that he loved her when she was planning a future with Seb? She had done so much for him. Drew didn't know what he and Molly would have done without her. It wouldn't be fair to tell her how he felt, how bitterly he regretted walking away three years ago and how much more he loved her now. Even if he could find the words, it would be bound to make things awkward. She might feel that she had to move out, which would mean that he had to move instead, and Drew's mind veered away from the thought of not seeing her and Jack every day.

No, he couldn't do that to Rose. Just accept it, Drew told himself. She had moved on, and he should do the same. There was no point in revisiting the past. It was over, so it was time to stop regretting and start looking forward. It was enough that they were friends and had this time together. He should be glad that she had the chance to make a family for Jack the way she wanted

It didn't mean he had to like it when Seb called, though.

Drew and Molly had arrived on a Wednesday evening, and by the following Monday Rose had decided that she could leave Jack and the baby in Drew's charge for an evening. Once he'd got over that hurdle, there seemed no reason not to take plunge and leave the three of them all day.

'Are you sure I'm ready for this?' Drew asked nervously, when she told him that she was going to the studio and would be back that evening.

'You'll be fine. You can always ring me if there's a problem.'

In spite of her brave words, Rose spent the entire day worrying and wondering how they were getting on without her. She missed them all, too. Drew had only been there a week, but already she had got used to having him around again.

It had been a revelation to see how naturally he had taken to fatherhood. Rose wanted to be angry with him for not realising how much he could enjoy being a father when they'd had the chance to have a baby together, but it was impossible to wish for something that would have meant no Jack and no Molly.

She should have known that Drew would throw himself into fatherhood so completely, though. He never did anything by halves, she remembered. That was what made him so irritating at times. Shopping, for instance, or endlessly quoting Dorothy Grebe, but it was also what made life seem so much more interesting and fun when he was around.

It made it hard to remember why she had made him walk away.

There was a little bit of her that was still in love with him, Rose knew. Perhaps part of her always would be. But it wasn't going to be more than a little part, she vowed. She wasn't going to risk all the heartache that would inevitably come along with falling properly in love with him all over again.

Drew hadn't changed that much. In spite of everything she had had to say about them being different people now, Rose thought he was pretty much the same—just a little steadier and more responsible. But not enough for her to trust him again. She had Jack to think about now, and she wasn't going to get involved with anyone who valued freedom and independence as much as Drew did. If she was going to get involved with anyone, it ought to be Seb, not Drew.

Besides, Drew hadn't given the slightest indication that he wanted to get involved with *her*. He was excellent company, he made her laugh and, to give him his due, worked much harder with Jack and Molly than she had expected. But he never made any attempt to touch her. He never talked about a future that included her.

So why was she wasting all this time thinking about him?

Rose tried to stop it by concentrating on the exasperating side of him instead—and there was plenty of scope there!—but there was no doubt that it was nice to have someone to do the practical jobs she had been putting off for so long. Everything was so much easier with two, as well. It meant you could have five minutes to yourself occasionally, or walk quickly down to the post office instead of stopping every minute for Jack to examine a pebble or a crack in the paving stones with intense interest. It wasn't that she didn't love watching him discover the world around him, but sometimes she really just needed to get to the post office and back quickly.

It was lovely having a baby again, too. Jack was at the wriggling stage, but Molly was happy to be cuddled for hours. She was a gorgeous baby, and Rose had fallen for her heavily. She had huge dark eyes, and Drew's odd hair, and the magical smile all babies have. Rose knew that Molly should be bonding with Drew, really, but she loved it if there was an excuse to hold her against her shoulder and breathe in her clean baby smell.

On the Wednesday Rose set off for her next full day

at Peter and Peter's studio. Bliss, she told herself. Time to get stuck into work, time to bandy ideas around with Peter and Peter, time to herself. She could have lunch. She could go to the loo on her own. A full seven hours without once having to change a nappy or wipe a nose. Yes, bliss. This was exactly what she'd wanted when she had fretted about finding childcare for Jack.

Only she hadn't bargained for how much she would miss being at home with Jack and Molly. She could barely concentrate, and had to stop herself ringing home every five minutes. They had agreed that Drew would call her mobile if he had a problem, but the fact that he didn't was almost more distracting than if he had been on the phone all day. Still, perhaps he was coping without her.

Rose could hear Molly's screams from the gate when she got home that evening, and she pulled a face. Something metal was being banged vigorously, as well— Jack had got hold of a saucepan, she guessed—and between that and Molly's crying there was no way Drew had heard the sound of the door opening.

'Molly—Molly, *please* shut up!' she heard him muttering as she hung up her coat in the hall. 'I'm going as fast as I can. I *know* you're hungry, I *know* Jack's making a horrible noise with that saucepan, but whose idea was that, I wonder? Oh, mine…you're quite right. I don't know what I was thinking of! Come on, now, try not crying for just a minute… Rose will be home soon, I promise.'

Rose suppressed a smile. 'I see you've got everything under control,' she said, as she went in and saw Drew by the cooker in the kitchen. He held a screaming Molly in one arm and was trying to put on some water for pasta while Jack sat on the floor, happily banging a saucepan and lid together.

Drew's face lit up at the sight of her. 'Thank God you're home!' he greeted her, with such heartfelt relief that Rose had to laugh.

Spotting his mother, Jack dropped the pan with a resounding clang and ran across the room to throw himself at her knees with such force that Rose staggered and almost lost her balance.

'Hello, darling.' She crouched down to hug him close, touched to realise that he had missed her. 'Have you been a good boy?'

'You probably won't believe me, but they've both been fine…for most of the time, anyway,' said Drew, jiggling Molly ineffectually.

'She's probably hungry,' said Rose, disentangling herself from Jack's grip on her legs. 'Here—let me have her.'

To Drew's chagrin, Molly stopped crying the moment Rose took her and crooned soothingly to her.

'Some daughter you are,' he pretended to complain, although actually he wouldn't have cared what she did as long as she stopped that crying. 'Where's your sense of loyalty? That's *it*,' he went on, wagging a finger at the oblivious Molly. 'You're not going to be allowed to go out until you're at least twenty-one now. I had thought you could go to parties when you were eighteen, but I've changed my mind after that little display of disloyalty!'

Rose laughed. 'Don't listen to him,' she said to Molly, and sat down gratefully on the sofa. 'He doesn't mean it. You'll be able to twist him round your little finger.'

It felt good to be home, with Jack clambering ecstatically over her, and Molly snuffling into her shoulder and clutching her hair. She looked around her,
belatedly taking in the mess. 'It looks like you had a
tough day!'

'I'm sorry the house is such a tip.' Drew rubbed a
hand wearily over his face. 'I did mean to tidy up before
you came home, but I haven't had a moment.'

'It doesn't matter. Jack and Molly are OK. That's the
main thing.'

'They may be OK, but what about me?' Drew col-
lapsed onto the sofa opposite her. 'I'm exhausted! How
do you do this every day?'

Rose laughed, her heart lightened just to be home.
'It's hard work on your own, isn't it?'

'You can say that again!'

'Well, I'm glad you missed me,' she said lightly,
tilting her head away slightly as Molly patted her face.
Any minute now she would be reaching for her nose,
and Rose knew from experience that those little fingers
could inflict quite a painful nip.

'We all did,' said Drew. 'Molly was cranky all day,
and I knew exactly how she felt!' He hesitated. 'I missed
you most, Rose.'

'I missed you, too,' said Rose, grey eyes meeting
green for a fleeting moment before she looked away.
'All of you.' All at once the air was charged with something indefinable, and her breathing had got all muddled
up for some reason. 'Still, I'm home now, so I can give
you a hand,' she said, making herself sound brisk to
disguise her sudden intense awareness of him.

'You've been at work all day,' he said, surprised.
'Aren't you tired?'

Rose shook her head as she got to her feet. 'Work isn't nearly as tiring as being at home with you lot all day!'

But by the end of the second week the non-stop pace was catching up with her. She got Jack up and breakfasted as normal, while Drew dealt with Molly, and then headed off to Peter and Peter's studio, where she worked without a break to make the most of her time there, before heading home to help Drew give the children their supper and bath before it was time for bed.

Even then she couldn't sit down until she had cleared up the debris of the day. Every day Drew was more confident about looking after Jack and Molly, but he was less good about keeping the house tidy.

'Why do you have to put everything away?' he asked, exasperated, as Rose knelt to gather up Jack's toys. 'Jack's only going to get them out again tomorrow. I don't understand why you bother.'

'Because I can't relax in all this mess,' she said, throwing bricks into the box. 'I can cope with the clutter during the day, but I like everything calm and orderly when I sit down.'

Drew rolled his eyes. 'God, you're so repressed!' he said with a grin. 'Let's see how you get on next week, when I go back to work and you've got two to look after all day!'

Rose wasn't at all sure that she *would* do much better than him, but she couldn't be any more tired than she was now, she thought as she let herself into the house that Friday evening. It had been a difficult day. A crisis on the project had meant frantic discussions with Peter and Peter and the client, and she had ended up having to work late.

'Don't worry about us,' Drew had said when she'd rung. 'I'll feed the kids and start putting them to bed. You do what you have to and come home when you're ready.'

All was quiet when Rose opened the door. Curious, she went into the living room and stopped and stared. It was immaculately tidy. All Jack's toys had been put away, the cushions had been straightened, and in the kitchen there was no sign of the chaos that was the usual aftermath of the children's supper. The table was wiped, the highchairs set neatly against the wall. A single pot was simmering on the hob and filling the room with an appetising aroma.

Rose's throat tightened. To walk into this calm, clean room after the day she had had was better than any present.

As she went upstairs, she could hear the sound of shrieking and giggling from the bathroom, and she smiled. It sounded as if all was normal up here at least. Jack and Molly both loved bathtime.

'Hello,' she said pushing open the door, and then stopped dead, just as she had done downstairs—but for a very different reason.

Drew was in the bath with the two children, dunking Molly up and down while she squealed happily. All three heads turned to look at Rose in the doorway, and Jack shouted a greeting.

'Oh,' she said, startled by the realisation that Drew was completely naked, and completely unembarrassed about it.

'Come on in,' he said with a smile. 'You're just in time! I was getting so wet trying to bath them by myself that I thought I might as well get in, too. We've been having a great time, but I was just wondering how I was going to get them both out!'

Jack chortled at his mother, splashing his hands in the water, and Rose pinned a smile to her face. 'Why don't I get Jack out first?' she suggested, hoping that she didn't look as disconcerted as she felt.

No such luck, though. Averting her eyes to lift her son out of the bath, she felt rather than saw Drew grin. 'Rose, you're blushing! I do believe you're embarrassed about the fact that I've got no clothes on!'

Rose pushed her hair away from her face. 'Why should I be embarrassed?' she asked, with a creditable assumption of coolness. 'I've seen it all before. It's not as if we haven't had plenty of baths together in the past.'

'Well, that's what I thought,' said Drew. 'But if it's not that, why the pink cheeks?'

'It's hot in here, that's all,' she said crossly, and he grinned.

'Then you won't mind if I get out now?'

CHAPTER EIGHT

'OF COURSE not,' said Rose coolly. She held out her hands for Molly. 'I'll take her.'

She wrapped a towel round the slippery little body and laid her gently down next to Jack, busying herself with drying them both carefully. It gave her an excuse not to look as Drew stepped out of the bath and casually wrapped a towel around his waist.

It wasn't that she was shy or prudish. That would have been easier to deal with than this desperate, aching awareness of him, Rose thought. She had known his body as well as her own once, had loved its lean, sleek strength and the warmth of his skin. She had used to want to burrow into him and lose herself in the hard maleness of him, and it was the memory of how glorious he had made her feel that was flooding her throat and face with colour.

So, no, she wasn't embarrassed by Drew's nakedness. It was her own reaction to it that made her cringe. She had tried so hard to think of him as no more than an old friend, but old friends didn't cause that disquieting pulse of response at the sight of bare flesh. A friend's hands wouldn't be tingling and twitching with the yearning to touch him, to explore him. A friend's lips wouldn't be dry with the need to kiss their way all over him.

Drew, though, was obviously drawing his own conclusions from her beastly flush. At least they were the wrong ones, Rose thought gratefully. That was something.

'You *are* embarrassed,' he said with contrition. 'I'm sorry, Rose. I didn't mean to make you feel awkward. That's the last thing I'd want to do. I didn't think.'

'Don't be silly,' she told him with a light laugh as she handed him his daughter. 'I don't feel the slightest bit awkward.' Not about the fact that he'd been in the bath, anyway. 'It's really not a big deal, Drew. Heavens, we've seen each other without any clothes on enough times! The fact that we don't have that kind of relationship any more doesn't change that. I just want to be friends, and surely friends can see each other in the bath without making a huge fuss about it?'

We don't have that kind of relationship any more. I just want to be friends.

Drew thought about what Rose had said as he finished drying Molly. Compared to that first day, he was quite quick about putting on her nappy and getting her into her sleepsuit. It was hard to remember now how nervous he had been and how strange Molly had seemed. He couldn't imagine life without her now, and he owed that to Rose.

Rose, who just wanted to be his friend.

Drew had seen her blush and thought that he *had* probably embarrassed her, whatever she'd said, and he felt horribly guilty about it now. He had known that she'd had a hard day, and he'd wanted to make her homecoming special tonight. It had taken him ages to tidy up, and he'd planned a nice supper. And then he had spoilt everything by being thoughtless. Drew shifted uncomfortably.

The last two weeks together had been so easy in some ways that it was hard to remember that they didn't have the same intimacy that they'd had before. He could hardly avoid knowing that their relationship had changed—sleeping alone in that narrow bed was a nightly reminder of that!—but he hadn't even paused to consider whether Rose would be shocked to see him in the bath.

He couldn't get the memory of Rose's painful flush out of his mind. Drew cursed himself for a tactless idiot. He had made things difficult enough for her as it was. The last thing she needed was to feel awkward about living with him. She'd made it plain that she only wanted to be friends, so a friend was what he should be. How many times did he have to tell himself that?

If she wanted to make a new life with Seb, it was up to him to stand back and help her, not embarrass her or remind her about what they had shared in the past. Rose wanted to look forward, not back, and if he was sensible he'd do the same thing. He needed to face up to the fact that he had to make a new future with Molly on his own. Rose had her own family to think about.

So, friends it was. Mentally, Drew squared his shoulders and tried to think of a way to show Rose that he had finally realised what he had to do.

'I've run you a bath,' he said gruffly as they kissed Molly and Jack goodnight and switched off the light.'

'A bath?' Rose's grey eyes were wary. She was probably wondering if he was going to invite himself to share it. Drew pushed the thought firmly aside.

'You've had a long day,' he said. 'I thought you might like some time to yourself. Supper can wait until you come down.'

Rose couldn't believe it when she saw what Drew had done to the bathroom. The packs of nappies and plastic ducks and everything else Jack and Molly needed in the bathroom had been hidden away some-where, and he'd found some candles and set them around the bath, turning off the light so that the room was filled with a flickering romantic glow. There was even a glass of wine sitting on the edge of the bath.

'It looks wonderful,' she said, but she was looking puzzled. 'You tidied up downstairs, too. What's all this in aid of?' she asked, striving to keep her voice light.

'I just wanted to say thank you.'

'Thank you? You're the one who's been looking after Jack and Molly all day! I should be thanking *you*!'

'I enjoy being here with them. The last two weeks have been amazing, Rose. Learning how to look after Molly, being with her…it's changed my life, and I know I couldn't have done it without you.' He paused. 'I want to say sorry, too, about what happened earlier. I keep forgetting about Seb, and the future you're thinking about with him, and that's not fair. I said we'd be friends, but I haven't been a good one to you.'

He drew a breath. 'I'm going back to work next week, and I know I've got to make some decisions about the future, and what I'm going to do with Molly, but in the meantime I want you to know that I'm going to try and be a better friend than I have been. We can still be friends, can't we, Rose?'

'Of course,' said Rose, wondering why she wanted to cry. 'Of course we can.'

It was all very well promising to be a good friend, but it was hard for Drew to remember when Rose came downstairs after her bath. She had changed and was ready for bed. No revealing wispy negligee for Rose. Just the loose stripy trousers and camisole she slept in, with a soft cardigan pulled over the top. Her blonde hair was damp and tucked behind her ears, and her face was scrubbed clean. She had made absolutely no effort to dress up for him, that was clear, but Drew had never seen her sexier.

She was gorgeous.

Drew's mouth dried. How could he be just a friend when she stood there looking like that? He gulped. 'Supper's nearly ready,' he managed in a strangled voice.

'That was a lovely bath,' said Rose, almost shyly. She glanced around her at the strangely tidy living room. 'Everything looks wonderful.'

And then every one of Drew's senses snarled as she came over and kissed him on the cheek. 'Thank you,' she whispered, with a little hug.

Her lips were soft against his cheek, very close to his mouth. Drew couldn't help himself. His arms went round her even before he had realised what was happening, and pulled her tight into his body so that he could rest his cheek against her silky hair for a moment. She smelt faintly of baby talc and soap.

The scent of her, the feel of her, made Drew's throat close with longing. 'We'll always be friends, won't we, Rose?' he managed at last, very low.

Rose nodded wordlessly. She couldn't speak. She could only cling to him and wish that this moment could go on for ever. She didn't want to step back and be sensible, didn't want to remember all the reasons this was the last thing she should be doing. She didn't want to think. All she wanted was to hold on to his warm, solid strength, to press her face into his throat, feel his arms around her.

They stood there, holding each other close, both reluctant to end the moment, until something between them shifted anyway and they stilled at the same time. Neither moved, neither spoke, but it was as if both were suddenly aware that they would only have to move their heads very slightly for their lips to meet. If Drew slid his mouth from her hair down the curve of her cheek… If Rose tilted her face just a little…

The possibility of a kiss sang and sizzled in the air. Rose was barely breathing, Drew was rigid and then, by a strange, unspoken agreement, they both pulled back at the same time.

Rose felt ridiculously shaky, torn between her shrieking senses, which urged her to reach for him again, to kiss him after all, it would be so easy, and her mind, which insisted on asking *but then what*? A kiss wouldn't change anything. It would just make missing him worse when this time was over.

They kept telling each other that they were friends. Much better to stick with that than to risk the heartache of losing him again.

From somewhere, Rose mustered a bright smile. 'What's for supper?' she asked.

Drew had cooked a pasta dish that was one of Rose's favourites, but she hardly tasted it. Her body was still thumping with awareness of him, and although they managed to keep a stilted conversation going, all she could think about was touching him, kissing him, being held by him again.

But they had agreed they would be just friends. That was the sensible thing to do.

All in all it was a relief when the phone rang just after they had finished eating. Rose leapt up to answer it. She didn't care who it was. She just wanted to stop sitting across the table from Drew and keeping her foot from sliding up and down his leg that was so close to hers.

'Seb!' she exclaimed delightedly when she heard his voice. It couldn't be better! Seb was exactly the person she needed to talk to right now. He would remind her about what was really important and make her sensible again. 'Jack's asleep, I'm afraid.'

'I thought he might be. I really wanted a word with you.'

'Oh?' Very aware of Drew listening from the table, Rose turned slightly away from him and leant back against the kitchen units. 'Is there a problem?'

'No, no,' said Seb, but he didn't sound quite him-self. 'In fact, I just heard today that my job's been made permanent.'

'That's great news!' said Rose, a little puzzled by his tone. 'Does that mean you'll be staying in Bristol?'

'Yes, and that's what I need to talk to you about, Rose.' Seb cleared his throat. 'I was thinking of coming up to London next Saturday. I haven't seen Jack for a long time, and we could have a proper chat then.'

'Of course,' she said after a tiny pause. Her heart was beating faster and she felt faintly sick. Was this it? Was Seb coming to ask her to make a decision about mar-rying him once and for all?

She had told Drew that she was thinking about the possibility, but she hadn't really let herself think what it would mean: leaving this house, moving in with Seb, sleeping with him. It would mean saying goodbye to Molly, goodbye to Drew.

Rose swallowed. It was good that Drew had come back, and that they had spent this time together. Otherwise she might always have been yearning for him, wondering what might have been if only he had changed his mind. Well, now she knew. He wanted to be friends. That was all.

It was time for her to leave the old dreams behind and start hoping for a new future—one that would give Jack the family he needed.

'Why don't you come for lunch, Seb?' she said. 'It'll be more relaxed with Jack that way. We can talk when he has a nap, and then take him to the park or something.'

She didn't look at Drew as she switched off the phone and put it back in its cradle.

'It sounds like I'd better make myself scarce next weekend,' said Drew. There didn't seem much point in pretending that he hadn't been listening when Rose had made it so obvious how delighted she was to hear from Seb.

'Would you mind?' she said a little awkwardly. 'He did say that he wanted to talk to me, and it sounded important.'

Drew had been studying his wine with a morose expression, but at that he lifted his eyes, and as always Rose's heart jumped a little at the clear green gaze. 'Is it about you going to Bristol?'

'Yes.' There was no point in lying about it. He had heard most of it anyway. She turned away and started rinsing the plates so that she didn't have to look at him.

'What are you going to say?'

I don't know, Rose wanted to cry. She wanted to

throw herself into his arms and beg him to give her a reason to say no again. But she had to do something. They couldn't carry on like this for ever.

'Are you going to keep Molly?' she asked him, instead of answering directly.

'Of course.' Drew was taken aback by her question. It had been less than three weeks, but already it was impossible for him to imagine a life without his daughter. 'Of course,' he said again. 'At least…I'll need to talk to the Clarkes. They have a say, too. Hannah made them Molly's guardians, so I'd have to take their wishes into account even if I didn't want to. I could go and see them next weekend when Seb is here. I hope we'll be able to agree that Molly lives with me, but that her grandparents are still involved in her upbringing and see her as often as possible.'

'Then you'll want this house,' said Rose, making her voice deliberately crisp and business-like, so that he wouldn't know that her heart was cracking at the realisation that Molly would grow up without her.

Drew frowned. 'Yes, but that's no reason for you to go to Bristol,' he added quickly. 'You and Jack could stay here if you wanted.'

'That wouldn't work, Drew. You're going back to work full time on Monday, and our arrangement was only for six weeks.'

Did she think he didn't *know* that? 'I hadn't forgotten,' he said coolly. How could he forget when she was always reminding him? 'I'll just have to get a nanny.'

'Where are you going to put her?' Rose asked, stacking the plates in the dishwasher. 'If you think a nanny will be prepared to squeeze in with Jack and Molly, you're in for a shock, I'm afraid. A good nanny will expect a decent room of her own at the very least, which means my room, and I can't see us sharing that tiny bed you're sleeping in at the moment, can you?'

Drew *could* see it. That was the trouble. He could picture lying close to Rose in that narrow bed with alarming clarity, and it took a real effort of will to push the image out of his mind.

'I'll get a nanny who comes in every day,' he offered, but Rose just shook her head.

'Easier said than done. No, you need Jack and me out of your hair,' she said, making up her mind as she wiped her hands and hung the teatowel carefully over the oven handle. She turned back to face him. 'It's not as if I don't have any options, and your need to find a nanny for Molly will force me to think about the future seriously, which is a good thing.

'Seb's visit next weekend may turn out to be perfect timing,' she went on, doing her best to talk herself into the idea. 'I've been thinking about myself for too long. Jack needs a father around all the time, not one who lives at the other end of the motorway and who he only sees every other weekend. It makes sense for Seb and me to be together for him. It's not as if we don't get on. We're friends, we share a son…there are worse bases for a good relationship.'

There were better ones, too, of course. Like loving each other, needing each other, wanting each other. Everything she had thought she had with Drew until he had walked away.

'So when he asks you to go and live with him in Bristol…?'

'I'll say yes.' Rose made herself meet his eyes and lifted her chin. 'It's the right thing to do, Drew. It's the right thing for Jack, and the right thing for you and Molly, as well.'

'And for you?'

'For me, too,' she said firmly.

Once the decision was made, she could think about making a life with Jack and Seb. Drew wouldn't be around, making her blood pound and her body thrum with memories. She might not be ecstatically happy, but at least she would be at peace, knowing that she had made the right decision for Jack.

'I've made up my mind, Drew,' she told him. 'I think it will make things easier for both of us.'

CHAPTER NINE

BUT it didn't feel easier, it felt horribly difficult, and they had a whole weekend together to get through. It wasn't too bad when Jack and Molly were up and awake, when there was no time to think about anything else, but Rose spent all of Saturday dreading the moment when the children were in bed and she and Drew would be alone.

'I think I'll try and get some work done this evening,' she said as casually as she could, when Jack and Molly were having their afternoon nap. 'I'll use the kitchen table, so if you want to go out I'll be here.'

'Out?' echoed Drew, taken aback. 'I've forgotten what going out is!'

'You might as well make the most of it,' Rose told him, emptying the washing machine. 'If you're only going to get a nanny for Molly during the day, you won't have many free evenings for a while.'

Well, why not? Drew thought. She clearly wanted him to go out, and the atmosphere was so strained that he'd just as soon not spend another evening like last night, when he'd been torn between wanting to shake her and longing to kiss her. Besides, he was going to have to start making a new life for himself some time if she was going off to Bristol. He might as well start now.

'OK, if you're sure,' he said, and looked around for his phone. 'I might give Caroline a ring and see if she's free tonight.'

Rose paused with a handful of wet clothes. 'Caroline?'

'I don't know if you ever met her,' said Drew. 'She's an engineer, too, and I've worked with her on a couple of projects in the past when I was in the London office. She was always good fun, but she hasn't had so good a time over the last year,' he went on, aware that he was rambling but somehow unable to do anything about it. 'Apparently she got divorced while I was away, and she's not getting much support from her ex with the kids. I saw her in the office that day I came back, and she was telling me that her social life has really shrunk since her divorce. She said she doesn't get the chance to go out much.'

It sounded like a blatant piece of fishing for an invitation if ever Rose heard one! Clearly, Caroline had barely allowed Drew to set foot in the office again before she made her move. Rose sniffed as she straightened with the laundry basket. Still, it wasn't her business, was it?

'Well, maybe you'll be lucky and she'll be able to find a babysitter,' she said, and was completely unsurprised when Drew told her that, yes, Caroline *had* been able to find someone to look after her children so that she could go out with him.

Surprise, surprise.

'Are you sure you don't mind?' Drew said later,

when Molly and Jack were in bed and he was shrugging on his jacket.

'Of course not,' said Rose, smiling brightly. 'Have fun!'

Drew did his best, but he couldn't honestly say that it was the best evening of his life. Caroline was a nice woman, and they had an excellent meal, but all the time he was supposed to be looking at her, listening to her, he was thinking about Rose, sitting at the kitchen table, hair tucked behind her ears and feet bare. There was a sick feeling in the pit of his stomach. It came from feeling that he was in completely the wrong place with completely the wrong woman, and it didn't do much for his appetite, that was for sure.

He had to get over this, Drew told himself fiercely, forcing his attention back to Caroline, who was looking very feminine this evening. He hadn't realised what an attractive woman she was before, but no matter how nice she looked she didn't make his heart lurch sickeningly into his throat the way Rose had done that evening, when she had come down in a faded T-shirt and baggy jogging pants. My work clothes, she had told him, mistaking his expression for surprise.

Drew sighed inwardly. Why did everything come back to Rose? Rose, who was going off to Bristol, who didn't want him around. Rose, who he could have spent the rest of his life with if he hadn't been so self-centred and short-sighted and *stupid*.

Enough. She had made her choice, and he was going to have to make a life without her. She wasn't the only woman in the world, Drew told himself. He would meet someone else. He would find a mother for Molly. He *would*. He just had to get over this desperate feeling that he had jumped on a train that was rattling off in quite the wrong direction first.

'How was your evening?' Rose asked when he got in at last.

'Fine,' said Drew heartily. 'Great.'

'Oh. Good.'

She longed to know whether he was planning to see Caroline again, but couldn't ask. It wasn't any of her business. She had made her decision, and once she had completed the project she was working on she would be able to take Jack down to Bristol and she wouldn't think about Drew again.

He would have this lovely house to himself, and would invite Caroline or anybody else he wanted to come round and sit at the kitchen table, to play with Molly or wander around her precious garden. She wouldn't know who was sleeping in her bed. The thought was enough to make Rose close her eyes in pain.

Because it wasn't her bed. It was Drew's. He could do whatever he liked with whoever he liked in it. She would be in Bristol. It would be nothing to do with her.

Rose had thought the weekend was bad, but the following week was even worse. Drew went back to work, and was assigned to a new project. She stayed at home with Jack and Molly. When Drew came home, she would hand them over to him and go out to Peter and Peter's, where she would sit in the quiet studio and try to remind herself of all the reasons why she should try and make a go of it with Seb.

She barely saw Drew, and when she did their conversations were limited to the children, what they had eaten or if one of them was in a bad mood. Rose told herself that it was easier that way, but the truth was that she missed him. She had got used to their evenings together, got used to having someone to talk to, someone who would share her delight in Jack.

Of course, Seb would do that.

Rose wasn't sure whether she dreaded Seb's arrival or longed for it. She wanted to make a decision, and had convinced herself that once she was committed it would be easier. At least then she wouldn't have this awful waiting and wondering if she was making the right decision. On Saturday all that would be over.

Drew's feelings were less complicated. He knew that he dreaded the weekend. Saturday loomed all week, towering blackly over his imagination, so that all he could think about was how he was going to feel when Rose agreed to marry Seb and reality crashed over him.

He did his best to think beyond it, but he just couldn't. It was impossible to imagine the house without Rose, empty of her scent, of her smile and her warmth. There would be no Jack demanding to be tossed in the air, or making a disgusting mess with his food. There would be no toys all over the floor, none of Rose's shampoo in the bathroom. Her bed would be empty. Drew's whole body clenched at the thought of it.

Molly would miss them terribly, too. What would happen to her with only him to look after her? He had relied so much on Rose that now the thought of being responsible for his daughter alone filled Drew with trepidation. How was he going to manage without her?

Well, he would just have to, Drew told himself bleakly. One way or another the future would come, and he would have to deal with it. He had to think about Molly.

He had arranged to take her to see her grandparents on Saturday, while Seb and Rose were talking. All he had to hope for now was that Seb wouldn't be there when they got back—that he wouldn't have to shake the other man's hand and congratulate him. He could pretend that he was happy for Rose, but he didn't see why Seb should have his good wishes. Seb would have Rose; what else could he want?

With any luck he wouldn't have to see the man at all. Drew's plan was to be long gone before Seb arrived, but inevitably perhaps it seemed to take twice as long as usual to get Molly ready that Saturday morning. He'd forgotten to put her seat back in his car, as well, which took up precious minutes, and then, just as he picked her up to say goodbye to Rose, a telltale whiff sent him up to the bathroom to change her nappy.

'Right, now I really *am* going,' he said when he came downstairs, to find Rose trying to distract Jack, who wanted to put his coat on and go with Drew and Molly.

The grey eyes were suspiciously bright as she kissed Molly goodbye. 'Be good,' she told her, and then glanced awkwardly at Drew. 'I hope you can come to some agreement with the Clarkes.'

'I'm sure we will.' He took Molly from her, and started for the door before changing his mind and turning back. 'I hope it goes well for you today, too, Rose,' he said abruptly. 'I hope you get everything you've ever wanted.'

'Thanks.' Rose's throat was so tight that she could hardly speak. She bent to pick up Jack. 'Drive carefully.'

Jack set up a wail of protest when he realised that Drew and Molly were going without him. His face red and screwed up with misery, confusion and frustration, he battered his hands furiously against Rose.

'I know, sweetheart.' She tried to shush him, understanding just how he felt at seeing Drew and Molly leave, and wishing that she could have a tantrum, too. 'I know.'

Drew winced at the sound of Jack's screams as he pulled the front door shut behind him. Poor Jack. Poor Rose, trying to calm him before his father arrived. Poor Molly, wondering what on earth was going on.

Poor him, knowing exactly what was going on, but unable to do anything about it.

He was digging into his jacket pocket for his car keys as he turned from the door, so it was only when he looked up that he saw the man with his hand on the gate.

He couldn't say that he recognised him, but Drew knew at once that this was Seb. He looked exactly what Rose had said he was—an attractive, kind, steady, reliable, genuinely nice man.

Drew disliked him on sight.

'Hi.' Seb smiled as Drew came down the path. 'You must be Drew.' He held out his hand. 'I'm Seb.'

Drew had little choice but to shift Molly to his other arm and shake the other man's hand.

'And this must be Molly. I've heard all about *you*.' Seb smiled and made a chucking noise that had Molly burying her face in Drew's neck. But just as Drew was silently congratulating her on her taste she peeped another glance, and when Seb grinned and waved, she ducked her head and smiled back.

Drew was furious. Not content with taking Rose away, Seb was flirting with his daughter, too!

'I've heard a lot about you both from Rose,' Seb was saying, apparently oblivious to Drew's disgusted expression. 'Jack's loved having you two around.'

Drew couldn't believe it. He had been living with

Rose and Jack for the last three weeks, and a lot could change in that time—as he knew to his cost. By rights, Seb should be seething with jealousy. He ought to be issuing veiled warnings, squaring up for a fight, or at the very least brushing Drew aside in his haste to see Rose and his son again. Instead, Seb appeared to be quite happy to stand here making polite chit-chat with his rival.

Except he obviously didn't think of Drew as a rival, Drew realised desolately. He must be very sure of Rose to be prepared to be so friendly to someone she had once been so close to.

'I must go. I'm late already,' he said, damned if he was going to stand there while Seb patronised him and flirted with his daughter. 'Have a good day,' he made himself add as Seb politely held the gate open for him.

A strange expression swept across Seb's face. 'Thanks,' he said. 'You, too.'

Squaring his shoulders, Drew stood on the doorstep and rang his own doorbell. He sincerely hoped that Seb would have gone by now, but just in case he hadn't it might be tactful not to use his key. He didn't want to walk in on a passionate clinch, or find Rose and Seb curled up cosily on the sofa, making plans. He had stayed as long as he could at the Clarkes, but Molly had begun to get tired and fretful, and Drew knew that he had to face going home some time.

This was it. It felt as if a cold stone were lodged in the pit of his stomach. He made himself take deep breaths and practised smiling at the door. *I'm very happy for you.* That was what he would say. *I hope you'll be happy*, perhaps. Anything other than, *Please don't leave me. Stay here and marry me instead*, which was what he was really going to want to say.

Was it only three and a half weeks since he had stood right here with Molly in his arms and waited for Rose to open the door? It felt like a lifetime ago. A lifetime that was about to end. The sick feeling intensified.

And then the door opened, and Rose stood there, and the sight of her was like a fist driving into his solar plexus, depriving him of breath and charging his whole body with the knowledge of just how essential she was to him now. He couldn't help smiling at her. But although she returned his smile, hers looked forced, and Drew saw with a trickle of unease that her grey eyes were shuttered.

Something was wrong.

Jack was clinging unsteadily to Rose's leg and crowing with delight as he recognised Drew and Molly.

'Hi, Jack.' Drew's voice sounded scratchy, as if he hadn't used it for some time. 'Can we come in?'

'Of course.' Rose seemed to recover herself and stood back. 'Come out of the way, Jack, and let Drew and Molly in.'

'Is Seb still here?' Drew made himself ask, and something flickered in the grey eyes.

'No, he's gone. I was just making supper for Jack. Molly hasn't had hers yet, has she?'

The trickling unease pooled into deep disquiet as he followed her into the kitchen. Rose was behaving as if everything was normal. She was talking and smiling and dealing with the children exactly as she always did. But it was as if she had withdrawn behind an invisible barrier where he couldn't reach her.

What is it? he wanted to shout, but Rose deflected

all his attempts at conversation, and eventually Drew had to accept that they wouldn't be able to talk until Molly and Jack had been fed and bathed and put to bed.

At least the bedtime routine was familiar enough now for Drew to go through the motions while speculating feverishly about what it was that Rose didn't want to tell him.

Was she going to Bristol sooner than he had thought? Was that it? But she couldn't go until her project was completed, and that would be another three weeks at least. Perhaps Seb was coming back to London and she and Jack were going to move in with him?

Drew's mind went round and round. But the truth, when it came, was the last thing he had expected.

Even if he hadn't sensed that something was wrong, he would have known for sure when Rose simply ignored the mess on the living room floor and dropped onto one of the sofas, tipping her head back against the cushions with a sigh.

Drew sat down opposite her, and for a while there was silence. Now that he had got to this point, he found himself wondering wildly if it would be better not to know. If she never told him that she was going, he could go on pretending that she would never leave.

But that was childish. He was a father now, and he had to face up to the truth. It might as well be now.

'So,' he said heavily, looking down at his linked hands, 'are you going to Bristol?'

Rose opened her eyes and looked at him. 'No,' she said.

'No?' Drew's head jerked up and he stared back at her, unable to suppress the quick leap of relief, even though he knew it was foolish. What did it matter whether she went to Bristol or anywhere else? She would still be gone. 'Where *are* you going?'

She hesitated. 'I don't know,' she said.

'Don't *know*?' Drew frowned. 'I thought that was what Seb wanted to discuss with you?'

'I misunderstood.' She closed her eyes briefly again, and then made herself face him directly. He had to know. 'He did want to talk to me about the future. But not about a future we would share.' She mustered a smile, and was very proud that her voice came out so steadily. 'It turns out that Seb is getting married. He wanted me to be the first to know.'

CHAPTER TEN

DREW couldn't quite believe what he was hearing. 'What do you mean, married?' he asked blankly.

'You know what married means, Drew!' snapped Rose, her unnatural calmness shattered at last by a flash of impatience. 'Seb has met someone in Bristol. He's only been there a month, but he said he fell in love with her at first sight and knows that he wants to spend the rest of his life with her. He wants to have a family with her. I believe that's often what happens when two people get married,' she added, with a touch of bitterness.

'But…what about Jack?'

Jack—her Jack—who wasn't going to get his happy family after all. Trust Drew to go straight to the one thing that had hurt her most.

Rose turned her face away so that he wouldn't see the pain in her eyes. 'Seb will always be Jack's father,' she said, trying desperately to sound reasonable, the way Seb had sounded when he'd explained it all, but she could feel her control wavering at the concern in Drew's voice. If only he would be cocky or arrogant or insensitive, it would be so much easier for her to hold this awful sense of confusion and humiliation in check.

'He wanted to reassure me about that,' she told him. 'He's going to pay me maintenance, as he won't be around to look after him in the same way, but he'd like to see Jack as much as possible. So next time he's going to bring his fiancée to meet him.'

She wasn't going to marry Seb. Seb was marrying someone else. It didn't make any kind of sense to Drew, but he could feel a heady mixture of relief and disbelief sloshing through him as Rose's words sank in.

Part of him wanted to leap to his feet and punch the air, but he restrained himself. It felt all wrong to be happy when Rose was sitting there with her face averted, her lips pressed together in a straight line, and her slender throat rigid with tension. She had lost another dream today. He had thoughtlessly destroyed her first one, and now she had had her second chance at happiness knocked out from beneath her.

And she was proud. It must be costing her a lot to tell him Seb's news without falling apart or admitting her own hurt the way she was surely entitled to.

'Rose?' he said gently, and although her chin tilted as she turned to look at him directly, he could see that the beautiful grey eyes were shimmering with unshed tears. 'What about *you*?'

His gentleness was the last straw for Rose. Ever since Drew had said goodbye that morning, leaving her with the sick feeling that she was making a terrible mistake and had left it too late to do anything about it, treacherous tears had been pressing against the back of her eyes.

She *wouldn't* cry, she promised herself fiercely, but the sadness and strain were clogging her throat so tightly that she felt she was being strangled, and in spite of herself a tear trembled on the edge of her lashes before trickling down the side of her nose. She brushed it away furiously, but it was too late. Drew had seen.

'Rose!' Without thinking, he moved to sit next to her and put his arm round her. Appalled at her misery, he pulled her close. 'Oh, Rose, I'm so sorry,' he murmured.

He felt terrible for reacting with such instinctive jubilation to the news that Seb didn't want to marry her instead of thinking about just what it might mean to her. 'I'm sorry,' he said again, conscious of how inadequate the words sounded.

For a few weak moments Rose let herself subside against his solid, incredibly comforting body, and gave in to the tears that had been clamouring for release all day. 'I don't know why I'm crying,' she wept, muffled by his shoulder. 'It's just the shock. I wasn't expecting it, that's all.'

Drew held her close. 'Does it hurt very much?'

'No…yes…I don't know…' She groped for a tissue and blew her nose, making herself straighten out of the reassuring circle of his arm. 'I don't think I'm hurt, not really. It's not like—'

Not like when you left, she had been about to say, before stopping herself just in time. 'It's not like I was desperately in love with Seb,' she said instead, after a tiny pause. 'But I'd started to think that we might have a future. I thought marrying him would be the best thing for Jack, and now…I suppose I feel a fool for not realising that Seb sounded different on the phone. That's what really hurts.'

She sighed, scrubbing her face absently with the crumpled tissue. 'It was my fault. I've been worrying about the future, and money and everything, really, and

I'd talked myself into believing that being with Seb would solve all my problems. But that wasn't the right thing to do. If I've got problems, I should solve them myself. I can't rely on anybody else.'

'You can rely on me,' said Drew, trying to draw her back against him, but she shook her head and moved deliberately out of his reach.

'No,' she said in a flat, final voice. 'I'm grateful to you for letting Jack and me stay here, and for making it possible for me to work on that big contract, but I have to make my own way now. I need to find a new home for Jack. A home that doesn't depend on any *arrangement* or on anyone else—one we don't have to leave if someone turns up unexpectedly or changes their mind.'

'But, Rose, you don't have to go. You can stay here.' He fought to keep his voice steady, so as not to betray how eager he was. He would have to be careful, though. Rose was in a fragile mood, and she was clearly still more upset about Seb than she was admitting. This wasn't the time to try and sweep her off her feet with a passionate declaration.

'We have had an arrangement that suits both of us,' he pointed out. 'Why don't we make it permanent? We could get married,' he told her impulsively. He grasped her hands, wondering how to convince her to say yes. 'I need you, Rose. And Molly needs you, too. I don't know how I'm going to manage her on my own.'

A welcome surge of anger was dissolving the numbness that had held Rose in its grip all day. 'I see,' she said tightly, wrenching her hands out of his warm clasp. 'So I marry you to save you paying for a nanny. Is that it?'

'It's not just that.' Drew could tell by the expression on

Rose's face that he was making a mess of it, and with every word he seemed to be making things worse. 'I mean, it's not that at *all*,' he said, with an edge of desperation.

'I'm thinking about you and Jack, as well. You told me yourself that you wouldn't be able to afford a house like this on your own. I hate the thought of you and Jack living somewhere grotty just because that's all you can afford. You won't even have to think about renting if you marry me. We can stay here, or buy somewhere bigger if that's what you want. And of course, it would solve the whole childcare issue for both of us once and for all.'

Too hurt and angry to sit still any longer, Rose leapt up from the sofa. 'Marriage isn't about childcare!' she said furiously, grey eyes stormy.

'That wasn't what you said when you were thinking about marrying Seb!' Drew's expression had cooled, and he got to his feet, too.

She flushed. 'That was different! Seb is Jack's father.'

'What difference does that make?'

'The difference is that if I had married Seb we would both have been doing it for Jack. *You* want to get married to save yourself the hassle of finding a nanny or having to pretend that you want to commit to a relationship in order to marry someone else!' Rose flung at him. 'You know that you can save yourself the bother if you ask me, as I know only too well how you really feel about marriage, and you can think of it as a nice business arrangement that you can dissolve whenever it suits you!'

'No!' Drew's voice rose in frustration and he raked a hand through his hair. He took a deep breath and made himself stay calm. 'I love you,' he told her, but Rose wasn't prepared to listen.

'What exactly do you love about me, Drew?' she demanded. 'I don't think you've ever even *seen* me properly! You've always just taken it for granted that I'll be there if you need me. We were only together for all those years because you were too lazy to go out and meet someone new, and the moment I asked you for some commitment you were off.'

She pushed her hair angrily behind her ears and glared at him, aware in a dim way that she was taking out the emotions of the day on him, but unable to help herself.

'But now suddenly you've got a baby to look after—and look who's handy! Why, good old Rose, who knows how to change a nappy and is struggling a bit financially! Marriage seems like a better deal now, doesn't it? Saying you love me is so much easier than paying through the nose for a nanny or going through the hassle of building a whole new relationship! Well, I've got news for you, Drew,' she finished. 'I'm a person, not a fallback position!'

If she stayed here any longer she was going to start crying again, and there was no way Rose was going to do that in front of Drew now. She had had enough of today anyway.

Scowling ferociously to keep the tears at bay, she headed for the door—only to trip over one of Jack's toys that she had never got round to picking up. She kicked it savagely out of the way. See what happened when you let the mess get out of control? Your whole life started falling apart.

'Find someone else to sort out your problems,' she threw at him as she reached for the door handle, only just avoiding a plastic train.

'Where are you going?' Drew was very white about the mouth.

'To bed!' She was halfway up the stairs by the time Drew reached the bottom.

'And tomorrow?' he called up to her.

'I don't know,' she snapped. 'But I'll think of something.'

Slamming the bedroom door, she threw herself down on the bed and gave in to the bitter tears at last. Seb's announcement had been a shock, but she had been secretly relieved, too, and then guilty at having failed Jack. It was humiliating, too, to realise how disastrously she had misinterpreted Seb.

Rose had spent most of the day dreading Drew's return, when she would have to admit how mistaken she had been. He had been so sympathetic at first, and she had begun to think it would be all right after all, but then he had made that crass proposal! Hadn't he *seen* how fragile she was feeling? He had looked so shocked when she had accused him of not seeing her properly, but there was a perfect example! All she had needed was for him to take her in his arms and hold her—but, no! Drew had seen no more than an opportunity to recruit a cheap nanny.

And the worst thing was that she wanted to marry him more than anything else. But not like that, Rose told herself. No, she might love him, like the fool she was, but she had Jack to think about. There was no way she was going to bring him up with a man who thought of relationships as no more than convenient arrangements as a role model.

But what was she going to do? Fear crept into her stomach, making it curdle and churn. It would be great to make a grand gesture and slam out of the house, but where could she and Jack go? Peter and Peter would let her stay temporarily, she was sure, but their house was totally unsuitable for small children, and she couldn't drag Jack away from everything that was familiar just to make a point. She would have to stay here until she could find somewhere cheap to rent, and how was she going to face Drew in the meantime?

Next door, Molly was crying. She must have woken up when Rose slammed her door. Rubbing her face with the back of her arm, Rose sat up guiltily, and was about to go to the baby when she heard Drew's step on the stairs. A few moments later, Molly's sobs subsided.

Lucky Molly, who could be so easily comforted. Who had Drew to pick her up and hold her until she felt better. Who didn't know enough to be afraid that he might leave her one day because he was bored or restless or hadn't really wanted her in the first place.

Rose slumped back against the pillows. She should get undressed, wash her face and try to get some sleep, but all she could do was lie there wretchedly, imagining the scene next door. Drew would be leaning over Molly's cot, soothing her with a warm, steady hand on her back, perhaps, or crooning softly so as not to wake Jack.

A few moments later there was a knock at the door. 'Go away!' she shouted.

Ignoring her, Drew went in. 'You'll wake Molly again if you yell like that,' he said mildly, and Rose glared at him.

'I don't want to talk.'

'You don't have to talk. You just have to listen.'

She pulled herself sullenly into a sitting position, wiping the tears from her cheeks with the back of her wrist. Her nose was red, her eyes puffy, her skin all blotched, but Drew's heart still turned over.

'What?' she said belligerently.

Drew sat down on the edge of the bed, not touching her. 'I'm glad Molly woke up. Trying to get a baby back to sleep is good thinking time,' he said pensively. 'Better than staying downstairs and feeling furious with you.'

'*You* were furious with *me*?' she said in disbelief.

'You walked out in the middle of an argument. Of course I was angry,' said Drew. 'But I calmed down when I was with Molly and thought about what you'd said, and I wanted to say that I'm sorry. I never meant to take you for granted. I know I've relied on you because you're such a true and dear friend, and I'm really sorry, Rose, if I ever made you feel that you were less than that.'

Rose sniffed and palmed the last traces of tears from her cheeks.

'But when you said that I'd never seen you…' Drew shook his head. 'No,' he said slowly, 'you're quite wrong about that.' He paused, and looked at Rose. 'Tell me, do you remember the first time we kissed?'

She eyed him suspiciously. 'Of course I do.'

'What do you remember about it?'

'We were in the kitchen in that flat I was sharing in Balham.'

'What else?'

'What do you mean?' she said crossly. 'We kissed. What more do you want?'

'I remember more than that,' said Drew, his voice very low. 'I remember that you were wearing a blue sleeveless top. It felt like silk and it was covered with tiny white daisies, and it had fabric buttons that took for ever to undo. I remember that your hair smelt like freshly cut grass. You told me it was your shampoo. Your friends were watching television in the other room, and I remember the theme tune of that programme you all used to watch the whole time.'

'Really?' said Rose, a little shakily.

'But what I really remember is *you*. I remember your smile, and how your eyes shone when you looked at me. I remember how soft and warm and sexy you were, how sweet you tasted. I couldn't believe how lucky I was to be able to hold you. You made me feel incredible, as if I could do anything, and my heart swelled and swelled until I thought I would explode with the sheer happiness of being with you.'

There was a tiny silence. 'It still feels like that, Rose,' Drew went on, very quietly. 'It feels like that every time I look at you. I remember every time. Like last week, when I came home from work and you were sitting between Molly and Jack, trying to get them to eat their supper. You were singing to them, and you were smiling and your eyes were so warm…Your hair was tucked behind your ears, the way you do it when you're being practical.'

Gently, he reached out and smoothed the hair behind Rose's ears, the way it had been then, and she quivered at his touch.

'How can you say that I never saw you, Rose?' he asked, and she stared mutely back at him, her grey eyes huge and still shimmering with tears. 'I love you,' he said simply. 'I love everything about you. I even love you when you're shopping!' He smiled at her, and her heart pounded with hope. 'And I love you now. Your nose is all red, and your eyes are all puffy and you're still the most beautiful girl I've ever seen.

I don't want a nanny or a housekeeper or a friend. I just want you.'

Rose swallowed hard and found her voice. It was a bit thin and creaky, but at least she managed to get some words out. 'Why didn't you tell me that downstairs?'

'Because I'm a fool,' said Drew. 'I knew you were upset about Seb, and I thought the last thing you needed was me declaring passionate love when you'd just lost the life you really wanted with him and Jack.'

Rose shook her head slowly. 'That wasn't what I really wanted,' she said, and her eyes met his very directly. 'You were what I really wanted, Drew. I just couldn't admit it to myself because I was afraid that you didn't really want *me*.'

A smile started in his eyes and spread slowly over his face. 'I've always wanted you, Rose,' he said. 'I always will.'

Rose's mouth wobbled, and with something that was half laugh, half sob, she reached for him. Drew caught her in his arms and at last—at last!—he could kiss her the way he had wanted to for so long. Sinking down onto the bed, they kissed at first with hunger and need and a kind of desperation at knowing how close they had come to losing each other again, but slowly their kisses became deeper, sweeter, less frantic, as they murmured endearments and let their hands roam blissfully over each other.

When they broke at length for breath, they were lying across the bed and facing each other, smiling between soft kisses. Drew stroked the hair tenderly from Rose's face.

'God, I've wanted that for the last three weeks. No, the last three years,' he corrected himself. 'I knew I'd made a terrible mistake almost as soon as I'd left, but I knew how much you wanted family, and I thought you should have the chance to do that. But being in London and knowing that you were with someone else was awful. Even going to Africa didn't help. I just missed you even more there, and when I was repatriated my first thought was that I could find an excuse to come and see you. And then you opened the door, and you were holding Jack. I could see at once that he was your son, and ever since I've had the sick feeling that I've left it too late to tell you how I feel.'

'It wasn't just you,' said Rose, drifting kisses along his jaw. It was so wonderful to be able to touch him again, to feel his hard, strong body against hers. 'I wished so much that I hadn't pushed you into leaving. It was easy enough to meet other men, but I soon realised that I didn't just want a baby, I wanted *your* baby. I'll never regret Jack, of course, but although I did think long and hard about marrying Seb to give him a family, I knew in my heart that I could never have with Seb what I had with you.'

Drew smiled as he rolled her beneath him and kissed her once more. 'We can have that again, darling,' he said, and nuzzled her neck until she arched with pleasure. 'Seb will always be Jack's father, but we'll be happy together, and Molly and Jack can have a family.'

'And we'll solve that childcare problem,' Rose reminded him, stretching luxuriously beneath his hands.

'Who cares about childcare?' Drew bent to kiss the lobe of her ear and began trailing kisses down her throat as he told Rose what she really wanted to hear. 'That's not why I want to marry you. I want you as my wife because I love you and I need you and when you're not there I feel like there's a bit of me missing.'

His lips had reached her clavicle, and he teased his way to the pulse that was beating frantically at the base of her throat. 'I want to wake up beside you every morning and come home to you every night. I want to see Jack and Molly grow up, and I want us to keep growing together, so we can share the bad times and the good times and all the bits in between. *That's* why I want to marry you,' he told her, as he retraced kisses all the way back up to her mouth.

'Also, I'm sick of that narrow bed in the other room,' he finished, and Rose laughed.

'You don't need to sleep there any more,' she said contently as she pulled his head down to hers.

The sun poured through the window onto Rose's bed the next morning. It had been Drew's turn to make the tea, and now he was sprawled across the bottom of the bed, letting Jack clamber excitedly all over him. Molly was propped up against Rose, watching with wide-eyed delight, and squealing and batting her arms occasionally with happiness.

Rose felt like doing the same. She was leaning back against the pillows, replete with loving and bubbling with joy, and looking, as Drew informed her, very smug.

'I feel smug,' she said, unrepentant. 'I've got you, I've got Jack, I've got darling Molly here…' she kissed the baby's wispy hair '…and I've got my childcare sorted out for the foreseeable future! What more could I want?'

'What about a wedding?' said Drew. 'Although now I come to think about it I don't think you ever got round to saying if you would marry me or not last night. We got…distracted.'

A faint blush spread along Rose's cheekbones and they exchanged smiles as the memory of just what form that distraction had taken shimmered between them. 'I don't think you ever got round to asking me,' she said demurely.

'Will you marry me, Rose?'

'Yes,' she said, and he leant across Molly to kiss her, while Jack jumped onto his neck and hung there, laughing.

'Isn't it funny how things have worked out?' said Rose a little later, watching Drew mock-wrestling with her son and wondering if it were possible to be any happier than she was at that moment. 'It's almost as if it were meant. I became a mother by accident, you were an accidental father, but somehow we've ended up together.'

Drew looked from Jack's bright little face to his daughter, snuggled safely against Rose, and then to Rose herself. 'We may have got here by accident, but the rest is up to us,' he said. 'The four of us have a whole future ahead of us. We've got a lifetime to make a family on purpose.'